SUMMARY

Book X in the Nature of Desire Series

Marius has all the things a Mistress could want in a one-night-sub encounter. Hot body, loads of charm and a willingness to get her off in any way she pleases. But Marius has a dark side. When he takes it too far, he's kicked out of The Zone club with only one way back in— Lady Regina.

Regina sees something in Marius. He doesn't know what it means to be truly helpless to a Mistress, but he needs it, more than any sub she's ever encountered. But Marius's pain, the secrets behind his bad behavior, will drive her into perilous territory. Bringing him back to the Mistress's control he craves will be the fight of her life.

TRULY HELPLESS

A Nature of Desire Series Novel

JOEY W. HILL

Truly Helpless

A Nature of Desire Series Novel - Book #10

Copyright © 2017 Joey W. Hill

ALL RIGHTS RESERVED

Cover Design by W. Scott Hill

SWP Digital & Print Edition publication April 2017

This book may not be reproduced or used in whole or in part by any means existing without written permission from the publisher, Story Witch Press, 452 Mattamushkeet Dr., Little River, SC 29566.

Warning: The unauthorized reproduction or distribution of this copyrighted work is illegal. No part of this book may be scanned, uploaded or distributed via the Internet or any other means, electronic or print, without the publisher's permission. Criminal copyright infringement, including infringement without monetary gain, is investigated by the FBI and is punishable by up to 5 years in federal prison and a fine of $250,000. (http://www.fbi.gov/ipr/). Please purchase only authorized electronic or print editions and do not participate in or encourage the electronic piracy of copyrighted material. Your support of the author's rights is appreciated.

This book is a work of fiction and any resemblance to persons, living or dead, or places, events or locales is purely coincidental. The characters are productions of the author's imagination and used fictitiously.

The publisher and author(s) acknowledge the trademark status and trademark ownership of all trademarks, service marks and word marks mentioned in this book.

The following material contains graphic sexual content meant for mature readers. Reader discretion is advised.

Digital ISBN: 978-1-942122-55-5

Print ISBN: 978-1-942122-56-2

ACKNOWLEDGMENTS

Often the research I need to do for my books is like a scavenger hunt. So I'm blessed, after fifteen-plus years of professional writing, to have readers and authors to assist me with their eclectic skills and resources.

A big thank you to Lisa for her help understanding the protocols related to maximum security prisons. And to the Florida Department of Corrections for their insights as well.

Thank you, fabulous author TJ Michaels, who helped me get Regina's "locs" right. TJ has this gorgeous hairstyle herself and noted her own preference was to call them "locs," rather than dreadlocks. One of the heroines of her books had demanded to know "what's so dreadful about them?" when a hero called them "dreadlocks" instead of "locs." That sold me on the term. So I primarily refer to Regina's hairstyle as "locs" during the course of this story, with only a couple references to dreadlocks to help readers understand a term that might not be so familiar.

Another reason I made that decision had to do with a college memory. My first encounter with "dreadlocks" was a boy who had these nasty ropes of hair matted with dirt and other horrible things. Yuck. It was a nice surprise to find "locs" can be quite beautiful and not like that at all!

Thank you to another fabulous author, Desiree Holt, and her son, Steven, for wandering around Tampa to help me find the right neighborhood for Regina's home and clarifying some issues related to the Tampa Riverwalk.

The usual but always heartfelt thanks to my current team of critique partners. A special thanks to Lauren and Judy, because they saved the opening and ending of this book, literally. Their suggestions for improvement also kicked off other observations from the team members that elevated the quality of the entire story.

Every book comes with a tremendous thanks, whether stated or not, to my wonderful readers. Thank you for taking yet another journey with my characters!

A last-but-not-least thank you to my husband, who has done all the other necessary things to get this book out to you. All while continuing to love his moody and disagreeable wife, despite her horrifying music preferences and unreasonable demands related to the publishing process.

AUTHOR'S NOTE

And it's a very sheepish one...

The Nature of Desire series was started way back at the start of this millennium. Since then, there have been a lot of books, in and out of this series, with plenty of overlap. My characters do not confine themselves to just one book or, for that matter, even one series.

If I had been a smart and forward-thinking author all those years ago, I would have been laying out timelines with every book to ensure things didn't get twisty and knotty. I've avoided a couple embarrassing snafus, thanks to my critique partners. Like correcting an error when Violet from *Natural Law* appeared as a side character in two books after her own. She was pregnant with the same child in both books—and the timeline between the two stories was about three times the normal term for carrying a human child. Violet would have been REALLY cranky with me.

I am not a math person. Despite my best (yet admittedly limited) efforts, I am positive I've made some timeline errors with Regina and Marius's story in terms of other Nature of Desire series relationships. Just roll with it and pretend it's a fictional world where timelines can magically be folded and shook out until everything falls just where it should for the best story possible (beaming). Forgive me for not having the patience to sort it out the way I should. I much prefer the idea of the magical timeline adjustment. That would be useful in so many ways...in real life as well as fiction!

PROLOGUE

*S*he was watching him. She did that a lot of nights. But she hadn't yet approached him for a session, and something kept him from asking. Maybe because he liked the watching.

No way to ruin that.

She came down the stairs from the mezzanine, her tall, lithe body all feminine elegance and strength in crimson corset, black poured-on leggings, and red and black boots. His eyes never knew where to rest because they were greedy. He drank in the quiver of her breasts, the sway of her hips. How her long, supple thighs transformed her stride into a primal dance that called to cock and deeper things.

Sometimes he studied her profile, the full lips and precise nose, the lines of cheekbone and jaw. Her throat was a fragile column to him. She wasn't a petite or fragile-looking woman, but he looked at her throat and saw that appealing vulnerability. She had a curtain of slim, soft-looking dreadlocks—"locs." That was what he'd heard her and other women in the club call the style. They were black with auburn highlights. Sometimes she strung the ropes with beads that shimmered in the club lights. Tonight she wore silver glitter in them. All of her glittered and shimmered. Her skin was like coal and heated chocolate mixed.

So he guessed he liked watching her, too. He managed to tear his gaze away before she noticed.

He was lying on his back on a bench in an intimate alcove, a good

1

trysting place for club members. He had his feet propped on the wall as he tossed a ball toward the ceiling. He hadn't been picked up by any of the unattached Mistresses, because most here tonight were hard psychological players or had brought their own subs, but he still preferred hanging out here to anywhere else. Especially tonight. He'd left his phone in the locker, not wanting to feel electricity shock his spine and his balls shrink up when it buzzed with a message. Which it would, sometime tonight. He didn't know why he was letting it bother him. Fuck it; the outcome changed nothing.

As he threw the ball toward the ceiling again, with an eye to hitting the same spot as he had the first twenty times he'd done it, Regina snagged the ball on the toss. She was standing over him, and he gave her points for stealth and hand-to-eye coordination. "Tyler wants a demo flogging," she said without preamble. "Says you're nominated because he's tired of you putting your damn feet on the walls like you live in a barn." Her gaze slid over him and rested on his upper arms. "Those are new."

"Just temps." He rubbed a thumb over the tribal tats on his biceps. "One of the sub girls wanted an excuse to play with my muscles and a magic marker." He gave her an easy grin. "You know I'm not into doing anything permanent."

Her lips twitched, but her brown eyes—liquid, soft but also sharp as sword points—were still doing that measuring thing. "Get your ass up, you idiot boy," she said without rancor.

Marius put his feet down. "Where do you want to do it?" This wouldn't be anything serious. A demo wasn't intended to be a session. Even so, it would be the first time he'd interacted one-on-one with Lady Regina. The first time she'd done more with him than look.

"The St. Andrew's Cross will do." She nodded toward it.

"Okay." He rose and gestured to her to precede him, but she shook her head.

"You first. I ogle your ass, not the other way around."

"Got it. Whatever makes you happy, Mistress." He headed for the cross. He was used to women looking at him, but her eyes held things he didn't entirely understand. He was good at reading people, but not good at reading her. His body didn't care about any of it. It responded merely to the idea that she was looking at him. Shoulders, back, ass. Taking him all in, deciding what she'd do with him.

2

When they reached the cross, he stepped on the foot rests and put his hands out to the sides and up so she could strap him to it if she wanted. Or he could just hold on for the ride. A flogging wasn't going to stretch him too much, but he could play it up, give a good show. He saw some people already drawing closer, ready to watch.

She moved behind him as he grinned and winked at a trio of young female submissives. The one in the center blushed prettily. Then she disappeared, because a blindfold was placed over his eyes.

"What—"

He bit it off, because it was Regina's call. But he hadn't expected it, not for a demo. She tied it securely and locked his wrists and ankles in the cuffs. As always, a shift happened inside him when restraints came into play, a pooling low in his gut, his cock stiffening. There were other reactions, too, ones that were felt more sharply tonight than he was used to feeling them. She leaned in, her breasts pressing against his bare back. All he was wearing was a pair of tight, stretchy black shorts that left nothing to the imagination, even when he wasn't sporting a hard-on. When he was, like now, it was pretty blatant. He expected the subs were getting an eyeful.

"Should I tell you my safe word?" he ventured, since demos were usually intended to reinforce safety measures at the club, as well as entertain and get more people playing on the public floor.

"I'll keep you safe," she said, her voice a queen bee's command, warm honey on a summer day. She laid her palm on the center of his back.

It was a quelling gesture, telling him to remain silent. But there was more to it. He shifted, uneasy. When first getting into a session with someone new, there was often some self-consciousness on both sides, as they adjusted into their respective roles. With the palm on his back, she centered him. The quiet words pierced him, restraining parts other than his arms and legs. She locked the two of them into the right place with merely a touch and four words. That rarely happened unless there was some serious chemistry happening. That happened to other people. Not to him. He made sure of it.

On top of that, her touch pulled other things to the surface. His need to go further, deeper. He wasn't known as a particularly obedient or easy-to-handle sub, but he was fun, charming. He'd give a Mistress a good time, give her pleasure. He enjoyed that. Even if he left most sessions feeling like he'd denied himself something, he knew it was best for him to stay in that safe zone. Too much dark shit in the wilderness around Disneyland. He might not be able to serve a Mistress to the depths of his soul, but he wouldn't let her take him somewhere he couldn't control. Where he could hurt her.

He didn't want to hurt anyone, and he knew the key to that was staying in the shallow end of his submissive cravings.

Regina had stepped back, and he heard the swish as she chose a flogger and tested it out, probably wrapping it around her lush body a couple times. His hands closed, opened, in the restraints. He'd like to see her doing what she was doing. He'd like to see, period, because in darkness, things could rise that might interfere with that good time he wanted to give her.

The first strike was easy, a sensual feathering with a light sting that slid down his back like a caress. He twitched under it.

"Nice. But I want something more."

She moved closer to him, her heeled boots making a click-click noise on the floor. Clasping the waistband of his tight shorts, she took them down with a sharp yank. She tucked them under his buttocks, leaving them only half off in front, his stiffening cock snagged in them. The pull on the elastic framed and lifted his ass, making him feel like a kid having his pants pulled down in front of the class.

She stepped back and struck again. This time she focused on his butt, hitting it in a repetitive, circular motion that built intensity fast, making him twitch under the blows. It wasn't unbearable pain; just a lot of sensation, and it seemed like every blow came with a message that drew a net tighter around him, making the audience disappear, everything disappear. He didn't let himself get lost this quick with anyone. Hell, he didn't do the getting lost thing at all.

She stepped closer again, and tucked the flogger between his legs, between flesh and shorts. He pulled in a breath as she wrapped her hand in the fall and yanked the straps taut against his balls, the handle imprinted against his ass along with the knuckles of her grip. Her forearm pressed against his side.

"Feeling safe, sweet boy?" she said, a husky whisper. Her breasts, clad in a thin, silky tee, rubbed against his back. He quivered.

That need kept rising. He suspected she could feel it, too, like he was a fish caught on a hook. Her hand was on the line, sensing the tension as she slowly pulled him in the direction that, unlike the fish, he desperately wanted to go.

"Yeah," he managed to mumble. Didn't even remember to say "Yes, Mistress," and he never forgot that.

She stepped back, pulling the flogger free, and went after him again. Sides, ass, back, shoulders, thighs. He was moving with her, like dancing, his cock hard, belly tight, and all his nerve endings reaching for her. Lips parted, breath whistling in and out.

He had no wings to fly like this, but she'd taken away his panic. He wasn't thinking about any of the things that had driven him here for refuge tonight, that had been stalking his mind these past few weeks, waiting for the other shoe to drop in his real life. She really was making him feel safe. Then she did something even worse than that.

He inhaled deep when she stepped close this time, and took in honeysuckle, a haunting fragrance that held him fast on a pin-sized point of nowhere-the-fuck-to-go-but-here. Putting her palm on the juncture between throat and shoulder, she simply stood there, connected to him.

"Breathe."

So he breathed. In darkness, with her touching him, with one firm, warm, substantial palm. The rush of feeling in his head muffled the sounds of the club, the way noise was muted when standing in the surf of an ocean. But each breath took him even farther out in the waters. Floating.

She was in those waters, diving deep into him without doing anything exceptional. No, that wasn't true. She picked up on what he needed at the right moment and pulled even more from him, keeping him unbalanced. It took Doms and subs a long time to get that point, even when they were open to one another. They were virtual strangers, and he didn't open up to anyone. Yet her timing with him was a hammer hitting a nail dead on with every stroke and touch.

He wanted to let go, feel more with her. But...he didn't want her to stop watching him. If he let himself go enough to get lost in this, treat it as something real, bad things would happen. Then she'd stop watching him.

It was pathetically ironic, what she'd said to him about a safe word. The way she watched him made him feel safe. Not safe like he was some chickenshit who needed protection. Different kind of safe. Safe

5

from the things inside himself. The things he was powerless to change. For months, he'd known a train was coming. His phone might be in his locker, but that wouldn't stop the message from coming. The train was almost here, but he couldn't get off the track.

She made him believe he could close his eyes, get lost in the bliss and never feel the impact obliterate him. And he shouldn't, couldn't do that.

"We need to stop," he said.

"Had enough?" she said in a neutral tone.

He nodded.

A long pause, as if she wasn't that willing to let this end. But it was a demo. She wasn't going to push things. She raised her voice. "Say you'll never put your feet on the walls again."

"I'll never put my feet on the walls again." If he was being his normal self, he would have added a teasing caveat to win himself a few more stripes. She must have realized it, because she waited an extra beat before she made a noncommittal noise and freed his ankles. Before she released his wrists, she rubbed his back gently with firm hands, making sure he was grounded. He didn't need that, didn't need that kind of aftercare, so he twitched enough to let her know, to make her stop. He didn't want her to stop.

When she took off one wrist cuff, he removed the blindfold himself. The first thing he saw were her eyes, dark pools. He'd never let himself look too deeply into them. Maybe because he could fall and be lost.

She braced a hand on his shoulder, rising onto her toes to release the other cuff. When she did, he found himself laying his cheek on her knuckles. Just putting his head down a second. Not really sure why.

He closed his eyes as she rested her hand on his head. It felt like all the things he would never have. Absolution, redemption, tenderness. A Mistress. Fortunately, he regained his senses and drew away. He stepped off the cross, avoiding further touch, and reached for whatever defenses that were still in reach of his grasping fingertips.

"Thank you, Mistress," he said in a raised voice, giving her a playful grin and turning away. He pulled up his shorts and rubbed his ass, making the cute sub girls giggled.

Regina watched him with those knowing eyes, and without smiling. She wasn't pissed. Just too aware. He added a respectful nod, conveying more serious thanks. When he did that, she nodded in return. His eyes lingered on her glossed lips, the gentle rise and fall of her breasts. The cocked hip stance, her meditative look. That was all he could have. He walked away.

As he made his escape, he saw Noah sitting against the wall in an unoccupied part of the play room, a good vantage point to watch several of the stations at once. Marius snagged a towel and a bottled water before sliding down to sit next to him. Everything in his back, ass and thighs was tingling. Everywhere she'd struck or touched.

He didn't say anything right off. Just ran the towel over his damp neck and chest. Noah had his head tipped back against the wall, knees drawn up to his chest, his eyes half closed. The lean man with long dark hair wore nothing but a pair of jeans and his tattoos. He'd been with Mistress Lyda for some time, long enough for their relationship to be considered a serious thing, but he never said anything about that. He had something to say about other things, though.

"That was some intense shit."

"You must have been watching something different." Marius took a swig of water. "That was just a demo, man."

"Yeah, sure. You should think about looking deeper into that."

Marius followed Noah's gaze to Regina, who'd met up with Mistress Lisette and was taking a seat with her at a courtside table. "You think she's looking for a boy-toy?"

Noah snorted. "I think if you pull that boy-toy stuff on her, she'll tear you to pieces and make you beg to be put back together again. Which she'd probably do, though she'd hold onto your dick for a few weeks to remind you not to fuck with her."

Because that twisted his cock and his gut in ways he couldn't interpret, Marius scoffed. "I've watched her play. She's not into that kind of meanness."

"That's surface stuff, and you're playing dumb. Her way of holding control has nothing to do with maximum force."

No, it didn't. It had taken him by surprise. Noah described it just right. When she touched him, she touched things far below the surface. Chemistry. Fuck. Had she felt it? He thought she had, but he could hope she hadn't.

"The boy-toy thing doesn't work forever, you know," Noah pointed out. "Not when you really do want a Mistress. The player routine is starting to look a little thin, Marius."

"I don't—" Marius broke off, his attention zeroing in on the activity at the suspension station. He glanced at the Dungeon Master on duty, Carlissa, but the DM was handling equipment instruction with a new member on the other side of the floor. "Hold that stupid and entirely off the mark thought. Back in a sec."

Noah grinned. "You're not on schedule to DM or do security tonight. You notice everything, man. Sure you're not a Mistress?"

"I'll come back and fuck you up the ass so you can decide for yourself," Marius said, already getting to his feet. He moved to the suspension station. The Dom was fortunately squatting over his open suitcase of ropes and clips. "Sir Guillaume?"

The black man with a runner's physique and a cauliflower top of short dreads shot him a look. Marius saw the usual flash of irritation that any Dom experienced when interrupted in session, so he got right to the point. He nodded to the slim Hispanic male sub, blindfolded and wrapped in an elaborate harness of jute, his feet off the ground since Guillaume had him suspended from the sturdy oak frame. Guillaume had found his passion with suspension rope play, and hadn't mentored long with the club experts before striking out on his own. He was smart enough to keep his solo play here at the Zone, though, where he was under the watchful eyes of the staff.

"He's having circulation issues in his right hand, and he's too deep to notice."

Guillaume rose. "There shouldn't be anything pinching him. I tied it—"

"When you worked him up earlier, this section probably tightened as he was squirming." Marius stepped closer to Tawn, the tied sub, and gestured. "See here." He guided Guillaume to grip Tawn's hand. "Feel how cold it is?"

Guillaume paled under his bisque coloring. "Shit."

"It's okay. He's not in danger yet. Skin color's still decent, though remember you have to keep a closer eye when your bottom's not Caucasian. Just fix the problem and massage the hand and arm, get the circulation going. Or, since you've already gotten him off and sent him flying, might be a good time to end the session." Marius gave Guillaume a dry smile. "Do aftercare and then let him have the chance

8

to suck his Master off to show his gratitude for giving him such a good time."

"Yeah." Guillaume was busy loosening the ropes, murmuring to Tawn, holding onto him. The sub's head tilted back, lips parted. Even without seeing his eyes, Marius knew they would show a subspace haze. Tawn was a dedicated rope bunny. All a Dom had to do was twitch some twine in his direction and he'd practically zone out then and there. Fortunately, the twitch of his fingers was what had caught Marius's attention. The unconscious mind had a way of staying on guard even when the rest of the brain was too fuzzy to compute danger. Until it was too late.

That wasn't the case here, and Marius was no longer needed. Easing back, he left Guillaume to handle his shit. As he crossed the room to Noah, he saw Regina watching him again. Though she was listening to Mistress Lisette, her eyes were on Marius.

He slowed under her regard. What would happen if he went and knelt at her feet? Asked if he could stay awhile, do anything for her? He could just sit, let her decide if there was more she might want from him. Maybe she'd put her hand on his shoulder and throat like she had before, that touch that sent him into a place that was similar but different, quieter but no less intense, than the subspace that Tawn was experiencing now.

What did he want from her? He didn't know, but a strong part of him wanted to find out. Noah was right, but being right didn't mean pursuing it was the best option.

Her gaze flickered, her lips parted. Fuck, it was an invitation. After all this time, when their schedules had never meshed, or she hadn't been approachable, or he'd talked himself out of it, maybe tonight...

"Marius."

Noah was waving at him, getting his attention. When he had it, he pointed toward the bar. Alex was working behind it, and he lifted the phone, telling Marius he had a call. He'd forgotten he'd left this as one of his backup numbers, because so often his cell was in a locker, or his car. He didn't really like carrying one. But he wished now he'd never given that number out, because his sense of sanctuary crumbled.

As he moved toward the bar, his gaze flickered up to the TV they kept on mute for people in the bar area who'd come to socialize rather than play. It was on the news, and the headlining story told him what that call would be about.

What were the chances they'd be on the right channel, at the right moment for him to see that shit? Right when the damn phone call came through? If there was any kind of sign in this bullshit world, it seemed like that was one.

He felt like he was in one of those video games where, when the player was killed, a gray pall came down on the landscape. Everything that was vibrant became dreary and lifeless. He found himself trying to draw in air, as if it was being sucked out of his world with the color.

Why did it fucking matter? It had been coming for months, right? He struggled to get past the gray, and he couldn't. It was like being struck blind, only he'd been struck color-blind, everything leached away, so it was an effort just to walk to the bar. He picked up the phone, spoke a word he didn't remember. Listened. Hung up.

He didn't remember going down to the locker room and putting on his street clothes. He didn't remember coming back and seeing the blushing submissive waiting by the door, hoping to catch his eye. He closed his hand on hers, tugging her out the door with him. He wouldn't remember that later either, or fucking her in her car like a crazed demon, trying to lift that gray pall. It didn't work.

The only thing he would remember was seeing Regina for one more brief second. When he emerged from the locker room, she was at the bar. As her eyes turned to his, he was going to fall in, get lost and do the wrong thing. He couldn't do the wrong thing with her. She pushed inside him too far. He wouldn't let himself hurt her.

The cute sub wasn't in danger. She didn't watch him the way Regina did. He needed to get out of here. Get out of his head. Give his dick a workout, and she'd do.

If that didn't help, he knew one other way. He'd heard somewhere that blood was gray until it hit the open air. Fucking poetic. He was ready to liberate some blood. His own or someone else's; it really didn't matter.

Fighting was the only thing that was going to bring back the color. Even if the only color it brought was red.

CHAPTER ONE

Eight months later

"You're smirking at me? You want me to break you, you goddamn asshole? Is that it?"

He started to laugh at her, the muscular man built like a gladiator. He was chained, his arms above his head, yet his laughter snapped something, forcing her into a place where she was the one without control. Her white-knuckled grip on the whip only drove the rage. She wanted to make him bleed, make him scream with the kind of pain that brought bowel-loosening fear, not pleasure. "You piece of shit, you arrogant, adolescent--"

In some tiny corner of her mind, the Mistress knew she should have ended this forty-five minutes ago. It had stopped being fun, it had gone over a line, and he'd dragged her past it, into this place with him. Somehow, he'd known where to press every trigger she had.

The thought increased her fury and she cranked the chains, yanking him off the ground. His feet dangled, his weight suspended brutally by his arms. It ended the laughter. If she kept him in the position long enough, his shoulders would dislocate. His muscles had to be screaming in agony already.

The snap of the dragon tail caught him mid-body, then lashed at his testicles. The blows wrested grunts from his throat, and his strong form writhed like a snake speared by a hook. Yet the light of challenge didn't die in his far-too-steady gaze. He was still sneering at her, the son of a bitch.

"Use it," she snarled. "Use it."

"*You* use it," he said in a soft voice. Almost pitying. That, and the contempt beneath it, dug into her like barbed claws. In a calmer moment, she might realize the infuriating pity was sincere, but the contempt was a goading tactic.

She was far from calm, however. Logic would return when she found herself again, the Domme she normally was. Not this Hyde-like monster he'd yanked out of her soul, twisting her mind and heart as if he were Lucifer in the desert, bringing out the worst and darkest parts of herself she'd never wanted to know were there.

Even while bound and seemingly helpless, a predator could take down a victim. She hadn't known that. She was destroying everything she cherished about herself, and he was reveling in watching her bleed. She hated him. She was going to make him suffer, goddamn it. If she was being dragged into hell, he was going with her.

Regina propped a booted foot on the lowest rung of the chair in front of her and sipped her drink. She had the tables in this section of the mezzanine to herself. On a weeknight, it was a quiet, less popular spot at The Zone, backed up to the executive offices and not as close to the public play areas.

She'd come ready to play, clad in latex from hip to ankle and calf boots. A sheer black shirt in a flowing fabric was held in place over her black bra by nothing more than a couple of buttons. Her lovingly cultivated locs, grown down past her shoulder blades, were loose, with a bit of corkscrew curl to them. The shimmer of the auburn highlights amid the black was accentuated with a scattering of sparkling silver and red beads.

She looked like a Mistress ready to kick and cherish some fine sub's ass. Once she'd hit the floor, though, nothing had grabbed her. Some nights were like that. She'd removed herself from the anticipatory gazes of unattached male submissives and come here. Many of them had been pleasant playmates on other nights, but right now she wanted to experience the club like the beach. By closing her eyes and absorbing it through all her senses, rather than actively seeking the waters.

It put her in a position to witness some club drama. She opened her eyes as Alex, one of the Dungeon Masters on duty, took the stairs to the mezzanine three at a time and put his head and broad upper torso into the open door of the floor manager's office. "Terry, we've got a problem in Room 7. I need backup to end it now, or he's going to do her real damage."

"Goddamn it." Along with the expletive, Regina heard a chair roll back and Terry emerged. The rangy woman with a blonde bob shrugged out of the fuzzy lavender cardigan she wore over her corset, snug jeans and stilettos. Regina was sure it kept her warm while she was sitting at her desk. Lower temps were a necessity in a club that generated a lot of body heat, particularly in the playrooms, public dungeon and on the dance floor, which even at this muffled distance was sending pumping bass through the table surface beneath Regina's fingertips.

"If you're calling for reinforcements, we're already too late on the damage part," Terry added in a clipped tone.

"Nobody has safe worded," Alex said. "And it's...well, fuck."

"Never mind." Terry brushed his shoulder with her own as she passed him, giving the long black braid down his back a tug. "It's not your fault. We both know what the problem is. Or who," she added darkly. "Let's go shut him down."

All Regina had to hear was a woman was in danger, and she was on her feet, following in their urgent wake. She wasn't staff, but she was a volunteer DM and gold star member of The Zone. The safety of a sub was everyone's responsibility. She wouldn't get in the way, but she'd be there to help. If Alex needed to contain an asshole, Regina had three years of past experience as a correctional officer to lend him a hand. Or they might require a skilled Domme to help calm and care for the sub.

It pissed her off, thinking a Dom had let things get out of hand and wasn't caring for his bottom. But it was an unusual occurrence at The Zone, which vetted its members carefully and had a diligent monitoring staff, so her curiosity was roused. Alex was a competent and experienced DM. What kind of situation could have escalated so far, and in such a way, that he'd called on Terry rather than defuse it himself?

Alex had left backup outside Room 7. The hallway was quiet, the open doors and dark interiors of most of the private rooms suggesting the bulk of tonight's play was happening in the public areas. Otis offered a short nod, arms crossed over his beefy chest. His neck was permanently brick red. While it was thanks to his fondness for fishing the Florida Gulf with no sunscreen, he claimed it showed Southern redneck was permanently baked into him.

"Still hasn't safe worded," he grumbled. "Was about to go in anyway, fuck it all. She's crying."

"I'm making the call. We're going," Terry said, and punched in a master code. "Head back to the main floor and keep an eye on things there with Georgia, Otis. Regina will be here with me for additional backup."

She tossed a glance over her shoulder, telling Regina she'd been aware of her presence. Regina wasn't surprised. Terry didn't miss much. She was a submissive herself in her off time, but Regina was sure that helped relieve the stress of her highly detail-oriented day job, that of a prosecutor with the Tampa DA's office.

Regina hung back until they entered, then she closed the distance. Terry immediately issued a clipped order to stop the session, but Regina saw it was protocol only, like the police identifying themselves to a perp who'd already given up.

Siren was collapsed in a corner of the room on a chair. She was trembling, her face rigid as if she was about to start screaming through stiff lips.

The situation wasn't what Regina had assumed, but when she saw who the sub was, it wasn't a surprise. It also hit her hard in the lower belly.

Goddamn Marius.

Marius's reputation at The Zone had been going downhill over the past months. Most Mistresses didn't even bother with him anymore, but when they did, the highest rating he earned was "frustrating-as-fuck." Topping from the bottom, an incorrigible brat, a misclassified Dom, a sub caught in the nebulous world of not wanting to be a Dom, but way too controlling to be a top. She'd heard all the speculations, and had wondered if he was an amalgamation of all of that. Plus one more, added by her good friend Lyda.

"He's become a total asshole," the Mistress had said bluntly.

Regina didn't disagree with the assessment, but the changes he'd displayed since the night she'd done a demo scene with him hadn't been able to completely erase the impact he'd made upon her that night. They had kept her in observation mode ever since, though. No matter how fascinating she found a question with no ready answer, she wasn't going to commit herself until she was sure he was worth her time. That he had the potential to be more than an asshole.

She didn't know if this would close the file on her interest, but it would be the end of something. As her gaze swept Room 7, the cold feeling told her what had happened here. It also explained Alex's frustration and Terry's anger.

Boy, you are so done. You finally pushed it too far.

Even so, his condition sent a spurt of angry incredulity through Regina. While Siren wasn't the most experienced Domme at The Zone, and she had qualities that Regina knew might have been rubbed the wrong way with a difficult power sub like Marius, she had enough experience to step back if she was losing control of her emotions. But she hadn't. Obviously.

Marius was off his feet, hung by his arms. His torso, legs and upper thighs were a mass of ugly welts, some inflamed enough to weep blood. The tools responsible were lying in a discarded stack on the ground. Fuck, she'd thrown everything but the kitchen sink at him. Dragon tail, violet wand, steel paddle. Even a frigging *sjambok*, a wicked-looking rubber cane.

The painfulness of the marks, the strain in his shoulders, should have been evident in his expression. Yet she only saw boredom, a mild annoyance. Until he turned his eyes toward her and she caught a flash beneath all that. A look which stopped everything and put her Mistress instincts on high alert.

Feral. Wild and violent, an animal in a trap. Then it was gone and the boredom was back.

Two things were happening. He was as spun up as any submissive would be, caught an intense scene that had gone bad. Yet another part of him, the part she suspected had contributed largely to that wrong direction, had iron control over his exterior reaction, making him look detached.

It was a dangerous deception, one she admitted she'd never had to defuse. Most times, a topping sub stayed in control. Marius was both in and out of control.

This boy shouldn't be within a hundred yards of a BDSM club environment. Not anymore.

Because another disturbing element in that buried-deep-but-not-deep-enough look was the desire to do harm. It made her cut Siren a little more slack, because it wasn't something that particular Domme would have recognized until it was too late. It was what a human predator emanated, emerging out of a cloak of shadows in a dark alley. But Regina was no one's prey.

"If the Mistress is done with me," Marius said to no one in particular, "it'd be nice to get some slack."

Siren had stayed hunched on the chair, shaking her lowered head as Terry spoke to her, the manager's hand on her shoulder. Yet when Marius spoke, the Domme's head whipped up like she'd been stung by a bee.

"You didn't give me any slack." She spat the words in a hoarse growl and exploded off the chair, taking Terry by surprise. Before she could grab Siren, the Mistress had charged Marius like a wounded animal, going after him with black nails and shoving hands, tearing a grunt from him as the impact jerked him against the chains.

Alex quickly subdued her in a neutralizing pin, and Terry moved to block her view of Marius. Regina stepped over the threshold, catching the manager's eye. "I'll handle him if you want to get her out of here," she offered.

Typically, the sub would have been the first person they attended. But Marius was being an ass, his studied indifference a passive attack, and they needed to get Siren away from that act now.

Terry had come to the same conclusion, prioritizing the care of the Domme to protect the interests of the club. "Appreciate it," she said shortly.

Siren was weeping in Alex's arms. In that condition, they could shepherd her out between them without further incident. Regina slid past them and approached Marius.

"Poor thing," Marius murmured. His tone was flat, not mocking, but Regina went with instinct.

She fetched him a sharp slap that boxed his ear.

It might not look like "safety first," but that hadn't made it any less necessary. He'd been moving his head, following the activity in the room, so she wasn't worried about neck issues. The rebuke served the right purpose, snapping his attention to her. Seizing his sweat-dampened dark hair, she jerked his head around and clamped her other hand on his jaw so he could see Siren being led down the hallway. Marius had a solid, strong-boned face, his jaw covered with a manly dark sandpaper stubble that rasped under her fingertips.

Alex had paused to give Siren a tissue from one of the liberally distributed dispensers before putting an arm around her again.

"That's your handiwork. Proud of yourself? Look at her. Unless you can't."

This time the aggression that flashed to the surface of his expression stayed. Good. She needed to spill off as much of that as she could, in addition to tending to the physical issues. Releasing him, she rested one palm between his shoulder blades and picked up the remote control to the suspension system. As she started taking him back to the ground, she could feel his explosive energy through her touch. If it wasn't defused, he could take this situation from bad to worse.

He'd stiffened when she put her hand on his back, and she noted he pinned his gaze to the top of the doorframe. She snorted. "Yeah, that's what I figured. You can't look at her. So just shut up," she added when his lips parted. His eyes narrowed but she ignored him. She brought him back to his feet, his elbows down around his ears. It eased the shoulder strain but not all at once, which would have been more hazardous.

Marius was close enough to six feet to be taller than most women. Not Regina, since in her high-heeled boots she was six even. He was built like a brawler, his thick dark hair chopped in a spiky style adding to the bad boy look. Tough facial features framed striking blue-gray eyes that went to silver when agitated, another way she could tell he was far less detached than he seemed. Right now the irises were the color of newly minted nickel.

He was clad only in a pair of latex shorts, his cock a thick curve under them even when not on duty. It wasn't the first time she'd noticed he had the proportions to please a woman at full erection. If only the rest of him didn't seem so at odds with that goal.

He only had one tattoo, a recent addition and nice work. Covering his right shoulder, the design looked like his skin had been torn away by claws to reveal armor beneath, a leather-style jerkin with buckles.

It was a shame he hadn't had actual armor to protect him tonight. But as she assessed his condition, she saw older scars and faded bruises. Cataloging past injuries, she suspected his nose had been broken at least once and possibly his right cheekbone. There were abrasions on his knuckles, mostly healed, layered over scar tissue.

That was another change in recent months. Before then, when he wanted to do so, he exuded pretty boy charm that transformed his features accordingly. He still had the charismatic looks to catch a woman's eye, but pretty no longer described him. He looked like a man who'd survived a lot of fights. Fights he'd gone looking for.

Siren was the first scene he'd had at The Zone recently, but there were other clubs, some far less reputable, that might allow rough play to exceed the boundaries of good sense.

She kept an impassive expression as she checked him for injury, but how he'd stiffened when she put her palm on his back took her back to that demo session they'd shared. Though he'd tried hard afterward to shrug off the obvious inroads she'd made during the flogging, she remembered when he'd rested his head on her knuckles. Only for a couple heartbeats, but it was as if a sudden weariness had come upon him, or he'd simply needed the connection.

She knew when a sub needed aftercare, and it had been like that, except she hadn't sensed the need came from their session. She'd had the unexpected thought that maybe the need had surfaced as a delayed reaction to a lot of past sessions, where he hadn't let himself ask for or accept it.

When his eyes had opened, something in the depths had reached out to her, a cry in the wilderness. Then it was gone. He gave her that shit-eating grin and stepped off the cross, turning his back on her. He'd thrown the obligatory "Thank you, Mistress," over his shoulder, and made the female subs laugh as he rubbed his ass in pained affectation.

If he was just an asshole, as Lyda had said, Regina would have put it to bed some time ago. But that moment he'd put his head on her hand had kept her gathering intel.

As a Zone employee, he worked part-time security and as a DM several nights a week. Over the bar were casual snapshots of staff members bantering with one another, posing and smiling. In those pictures, he displayed a whole different persona from what she had under her hands now.

However, those images were older, the most recent one of him taken well over a year ago. Lyda's assessment "He's *become* a total asshole" was key.

Regina thought of her first impressions of him. He'd always been hard to top, but he'd avoided causing frustration with powerful sex appeal and a playful, prankster's charm. The combination left a savvy Mistress shaking her head but amused with him, cutting him loose after some mutual pleasure taking. Often they came back for repeat business, particularly when they wanted to try some new stuff on an experienced sub. Marius's only real limit was he didn't do men.

While Regina always suspected his charm and flirty nature were a defensive act, there'd been a more genuine quality to them then. Kind of a, "Yeah, you're not getting deeper into my head, but we can have a lot of fun if you stay in the approved area. Don't knock too hard on the doors and we'll be all good."

As a staff member, he was a valued member of the security team and an excellent, even handed Dungeon Master, able to defuse or reroute sessions into safer and healthier waters when inexperienced players or those in the wrong frame of mind went awry. Ironic, to say the least. His sharpness and intuition as a DM were also why he could fuck with Mistresses the way he was doing now.

It was obvious something had changed in recent months, and had reached a breaking point tonight. He'd used that charm as bait for a trap, and lured Siren into those darker rooms. Then he'd shut her in there all by herself and turned her fear and insecurities on her. He'd mindfucked the mistress. Until she'd seen that feral look, Regina wouldn't have put it together, but she came to the unsettling conclusion he'd developed a sadistic streak, and not the pleasurable kind.

That didn't make sense, especially not for a true sub. She was certain that was what he was, no matter what smokescreen he put up to confuse the issue. The man who'd rested his head briefly on her hand might be a wild animal, with no capacity for trust. But the gesture had expressed a fleeting wistfulness, a wish that he *could* trust her, with everything happening in his fucked-up head.

Speaking of fucked-up... His firm lips had curved in a half smile now. The gesture was crooked because of a scar across the corner. She remembered when he'd shown up with the busted lip, though she didn't know the cause. She just remembered he'd had stitches in his chin and along his cheek.

The smile brought the right touch of concerned and rueful to his expression. His slate-colored eyes would have been mesmerizing except for that hardness in them, a calculating watchfulness that said he never completely stepped out of the picture and let go. It made the discerning woman wary, instead of melting with need. Until he turned on the charm, which he did now, masking the earlier flash of attitude.

"Sorry, Mistress. Didn't mean to be disrespectful. Was coming out of the zone," he said. "Hope she's okay."

"Do you now?" she asked coolly, rubbing the muscles in his shoulders, working out the knots, making sure he hadn't been injured. If he had, she suspected he wouldn't have revealed it with a single word. It took time to convince a male sub to admit when he was hurt so he could be properly tended, and Marius resonated with the tough-guy vibes. So she was thorough.

He tilted his head unconsciously to give her better access, and a breath escaped him, making her suppress a tight smile. *There you are, bad boy.* She had good, strong hands. She knew how to mix power and tenderness together the right way.

"Yeah." He recalled himself enough to answer her question. "I don't mean her any harm."

"Just worked out that way, hmm? Interesting choice of words. Most subs would be upset with her for losing control like that, for not keeping them safe. Sounds like you hold yourself partly to blame. A humble or insecure sub might incorrectly do that, but you're neither of those."

"Sounds like you got me all figured out." The broken lip curled. "So tell me what I am, Lady Regina."

He moved so his ass brushed her thigh. Not only an insolent move, but inappropriate, both in timing and situation. That didn't stop sparks from igniting wherever their flesh touched. Fortunately, her libido didn't do her thinking for her. Her Mistress side did.

She dropped the slack on the chains so he could lower his arms fully. In the same motion, she gripped his wrist, twisted, and bumped the back of his leg, shoving him to one knee. She ignored his grunt.

Yeah, he was hurting, but he wasn't injured. As Keanu Reeves á la *The Replacements* said: *Pain heals.*

The wrist pin kept him in that position. With the threat of excruciating pain if he tried to get out of it, it would keep most subs still. At the height of his session with Siren, when the air had likely crackled with violence, Regina suspected he'd have been one of those who'd risk a broken bone rather than be subdued. But for now, he went still as she bent over him and spoke against his nape. It was easier to keep his head bowed with the hold she was employing, but she wondered if he was doing it purposefully to play her. That wouldn't interest her. If his true sub part was responding, that would, but neither route had her attention right now. He wanted an answer to her question; she'd give it to him.

"You're a fucked-up soul," she said flatly. "Been lost in the woods for so long you stopped calling for Mommy, even though the need to do it is still there, pissing you off so you blame everything female for it. It digs into your heart and squeezes until you think the blood's gone, leaving stone. Probably why your eyes are the color of poured concrete."

They flashed. Feeling the thrum of tension through his shoulder, she tightened the screws, her hold on his wrist, before he could do something inadvisable. "But stone is what you better get used to feeling, boy, because you just hit rock bottom here."

He stared at the floor. A muscle in his jaw twitched, a quiver of reaction going through his body. As if he knew she'd detected it, he tensed from head to toe. The surge of reaction she felt like an impending explosion told her he was going to do something stupid, like break his wrist trying to throw her hold. Releasing him before that tension could translate to action, she shoved him forward, forcing him to catch himself on his palms.

She left him on his hands and knees and moved across the room, refusing to look at him again. "You don't have any injuries requiring formal medical treatment, though you're going to be sore as hell the next few days. Won't be the first time, so I expect you know how to handle that. Put something on those welts to minimize the chance of infection."

It wasn't until she closed the door behind her that she let her own reaction surface. Leaning against the door, she blew out a breath. *Shit and double shit.*

Over the years, she'd explored and binged on a lot of BDSM practices. Primal play, Mommy/boy, rope, electric, wax, impact, interrogation, pony and puppy play. All the basics in restraint and pain for punishment and pleasure. The Zone had been her place to indulge and learn, and network into other opportunities in private homes and at BDSM events during her work travels. The skills had earned her the regard of others, a resource in her own right for other Masters and Mistresses.

Her work as a correctional officer had helped pay her way through engineering school. Now, as a consultant in the technology and manufacturing industries, staying on top of all the latest advancements was critical. She had the type of mind that sought and devoured new information. If she had interest in acquiring a new skill set, she wasn't a dabbler. She wanted to master it and did.

Yet there was a type of interaction with a sub that had nothing to do with the mechanics, and it had kept BDSM an enduring passion long after she'd mastered and moved on from other interests. That connection simmered beneath the surface of scenes, a potential treasure that could surface during any of them. She'd played along the edges, dipped her toe into it now and then, keeping it a casual addiction. She was too busy and had far too many other pastimes to bog herself down in a relationship.

Yet when she'd seen others experience it at far deeper levels, she'd felt the twinge that told her one day she would want to go deeper and find that treasure for herself.

She was aware that emotions were her unknown frontier. She wasn't averse to the idea of getting involved with someone; in her practical way, she simply knew it would take the right opportunity to motivate her in that direction.

Months of studying him, chewing on the enigma in random moments, should have told her that she wasn't yet done with him. The thrum that went through Regina's bones now was a message easy enough to read.

"Yeah, he's trouble. But there's something shiny hiding under the heap of hurt he'll dish out."

His violence and Siren's distress had packed the room with dense negative energy, but that glimmer remained as hi-def clear as the cold starlight in Marius's gray eyes, impossible for her to ignore. A diamond dug out of a septic pond was still a diamond. The question was how dirty a person was willing to get to obtain it.

She wasn't a romantic. She'd rarely seen that glimmer of treasure and, when she did, often it was fool's gold. But she could feel the difference in that part of herself that knew such things. If she doubted it, she only had to defer to the equal surge of "oh shit no" that came along with it now, afraid she was right.

Yeah, the timing might suck, or it might be where it was supposed to be. Didn't matter anyway, did it? His ass was so done here. As quickly as the realization of her serious interest had happened, the optimal conditions in which to pursue it were going to close. She wasn't going to chase the boy down in whatever corners of the world he inhabited outside The Zone.

She strolled back to the floor, to all appearances dismissing the whole thing. Yet she kept a close eye on the corridor until Marius emerged from it, moving stiffly. Alex intercepted him on the way to the locker rooms. Marius balked at whatever the DM told him, but Alexander set his jaw and put a hand on his arm. An ultimatum had been delivered. When he pointed, Regina glanced up to the third level and saw the light on in Tyler's office. Fuck, she hated to be right. They'd called the boss man himself. She suspected Alex was saying Tyler wanted Marius in his office now, no time to change. He could either comply or clean out his locker and leave, period.

Forfeiting his membership, one of the perks of his employment, wouldn't be the only penalty for noncompliance. He'd broken the common-sense rule of not shitting where you work.

Marius's gaze flicked to the contact point between the two men, an obvious warning. The DM removed his hand, but he kept his hard gaze pinned on Marius.

Even at this distance Regina felt the crackle of electricity she'd experienced when she'd laid her palm on Marius. He was still in high rev mode from the scene, the whole situation. Guilt twinged through her for leaving him so abruptly, though the proper aftercare for a sub who'd shoved himself into sub drop through his own sadistic behavior wasn't in any BDSM play manual she'd ever read. Chaining him to the back of a car and making him run to keep up for a couple miles, naked and barefoot, came to mind, but local law enforcement would frown on the tactic.

Still... At least one club Domme was a state trooper. Maybe Violet would provide a police escort.

Regina wanted to shadow him up to Tyler's office. Maybe she could devise an even less plausible scheme to get herself into the meeting, or within hearing distance.

It turned out such strategies were not necessary. When Alex saw her, he held Marius in place with a gesture and crossed the room to her. "Lady Regina, if you're willing, Mr. Winterman has requested your presence. He feels your insight and participation would be valuable."

An interesting way of phrasing it, and one she was sure was deliberate, knowing what she did of Tyler Winterman.

"It would be my pleasure," she said.

CHAPTER TWO

$\mathcal{T}$yler replayed the feeds, the two tapes displayed on side-by-side monitors. He'd already digested the full session between Marius and Siren, confirming what he'd unfortunately anticipated the situation would be when Terry gave him the high points. But it was the end of both feeds that had his interest now.

Pressing play, he watched Regina take Marius down to one knee. Plenty of Mistresses had the ability to manhandle an unruly male sub, since some of them craved that, but what she'd said to him... Tyler hadn't heard it, but whatever she'd said had compelled an interesting reaction from the pain-in-everyone's-ass that Marius had become.

Tyler had been a practicing Master nearly all his adult life. He'd employed some of those skills for the CIA, in ways that still gave him bad dreams. It was not his preferred way of exercising his Dominant side.

But whether to extort information or give pleasure, he knew the significance of every movement or expression, the smallest ripple of muscle, the flash of an eye. Typical for most security cameras, the feed offered wasn't hi-res, but when their gazes had locked, Marius's body language suggested Regina's words had struck a nerve. Even more importantly, Regina had known it. It might have been a blind shot in the dark, but intuition had guided her arrow with accuracy.

The other tape was Regina's public flogging with Marius from a few months ago. *There.* Tyler stopped it at the point where Regina was releasing Marius and watched the man rest his cheek on her hand. In this instance, Tyler was more interested in Regina's reaction, the stillness that gripped her. How she'd touched his head with a tenderness the practical Mistress didn't often display in her Zone sessions.

He should throw Marius out on his ass with extreme prejudice, no more chances. Two taped moments wouldn't have changed his mind about that, except another factor had to be considered. Marguerite.

Tyler's wife was an indomitable Mistress and yet also his committed submissive, wrapped up into one complex, damaged but precious soul. His angel. Out of all the Mistresses at The Zone, she was the only one who had ever successfully topped Marius, meaning she'd achieved deeper levels than a simple, shallow orgasm exchange, usually the best-case scenario with him.

That had been well before Marius's downward spiral, which had come to a head tonight. Being a frustrating submissive wasn't against club rules. Mistresses could choose not to play with him, and they talked among themselves enough to know his M.O. even before trying him. But tonight he'd crossed a line, and Tyler protected his club members, whether Masters, Mistresses or subs.

His jaw flexed as he thought of Siren on the tape, shivering and crying. While just a few notches above novice-level, and sometimes taking herself a little too seriously in her Domme role, she was usually an even-handed Mistress who'd brought pleasure to many male subs in her same weight class.

Even behind closed doors, cautionary tales like this one leaked. It was a fair bet the subs who'd enjoyed Siren's company would be happy to handle Marius's punishment. Probably by taking him into the back lot, beating him bloody and dumping him into the trash. Tyler had to get out ahead of it before Marius was done permanent damage, no matter how much the idiot deserved it.

He sat back and thought about Marguerite's advice, which he'd solicited several weeks ago when he'd noticed the problems with Marius increasing.

~

"I'm going to have Mac shoot him. Every time I issue a warning, he says and does the right thing. When I call him on that shit, he clams up and tells me 'Understood, sir.'"

"Mac hates the red tape when he shoots someone," Marguerite pointed out serenely. "Using your covert CIA clearance to dispatch him would make far more sense."

Tyler snorted. They were sharing breakfast on the sunporch of his plantation house. His angel was in a short white silk robe and reclining on her hip against colorful pillows on the chaise lounge. The sunrise reflected off her moonlight-colored hair. Sitting across from her at the glass table, which gave him an unimpeded view of her long, bare legs and pearlescent toenails, he thought all she needed was a pair of wings. Though his second thought was far more earth-bound. He considered when he would order her to open the robe and lie there naked for his viewing enjoyment. The fabric was already slipping off one silken shoulder.

"Marius possesses as many layers as a brick wall. And he'll never open up to a male authority figure." She cocked her head, a smile touching her serious lips. "You're not listening, Master."

"I'm listening. I'm just fantasizing at the same time. By calling me that, you just pushed it into a higher gear, as I'm sure you're quite aware." He put down his coffee cup, though, and folded his arms on the table, nodding at her to continue.

"One side of Marius is a reasonably decent man with a good heart," she said. "The same Mistresses he drives crazy in scenes have complete confidence in him as a DM and security. The problem starts when you hit his triggers."

"Which seems to be happening more often."

"Yes," she confirmed. "When it does, he morphs into a mean-spirited bastard."

Tyler's eyes narrowed. "I didn't see your session with him back then. Did he get mean?"

"He tried." She met his gaze with eyes the color of a blue sky veiled with gossamer clouds. "Which I handled, quite effectively. That's why you're asking my advice."

He was sure she had. It didn't defuse his protective instincts, even in retroactive application. She gave him an amused, knowing look, but continued her explanation. "After our session, he made a conscious choice to limit himself to the Mistresses who don't push. Or the ones who cut him loose when he starts to be an ass, not interested in that kind of drama. Until recently."

"Yeah." Tyler shook his head. "Probably why I've let this go on longer than I should have. And because I used to like and respect the kid."

"He wouldn't be working for you otherwise." She nodded. "The more a Mistress tries to penetrate his shields, the more acrimonious he gets. His shields protect what's at his very center. At his core, he's deeply troubled. Damaged. Perhaps damaged in a way beyond repair."

She paused. "His wounds run deep—possibly deeper—than what you found in my heart."

He knew the depth of those wounds, the hell she'd gone through and to which he'd nearly lost her. "Are you sure?" he asked quietly.

"Yes. Whatever set him off in recent months has made it harder for him to keep up his façade. Or maybe the attempt to be something he's not is wearing thin, which happens as the years pass and we realize those demons aren't going away without the aid of something we do not possess alone."

She reached out, something she wouldn't have done at one time, and laid her hand on the table, like a bird landing at the corner of his place setting. He collected her fingers into the shelter of his grip. Whether she'd intended it or not, it was the hand that bore a scar that looked like a starburst, evidence of that hell she'd faced.

"Perhaps that's how he and I connected," she said slowly, gazing at the link between them. "How I found an open doorway. But there was a point during my session with Marius that I felt like a neurosurgeon who opened the body and saw a cardiologist was needed instead. He's not mine to fix." She lifted her eyes to meet his. "The one who needs to perform that operation is the one who wants to hold his soul in her hand. The way you wanted to do with mine."

He needed to be closer to her. Rising, he came around the table, continuing to hold her hand. "Robe off," he murmured, his chest and loins tightening at how she complied, with such quiet obedience. His own personal miracle. A woman with the soul of a Mistress and the heart of a submissive. He released her only to allow the robe to drop all the way free, then he folded her down on the lounge again, stretching himself out behind her, their bodies spooned together.

Propping himself on his elbow, he ran a proprietary hand over her body, her backside, her upper thighs. She laid her head down on his biceps, her short, manicured nails stroking a trail up his propped forearm. He dipped his head to smell her hair, nuzzle it.

"Do you think there's such a woman out there? That's a tall order, finding the perfect Dominant for such a difficult sub."

"I won't inflate your already massive ego," she said, but added a teasing rub of her ass against his groin, emphasizing the innuendo—and inflating it. He wrapped his hand around her hair and tugged.

"Tell me more about this mystery Somme, then."

"She won't be driven by a sentimental desire to save him, though she may very well do that. She'll first be interested in the challenge he offers to her skills." Marguerite laid her head back down on his arm, her body shivering as he idly cupped her breast, stroked over her navel and down to her smooth sex. He noted with satisfied male interest her next words were more breathless. "That's what will draw her to him and will be the only thing that works, because she has to stay detached enough to stay ahead of him on every level."

"She'll have to be stronger than I was. I couldn't stay detached from you. You had my heart from the first time you tried to stab me with a cake knife."

"You wouldn't have said that if you were a hair less quick," she said dryly.

"Yes, I would have." He pressed his lips to her throat, used teeth, and felt her pulse elevate. "As I told you then, I'm not afraid to bleed for you."

Her hand gripped his forearm in aroused reaction and he saw her lashes lower as her eyes closed. "Keep explaining," he said. "You're not done."

Her lips curved, even as her fingers quivered on his at the command. "Sadist. For her to reach him completely, at some point she'll have to love him. Because love is the only thing that saves a lost soul. But I don't think it can start that way. I was wounded, but I'd reached a balancing point in other aspects of my life, like running Tea Leaves, and my tentative friendships with Chloe and Gen. When I struck out at you, it was more from fear than hate and the need to do violence. Marius...I'm not sure he's there yet."

Her expression became more serious as she turned her face to him. Her hand stilled his on her stomach. "If there is a woman who decides to walk the path with him that you walked with me, she'll be risking herself in ways I'm not sure are wise. But that's the risk of loving a lost soul. They can drag whoever's trying to love them into hell and destroy them there."

"Or pull them out and save them," he reminded her, wrapping his arms around her. "We're going back to bed soon. I need to be inside you again."

She made a soft noise of pleasure as he sipped from her lips, teasing her tongue with his own. "I'm yours to command. And no one else's."

"I'll make sure you remember it all day long," he promised.

At the taste of her mouth, the press of her body, and with all his senses immersed in her, he decided he wasn't waiting to have her. He reached down between them to open his slacks, and felt the tremor go through her body. Her head tipped back against his shoulder, eyes half closed. She moistened her lips.

"Master," she whispered.

"Always," he responded, with authority and need at once. He gripped her throat as he guided himself into her. He took her from behind right there, his other hand shifting to her waist and hip to grip. Her body arched up, moans caught in her throat as he seated himself deep and then began to thrust, slow, torturing them both.

He made her silken skin damp with perspiration, and those tremors took over, quivering all along her lovely limbs. He buried his face in her hair, found her throat and set his teeth to it, causing her to cry out at the sharp clamp, the demand that he knew she needed as much as he did.

It didn't take long to bring her to climax, his fingers stroking her clit, his cock thrusting inside her. She spoke when she was still breathless.

"Please come with me."

He could refuse her nothing. When he spilled himself in her cunt, those muscles clutching him like a vise, he couldn't think of a better way to end the discussion. Or start his day. Being inside her was the best way to start or end anything.

It seemed slow, ticking moments later that they were curled up in one another's arms, her still naked as he preferred, him with his shirt open and trousers unhooked so she could stroke his damp shaft, curl her fingers in the coarse hair around it.

Half asleep, her mouth moving against his chest, breath heating his nipple, Marguerite softly sung a few bars of the *Sound of Music* tune, changing the words to, "How do you solve a problem like Marius." It planted a vision in his mind of all the nuns singing the chorus, only they had the faces of the club Dommes, like her and Violet, Lyda, Regina...

She smiled when he told her that. He liked making her smile.

Marguerite's assessment had startled him, her belief that beneath Marius's ten-foot deep layers of charm and humor bullshit lay something as dark as what Tyler had found devouring her soul. At the time of that conversation, nothing as blatant as this had happened. Now, even with the grainy feed, he could see the truth of it in the session with Siren.

Marius had likely noted Siren's relative inexperience and mild character flaws while he was working as DM and security, because he was second-to-none for noticing the details when serving in those roles. Which only increased the depth of the cold anger Tyler felt as he'd watched the feed and saw how Marius used that intel against her, the same intel he would have normally used to protect her and her subs when he was working.

Those weaknesses that could be groomed into strengths, he'd instead exploited to make her doubt herself, make her insecure, put her on the defensive, and ultimately lose control.

Tyler's anger about that made him stop and give serious second thought to the plan that had started to form, the idea that had taken hold, as he studied the two key moments between Regina and Marius. He could cut Marius loose. Keep Regina out of it. Her play was mainly within the scene, with resources provided by club members at several reputable private establishments in the area, like The Zone. If Marius was kicked out of The Zone, the decision would travel fast within the closely networked BDSM community, such that he likely wouldn't be welcome anywhere else locally.

Yet Tyler knew Regina and had a tremendous respect for her skills as a Domme. While Siren was competent, he believed Marius wouldn't have gotten so far along such a destructive track with Regina. There were tough Mistresses, hard Mistresses. She was tough but not hard. Just impossible to bullshit. She gave a great deal to her subs, satisfying experiences, with the parts of herself she was willing to give, and yet never left them feeling denied. She guarded herself closely, but not because of skeletons in her closet, Tyler was almost sure. It was because she had self-confidence and high expectations.

If he had to make an educated guess on her views about a long-term relationship, he expected when she gave her heart, she'd give herself above and beyond to the effort. But it wasn't something she'd do lightly. In the meantime, she took genuine pleasure in exercising control over her subs, her discipline and practicality keeping close rein over both their emotional responses.

Which came a little too damn close to exactly how Marguerite had described the right kind of Domme for Marius. It would be easier if the man was gay and Regina was male, because Tyler's first reaction in any situation where a woman might be at risk was to protect her. His lips twisted ruefully as he imagined Marguerite or Regina's expression if he said that aloud. He'd lost count of the times his indomitable wife had chided him about the line between chivalry and sexism.

If Regina was interested, *and* if he could satisfy himself that she knew what she was walking into—as much as anyone could predict an unstable submissive personality—she would deserve the opportunity.

Then there was Marius himself. If only tonight's behavior was taken into account, he didn't deserve any consideration at all. But he was one of theirs, too, and it was as obvious to Tyler as it was to Marguerite that the man was on an accelerating crash-and-burn slide. If he needed fixing and there was a way to do it, Tyler couldn't bring himself to turn his back on him.

He thanked God every day for the skills honed over a lifetime that had helped him reach his wife's heart. He'd found the way with his angel after they'd skated so perilously close, not only to the destruction of her soul, but her very life. They'd come out the other side, full into the light of the blessings that shone upon them now.

But it wasn't just practicality and skill that had taken him there. He'd learned to believe in signs. While he wasn't converting to crystals and rainbow aromatherapy anytime soon, he couldn't ignore the connection between Regina and Marius the tapes showed.

A knock on his door brought him out of his musings. Alex put his head through the opening. "Ready for them, sir?"

Tyler closed the two files. "Did she agree to come?"

At Alex's nod, Tyler pursed his lips. Another sign. "Good. Bring them in together."

Tyler noticed Marius sauntered in ahead of Regina, deliberately stepping in front of her before Alex could stop him. Interesting. Even at his worst, Marius always played the gentleman, at least in the predictable ways. Regina's russet eyes flashed, but her lips tightened against what Tyler suspected was a grim smile.

Rising, Tyler gestured to a chair. "Please sit down, Lady Regina." He cut his attention to Marius, deliberately evaluating him from head to toe in the revealing shorts. Tyler was straight, and so was Marius. However, since The Zone had a higher percentage of gay males than the norm for a mixed orientation club, Marius handled his fair share of offers. As a result, he didn't have hang-ups about being under male perusal. Usually. Being called to task nearly naked before a male Dom who was about to chastise him clearly didn't please him.

"You stand," Tyler said sharply, and got right to it. "How many warnings have I given you about this shit?"

"It isn't my fault if a Mistress bites off more than she can chew."

Oh yeah, the man was worked up, emanating a hot-blooded stress even through a sullen mask. Tyler noted a slight tension in Regina's hand, resting on the chair arm. Her eyes were on Marius, watching him with the unwavering focus of a Domme who knew he needed some type of grounding.

Well, he was going to have to do without. Sitting down, Tyler leveled a cold gaze on Marius he knew was effective, since Alex and Regina responded to it by going more still. Even Marius looked as if he knew he should step down on the attitude.

"Was that my fucking question?" Tyler asked pleasantly.

"No. No, sir." Marius might have pulled off the honorific if not for the biting edge. Regina crossed her long, beautiful latex-clad legs, her manicured nails tapping the chair arm in a meditative manner. She was absorbing him like a sponge, Tyler realized. Which was what an experienced Domme did when she'd decided she was very interested in something. In someone.

"Then answer it," Tyler continued. "I wouldn't suggest you ask me to repeat the question."

"Yes. I've been warned three times." Marius's tone went wooden, his eyes flat and focused on the wall above Tyler's head. He was bracing for impact. A wise decision, since it was coming.

"Thank you. That's it, then. Your membership is terminated, effective immediately."

Marius stiffened. "I work the floor tomorrow night—"

"No, you don't. Your employment is likewise terminated. You've alienated your last Mistress in this club. Tonight you crossed the line into abusing one."

Marius's gaze snapped to Tyler. "I didn't touch her."

Tyler leaned forward, pinning him with a dangerous look. "Abuse doesn't come only from a fist."

Marius's face went white. For an instant, Tyler saw a dark flatness in his gaze that reminded him of a suicide bomber he'd interrogated.

Forget it. Damaged or not, angel, he's done. Yet a tone of desperation entered Marius's voice Tyler couldn't ignore.

"There's nothing in the session between me and Siren to show me at fault."

"Everything in that video shows you at fault." Tyler's voice cut across his, slashing steel. "This isn't a democracy or a court of law. It's a benevolent dictatorship, and you are not in control."

Tyler leaned back again as a weighted silence descended on the room. Regina's eyes met his. Her face was impassive, revealing nothing, but the lock of her gaze was a message itself. He bit back a sigh.

I don't like this. If she gets hurt...

It is her choice to make. Give her the opportunity. Good Goddess, Tyler, she was a C.O. at a maximum-security prison. Who conducted The Zone workshop on physical takedowns? She did.

A man knew he was irrevocably married when he could conjure full conversations in his head with his wife, even when she wasn't present.

"Your membership termination may not be permanent."

With that statement, Tyler shifted back to Marius, capturing a flash of surprise among the resentment. "It's incontestable for three months. After which time, Lady Regina may re-apply on your behalf. You may not approach her about that. It is wholly her decision if she wishes to work with you."

He'd startled Marius, no question. The man's regard bounced fully to the Mistress. Even Alex looked startled, and like he thought his boss might have lost his mind. Alex had a special fondness for Siren. He probably would have led the group to beat Marius into unconsciousness behind the building.

The only one who didn't look shocked was Regina. Tyler gave the Mistress credit for aplomb. Except for a slight twitch of her facial muscles, she didn't give anything away, even though he'd sprung that on her at the same time he had Marius. But he'd phrased it the way it was meant. She could pick up the gauntlet or not, but regardless, she was Marius's last chance here. If she was as interested as Tyler suspected she was, and if the membership meant anything to Marius, Tyler had given him a reason to respond to the Mistress's attention. If not, or Regina wasn't interested, or decided it wasn't worth it, then that was the end of that.

His angel's words counted for a great deal, but she was as much Mistress as he was Master. If you led a sub to water, held his head under to the point of near drowning, and he still wouldn't drink, well... Free will meant the right to throw your life away.

Case in point. Marius's eyes smoked over like a hot ash fire.

"Fuck all of you," he said.

He pivoted, shouldered roughly past Alex and left the office. Pursing her lips, Regina raised a silken brow. "Did that go as well as you'd hoped?" she asked Tyler.

"As expected," he said, with a sigh. He nodded to Alex. "Give him breathing room, but make sure he gets his locker cleaned out and reaches the parking lot without causing any more trouble. Or incurring any."

"Yes, sir." Alex's tone was stiff. Tyler sharpened his glance upon him.

"Something you want to say?"

"I wouldn't want any woman I care about near him," Alex said.

"No disrespect, Mr. Winterman, but I don't think I'd have put that option out there."

"None taken. I'm questioning it myself, which is why I'd like Lady Regina to stay a few moments, so we can discuss some additional things. Thank you, Alex."

It was a firm dismissal. Alex acknowledged it with a troubled look and disappeared.

"I'm surprised he didn't charge into the room without Terry," Tyler observed. "It speaks to his professionalism, that he followed procedure despite his feelings for Siren."

"Alex is a good man." Regina studied him. "Did you just throw me to the wolves, Tyler Winterman?"

"No." He smiled at her patented *don't-bullshit-me-boy* look. Considering the circumstances, it injected him with an extra dose of reassurance. "I listened to my wife's advice, rather than my protective instincts, and gave you the key to his cage. It's up to you whether to unlock it or not." Pushing his chair back, he put an ankle on his knee. "I'll support your decision a hundred percent. At this point, his behavior doesn't require my advocacy or loyalty."

"Yet your sense of fairness, and how long you've known him, is providing a chance for fate to intervene."

Tyler cocked his head. "The intuition of a beautiful Domme is a scary thing."

"I'd say the same about a handsome one like yourself. You could have given that key to any Domme in this club. There are reasons you chose me."

"There are." He templed his fingers. "You've had him on your radar for some time. I'd like to hear your assessment."

Regina uncrossed her long legs and hooked them at the ankles, lacing her fingers over her flat stomach. "You have a lot of spies in this club. It could make a paranoid person nervous."

"I have a lot of people watching out for the welfare of everyone here, including you," he corrected. "And we live up to the reputation, which is why so many sign the waiver accepting that we maintain cameras in all club areas. It ended up being a fortunate decision tonight."

"Yes, it did." She sobered. "My opinion is still forming. But my current take is he has a touch of meanness and rebellion under a mountain of pissed off. The whole package is coated in melt-your-panties bad boy charm, with a wicked sense of humor that can turn around and cut to the quick in a blink. It all comes with a huge shoulder chip on the side."

When offering her opinion, Regina didn't pull any punches, and her flair for words provided a picture clear as a photograph. Tyler sighed and ran a hand over his face. "Marguerite deduced much the same. My concern is the escalation of the meanness. He may be unstable."

"He is unstable." She confirmed it with quiet frankness, surprising him. "Before tonight, I wasn't certain enough of that to bring it to your attention. It could have been chance, him and Siren coming together. Most of the Mistresses have lost interest in him and maybe he was jonesing for a sub fix. But I think whatever is broken inside him sent him after her deliberately tonight, knowing she had the right chinks in her armor. We all know she's still new enough to this she gets wound a little tight in session. She was a Mistress who had the right weaknesses he could exploit to a dangerous level. Siren was his prey from the moment they stepped into that room."

His jaw tightened. "So that's that, then. He's out of here."

"In his current state? Oh yeah. He's nowhere near the proper headspace to be playing at The Zone. That was the right call."

"So that means you won't be pursuing his re-application."

"Not necessarily." At his sharp, surprised glance, she shrugged. "Jury's out on that. The problem is, there's something else inside him. Something real. It's the bait that's lured too many Dommes into his traps. Fortunately, most of them got out before they reached the point Siren did. They didn't feel he was worth the aggravation."

A smile touched her lips. "I can't say I blame them. A normal sub, a normal man, is a lot of work to train properly. Marius has walked deep into no-go territory and fortressed himself there with quicksand and mud bogs. Somebody's going to have a real workout to get to him."

She stretched in the chair, a relaxed move, twisting her hair into a knot on top of her head and then letting it fall again as she re-crossed her legs. "Stop imagining me mud wrestling with your wife," she added.

Tyler chuckled. "It was Lyda. You two are a better physical match."

"I could take her." Regina sniffed. "She may be Selene in *Underworld*, but I'm Black Xena."

"Thanks for giving me more fantasy material."

Regina laughed then, a throaty sound that could inspire plenty of fantasies alone. Tyler's real life desires only involved his wife. However, since Marguerite on occasion had sessions with young, muscular submissives in this very club—though always under his supervision or observation—sharing his fantasies with her about other Dommes and subs he had no intention of touching helped balance things. And added an additional spice to their already flavorful sexual intimacy.

"So if he's too much trouble for most Dommes, why would *you* want to go after him?" he asked.

"Hmm." Her expression darkened, her long fingernails unconsciously stroking the chair arm as if it were a man's. "Just a feeling I can't ignore. If I can get us both through that bog, I think he's the kind of sub who will be waiting with a towel and a bubble bath. One who has a hunger to serve a woman with everything he's got. If it's there, it's built up in him a long time, untapped. He's Sleeping Beauty caught in a nightmare until the right Domme zaps his ass awake."

"Now I've moved right into lesbian sex fantasies about Sleeping Beauty and her evil stepmother." Tyler enjoyed another cock-teasing dose of Regina's laughter, but then all humor dropped from his expression, leaving only his concern for her.

"What's to keep you from being sucked into the nightmare? I care about you, Regina. So do Marguerite and many people here. It worries me, the door I've opened for you."

"That door has been there for me to open for months. I'm a big girl, Tyler." Her gaze slid down her long form. She was large-boned, elegantly made and as feminine and intimidating as a warrior goddess, a Black Xena in truth. "Bigger than most. What you've done is set it up so I don't have to chase him. If I initiate, from that point onward, he has to work with me. Which gives me a foot in the door, if he truly wants to get back into The Zone."

She rose. "My choice. My decision. Your conscience can rest easy on that."

"If it was only my conscience I had to appease." Leaving the chair, he came around the desk to emphasize his final point. "Watch your ass, Mistress. And know I'm here to help with that. You don't reach out to me and I find out you needed to do so, I'll be a mountain of pissed-off myself. I'm not as easy to handle as a male sub."

She chuckled. "Don't let a male sub hear you say that. It's a vast misconception that their testosterone poisoning is less than that of an overprotective Dom."

"Don't I know it." Tyler snorted. "I work out at the same gym with Mac Nighthorse. Still can't believe the man has never taken steroids."

"Oh, no. That is 100%, Grade A, organic beefcake." She flashed a wicked smile. "Violet is well aware of my lust, so I'm not telling you anything Tinkerbell doesn't already know."

"Except that you called her Tinkerbell, which we all know gets her hackles up."

"She's so cute. I just want to stick her on my dash with my Daenerys *Game of Thrones* bobble-head." Sobering, Regina touched Tyler's arm. "Your concern is noted and appreciated, Tyler. I'm not only a big girl, but a smart woman, too. You know my background. I won't get in over my head. But if I did, you'd be the first I'd call. I promise. If you don't mind, email me his contact info. That way, when I decide what I want to do, I'll have what I need at my fingertips."

When he agreed, she took her leave after a few more pleasantries. Tyler noted her step was smooth but bore a touch of urgency. She was already hatching a plan.

Sitting back down at the desk, he rubbed his temples. Yes, she was a smart woman. A fearless one, the kind of Mistress who *would* get in over her head if she thought the risk was worth the reward. He was married to one of those. And she would claim he had plenty of that reward-worth-the-risk mentality himself.

It was that way sometimes, for Master or Mistress.

It wouldn't stop him from worrying. Or from keeping as close an eye on the situation as his "network of spies" allowed.

⁓

Regina changed out her sheer blouse for a silk blue tunic over the latex leggings. Still a sexy outfit, but more street-appropriate. She wasn't sure if she'd beat Marius out of the building, but when she emerged, she saw his car was still there and it was empty. Good.

He drove a blue Honda Civic with a few minor dents in it, to be expected since it was an older model. One of the doors had been replaced, probably through junk yard parts, since it was a different kind of blue from the rest of the vehicle body. When she passed the car on the way to her own vehicle, she glanced inside, surprised to see the interior was pristine. From its aged appearance, she would have expected discarded fast food bags or soda cans, old crumbs and dirt on the carpets, receipt scraps. Though the upholstery was worn, duct tape neatly mended a couple rips.

He took care of his car, which meant he had a regard for his possessions, no matter the age or condition. Perhaps because he didn't have a lot of money to spend on repairs or getting new things. But she'd seen plenty of poor people with junk cars and rusted bikes in the yard, or trash and old furniture piled on the bowed and rotting floor boards of the front porch. He was an interesting mix of puzzle pieces. Would she want the finished picture, after she assembled it? Would there be vital pieces missing?

His employment at The Zone explained how he afforded the pricey membership, since employees received a deep discount after their first full year. Before that, they could offer themselves as a sub or Dom loaner if a customer was interested, but otherwise they had no membership privileges.

She moved to her Mercedes, a few rows over but fortunately parked in a position that allowed a line of sight on his vehicle. While she had no intention of talking to him in the parking lot, she would take her current advantage to gather intel.

With time to kill, she reviewed what prep work she wanted to do before she decided to initiate. If the other Mistress was up to it, she'd talk to Siren about what had gone down, at a neutral place like a coffee shop. Though he'd given her quite a bit of info, she didn't expect Tyler would allow her to watch the tape.

That thought made her think of Marius in Tyler's office, the energy pouring off him explosive as a stick of dynamite. *Fuck all of you.*

"Yeah, baby, it pissed you off, didn't it?" Regina spoke softly inside the silence of her darkened car. "You don't like being handled. Or depending on someone else for the things you want. Yet you want to be a sub. It's like an oil coating all those fine muscles, head to toe, inside and out. Can't figure it out, can you? And the longer it's gone on, the meaner it's made you. You're just about on the ruined side of it. Are you worth bringing back?"

If she was being honest with herself—and she always was—becoming involved in this decision was secondary to her interest in the man and seeing where that would take her. The rest would resolve itself. She didn't stress over his fate at The Zone. She was a fair, even-handed Domme, mindful of the right frame of mind needed to deserve the privilege of playing at a place like it. He'd either work that shit out with her enough to prove he belonged there, or not.

She settled into her seat, pushing it back to give her more relaxed leg room. Her Mercedes was as old as Marius's Civic, but in far better exterior condition. She'd bought it after she'd graduated Georgia Tech with honors and landed her first engineering job with a salary that allowed the indulgence. She'd lovingly cared for it ever since. No reason to get rid of something that had served her so well for so long, and was still doing the job.

There he is. She remained motionless as he emerged from the club. He might know where her car was, but at nighttime, she shouldn't be noticed. Though if he saw her, she'd use whatever openings that turn of events gave her. She wasn't hiding.

She had no problem taking the opportunity to observe him when he didn't think he was on anyone's radar, however. He was dressed in jeans and a dark blue T-shirt that etched out his upper torso damn well. Jeans did a good job of it, too, defining an ass as tight with tension as the rest of him. When he threw his gym bag in the back and put himself into the front seat, the car rocked from the door slam.

Still angry, though he also seemed deep in his head. He was staring through the windshield. His hands appeared on the top of the steering wheel. From the flex of his shoulders, he was gripping it as tightly as he could, fighting whatever was going on within him. He pressed his head back against the seat. Tattoo beat, one, two, three.

The grip on the wheel showed external anger. Who to blame. Tyler, her, Alex, Siren. But the head beating thing, she believed that was self-frustration. Loss of control. Deep inside, he must have known taking it so far would have bad consequences, especially after three warnings. But that was how a self-destructive personality worked. They just couldn't help themselves.

She'd been developing a theory since she'd felt that energy vibrating off him when she lowered his chains. She believed he hadn't intended to go as far as he had with Siren. If he was truly as detached as he tried to appear, he could have called himself back. But maybe the true submissive's need under all the shit had pushed him forward, convincing him he could get there, could get where a Mistress wanted him to go.

Then that other side of him took over again, blew it all up and caught everyone, including himself, in the shrapnel. Another sub would have come out of such an experience dazed, craving a nurturing form of aftercare. He'd come out angry, closed and defensive, unwilling to accept good or bad shit from anyone.

He was not going to be an easy project.

"You better be ready to see this one through, Regina," she advised herself. "You go at this half-assed, he'll cut you to ribbons. He might do it anyway, but if you're all the way in, you'll have your hand on the same knife."

Regina jumped when he erupted into motion. Marius hit the wheel with a closed fist, surprising her with the vehemence. One sharp blow, two. Then he rummaged in the glove compartment and produced what looked like a cheap flip phone. After dialing, he spoke to whoever answered in short terse sentences. A nod, and he tossed the phone on the seat before turning over the engine.

When he put the car in drive, his set countenance suggested he had a destination in mind.

Well, she had a free evening, didn't she? She'd see where he went to blow off steam.

As she navigated through traffic, she didn't have trouble keeping him in sight. He drove decently close to the speed limit and he didn't drive like an angry man. After he'd made the phone call, he'd settled. Or maybe he'd channeled his aggression toward a different target.

Since The Zone had to accept the same zoning restrictions as much seedier adult businesses, it was on the fringes of the less desirable side of Tampa. Marius was headed deeper into that area. After a few miles, she followed him down a narrow, dark street that in crime shows would have had men huddled over oil drums of burning trash, the flames and their figures throwing eerie shadows up against the brick. Well, if it wasn't a balmy Florida night.

Regardless of her dramatic imaginings, only homeless people or those with criminal intent would be wandering this area without purpose. Marius took a right and disappeared down another alley. She waited a moment and then followed, making sure her doors were locked. If there was nothing down here but darkness, she was prepared to reverse and end her sleuthing days before they began. She had no desire to be carjacked.

The alley dead-ended at a boarded-up, abandoned warehouse, a backdrop that would have confirmed her concerns, except for the type of vehicles in the parking lot. Whereas the asphalt was so cracked it might as well be gravel, a variety of shiny, expensive cars mixed with upscale SUVs were parked upon it. Directly in front of Regina, a man circled the front of a red Ferrari to hand out a woman from the passenger side. She wore a white sparkling dress that barely passed legal in either direction. Her blond hair was as white as the dress, except for a vivid blue streak down the right side that matched the sapphires on her neck and ears.

Marius had pulled past all the flashy vehicles, and been waved into a roped-off area on the side of the building where more modest cars were parked. He exited his and entered the building through that side door. As Regina pulled into the lot, intending to follow him, she was intercepted by a ponderously built man approaching her car. He was dressed in an impressively well-cut suit and looked enough like a security detail to give her confidence he didn't have murder on his mind when he gestured to her to lower her window.

Yet since his responsibilities could include protecting a drug lord, she put her hand on the Glock she kept tucked into the cushioned pocket between seat and console. Better safe than sorry.

He leaned forward and gave her a thorough appraisal that would have been rude if it didn't appear more functional than appreciative of the view, though he managed to work in the latter in an inoffensive way. "Hot lady looking for a hookup with the fight talent?"

Fight talent. She thought of the fading bruises on Marius's body, the abrasions on his knuckles. Covering her sinking feeling, she raised a brow. "Is that what I look like?"

He gave her an easy grin. "No man in the car, and nothing about you says show pony. You looking for a show stud if you're here. Or got some serious money riding on the action."

From the steady look in his brown eyes, she expected her answer was going to get her in or kicked out. She chose honesty. "I'm not betting on anyone. I followed a guy I want here. Though I do think he's one of the fighters."

He hadn't gotten in the door by placing big money bets with bookies, like she expected the people in fancy clothes and stepping out of their Ferraris and Porsches had. His entrance fee was paid by his fists. And blood. She took a breath.

"In fact, I'm pretty damn sure of it."

CHAPTER THREE

*T*he man gave her another close look, then shrugged. "Boss says sexy women are always welcome at our fights, even if they don't have anything riding on the action. Park over there." He pointed. "Entrance and exit are where you see the people going in. You'll be searched for recording devices and wires and you have to check your phone, so if you don't want anyone handling that, leave it in the car. First fight's already started, so you're going to have to work to get a good seat. Tell them Freddie said to take care of you and you'll be able to see."

"Appreciate it."

"My pleasure."

When she parked, she noted a handful of men similar to Freddie strategically placed around the lot. They appeared to be providing the same courteous guidance and sharp-eyed new guest vetting that he had for her.

She guessed if the police came by, those responsible for that possibility would be armed with paperwork and answers to questions that would neatly skirt any probable cause to search the premises. She came to that conclusion because they didn't look ready to scramble like cockroaches at the first hint of trouble, the way members of a corner drug deal would. And from what she knew about illegal betting events, the key was making sure all the big money transactions happened elsewhere.

Who said working in a prison couldn't be educational?

She'd learned as much from that job as she had from the engineering classes the work had funded. Plus, the skills she'd acquired there had neatly dovetailed into her pursuits as a Mistress. She was a very well-rounded person. Glancing down at her curvaceous figure, she chuckled. "In more ways than one, hot lady."

She sobered. She was about to attend an underground, illegal fight. Well, if it was raided, she hoped the attendees faced less stringent consequences than the organizers. Regardless, she knew who to call for bail. While she'd rarely used Tyler's private cell number, she did have it, and since he was partly responsible for why she was here, she wouldn't hesitate to get his ass out of bed to come get her. He'd offered to watch her back, right?

Based on the snazzy dress and enthusiasm of those converging on the nondescript door, it was as if she was entering an exclusive nightclub. Expensive cars, expensive people. They probably had thousands riding on tonight's fights. She wondered how much of that Marius got if he won. Probably not anywhere as much as the bookies and their bosses would.

Most of the attendees were probably carrying wads of cash to do some side betting with friends. She thought she had enough on hand to cover a two-drink minimum, because she was very certain they wouldn't be handling credit cards.

But Lord, she hoped they had some alcohol. She was going to need it. She wasn't squeamish, but as she approached the entrance, she picked up the tang of violence in the air. It had her pulse beating high in her throat, particularly as she thought of why Marius might be here. Yes, he'd engaged her interest, but she hadn't expected to feel this level of concern. A reaction clearly too precipitous for this stage of their non-relationship. A nice fiery drink to her gut might settle that down.

Her lip curled at her self-chiding. She nodded to the doorman, a wiry guy with a knit toboggan hat pulled low over what she suspected was his cue ball smooth head. He looked like a fisherman from a shrimp boat reality show, but he pulled open the graffiti-covered steel warehouse door with a flourish, like the bellhop at a pricey hotel. His dancing hazel eyes made her smile and relax a little more. She was used to handling men in a lot of volatile situations, both professionally and personally. Though she was obviously stepping into an illegal situation, these men weren't a threat to her. As Freddie had made clear, she was a commodity they wanted here for repeat business. Also like at an exclusive nightclub, a woman with the right looks and attitude was always welcomed and pampered.

Inside, tall panels had been put up to filter people past the security check, but behind the panels she could hear an excited crowd, a tidal roar of sound punctuated by shouts and cries, people watching a sporting event in progress. The air was saturated with heat.

A man with skin so dark he almost blended into the shadows, thanks to a matching black suit, shirt and shoes, scanned her with a device she expected was checking for electronics of any kind. She was patted down thoroughly by a female counterpart to him, though she was fair Irish, her red hair sparkling with glitter. The festive look didn't detract from her ice-cool eyes.

With this investment of manpower and security equipment, she wondered that they didn't have the event in more posh surroundings, perhaps at the mansion of a sympathetic mogul's estate. They probably did move the event around, but part of the allure was this kind of setting. A warehouse with a concrete floor, exposed metal rafters. Raw, unfinished surroundings to match the nature of the spectator sport.

After being searched, Regina was directed politely to a ticket window to hand over a fifty-dollar cover charge, something Freddie had neglected to mention. There went her drink money.

"Let me stamp your hand, love." That came from a man next to the cashier's booth. His broad Australian accent was complemented by spiky bleached hair, earth green eyes and a scar that ran across his nose and left cheekbone like a bold underscore to that eye. The cut had come close enough she suspected the bottom lid had needed suturing and his eyeball had been in danger of rolling right out. "You new to us?"

At her nod, he grinned. "I could tell. Welcome to the show."

He had cauliflower ears, she noticed, and big gnarled hands that would give him arthritis as he aged. Perhaps already, since he appeared to be in his forties.

"You look like a fighter yourself."

"Semi-retired," he confirmed. "Sometimes they'll match me up with someone in my condition, an old geezer opening workout to make all those aging Viagra blokes in the audience feel virile by association." He winked. "But I got myself a lovely girl, and she put an end to it the night this happened, the straw that tipped over this aging camel." He tapped the scar. "Bastard I was fighting put a razor blade between his knuckles." He made a fist and did a gentle pantomime of a swing before her nose. "He was trying to open up my forehead to get blood in my eyes, but he misjudged. Or I was too slow or too quick."

"Is that kind of thing allowed?" she asked, her heart kicking up into her throat.

"If I couldn't tell it's your first time, that would have proved it. Though it's also your scent and look. Fresh and lovely. A bit wide-eyed, which I expect isn't a look you have too often." He chuckled, eying her appreciatively. "Not too sure what it is you've stepped into, eh? But don't worry none. We're the upper scale of this type of independent enterprise. All the women who come here are safe. Good for business as well as just plain good. Men like to come with someone on their arm. If she's not comfortable, she's not coming back. We've got some female high rollers, but men are our staple."

"Like strip clubs."

"Just so. It's entertainment that gets their dicks hard. Some of them don't make it out of the parking lot before they're already all over their show pony of the night." He spoke matter-of-factly, not as if he were attempting to shock her with the crudity. It didn't offend her, though she didn't care for the image he'd conjured, of fight groupies crawling all over Marius in the parking lot, wanting to taste the sweat off his muscles.

"There aren't many rules," he continued. "You can't bring a knife, but the occasional razor blade? That's just initiative. We got all styles of fighting, but it can get down to brutal street brawls for any of them, if they want to win bad enough and their opponent is just as tough. That's really what most of this crowd pays to see. Like the ones who go to Daytona to see the race cars wreck."

She arched a brow. "Why are you telling me this? I could be one of the bloodthirsty ones."

He ran his gaze over her. Her sex appeal had never been assessed by so many in such a practical way. "No. You're not here for the fighting. You're here for someone. Which one?"

"I don't know if he's using his real name, so I don't want to betray his privacy." Hell, she didn't even know if Marius was his real name at The Zone, come to that. She wondered if Tyler would include that in his email. "He has short, dark hair, a bit spiked, and blue-gray eyes. He's not as tall as I am in these boots, but he's built solid so he looks bigger, like..." A fighter.

At the flicker of humor in her listener's craggy visage, she realized she was giving him nothing useful, unless he wanted to know how closely she'd studied Marius from head to toe and how often. She wasn't usually caught being sentimental. "He has a tattoo on his left shoulder that looks like there's battle armor under his skin," she said briskly.

"Just so." His gaze cleared as he repeated the phrase. "That's Rabid. He's my boy."

At her raised brow, he grinned. "No, not my son. Pretty sure he was spawned by wolves. I manage him, much as he'll let anyone. Set up his fights. I'm Tal. You've come on a good night. The bookies stopped taking straight bets on him winning or losing, because no money in it. He always wins. Unless they come up with a new twist to make it a bigger challenge, you can only bet on how far in he'll be when he'll take down his opponent, or what kind of blow will do it. When he's down and getting the shit kicked out of him? That's when he's the meanest and most dangerous. Hence, Rabid. A rabid animal backs down from no one."

Because the animal is suffering so much pain, he turns savage, Regina thought.

"He takes pain and uses it like rocket fuel," Tal said, unwittingly confirming her thought. "But they'll make money on him tonight, because he's agreed to something he hasn't done before. Three consecutive fights, no breaks except to haul his previous opponent out of the ring. They've lined up a trio of our best against him."

As her gaze darted toward what the panels concealed, he misconstrued her alarm. "Don't worry, you haven't missed him. He's third in tonight's line-up. They're still on the first bout." He gave her a considering look. "I'm fond of the tough little bastard, so I'm going to put you in a choice place, right where he'll be able to see you. Don't worry, you should stay clean. Blood spray doesn't usually hit the catwalk.

Better to put you there anyway. You might be too distracting to him on the ground level, in his direct line of sight."

Regina wondered if she should ask how close the nearest restroom would be, since she thought she might be sick. Once she accepted the escort Tal assigned to her, and that man positioned her in a front row position on the wide metal catwalk with a good view of the fighting ring, she was certain of it.

As a correctional officer, she'd faced the simmering potential for violence every day. That was her work environment, and it kept her on full alert through her shift. Her pep talk from her boss when she was hired had run along the lines of, "Stay focused at all times. They watch for a careless moment. You have one, that's when you'll get injured, raped or killed. Have a nice first day."

Her job was as much to maintain calm and order, to keep the inmates on the same even keel, as it was to be ready if that calm and order was disrupted. Even though rationally she knew this was different, the edgy excitement of the crowd, their anticipation of danger and the forbidden, had a similar tenor. She felt like she was back at the prison, particularly on the handful of days when there'd been rumors of an impending riot, usually started and provoked by rival gangs.

She'd had a variety of coping mechanisms. Breaking things down into logical pieces was one of them. This is an organized fight, she reminded herself. Illegal, yes. Out of control, no.

Remembering the cut under the Aussie's eye, she wondered how much of a lie she was telling herself. One thing she knew for sure, though. Based on what she'd felt from Marius earlier in the night, this was an even worse place for him to be than a BDSM club.

The atmosphere was smoky, dirty yellow light illuminating the crowd, the spotlights on the cage style ring throwing their shadows on the high walls like dancing flames. Despite the large space, it was hot.

The man emceeing the fights was a dwarf in a green velour top hat with a purple feather. With his jaunty strut, he reminded her of a character in a Dickens novel.

She guessed she was well and truly committed to figuring Marius out. Else she wouldn't be staying in place now, watching two men hammer on each other with thuds against meaty flesh, their grunts hitting her ears like thunder. The sweat spraying off them from the punches reminded her of children stomping into puddles. The crowd shouted in delight when a blow made solid contact, and even louder when a follow up knocked the man to one knee. There was no referee to call the opponent back. When the man went down, his combatant was on top of him, punching, kicking and hammering. The other man somehow managed to throw him off and get back to his feet, but she thought he was on borrowed time.

She'd had female friends who'd been to boxing matches or MMA fights. Laced with just enough barbarism to make them feel a little guilty about the surge of physical excitement, they'd admitted it had been mesmerizing, watching two men in premium condition hammer and strain against one another.

But that was because the safety net of structure allowed them to rationalize that it was okay, the fighters protected as much as the formal dictates of their sport allowed. This had none of that. It was two men thrown into a ring to beat the hell out of each other in whatever way put one on the ground first, hard enough he wouldn't get up.

Whether for the adrenaline rush, money, validation, a chance at fame or something darker, desperation would be the key to why someone stepped into that ring. She wondered what flavor of it drove Marius here. It wouldn't be about money, even if that was his front for it.

The spectacle attracted all kinds. On her left was a group that looked like a rapper with his entourage; on her right, a Bill Gates style geek with his latest trophy wife. Both sets of people were hanging precariously over the rail, shouting and urging on their chosen one, erupting into cheers or boos as one man struck the other hard enough in the face that his lip split and arced blood over them both. Before it was all over, she expected the floor would be slick with sweat and blood, posing a footing challenge for the later fights. Like Marius's.

As the metal catwalk vibrated beneath her feet from all the excited stomping and motion, she turned her attention to those gathered closest to the cage at ground level. Marius might be there, queued up for his fight. But there was too much movement, too many shadows clustered outside the cage, too many...wait.

If he hadn't moved when her eyes were passing over him, she would have missed him. Like *Name That Tune*, it only took a few notes —or movements—for her to latch onto his familiar form.

The pair of shorts he wore were as revealing as the ones he'd worn for Siren. They clung to hips, ass and upper thighs. When he came into the spotlighted ring, the bulge of his genitals would be equally on display, to the appreciation of every female or gay male present. No need for modesty. This was all about exposing and praising the primal male form at the top limits of his endurance.

The current bout was over. As the man in the top hat announced the next set of fighters, Regina tuned him out, because one of the men at the opening to the cage called Marius over. Marius was bouncing lightly on the balls of his feet. He kept shrugging his shoulders as the man talked to him, tipping his head from shoulder to shoulder, warming up for his fight. Or fights, since there would be three.

A bell clanged, the crowd shouted, and the next fight was on, two combatants charging one another like wild animals in rut.

What happened if someone was killed? Was part of Freddie's job to dispose of the body, while a manager like Tal left some money, a severance pay of sorts, on the doorstep of a grieving mother, girlfriend or widow? Deaths were probably rare in the ring, though. Small comfort, since a concussion or brain bleed was far more likely. A man might be smart enough to go to an Urgent Care if he noted the symptoms. But more likely, he dropped like a stone at his job, as he ignored the effects of dangerously familiar injuries.

Marius nodded at whatever the man said and bounced back into the shadows again. A burly-looking spotter provided a pair of target palms for him. The speed of Marius's punches, the grace of the spinning kicks, took her breath. The man was in top fighting form.

Her Mistress side pushed aside her disapproval, her concerns and moral wrangling, to note other significant factors. At The Zone, he moved like a captive tiger, his energy too closely contained, his senses hyperalert to threats. Here he moved like one on a savannah, his movements fluid and unguarded. Here, he *was* the threat. The beast was fully out of his cage, no façade necessary. Here they wanted the beast in all his savage glory.

And this was why *she* was here. Key pieces were required to start solving a puzzle.

The current fight was done, the victor doing a whooping, jumping lap around the inside of the ring, egging on the crowd with his own exultant yells while the fallen was helped up and out.

The man with the top hat came back after the winner exited. He was wearing a pair of heavy Goth-styled boots with buckles up to the knee. As he held up a hand, the crowd settled to a low roar so he could effectively use the megaphone he carried. He hooted his first line like a rap song, waving one arm in rhythm.

"Rabid is in the houuuuuuse." He paused as the warehouse thundered with cheers. Looking around at the faces around her, suffused with a manic enthusiasm, Regina deduced Marius was a favorite, and blamed twisted human nature on why she felt a surge of possessive pride. "You all know Rabid as the beast that won't be beat. Tonight, though, he faces a new challenge. Not only will he fight three opponents back to back, no breaks, he'll be taking on three of our best. Tank, Killjoy and Skullface."

Whistles, boos and sounds of incredulity added to the din. "In the interests of full disclosure"—the emcee raised his voice and rolled his hips suggestively to jeers—"Rabid is the winner of fourteen consecutive fights in our series, which includes five complete knockouts, against such star quality fighters as..."

While the man ran down the stats on Marius and his opponents, Regina's gaze went back to him. He was still working with the spotter, not paying any obvious attention to the comments about him or the competition. She got that. She'd played basketball in high school, and they'd made it to the division finals. She recalled that absolute focus before the key game, tuning out everything except her teammates and the coach.

The coach told them the same thing before every game. *"You don't let yourself hear those cheers until you've earned them, and that won't be until that final scoreboard."* Regina had often wondered if the woman meant life in general, not just the game of basketball.

The trophy wife was a little too pouty about her date having placed his bet against Marius, not only in Regina's sour opinion, but in the estimation of her Bill Gates sugar daddy too. Regina gave him points for being unaffected by the exaggerated heave of her augmented breasts.

"He'll win all three," she murmured, gazing down at Marius. Somehow, she just knew it.

"You sound pretty sure of that."

She'd caught the sharp ears of a young man sliding along the top row of bleacher seating just below the catwalk, his hand gripping the rail at her waist for balance he didn't really seem to need.

Despite his youth, he had the shrewd, pointed face of a ferret. His comfort in the environment showed he was a regular visitor, his sense of purpose suggesting he might work for the organizers, doing whatever running through the crowds was needed for this kind of event. His skinny body type was certainly a good choice to be squeezing fast through them, and he had the height to be seen above them. He wore a neon orange vest over a purple Saints T-shirt and stressed jeans.

"High stakes, pretty mama," he said in a deeper voice than she would have expected. "Hope that's money you can afford to lose."

"I'm not a bettor. But if I had placed one, I would bet on him for all three rounds. I can predict how fast he'll take down his first opponent."

"Really? How fast?" He leaned on the rail, jutting out a bony hip as if he had all the time in the world, though the way his eyes continued to scan the crowd said otherwise.

"He'll take him down with the first punch."

His eyes came back to her fast, slim brows rising to his buzz cut hairline. Her comment drew the attention of the people on either side of her. "Tank is his first fight," one of the rapper's entourage declared. "Tank don't go down like that for nobody."

"He does tonight," she retorted. Her heart was thumping wildly again. What the hell was she doing?

The runner checked a handheld device and pursed his lips. "I'd say there'd be twenty-to-one odds on that at least." With a grin, he pulled out five dollars. "Side bet, mama. My own personal money. Boss got a strict policy about any action happening ringside, but small stakes are just considered tips for low-paid runners like me. You got a hundred dollars to lose on that? I also take other forms of currency."

He gave her an appraising look with a bump of his brows that had her considering whether to slap him upside the head to teach him manners. "Or we can lower the bet," he added, quickly picking up on her warning look. Fast learner.

"You're going to lose a hundred bucks. Sure you have that in your pockets?" she asked, passing her gaze over the voluminous pants held up only by a belt.

"I've got all sorts of things you'll like in these pockets, baby." But the quip was kneejerk now, since he said it absently as he put something down on the handheld. "Yeah, I've got it. If you're right, that'd be something to see. Even worth losing the hundred bucks. Maybe."

Tossing her a cheeky grin, he slipped away, though she noted he threw a speculative look over his shoulder, one reflected in the expressions of those around her.

Just hide and watch, babies. She didn't know how she was so sure, but she was thinking of Marius in the car, him hitting the steering wheel, the look in his eyes. Her whole body was taut as a wire, knowing her certainty was central to her reasons for staying here, for why she was digging herself deeper into this.

Marius had climbed into the ring. He was barefoot, unlike his opponent, who wore laced up boxing shoes and traditional gold shorts with a white stripe. Tank was predictably built like his name. He had a tattoo across his back, a detailed Sherman, to add to his brand. Nothing like good marketing. Comparing body mass, Marius looked like his kid brother. But when the eyes of the two fighters locked, the size seemed less significant. She kept her attention on Marius, realizing she was cataloging everything as if they were in a session together, just the two of them.

Whereas he'd been in constant motion since she'd seen him outside the ring, now he stilled. Arms loose at his sides, eyes so fixed they were eerily like a dead man's. The only betraying movement was a slight flexing of his shoulder beneath his tattoo.

The movement of the muscles guided her gaze to his hand. Loose, but two fingers double tapping each other, forefinger and thumb. One-two, three-four...

The bell rang and he was in motion. A blast of speed took him across the ring in one stride, two strides, and then he was in the air, his foot connecting hard with the midriff of his opponent, driving Tank's breath out before he could deflect Marius's swift frontal attack.

Marius landed in a spread stance, but his upper body kept twisting, one continuous flow of motion. He punched Tank squarely in the jaw, a hard ripple along his back and arm muscles showing the force behind the blow.

Tank swayed, his eyes glazed and spinning, his mouth tight on a curse, half muttered and lost as he crashed to his knees. One indrawn breath from the crowd, and he toppled to meet the concrete, his head rocking back and forth like a clock that had been overwound.

The crowd erupted, screaming its appreciation. Even the booing losers were jeering with enthusiastic gusto. There was no way to call it a dive. Marius's punch was so decisively powerful she'd felt the concussion vibrate through her own body.

Marius had moved to his corner, not pursuing a vicious follow up attack like previous fighters. By deliberately giving his opponent space, and time to get up if he could, he emphasized his total mastery of the moment. He had two more fighters pending and watching. No harm in a little psychological warfare.

It was when he was pressed against the wire cage that he saw her. She wasn't sure how, because the fierce gaze he swept over the crowd seemed more for effect than to notice who was watching. Yet his gaze came to a full stop upon her.

Did he realize he had his teeth bared like a wild dog? His chest rose and fell, an eye-catching bellows. It was only getting hotter in the crowded warehouse, and he'd already been warmed up enough to be coated with a gleam of perspiration. His cock was temptingly hard against the hold of the shorts.

Fucking hell. Aroused and agitated. He was like a tornado. He didn't want to defuse what had started with Siren. He'd come here for more fuel to keep the deadly twister within him going.

She kept her expression impassive. She wasn't sure what reaction would make sense anyway. Congratulations, bloodthirsty exultation like those around her, disappointment, horror, disapproval? Desire, need. Interest.

Deep, abiding interest.

Because she felt all those things, she showed none of them. No way was she revealing any of it until she could make sense of that cacophony of response.

He rubbed a hand over his chest, and slid his slickened palm down into the front of the shorts, giving his cock a hard, lubricated tug that had the women squealing with feigned shock, edged with pleasure, and the men guffawing. She didn't think he even noticed. He curled his lip at her in a sneer.

Nasty, wretched boy. There wasn't a punishment in the world that would turn him into something worth having. Or was there?

She considered keeping her cool mien in place, but decided differently. Yawning, she glanced at her wrist as if checking the time, even though she wore no watch. The muscles around his right eye tightened. Then the sneer became a dangerous smile, until her runner returned to her, a hundred-dollar bill in hand.

"Think you had some vital inside info, mama," he said affably, putting it in her outstretched hand and clasping her wrist. He executed a calculated and skilled stroke across her pulse. But behind the flirtation, there was real curiosity in his eyes. "How did you know?"

"My secret," she said, offering a feline smile and extricating herself from his hold with the ease of long practice.

"Secrets only add to the spice." He winked. As she tucked her winnings away into her bra cup, he made no pretense of not looking at the swell of her breasts. "Let me know if you want to take me out for dinner with those winnings, mama. I can earn them back."

Though she tossed him a dubious look, she couldn't help smiling. "Boy, I would break you like a twig."

"No way, baby. I'm like Stretch Armstrong, full of surprises." He did a Michael Jackson snake move and left her chuckling. "Don't be staring at my ass now if you don't mean it."

He gave his pants a hitch as he moved away, showing the first evidence of a butt being there. It was a compact one, if on the narrow side for her tastes. She sent him off with a wave and another laugh, then her gaze went back to Marius and his superlative ass.

He looked as if he'd been tracking her conversation with the runner, his mouth firm and hooded eyes still fixed on her. She formed one word, not knowing if he'd make it out or not in all the noise.

"Focus." A command, demand and imperative. If she couldn't break him out of the session mode in which he seemed to be stuck like an engine on high-rev, she could try to modulate it by treating him as if he was still in session. He stared at her a long moment. She could almost feel the heat of his body against her, the power of it quivering, wanting...something.

His gaze flickered. From this distance his eyes seemed far darker, dominated by pupil and shadowed by the dark line of his brows pulled down over them. He nodded to her, a barely imperceptible move, but one that shot heat straight to her core. He spoke his own response.

Two words she recognized, having seen them on countless lips before, but never containing the impact they had on her in such unusual circumstances.

Yes, Mistress.

The bell rang, and Killjoy was in the ring.

He wasn't as big as Tank, but he was a far faster and more calculating fighter. Tank had likely been chosen as a dramatic opener, one whose size and strength were intended to wear Marius out, not defeat him.

So it was possible more than banked rage had taken him down. If her boy was this good of a fighter, he had tactical skills as well as brawn. Knowing the skills of all coming against him, Marius had addressed Tank the best way to conserve his energy. It hadn't been without cost, though. When he'd made the winning punch, she'd seen a shiver of reaction go through the shoulder, all the way up the neck and across the back. A Mistress watched for those signs of strain. And Marius had started the night bruised and battered.

It didn't matter. He couldn't afford to coddle himself. Even though the dramatic nature of the opening hadn't displeased them, for this next fight the crowd would demand more time to savor. Marius and Killjoy didn't disappoint.

He and the other man circled one another, grappled, kicked, punched, wrestled. She heard the people around her debating fighting styles, martial arts and boxing terms that went over her head, but she got the gist of it. Both men were well-versed in a variety of styles, including street brawling, as Tal had said.

They came together, grunting and straining on the concrete, and then danced back again, sometimes more bloody and bruised than before. In the two earlier fights, it seemed the fighters had divided their time between the battle itself and playing the crowd. These were two gladiators unaware of anything but the task of defeating the other. As the blows grew faster and the fight more intense, the cold knot returned to Regina's stomach.

Killjoy pinned Marius against the cage with a clang of metal, landing several, horrible thudding blows in his mid-section. Marius twisted free and shoved him back, plowing into him and taking him down so they tumbled and rolled, bones jarring against the blood- and sweat-stained concrete. When they were back up again, some of the blood was on Marius's shoulder tattoo, making the leather armor artwork look even more real.

Killjoy's next face punch took Marius to his knees. Regina found herself straining against the rail, gripping it in tense fingers. What did she hope for here? That he lost, before more serious damage was inflicted upon him? Or that he'd get up, succeed over impossible odds, because something inside her wanted that for him? Because under the arrogant prick routine, she sensed a soul needing to prove something.

It was the wrong way to prove it, no matter what it was. Fuck it, she wanted him out of that ring. But her wants didn't count here.

Snarling, Marius swept his opponent's leg and flipped them both, landing on Killjoy. Using elbows and fists to good effect, he spun around to straddle him, punch his face, his torso. He went after him like Rocky Balboa after a slab of meat. Blood, more blood, and then a muffled shout from Killjoy that had several brawny men lunging into the cage to pull Marius off Killjoy. Marius shoved away from them immediately and paced the other side like a caged animal as they carried Killjoy out. His teeth were bared again and he was snarling a word she couldn't make out until he looked up at her with eyes made up of hellfire.

"Next."

Did he view Mistresses the same way?

He hit his chest with both open palms, a quick, demanding slap, and shouted it even louder, until the crowd, probably even those betting against him, were chanting it.

Skullface had a tattoo on his visage that matched the name. Though he and Marius started out much as Marius had with Killjoy, it wasn't long before she went past the point of any mixed emotions to one emphatic one.

Stop. Please just stop.

They'd obviously saved their best opponent for last. Skullface bided his time, drawing it out longer and longer, taking advantage of short openings to land blows on wounded areas and important motor points. He made Marius work for every return strike. Though Marius had showed he had the ability to think and strategize when he fought, Skullface was better at it. When Marius's bloodlust was up, tenacity and brute power took over as his strongest fighting assets.

At the beginning, she'd wondered if the organizers fixed some of the fights to ensure the house took home enough of the profits, but not so much that their audience wouldn't leave satisfied enough to come back. It probably did happen, but nothing in this event with Marius suggested the four fighters had anything on their minds but winning. Marius had been aware of her earlier, but now, she expected the two fighters were as isolated as if they were on a mountaintop together, seeing who could throw the other off the edge.

The crowd roared as Skullface spun and hit Marius mid-body with a kick that knocked him back, then rushed him like a roaring bull. In a move worthy of a professional wrestler, he caught Marius about the waist and thighs and heaved him against the cage door so hard it gave way. Marius slammed into the floor on the outside, shoulder and face thudding against the concrete.

Those clustered near the gate had scattered. Good thing, because Skullface pounced, not intending to give Marius any breathing room. But Marius somehow was already up on one knee. He bulled into Skullface with an enraged roar of his own, and reversed their momentum, taking them both back into the ring. They rolled, and Marius ended up on top.

She saw it happen, exactly what the Aussie had described. Marius hit a different gear, raw power called up from a reserve inside him that simply refused to be beaten, no matter the cost.

He was hammering Skullface with his fists, the blows a blur of motion. He grabbed his opponent's slick cranium and slammed the man's head against the floor, hard enough to daze him.

If Skullface wanted to call it, Regina didn't see how he could. Marius was punching him again, turning his face into meat. Surely... good Christ, she wasn't going to stand by and watch him kill someone. Up until now, the fighters themselves had seemed mindful of just how far they should go, even in this environment. Until one of them was past the point of caring.

She was pushing, shoving, moving along the rail. Then she muttered "screw it" and went over it, onto the top of the bleacher seating just below. She ignored the startled glances of those crowded upon it, gripping shoulders as needed to keep herself steady, get to the ground level fast and push closer to the cage. She was a tall, big-boned and powerful woman, and she wasn't shy about using that when needed.

She emerged right where she intended, at the corner only a few feet from where Marius was going after the nearly unconscious man. Thank God, they'd realized the same thing she had, that Skullface couldn't call mercy to save himself. Now the same men who'd retrieved Killjoy were in the ring, pulling Marius off. They'd left the cage door open, and she had an odd sense of déjà vu from earlier in the night, when she'd stood in the doorway of Room 7 at The Zone.

The man in the top hat shouted for—had she heard that right—a shot of freaking ketamine? A horse tranquilizer? She was pushing through the doorway, not thinking about it, just acting on instinct. Perhaps she was as insensible to the wisdom of her course as Marius seemed to be toward everything right now. She wouldn't realize until later her skinny runner and Tal helped her get into the cage with him, obviously deciding something else beyond the norm was required to defuse the situation.

She was driven by conscience, an unsettling feeling she'd somehow caused this. First by not defusing him properly after his session with Siren, and then triggering something in her boy with her presence and that *Focus* command.

Her boy. Christ, yeah, she'd made her decision, hadn't she?

She put her palm flat on Marius's heaving chest, the only clear space between the arms of the three men holding him. Her touch snapped his gaze to her, his silver eyes as brilliant as lightning in a black sky.

"Stop," she ordered. "That's enough."

CHAPTER FOUR

*S*he'd had subs who called her a sorceress for her ability to command obedience from them. But those were men who ultimately wanted to obey, no matter what personal shit they had to wade through. She thought Marius had that in him, but in comparison, her other subs had been jumping a babbling brook to get to a compliant state. He was in the center of a vast, churning whirlpool ocean of sewage. She could almost smell it coming off him. It took three times for the sharp command to reach through the violence and hook his attention.

She felt it when it happened, when he wasn't merely looking at her blindly through that haze. His gaze sharpened and locked. A runner arrived with a full syringe of ketamine, she assumed, and she pointed an emphatic finger at him, a *don't touch him with that* gesture she backed up with a look. Maybe that alone wouldn't have succeeded, but since each time she'd issued her command, Marius's struggling had lessened, Top Hat waved off the tranq.

The crowd loved the drama, since to them that was what it was. She supposed they interpreted it like an action film, the hero caught up in a just rage. They didn't see the reality, a man so lost to his most base instincts he would have killed the man who was there for no different reasons than himself. Skullface had been transported out of the ring on a stretcher, probably to be placed in the back of some van and taken to a hospital.

The dwarf snapped his fingers in front of Marius's face, drawing his eyes. "Good, Rabid? Can we let you go?"

When Marius jerked his head in assent, the man wasn't completely satisfied. He turned to her.

"What do you think, Legs?" Since his head barely reached her waist, she was relieved he came up with a nickname based on the most evident part of her anatomy, rather than what was at eye level.

She was studying Marius's face. Skullface's removal had defused his most obvious trigger. But to be sure, she laid her hand back on Marius's chest. His heartbeat was still fast, his pulse jumping in his throat as she shifted to a light clasp over it. His gray eyes swiveled down to her arm and back up to her face. When she lifted her thumb to his mouth, brushing his split lip, he didn't flinch. His tongue flicked out and took the blood that had been transferred onto her skin. A spark in his gaze told her he'd done it consciously, but maybe not entirely to be a smartass. When he dropped his head back and closed his eyes, she felt him draw a couple deep, leveling breaths.

"He's good," she confirmed. "But can he go somewhere halfway quiet here?"

"For the money he earned us tonight, we'll give him the champion's suite," the emcee said dryly.

His affable sarcasm made sense when she saw it. They had a sectioned-off area next to the locker room for the fighters, made possible by more of the temporary divider panels they'd used in the foyer. There was a padded table, a cabinet, jugs of water and a big basin. All the men but Tal left them there. Barely a moment later, she heard the dwarf announcing the final fight of the night over the dull thunder of the crowd. She thought anything else would be anticlimactic after Marius's performance, but there was no telling what spectacle they'd arranged. Probably a fight between a pair of paraplegics in high-powered wheel chairs, one knife thrown down between them.

Tal slapped Marius on the shoulder. This time Marius did flinch, but not from pain. It was as if the friendly contact was startling. Tal overlooked it with an understanding expression.

"Good fight, Duncan. You did good. Top Hat about shot his load when you took down Tank."

Duncan? She glanced at Marius.

"Don't give a shit." Marius grunted the insult and acknowledgment as he moved toward the padded table.

"Which is why I handle the money and your fight schedule. So you don't piss off the wrong people and end up chained to a bunch of concrete blocks at the bottom of the bay."

Marius didn't bother to respond to that. He bent stiffly to pick up the basin and one of the jugs of water, putting them on the table. Regina met the Aussie's gaze. She could handle this part, and she wanted some privacy. He picked it up so quickly she thought he'd be an excellent submissive. Who knew? Maybe behind closed doors, he was. With that "lovely girl" who'd made him stop fighting.

"First aid kit and cloths are in that cabinet." He pointed. "Along with a shitload of peroxide for cleaning out wounds. Got some broad-spectrum antibiotics and ibuprofen in there. He can help himself."

Was Duncan Marius's real name? If he and Tal knew each other well enough, perhaps the older man had used it to help ground him further. Calling him Rabid right now definitely didn't seem to be a good idea.

As the Aussie took his leave, she drew Marius's attention with a gesture. "Sit on the table," she said. "You're in no condition to tend to yourself."

"I always do," he said, his tone flat.

"Yeah. I bet you do. But I'm offering. Once the adrenaline leaves you, you're going to be close to collapse. So don't be a shit. Sit your ass on the table."

He pivoted to square off with her. "Women line up to fuck fighters fresh out of the ring. You're at the front of the line, Mistress." He lifted his arms to his sides, sweeping his gaze down his own body. "Have at it, sweetheart."

"You call me sweetheart ever again, I will feed you your own nuts." She leveled a stare on him. "Hard as it may be to believe, a man stinking of sweat and blood is not my dream come true. You can't manipulate my emotions, Marius. I see you coming with that shit from a mile away. So accept my help, or go fuck yourself."

Some or all of that might be a lie, but one part wasn't. She wouldn't be played by a sub. He might pull this shit on a Domme who expected fair play from her partner, but Regina was forewarned and forearmed. He didn't know the meaning of fair play. Not yet.

She didn't know which way he'd go on it, and so was prepared to turn on her heel and depart, no matter how difficult she might find it to leave him in this state. After a long moment that stopped short of her doing just that, he moved to the table and lifted himself onto it. Spreading out his hands in another exaggerated motion, he gave her a look that said, *"Here I am. So?"*

There was a case of drinking water in the bottom of the dusty cabinet. She brought two bottles of it, the first aid supplies, peroxide and meds to the table. "Here. Hydrate. Slow so you don't vomit."

"I know that."

"I don't have the best opinion of your brain power. I'd rather tell you the obvious and remove any risk."

He muttered something uncomplimentary into the top of the bottle, but he was drinking. He did know what needed to happen after a fight, she could see that. That was somewhat comforting, when so much of this wasn't.

She cleaned the blood off his face and dabbed peroxide on one nasty gash. Killjoy had been wearing a ring with a spike on his left hand. "This could do with a few stitches."

"Naw, it'll be fine. Just use the stitch tape. I'll sew it up later if that doesn't work." He used the back of his hand to wipe his nose, which was also still bleeding sporadically. The graceless gesture made her cluck and take his hand, wiping it clean before she rolled up two small pieces of gauze.

"Here, stick those in your nostrils. Tip your head back. Barbarian. In the habit of giving yourself stitches, are you?"

He complied with the head tipping, his gaze moving to the ceiling as he packed his nose around her ministrations. "It's easy. Like fixing holes in socks, if the socks were a tough-skinned kind of Jell-O."

Her gaze slid to his face. He'd offered a faint, lopsided smile when he said it, thanks to the split lip. Strange as the setting and topic was, it was the first dialogue they'd had as normal people in the vanilla world, a side of him she'd not yet discovered. If his behavior now was real, not charm.

"What's your favorite flavor of Jell-O?" she asked. She turned her attention to wiping the blood off his left shoulder and arm, but also took the time to tuck another gauze pad in his callused hand and guide it to his lip to put pressure on it. It kept bleeding. The gesture muffled his words, but they were still intelligible.

"It's a non-food."

"What does that have to do with anything?" she asked. "So's a Twinkie. Everyone loves that. And you can play with Jell-O. Make molds."

He grunted. "Black cherry, then."

She slanted him a glance. "Seriously?"

That half smile came around the gauze pad. "Seriously. It wasn't a line, no matter that you are a fine black woman."

"With you, everything is a line. But black cherry is a good flavor. Particularly for wine slushies."

"Don't know. I don't drink, except for an occasional beer."

She screwed the top back on the peroxide. His words surprised her, but so did he, when he collected the assortment of stained gauze pads she'd left next to him to toss them into the trash. The fighters were probably required to clean up after themselves, part of the deal of getting their cut from the fight. However, letting her do it would have been an excellent way for him to snub her, the way he had when he cut in front of her at Tyler's office. This time, he hadn't taken the opening.

"Why don't you drink? Recovering alcoholic, health nut, control freak, or you just don't like the taste?"

He blinked. The silver and red beads threaded through her hair seemed to have caught his attention. His eyes tracked the sparkling movement as the black locs spilled over her shoulder. "What do you think?" he asked in the unreadable monotone he was favoring.

"Control freak, definitely." She put the first aid supplies back in the cabinet. "I can't imagine what amount is worth going through all this, but I hope you get paid well tonight."

He grunted. She wondered if it mattered to him if he was paid at all. Whatever his day job was, it didn't visibly pay him well, if the condition of his car meant anything. During his playtimes at the club, he wore street wear and stripped out of it. If he wore any "fetish wear," it was either the clingy style shorts, or an outfit provided by the Domme. For his job there, he wore The Zone staff shirt with his jeans.

So he didn't spend his money on fancy sub outfits like some of the other males. He didn't seem to spend money on much of anything. Except the tattoo. She wondered what had inspired him to get it, because she was sure something had marked the occasion. He had no other body art.

She touched it with light fingers after making another pass with the gauze to wipe a missed smear of blood off the shoulder. "That's some good work there."

Another grunt of assent and an irritable twitch. She stepped back. "You'll do. I suppose you know a hot shower when you get home is the best remedy, on top of the ibuprofen you just took. Though I'd highly recommend a tetanus update and having your head examined."

He kept staring at her. He wanted to make her nervous with his silence. *Tough luck with that, boy. You want to self-gag, it doesn't bother me.*

Answering in kind, she tossed one final wipe into the trash and headed for the door. Embracing her Mistress side meant understanding there was an energy flow between Dom and sub once a connection was made, even if the connection was the rope in a tug of war. She rode that energy the way it was meant to be ridden, not forcing her own expectations on it. It worked better that way. She'd accomplished what mattered most to her here, which was confirming he'd released that surfeit of potent energy from his session. He was leveling out. While he could use a lot more aftercare, they were quite a distance from him welcoming or earning that kind of treatment from her.

"You don't want to talk about what happened in Tyler's office?" he said abruptly. "Or why you followed me here?"

"No." She continued to move toward the opening between the panels that would lead back to the cage and, even better, out toward the parking lot. She didn't need to stay any longer, and what she really wanted was a deep breath of clean air.

She didn't anticipate that he would do or say anything to hold her there longer, so it was a pleasant surprise when he did.

"You didn't say what you thought of the fight."

She pivoted at the opening and met his gaze. "No, I didn't. Would you like to know?"

He could look wary, like an animal being baited into a trap. He had thick, dark lashes. Though he'd let his face get pummeled too often, nothing could dim the impact of his eyes. They were like the mirror surface of a lake. "Yeah," he said at last.

"Okay." There was a pen sitting next to the tray of gauze. Returning to him, she picked it up and extended her hand, looking pointedly at one of his. When he offered it, she clasped his wrist and wrote an address on the inside of his forearm, along with Friday, 6:30pm.

His fingers flexed above her grip. She was aware of his breath stirring tendrils of hair against her cheek. Her hip pressed against his knee. She let herself imagine sliding between his spread thighs, tasting the metallic flavor lingering on his lips, feeling the flex of his shoulder muscles under her splayed fingers and firm palms. His hands would curve over her hips, his own fingers digging in, showing he wanted and needed her.

Careful, girl. Don't fuck with your own head. He'll do enough of that without your help.

"Meet me there and I'll tell you." Setting the pen aside, she laid a hand on the side of his face. "Get some rest. Take care of yourself."

When he tried to clasp her arm, she drew back and shook her head, a denial. His lips set in a thin line. "That a command, Mistress?" he asked tonelessly.

"Take it however you want."

He curled his fingers around the edge of the table, body leaning forward, eyes suddenly cold and hard. "It wouldn't matter anyway, since you don't really like me."

"No. I don't," she responded frankly. "But I care about you. That doesn't require that I like you."

Maggie O'Day was a woman of considerable wealth. Currently in her seventies, she'd decided a decade ago to establish "The Preserve," a Dommes-only playground of over seventy-five acres. The property was populated by trails and woods perfectly suited for primal scenes, slave hunts and capture fantasies. The two roomy barns were stocked with stalls and a few carriages for pony play, adjacent to a dirt track for Mistresses to race their "ponies." Covered shelters scattered throughout the property offered other outdoor setup options for equipment, or there was a fully stocked dungeon room in the "clubhouse," along with sitting areas, kitchen and wide screen TVs with full cable hookups. A library of adult films catered to female tastes.

Like The Zone, The Preserve's membership was intended to weed out dabblers. The vetting process was handled by Maggie's savvy personal assistant and collared slave, Emile, but Maggie always had final say and reviewed his every recommendation. If she took a shine to a Mistress of lesser means, she would offer a membership proportionate with the woman's income. She'd been known to say, "I don't really need the money, but people appreciate what they have to pay for or earn. If they don't," she'd add, "they'll be out the door. With my size ten Army boot up their asses."

Maggie had been out as a lesbian since her teens, and was a vast resource of laywoman history on lesbian rights and struggles to be accepted by mainstream society. She was also a strong champion of women in general. From the beginning, The Preserve welcomed Dommes, gay or straight, but the only men allowed through the gates were submissives under the supervision of a specific Domme. "Children must be accompanied by an adult," Maggie would quip. The men and women who maintained the grounds were all submissives and slaves loyal and bound to Maggie.

She'd imposed The Preserve's gender restrictions with an unapologetic and succinct explanation. "Girls need a place to be girls." Twice a year, she held an eclectic fertility festival that also honored the Greek poet Sappho. Regina was on the invitation list, along with about a hundred other Dommes Maggie counted as her friends. They could each bring their chosen subs for a weekend of fun, frolicking and debauched revelry.

But Maggie believed in committed relationships, and it concerned her that Regina didn't have one. Sometimes her grandmother and mother side emerged, as much a part of her matriarchal personality as her Mistress traits. At the last event, Regina recalled Maggie cornering her about her long-term relationship plans.

"You like the challenging ones, but you train them to be better for the next Mistress and don't keep them for yourself. You're looking for the right one, aren't you?" The older woman had adopted a dramatic tone, clasping her hands over her heart. "Your soulmate."

"Maggie, if you're taken, there's no one else for me," Regina teased her. But fueled by fertility festival moonshine, she'd allowed some truth to come out. "Nothing wrong with having my own personal treasure hunt. I'm happy single, but when I find him, I'll know he's who I want."

Maggie had sighed and hugged her. "Dumb, sentimental bitch. Just don't be too picky."

Regina smiled at the memory, but the smile disappeared as she thought about Marius. She might be a little more absorbed in him than her recent past engagements. But that didn't translate to him being "it," "the one," or choose the romance novel term of choice. She'd committed to this much, this day, and she'd see where it went. If he even showed up.

When she pulled up to The Preserve's gate at 6:30, he was waiting. That was a mark for him, his understanding that she wouldn't take any disrespect up front tonight. If he'd been even a minute late, she would have turned the car around and been on her way. So he'd decided to see where this was going to go. Or he wasn't giving up on the question and challenge she presented, seeing whether he could fuck with her the way he did other Mistresses.

He'd healed up some. The bruises from the face shots weren't so purplish, and the cut from Killjoy's ring had scabbed over. However, he'd still be feeling some aches and pains from the overall battering, and she'd use the physical and emotional effects of those for her own purposes.

He'd shaved earlier in the day, and wore jeans and a button-down dress shirt. Southern straight white boy's way of "dressing up" for a girl on a casual date. It didn't displease her.

She rolled down her window and gestured. He came to her, a saunter of motion that was part deliberate cockiness and part just the way a man moved who was in superior shape. A fighter, who walked light on his feet with full awareness of his physical capabilities. She'd been around cops and former military who had that vibe, but there was a different quality to it for Marius. His version had an edge, like he'd honed the skills for personal survival and retaliation, not protection and specific service to a cause greater than himself.

He looked good, though. No matter his fucked-up nature, Marius had a body meant to be used hard by a Mistress. If she got nothing else out of this, she would get that. But he was more than willing to provide that to any Mistress who hooked up with him at The Zone. Maggie was right. She was looking for more. If she didn't find more than that tonight, she'd probably be done with this.

"Mistress." He spoke the one word as a greeting.

"Marius. Are you familiar with The Preserve?"

"Heard of it. Never been here."

"Follow me in. There's parking at the clubhouse. I'll take you where we're going from there on foot."

She rolled up her window and eased forward to the gate. In her rearview, she saw him pause and then move to his car. He'd probably expected more chitchat. She saw no reason to delay the program she wanted to execute tonight. Until then, the only thing she'd be getting out of his mouth was bullshit.

Yesterday, she'd stocked the area she would be using with the equipment and supplies needed, so it left her hands free as she exited her car. When he left his own to join her, Marius looked at her like she looked at a cupcake. He didn't try to hide his interest in a deeper exploration of her body, showcased in snug jeans and a red tank that clung and caressed her curves. A ruby pendant winked in her cleavage, drawing his gaze there.

"Seen enough?" she asked tartly.

"Not nearly. Mistress." He added it with a grin she wanted to slap off his face, but she logged the data it gave her. The smile at the fight, that lopsided gesture when he'd told her his favorite flavor of Jell-O? That had been real. This wasn't.

"Does it get exhausting?" she asked. "Always playing a part? Or do people falling for it energize you? In the right kind of way?"

She meant it seriously, not in anger. Though he didn't appear to expect that, he shrugged in answer. Letting it go for now, she strode up the dirt road to the nearest barn. Once there, she led him down the wide corridor of stalls to the one at the end, next to her personal supply cabinet.

She saw him noting the tack mounted on the wall, the array of combs and brushes. His expression became wooden. Stoic.

"Are you familiar with pony play?"

"Yeah. Done a little bit. I'm not usually a fave for the pony play

Mistresses. I don't get into it the way they want. Just because I'm hung like a horse doesn't mean I know how to be one."

She rolled her eyes. "Your cock has the proportions to please a woman, but I've had subs who *are* hung like a horse. They'd put you to shame."

"So why aren't you with them?" he asked with a touch of belligerence that made her hide a smile.

"Because it's not about size." She drew him into the stall that had a knee-high wooden platform covered by a rubber mat. An array of rings were driven into the platform to allow for tie-down straps. "Take off your clothes and get on your hands and knees on the dais."

"Just like that? No preliminaries, no talk of safe words?"

She moved toward the shelf of supplies. "I've watched you plenty at the club. You don't ask for limits, and you never volunteer a safe word. A Mistress can impose one on you, but you never use it, so why would I waste my energy? What I'm going to do to you here won't be half as physically demanding as other sessions I've seen you handle." She arched a brow. "Or are you asking for a little romancing? You don't seem the type to need pointless reassurance."

"A woman who thinks romance is pointless reassurance." His voice was dry. "Sure I haven't died and landed in male heaven?"

"I haven't killed anyone in a session, but there's always a first. Enough chatting. Clothes off and on the platform, hands and knees."

She pulled a stool over and took a seat, hooking a boot heel over one of the slats as she crossed her arms and leaned back against a pole. He stopped in the act of unbuttoning his shirt. "You like to watch, Mistress? Want me to make it a strip tease?"

She shook her head. "Take off your clothes the way you do it when you're alone, Marius. Are you capable of not performing?"

Tossing her a cheeky grin, he started to swivel his hips, like a male stripper. Sighing, she rose and put the stool aside, turning toward her supply cabinet.

"Okay. Jesus. Fine, I'll do it the way you want. Boring."

"I don't have patience for second chances or attitude, Marius. Let me know when you're on the platform the way I ordered you to do it, or head back to your car."

She perused her liniment choices and thought the one with eucalyptus would be excellent. She ignored his grumbling, because she'd made enough of an impact he kept it low so she couldn't hear the words. She would have liked very much to watch him undress, shrug out of the shirt, wriggle the jeans off his hips, hook the underwear beneath and drop it to the floor, showing off the whole man. But the first part was often like this, both of them having to be denied until he got with the program.

She hadn't considered her previous pet projects easy—pun intended—but he was already more of a challenge than any of those had been. She wasn't going to anticipate it going in a right direction any time soon. Hearing him kick the clothes to the corner with definite attitude, she was certain of it.

"I always figured the Mistresses who are into this never got their birthday pony from Daddy," he said. "I'm on the platform. Buck naked, by the way. On hands and knees."

She hummed a note of acknowledgement, but selected and arranged her supplies to her satisfaction before she at last turned.

Oh, Lord, what a fine creation You have made. It was something her mother said when she saw a particularly good-looking specimen of manhood.

Marius was in an acceptable hands and knees posture on the raised platform. Head up, eyes forward, back straight, knees spread to shoulder width, palms braced flat, weight distributed evenly. The position showcased the layers of muscle over his ribcage. Hip bones and ribs were more prominent in this position, making her wonder if he fueled his muscles with protein shakes rather than actual food. His buttocks were taut and begging to be marked, his thigh muscles flexing as he shifted. Siren's marks were still there among the fight bruises, but fading. She wished they were gone. She wanted a blank canvas, no evidence of another Mistress's hand upon him.

The hair on his neck was groomed to a small point. He'd gotten a haircut. It had been longer, spikier, at the fight.

Picking up a handful of short straps, she ran them over his knees, calves and ankles, fixing them to the rings embedded in the platform to restrain his legs. Cuffs around his wrists were likewise snapped to rings. The cuffs were a temporary measure, but would limit his ability to quickly resist what she had in mind next.

He was watching her closely out of his peripheral vision. She'd take care of that, but first she'd put the piece on him that was most difficult for her to add without betraying her emotions. A collar wasn't part of the usual tack she used for pony play, but something told her she should use it on Marius, as another essential way to alter his headspace.

Maggie wasn't entirely wrong about Regina looking for a particular kind of sub. Or being picky. Regina merely refused to settle for less than what she wanted. A lot of women did it and made it work for them. They figured out how to chisel pieces of themselves away to fit with a lover who likewise chiseled at himself to make that fit happen. It could be a lovely way to show love growing and adapting.

The problem was—no. She wasn't going to call it a problem. It wasn't a problem to be a woman who was enough for herself. She liked every bit of who she was, and had never met the man who made her want to adapt any of that to his nooks and crannies. If she found one who did, she'd expect a similar sacrifice from him, a meeting in the middle. If she didn't, she could live every fascinating, glorious moment of this life without a lover at her side. But that resolve didn't mean she didn't want to find that man.

As a Mistress, she wanted to collar a sub and call him her own forever. It was one of the deepest wishes she had, and one she'd never said aloud to anyone. When she put a collar on such a man, she'd finally let her fingers tremble, her heart leap. She'd trust him enough to let him see her eyes and mouth go soft with need.

Every time she buckled a collar on a sub, it reminded her of that soul-deep wish. With Marius, she wanted to keep her fingers under the strap, hold and tug him to her lips. Indulge in his sweet mouth, feel his hunger grow with hers.

To keep that compulsion at bay while she strapped the collar around Marius's thick, corded neck, she ran through her domestic to-do list. The Mercedes needed to be serviced. She should add detergent and dark cherries to the weekly online grocery order. Her fingertips might be lingering on the faint rasp of a few hours' growth of beard, but that was permissible.

It was done. She withdrew her touch. Aware of his gaze on her face, she tugged his hair, an absent affection, though what she really wanted to do was take a handful and yank his head back. She'd pull on his scalp, letting him feel the sharp edge of her nails.

Shifting behind him, she ran a hand down his back, slow, learning the shape of him, all the way over the rise of his ass.

"You could keep going," he said. "I'd prefer to feel your hand on my cock rather than any of this horse stuff."

"Hmm." She brought the additional tack to the platform. First the shoulder harness, which she enjoyed securing over that broad terrain. Then the saddle. She cinched the chest strap but left the one that went across the abdomen dangling, for now. And resisted the compulsion to reach beneath him and caress his cock, aroused and stiff. His erection had grown from the moment she started to restrain him, but a significant extra jump had happened when she'd put the collar on him. It probably explained the mouthing off. He didn't want her to notice that.

Tough, baby. I notice everything.

She picked up another piece of tack with a clink of metal, the straps falling together as she lifted it. She asked him to open up the same way she would a horse. Not with words.

Inserting her thumb in the corner of his mouth, she pushed the bit against his teeth. Before he could resist, she'd forced the piece back to the furthest set of molars it could reach and tightened the head straps to keep it there. When he tried to pull away from her, she merely jerked his head down, forcing him to an elbow while she finished the adjustments. The bit had a port, a flat piece to keep his tongue from getting over the bit. It also enhanced the bit's ability to prohibit speech.

"Now, where was I?" she mused. "Before my horse decided he was Mr. Ed and could talk?"

~

What she was doing wasn't going to work. Marius wasn't into this pony bullshit. He wasn't going to "become a horse" just because she slapped tack on him like one. He for sure wasn't going to let go of the million-and-one calculations his brain was doing to stay on top of the situation.

She connected the rings of the bit to cross ties hooked to his left and right on the wall in front of him. Now he couldn't turn his head.

She returned to the supply cabinet, because he could hear the faint squeak of the doors as she opened them and slid something off a shelf.

"Here we go." She hung a mirror on the wall in front of him. It was like a locker mirror, about a foot square, but it let him see what she was putting on his head.

He'd seen the full pony masks employed at the club, which were mostly featureless. This was not that. This was a custom-made fetish piece. As she slid it over his face, the mirror before him showed a proud stallion. The rakish fall of mane and the molding of the features around the eyes and long nose conveyed a badass attitude. The decorative browband across the forelock was embellished with silver chain and spikes.

The mask blocked his peripheral vision. Now he could only see directly in front of him. The mirror provided him a scant few inches of rear view on either side.

"Yeah, you're realizing I've taken care of those wandering eyes, haven't you?" Her fingertips slid down the valley between his shoulder blades. "Putting blinders on a horse narrows his distractions, minimizes what makes him nervous."

He wasn't nervous. If she couldn't read him any better than that...

"You'd deny this makes you nervous, and I'd agree. That's not the word I'd use for you. Any emotions you perceive as weak—nervous, afraid, defensive—you merely channel into aggression, taking the offensive tactic. You seek the high ground, in the battle sense, not the moral one. It's what a predator does."

She used additional straps to secure the mask to the harness she'd put around his shoulders, and did the same with the saddle, so it couldn't slide back.

Her fingers slid over the collar on his throat as she did that, but didn't linger. He'd looked for some hint of her feelings about putting that piece on him, because most Mistresses went a little starry-eyed over it, even if they only intended to keep him for a night. He hadn't picked up anything from her but efficiency in getting the task done. She appeared so not-engaged in the act, she could have been going through a laundry list in her head. A stab of disappointment about that irritated him. Why should he care? He didn't get starry-eyed over that kind of shit, either.

Whatever she'd done to secure the mask had also locked his head in a raised position and increased the tension at the corners of his mouth. Now, in addition to being unable to move his head side to side, he couldn't drop it down, either.

She shifted back and attended to the stomach strap she'd left loose. A clink of metal, a whisper of straps against his leg, and he realized she'd threaded the band through another strap. He grunted as she tucked his cock beneath the crisscrossed pieces and bound his rigid organ to his belly with the girth. She then pulled the other piece up between his legs, his balls and buttocks before securing it to the back of the saddle. When she tugged on it, he bit back an oath as it compressed his hardening cock against his belly further and dug into his ball sac, separating his testicles.

He growled against the bit as she positioned a wide ring, sewn into the strap, between his cheeks, right where it would give her access to his rectum. He didn't need a fucking safe word for this? Okay, yeah, everything she'd said had been right. He wouldn't use it, but skipping it, not giving him the choice, that was wrong. No matter how stubborn he was, she was supposed to be the responsible one. She didn't usually go this route. He thought he'd known what to expect from her.

She put her hand on one of the lines running to the bit, so he felt the tug on it, the degree of restraint. It tilted the stallion's head toward her. His head. Bent in such a way that it looked like he had it bowed to her. "Your only task is to obey my commands, heed my touch. You are not Marius, the man that fucks with Mistresses' heads for reasons that don't bring you any pleasure or peace. You are a horse. My horse."

Now what was she doing? She retrieved another thing from the cabinet. As he watched, gagged from speaking and mostly blinded, he saw only glimpses of her face when she bent before him. He did feel the incidental brush of her body from her movements. She curled his hand into a fist, her fingers too-briefly upon his flesh before she released the cuff on his arm and replaced it with a glove-like piece that enclosed his fist and forearm up to the elbow. Hoof mitts, designed to look like a horse's front hooves, depending on how much the pony player spent. He expected these looked pretty damn realistic. When he shifted, the bottom piece, where the knuckles of his fist were resting, clopped against the boards of the platform.

Velcro straps secured the mitt to his wrist, arm and elbow, effectively restricting the use of his hands. She'd given him hooves.

Now that he was properly outfitted in mask, hooves and tack, she returned to touching him, a thorough and maddeningly dispassionate evaluation of his shoulders, biceps and forearms, as if she were a trainer testing the soundness of his "legs."

It made him feel restless and he tossed his head. The lifelike reaction of the mask and hooves were unsettling, melding with his physical movements. Damn if he wasn't feeling like a damn horse. She crooned to him, her big, powerful animal, her stallion, one that would need a good rubdown after she gave him a hard workout. She slid her hand from his shoulder to his upper back above the saddle, fingernails scraping his flesh there before moving to his buttocks and upper thighs. She pressed gently on the fading bruises, and somehow she seemed to know which ones were from Siren and which were from the fight, because she passed over the former, refusing to acknowledge another Mistress's attempt to claim him.

He could assume that possessiveness was there, use it to his advantage, but he didn't have enough information. He tried to lower his head, throw it back, adjust his hips. The visual seemed to please her, because she chuckled softly, a hint of her throaty laugh that went straight to a man's cock. She slapped his flank, a stinging blow.

When she followed it up with a caress of his side, she came so close to his stiffening cock that his hips flexed, trying to force himself into her hands despite the binding straps. A breath later, a riding crop popped his flank, hard enough he jumped and hissed. "None of that now," she chided.

He pulled against the restraints in angry reproof. All he earned was her amused chuckle and the uneasy confirmation of how securely he was tied.

"You're a spirited mount. I'm going to enjoy that while I'm fucking you. I need to go and change, but there are cameras. I can see you in the dressing room. You're not alone." Her fingertips slid in one more lingering caress over his shoulder and backside.

Good. He knew how to handle fucking. She'd be done with him after that, and she'd let him go. She wasn't so different from other Mistresses. But he didn't like this. He was becoming far too aware of the restraints, the quiet she'd imposed on him, how little she was asking. He needed the bitch to ask for more, hurt him, demand every-thing from him. Then he could take all the pain, give everything to her she thought she'd wanted and spit in her face. Laugh at her, and let her see he'd given her nothing. What the hell was the matter with her?

What the hell was the matter with him? Reining in the odd surge of emotion—and ignoring how he was falling into horse metaphors—he focused on baser interests. He wished those cameras were two-way so he could see what she was doing, how she looked as she removed that tit-alicious tank. She had a powerhouse figure. Generous breasts and a taut, round, high-set ass. She didn't have stick legs, her thighs strong and healthy, toned pillows to cradle a man as he was plowing her cunt. Her slim auburn and black dreadlocks reached the middle of her back, the beads she seemed to like to use as embellishment clicking when she moved. She had long, elegant fingers, but her hands were surprisingly strong.

Her eyes...so dark. They were a rich maple syrup kind of color that had a touch of red when the light hit them the right way. Then they were back to being dark, coated in shadows hard to interpret, but sucking him in regardless.

Okay, he wasn't thinking about sex. He was thinking about her freaking eyes.

He stared at himself in the mirror. For a blink he forgot it was a mask and saw himself as a restless, angry horse, one that yanked against his bonds. The pull on the bit made his cock harder, and he stomped the hooves. He imagined covering her, driving into her, baring blunt teeth and latching onto her throat.

A peculiar feeling was coiling and uncoiling in his belly, like an agitated snake. Horses didn't like snakes. He stomped again, harder. He shook his head. The mane pattered against the mask and the tack jingled. The hooves made the dais vibrate, thanks to the wood beneath the thin rubber mat. His trapped cock convulsed beneath him, balls hanging heavy and loose on either side of that cutting strap. He had to suppress an animalistic urge to hump air, his rutting need to mate. Where the hell was she?

The bite of the bit at the corners of his mouth, the hold of the ropes keeping his head up, increased his agitation. He rocked, trying to loosen things, but she'd secured him too well. He was held fast.

It seemed like she'd been gone forever, but he knew it was only minutes. He needed to calm down, get a grip. He couldn't. Fuck it, what was happening? He didn't panic over hardcore shit, and this wasn't even half hardcore. He needed...

"Easy..." Her voice came through an intercom near his head. She'd said she had cameras in the room. She'd neglected to mention the audio function, but it was welcome. Too welcome. His senses strained to absorb her words.

"Settle down." Her tone became firm. "Your Mistress will be back with you in a minute. Behave for her."

He behaved for no one. He wanted to lay back his ears and pluck the intercom from the wall, smash it under his hooves.

Then he heard her coming back and need lashed him harder. He tried to see more of her in the mirror, but he could only see a piece of her. It confused him. Pink latex, black rubber.

She was moving. Her heels made a delicate clip, clop sound, a measured, echoing rhythm he understood when she moved into his field of vision and stood before him. She was moving like a horse, one foot up, then the other, a subtle prance that made her breasts quiver.

She was wearing a pale pink latex mini dress, sleeveless but with a high neck. It clung to her breasts like a second skin, showing off large, firm nipples that made him have to swallow several times to keep drool from escaping around the bit. The skirt creased high up on her thighs. Her stilettos were designed to look like hooves in the front, ladies' heels in the back, showcasing her long, toned dark legs all the way to the upper thigh. Her body was everything he'd want to fuck, even as it looked too good for him, inaccessible. No mortal man was worthy of fucking a goddess.

Snapping himself away from that crazy thought, he lifted his attention to her face. She wore a horse mask, too, as detailed as the stallion's head she'd put upon him. Only hers had a long elegant nose and feminine lines, including a long, silky forelock that fell along the jaw of the mask, emphasizing the column of her neck beneath. The dark eyes he'd been describing to himself were even more unsettling, the shape of the eye holes emphasizing how much her liquid brown irises and large pupils were like a mare's, vibrant with life and intensity.

She was an erotic meshing of horse and human. He'd said he didn't get this. She'd just forced him past that line and shown him that he could get this. All he had to do was let it happen...or have a Mistress who gave him no other choice but to do so.

He'd gone rigid. He had no ability to talk, to get loose, to even utter a freaking safe word, if he used one. He could handle pain and fucking. He didn't like this unfamiliar territory. She was testing the boundaries of what he normally was with a Mistress. She'd made him into a horse. A stallion that chewed on the bit, stamped his hooves, pulled against the reins, snorted his anger and lust. If she let him go, he'd be on her in a heartbeat, just like an animal, taking whatever he wanted. She was a physically capable woman, but she was still a woman. He was stronger. He could take her by force, make her submit.

He suspected she knew all that, and yet she showed no fear. It made him hotter, harder. It made him want her more.

"You asked me what I thought when I watched you fight." Her voice was a muted purr from the confines of the mask. She moved behind him, that feminine clip clop gait. She was placing an object on the dais next to him. She must be leaning against the platform, because he felt her body as she did something, slight rhythmic movements. In the mirror, he could see a piece of her smooth brown shoulder, the tilt of the mare's head.

"I was horrified. Worried about what would happen to you. Worried you would be seriously hurt. Yet I was also aroused by your strength and raw ferocity, the beauty of how you fight. That primal part of woman that responds to certain kinds of strength and violence from a male? I wanted to bind all that power beneath me, feel it plunging. I wanted to take you to your hands and knees and make you my mount. So that's what I'm doing."

He chewed on the bit and made a strangled noise that sounded a little too much like the angry snort of a steed for comfort, especially when he did it again, warning her. She gave him that soft laugh and struck his flank with the crop once more.

She stepped up on the dais behind him. This time, he caught enough of a glimpse to understand what she'd been doing. She'd been oiling up a black rubber phallus, one she'd strapped over her hips and waist. This was what he'd anticipated, but he resisted, yanking against the ropes. She ignored him.

"I'm glad I made sure your head has to stay up. I want you looking at yourself while I fuck you."

Taking the phallus in her hand, she pressed it through the ring that had kept his ass accessible to her. At the first touch of it against his opening, he clenched up and fought her in earnest, but she'd left him no way to refuse her. His cock was pulsing, leaking pre-come he could feel dampening the tip. The sudden explosion of physical response as she began to enter him was so unexpected, he was afraid he might spew. He'd been so much in his head he'd ignored how his body had been readying itself, reaching for this, wanting it. Which lessened his control with her even further.

"You know, when a mare is being bred, and there's concern that she might resist the stud to the point she'll do him damage, they sometimes temporarily hobble her, or strap one leg. It's to ensure she's receptive, get things moving in the right direction."

She dropped forward, her hand between his shoulder blades, and teased the valley of his spine with the tip of her tongue, sending a starburst of sensation through all his nerve endings. It converged on his cock, making him groan as the straps bit cruelly into the thick shaft.

"I can feel how much you want me, Marius, when I strap down all your shit, inside and out." Her other hand slid beneath his belly, traced the side of his steel cock. "Feel how big you are. My beautiful stud."

She straightened and kept working the dildo into him. He'd been fucked up the ass before, but not recently, so he was tighter than usual. Staring at the small part of her he could see in the mirror, he imagined the rest. The arch of her back, the jut of her nipples. The quiver of her breasts and crease of latex over her undulating hips. The way she was probably moistening her lips beneath the mask. Her cunt would be gushing, blissfully wet.

While he had to envision all that, he saw the hard quiver of his own muscles as she fully penetrated him and sunk deep. His mind might not be sure how to react, but his cock wasn't having the same problem. Despite the pain the strap was causing him, it was pulsing like a countdown on a bomb timer. Lust fueled by the unspecific rage churned inside him.

When he yanked against the ropes, she grasped the straps between harness and mask, increasing their tautness. He made a rebellious noise of anger and need.

"The stallion doesn't like being mounted by the mare, does he? But oh, the mare loves it, all that rage of the alpha who won't submit, but he's going to. What a tight, hot little ass you have, my sweet, sweet boy."

Fuck, he was going to come just from her talking. He snarled against the bit. He struggled, hoping to force something to twist or slip so she'd have to stop and loosen it before his circulation was cut off, but she was too damn good at this. She was starting to thrust in a diabolical rhythm. He could feel his climax rising, commanded wholly by her. He made a noise of furious frustration as the reaction boiled up from his balls. He kicked his back feet against restraints that wouldn't yield to his temper.

"You've no control or influence at all here," she said in that same steady purr, one laced with enough desire he could tell how turned on she was. But it gave him no power. He had no way to turn it to his advantage, since she had him bound, gagged, and had pulled him to the brink of climax without any element of persuasion. She was making him do her will.

"You'll come when I want you to come," she said, echoing his thoughts in that same even, relentless tone. "You're my breeding stud, my property, my responsibility. I know what's best for you in a way you don't. You live by your fighting instincts, but they take you into a place where you do yourself and others harm. I won't allow that anymore."

She was punctuating her breathless monologue with rhythmic, slow strokes that were cutting every line he had on his own reaction. "When you have a Mistress that's broken you, ridden you, and who fucks your ass when you need it, you're protected from everything, including yourself. There are no choices. You're my mount and that's it. You serve me. I own you, Marius. Come now."

He strangled on a roar, fighting the orgasm that rose and crashed down upon him. Even knowing his resistance played right into her hands, he couldn't make himself let it go, play the game, because she'd knocked him too far out of his normal headspace.

"Now," she repeated sharply, and he groaned, hips jerking as she reached beneath him and wrapped deft fingers over the crisscross of girth and strap to grasp his cock and balls. Semen instantly spurted wet heat over her fingers, against his chest and upper arms, his abdomen. He dug in to the platform on the hooves and almost buckled to his elbows.

His hips worked just as he'd shamefully imagined it earlier, a male animal humping air as she fucked him with harder thrusts, her other hand seizing his mane and twisting. In the mirror he saw two horses. The stallion's badass countenance turned dangerous from the angry flame in his eyes, the way he was fighting his restraints. Whereas the mare's head moved in a steady feminine dip of motion, her dark eyes luminous upon him, pleased with his response, alive with her own lust. Knowing he was making her so hot, without having had a thing to do with it himself, with no control...it was fucked up.

"That's it. That's my beautiful boy. Beautiful stud. All done for now." She spoke in a quiet hum as he finished, as his body shuddered beneath her. "What a mess you've made, but that's all right. That's exactly what your Mistress wanted from you."

As she slid from inside him, a hard aftershock jolted his muscles. He was trembling with the force of his reaction. His physical reaction. That was what he told himself.

Yet his gut clenched when he heard the whisper of straps and clink of the buckles that told him she'd removed the strap-on and set it aside. He confirmed it when she moved in front of him again.

He didn't know if it made her merciful or even more cruel when she removed the dress. The hoof stilettos were thigh high boots, and she wore nothing under the dress, so she stood before him in the boots and head mask alone. Her breasts, big, round and tipped with nipples that reminded him of black cherries, captured his gaze. He'd sort of lied when he'd said black cherry Jell-O wasn't his favorite because of her. He'd been thinking about that flavor a lot lately.

He was hungry to suckle, never mind his cock had just been drained. Christ, she wasn't done.

No, this was good. Of course she wasn't done. She hadn't come yet. She would want him to make that happen for her, which would put him back on familiar footing. She wouldn't keep him in this ridiculous get up. As he counted on that, he didn't let himself miss out on the view.

Her trim thatch of pubic hair was ebony as her hair. The soft ropes of her locs fell down her back below her mask, an enhancement to the mane.

She tsked, her gaze coursing over him. "Before I go for my ride, I think one very important thing is missing." She left his view, though he angled his head as hard as he could to get a brief glimpse of her bare ass twitching in a saucy walk as she circled him again. Wearing those boots, Christ, she was a picture. If he ever got free of this...

The cabinet door rattled, and she was back behind him. Silky, thick hair brushed against the back of his thighs. Oh, fuck, no. She was giving him a tail, one that was put in place with the help of a rosebud butt plug. It felt twice as thick as what she'd used to fuck him. He was too lubricated to resist her, no matter how he tried.

"My stallion's still so slick for me," she observed in a pleased tone. "Look at that. No, don't tighten up. You can take this. Don't be stubborn." Her fingers curled around his cock again, a sensual stroke and tug, stroke and tug, that was disturbing, but oh hell... Okay, yeah, it was big, but she coaxed and teased, and it was going in, stretching, burning, and he was working with her, despite his initial resolve to resist.

When it was seated, it wasn't comfortable, but his dick didn't care, still floundering toward an erection again like a drowning swimmer determined to reach firm footing. It messed with his theory that if she'd used the big plug first he could have kept better control of his response.

"There it is, all the way in." The tail fell against the backs of his legs, and the burning had him fidgeting, making it swish more, adding to the whole equine identity crisis. God, he was himself, but he was this beast, this powerful beast she described, caught up in a fantasy where he belonged to her, where he had no rights beyond being her property. The more he chafed against it, the more she soothed and stimulated and messed up his head.

Stepping back up on the dais, she swung a leg over him. She didn't put her fine ass in the saddle right away. First, she straddled his shoulders. The feel of her round ass, wet cunt and springy hair, rubbing against his flesh, provoked the hard, angry need inside him.

When they'd come into the stall, he'd noticed there were a couple chains with stirrup-style loops hung from the ceiling. She grasped one now with one hand so she wasn't putting her full weight on him. It also gave her the leverage to rub herself over him lighter or harder, depending on her preferences. Her thighs clasped his upper body while she curled the other hand in the reins and his mane, and started to rock. As she rubbed her clit against him, her arousal dampened his flesh. "This is one way I can come," she mused. "Or maybe..."

She moved back onto the saddle. The brief glimpse he'd had of the pommel when she'd put the saddle on him had shown it was designed for other purposes. It was shaped like a phallus, with a rabbit ear clit stimulator. Since it seemed like she was manipulating it back and at a different angle, it apparently could be adjusted so she could work herself on it while comfortable in the seat. It probably also goddamn vibrated. A sudden tingle through the saddle told him he was right.

The plug in his ass, something about it was making him shift and rock and, oh God, what the fuck now? He wasn't ready to get fully hard again, but suddenly it felt like he could, he was. What kind of stimulant was in that lube?

Adding to his aroused state, she'd lowered herself onto the pommel. He was watching her fuck it, push herself up and drop back down. She'd chosen an inanimate object over him, a man who could fuck her to pleasure. A stallion that could cover a mare, bite her neck, hammer into her until he spilled his seed and possessed her completely.

He tried to jostle her, buck her off, and didn't succeed at all.

"This is how it's going to be, Marius," she said. "I take care of my own needs. I'll make you come whenever I wish, long and hard, drain you dry, but you don't get to take the lead in giving me pleasure until the day you want the privilege badly enough to mean it. Oh..." She let out a sigh that evolved into a moan, which felt like velvet against his frayed nerves. "You feel so good beneath me when I'm getting off. Nothing better than riding a horse..."

He was growling in anger, groaning in sexual frustration, watching her pleasure herself, feeling the rock of her through the saddle. She'd even denied him anything more than that brief contact with her cunt. Some of his more creative cursing came through, because she reclaimed the crop and started using it, smacking his ass, his balls, hard enough he was jumping against his bonds for different reasons. She was laughing breathlessly at him, calling him her bucking rodeo mount. He couldn't get away from any of it. His cock got fully stiff again as her husky laughter became longer, deeper moans.

Something was cracking inside him, the pressure of his emotions building in an alarming way.

She'd turned him into a fucking horse, made him feel like a horse, one she'd fucked up the ass before giving him a tail and pleasing herself with a damn rubber dick. She was arched back, her beautiful throat exposed, breasts bobbing. He couldn't see that far down, but he imagined her long, flat but soft stomach contracting, her cunt lips and short curls becoming wet as she came at last with low, throaty cries. Her legs, encased in the thigh high hoof boots, flexed with her movements.

He wanted, he hungered, he needed. He was going to fucking kill her. Or kill something to have her.

He needed to pull himself back together. She was just a clever bitch trying to take what he hadn't given her. Yet he could only stare hungrily at her as she went over her peak and came, gasping, moaning, claiming her full measure of satisfaction from him. He could watch her come forever. He wished he could be what made her come all the time. Every time.

Stop this shit.

But he was tied and could do nothing right now but watch. And feel. He hated it. Yet he never wanted her to untie him, so he couldn't ruin it for her. For either of them.

When her orgasm was done, for some inexplicable reason he was shuddering as much as she was. After a few long, steadying breaths that did interesting things with her breasts, she unstrapped her mask and pulled it free. As she bent behind his stallion headpiece, her lips touched his shoulder, where the tattoo armor was. He didn't want that either. Mistresses weren't tender to him. He had a few that he got along with well enough it was a fun fuck, and they were affectionate afterward. This wasn't that. He wanted to tell her to get off him.

But instead of spitting curses at her, he closed his eyes behind the mask, experiencing the touch of her lips through every nerve ending. She straightened, running her hands over her hair. Even with the compression of the mask that had somewhat mussed her features and hair, she was still beautiful.

She dismounted, removed the saddle and the harness, but left on the mask and straps that held his head and body in place. She was humming a little tune to herself.

When she came back, he tensed, not sure what was next. But she began to run a curry comb over him. Tiny rubber teeth massaged his muscles as she moved it in circles over the base of his neck, his back and shoulders, down over his ass and upper thighs, his stomach.

He thought of her hands on him the other night. This wasn't quite as good as that, but it was close. He tried to drop his head again, responding to the massage, and was thwarted by the straps pulling against his mouth. Murmuring a reassurance, she released those lines and rubbed his shoulders where they fed into his tense neck muscles.

Threading her fingers through the mane on the back of the mask, she tugged, then found the point of hair at his nape beneath it and caressed that.

After she worked him over with the rubber grooming tool, she started using her hands, coated with a liniment that smelled of eucalyptus. As she kneaded him with bare palms, he couldn't bite back a noise of bliss. Under her touch, the knots he seemed to carry more often than not started to loosen.

When she worked on his shoulders, she pressed his head down and held it there with a grip on his forelock and the decorative brow band. The position let him feel the full effect of her touch through his shoulders and neck. Then she brought his head back up. For a pleasurable moment, he was staring right at her breasts, soft round temptation. Moving toward his legs, she worked down his side and along his abdomen.

When she was done, his whole body felt better, while everything inside was tied in knots, though it wasn't without effort. His insides wanted to become just as malleable under her hands as his outside was. He forced himself to resist that urge, but when her eyes met his in the mirror, the shuttered finality he saw there speared him through his soul.

They were done for tonight. She'd give him nothing further in this session. Could he blame her?

He hated that part the worst of all, the emotions that surged up in him at the end of a session, even the fun fucks. She hadn't allowed him to turn this into that, and that only seemed to make his descent into a dark well of emotions all the more inevitable.

As he stared at her, he thought of what he'd do if he was free. Maybe he'd reach out and touch her chin, run his fingers along the creases the mask had left on her cheeks. His questing fingers would trace her collar bone. *"You're so beautiful,"* he would whisper, before he knew he'd said it.

He'd just come; she'd just come. So why did he hurt and yearn? Fuck, he didn't let himself feel that kind of hunger outside the fighting ring. He certainly didn't allow those feelings to slip into a session with a Mistress. His time with a Domme was supposed to be about getting her off. He hoped Regina would agree to that next time so he could fuck her and be done with this.

He hoped for that almost as much as he wanted her to never give in to him. But they always did. Or they broke. He was the child that always broke his toys before he could figure out how to play with them.

Sometimes he preferred not to come when he was in a session, letting all the orgasms happen to her. Not just because it kept power on his side, but he'd discovered unreleased passion had weight, something that could fill him and disguise what was empty.

Maybe there'd be no next time. Even if there was, this tug of war couldn't go on forever. She'd be done with him before long. He wasn't worth a lot of effort, and those that tried too hard just earned his contempt, while contributing to his well of self-loathing, freak that he was.

Shut the fuck up. Was there a lobotomy to remove one's inner voice?

She unhooked the cross ties, which allowed him to turn his head to see her. With the mask on he still had tunnel vision, but now he could turn that limited view on her wherever she moved, as long as she wasn't directly behind him. She moved to the sink wearing only the hoof boots, though she unzipped and stepped out of them, so she was entirely naked.

Most women, even the most formidable Mistress, looked more vulnerable that way, devoid of any trappings to enhance their power or allure, all imperfections visible to all. She moved the way a woman moved who had never viewed clothes as a shield. If she was walking down a busy city street right now, he expected she'd have the same sensual confidence and indifferent awareness. He'd never really understood why there were two terms for being clothes-less; *nude* and *naked*.

But seeing her, he realized they weren't the same word. Naked was about vulnerability, imperfection. Nude was *this is what I am, and it's so damn awesome I don't even think about it.*

A lifetime ago, in his sixth-grade class, they'd visited a bakery on a field trip to a local museum. The baker set out hot cinnamon rolls. Marius remembered having his nose pressed to the glass shield over the baker's work area. The cinnamon, sugar and butter had mixed together in the spiral crevices to form a rich, dark syrup. That was the color of Regina's skin, such a close match that if he closed his eyes and inhaled, he thought he could bring back the scent of the bakery. But he didn't want to close his eyes.

He'd worship the line of her back alone. Smooth and long, a graceful curve that disappeared into the crease at the top of her buttocks. And her ass...he wanted to kiss, squeeze and bite his way over every inch of it. Tease her rim and make those long, strong legs tremble, her round ass push urgently against his face. She'd turn, swinging one of her smoothly muscled legs over his head and bring him to her breasts, letting him suck and bite there...

She hadn't spoken, and with him still gagged, he had no chance to affect the mood or break up the intensity that still vibrated in the air. Or maybe he was the only one still feeling it. She looked relaxed. He stared at every part of her he could, but he couldn't get enough.

Putting on her panties and matching bra, red cotton with a trim of lace, she shrugged back into the tank and pulled on her jeans. Staying barefoot, she tied her locs back into a tail before she approached the dais again.

She released all the ties holding his legs, then moved forward to remove the mask. As she pulled it off his head, it was weird to see his human face in the mirror but the same eyes staring at him. Regina removed the bit and head straps, setting them aside before she combed his hair back with her fingers. He expected she did it to get rid of that hat hair feeling that came with wearing the tack and mask. It felt good, but before he could stiffen up against that vulnerability, she took the touch away. It had been an automatic, functional gesture, no time to reject or take advantage of it.

"You can use your teeth to pull off the straps holding the hooves in place," she said, pointing to them. "Wipe down the platform with the sterile wipes under the sink. There are detailed instructions there for cleaning the other tack. Be sure and use the proper cleaning agents with those instructions. Put everything back where it belongs, and then get dressed and leave. You have forty-five minutes to do all that and drive out the gate before I set the alarm."

"I—"

She shook her head. "No. You don't get to talk. Just nod if you'll obey, or leave. Before you think about being a smart-ass, remember the lesson I taught you when you were taking off your clothes. I have no interest in game playing. So nod if you'll do as you're told."

He could cheerfully tell her to fuck off, that all of it was game playing and who the hell was she to act as if he couldn't do exactly what the hell he wanted? But in a weird way, him acting out right now would mean she had won. She'd pulled something over on him. He just couldn't figure out exactly how she'd done it and he needed to think it through. He could exercise control. Even if he thought she smelled like cinnamon rolls.

"Are you..." He shut his mouth. She cocked her head.

"I'll allow one question. Am I what?"

"Are you wearing cinnamon?"

"I have a skin dust flavored with cinnamon. Yes. Is your real name Duncan?"

Duncan Marius Walczak.

Fuck. Tal, the big Oz asshole, had used his first name. He'd forgotten that, but she hadn't. The way it sounded on her full, glossy lips...he remembered a lullaby, a call to dinner, a harsh cry.

"That's two questions," he said carelessly. "I'd answer, but I'd hate to see you break your own rules, Mistress. Especially since you've worked so hard to put me in my place tonight, playing horsey."

She glanced at the slim watch she'd put on her wrist. "Very well. You have ten minutes to get out of here before you'll set off an alarm. Better put your clothes on and get to your car."

"No need to get pissy. I can clean up— "

"Go home, Marius," she said shortly. She was moving, striding down the wide corridor of the barn and toward the arched opening. She paused only to shut off the lights, leaving dim emergency lamps to illuminate his space.

He watched her head toward the building where they'd parked.

Wearing her jeans and tank, she was a cock-hardening, deep-into-temptation play of feminine curves.

It must be the lingering sense of the horse, because for a single moment, those wild instincts took over. He'd chase after her, shove her to the ground and take her the way she'd taken him, with such ruthless lust and need. He'd make her come the way she should have allowed him to do it.

He trembled with the rage, and it was a close thing. What would she do? Would she fight him? Would he like that?

His hands bunched into harder fists inside the hoof mitts. She didn't toss him even one backwards look. The distant sound of the clubhouse door shutting echoed in an inexplicably hollow place inside him.

Fine. Using his teeth, he removed the straps to take off the first "hoof," and then yanked the other free. He pulled on his jeans and shrugged into the shirt, not buttoning it. He dug out his car keys, but paused. He didn't like leaving the space like this, the strap-on, the crop, the saddle and other tack, none of it properly cared for and put away. It felt wrong, irritating him. They'd had a good time. Why couldn't she handle a little mouthing off? She'd ruined it.

Yeah, right, she'd ruined it. That was total crap. Looking bleakly around at the wreckage of their pleasure, thinking about how he could have cleaned it all, hung it up and won a look of approval from her...

"You know what?" he muttered. "Fuck it." So she'd set the alarm and lock him in here. The cops might come. Wouldn't be the first time he'd been on their bad side.

It took him thirty-eight minutes. He cleaned everything the way she'd directed. He had to do some switching around to remember exactly where everything went, but he thought he got it right. He'd have to pay closer attention next time. She was apparently the type of Mistress who liked to give quizzes.

He put the horse masks side by side in the cabinet after carefully wiping them down. His fingers lingered on the long, slim nose of her mask. "You are beautiful," he said quietly, thinking of all he'd imagined doing to her while she was wearing it. And while she wasn't. Then he closed the doors, and turned the latch.

When he walked to his car, hers was still there, and there was a light on in the clubhouse. It looked like she might have the TV on and was drinking a cocktail. But if he knocked, it'd be like he was begging. She hadn't invited him anyway. Hell, she'd told him to have his ass out of here thirty minutes ago. For all he knew, she'd coded the alarm as she'd threatened and he'd set it off when he left.

He got into his car and drove away, because that was all he knew how to do. When he reached the gate to the property, he hit the buzzer to exit, bracing himself for a shrieking alarm blast. Instead, the intercom near the gate emitted a short crackle of static before her voice came over it.

"Be at Safe Word tomorrow night," she said. "Nine p.m."

Swallowing a million different responses, he went with the only one he really wanted to say.

"Yes, Mistress."

CHAPTER FIVE

*W*ould he show? Regina figured it was a fifty-fifty bet. He'd been rattled by the whole pony play scene. After having time to think, he'd be all kinds of conflicted about it, tangled up with a bunch of rationalizations about his behavior and hers.

It was a decently active night at Safe Word, for a week day. The club was not as upscale as The Zone, but safe, clean, and with enough amenities to cater to middle-class BDSM lifestylers. An enthusiastic group of mostly naked subs were being directed through various line dances on the small dance floor, and cheerfully punished by a trio of patrolling Dominants when they had missteps.

The DJ was playing Alan Jackson and Jimmy Buffet's duet of "It's Five O' Clock Somewhere," so as she went by, she hooked her thumbs in an imaginary belt and did a decent two-step and twirl. It made Mistress Zoe, one of the Dommes directing the action, grin and do a little pirouette in sisterly response. When she invited Regina to join them, Regina shook her head and gave her a friendly wave, letting her know she had other plans tonight.

About half of the handful of private rooms were occupied, while other Masters, Mistresses and subs enjoyed the equipment in the public dungeon. Her destination was the lounge and bar area, where there were scattered couches and comfortable chairs, seating areas for people to socialize. One of the things Regina looked for in the BDSM clubs she chose was evidence that the long-term membership used it as much for a social gathering spot as a place to get their kink on.

Case in point: Kristoff and Janice, Master and sub, both in street clothes, were relaxing in one set of facing chairs, playing a card game. Janice had her bare foot propped on her Master's knee, her casual heels tumbled on the floor. When they both suddenly lunged forward and tried to slap the card on the table, Regina grinned, realizing they were playing Slapjack. Janice won, laughing, while Kristoff gave her a mock scowl and they started again.

Though they were in an environment where they could make it about more than a card game, they might or might not. Lifestylers often hung out at their favorite club the way other people went to their favorite bar or coffee shop. It was their place, their people. While The Zone was her first choice for serious play, Regina had always liked the energy here as a good runner-up. Since Marius was currently banned from The Zone, this was the best option for what she had in mind. She'd left his name up front as her guest, so they'd let him in. If he decided to show.

She glanced at her watch. 8:55. He was cutting it close. So yeah, he'd fucked his head up over the other night. If he showed tonight, he'd be spoiling for a fight. Fine. She'd position herself accordingly. The Throne corner was available.

The tall wooden chair placed there had earned the name with its carved floral back and velvet seat and arm rests. A center board and cushion could be removed to reveal a strategically placed hole beneath the Mistress, if she wanted her sub to eat her pussy or tongue her ass while she was in the chair.

The Throne was flanked by two shorter stools, which could serve as seating for bottoms or a prop to do other things to them. One night, she'd put a sub over each one while she took the center seat. Both men had donned thin body suits lined with metallic thread. The suits had an opening that allowed their cocks to hang free, and she'd ordered both to don a seven-ring gates of hell to contain their erect shafts until their queen allowed them to climax.

As she enjoyed holding court that night with Mistresses who visited her for the fun of joining in the role play, she idly stroked the men's bodies with her scepter, a violet wand that crackled electric energy over their flesh. Thanks to the metallic thread, the enhanced sensation sent hard shudders through them. When she applied it to the rings around their hard and needy cocks, the response was particularly volatile. But her favorite part had been running the wand over the stretched fabric around their testicles. Leaned over the bench, legs spread, arms braced on the floor as they faced outward, they never knew when to expect that.

Speak of the devil. One of those subs, Rob, was here tonight. He was at the bar, chatting with the bartender, but when he saw her, his eyes lighted with pleasure. Before she'd had her gradual shift toward problem subs, he'd been a favorite hook-up for her.

Rob was married to a woman he adored, but who had no interest in BDSM. He'd brought her once when they were engaged, but not to see if he could change her mind. They'd already tried that route. Regina thought favorably of Rob, but her regard increased that night, for both him and Thea. Rob's intent in bringing her was to introduce her to the Mistresses whom he might seek out for play, and say in front of each one: "My fiancée has given me permission to pursue those interests here." None of that "she knows about this, but hey, you don't get to ask her directly because I'm lying my ass off" bullshit that so many men tried to pull.

In the BDSM world, people didn't pass judgment, but Regina had no interest in playing with attached people who were lying to their other half about it. Didn't matter if sex happened or not; everyone knew BDSM play had a vital sexual core, so if she was playing with a man or woman who hadn't told a committed partner about this part of their life, and she found out about it, that was it. It didn't sit right with her, so she passed on future sessions with them.

Rob had cleared the purpose of the visit with his Mistresses ahead of time, so they'd been surreptitiously watching him make the rounds with his wife as soon as they arrived. Thea was a little thing with a powerful presence. Lots of curly red hair and big brown eyes. Her clothes were well chosen for her slightly plump figure, neat and fashionable.

At first, she'd been quiet and watchful, but by the time Rob introduced her to Regina, the acceptance and friendly nature of his other three regular Mistresses had relaxed her enough to show her feelings more openly.

"And he won't be playing at any other club," she added to Rob's declaration. "Outside of Safe Word, he belongs to me." Regina saw a trace of vulnerability in her expression, but the set to her chin was steady. Rob had his hand on the small of her back, his body pressed close to her, a reminder of love and support. He sent Regina a half-smile, though his eyes conveyed his worry, which told Regina that coming here had been Thea's idea. Another point in the woman's favor.

Though Regina was almost half a foot taller and far more physically imposing than his bride-to-be, Rob rallied enough to give Regina a meaningful head-to-toe look. "Don't make my future wife kick your ass to prove it, Mistress. She's a dispatcher with city sanitation. I've seen her keep those guys in line in ways that would make your knees shake."

"I believe it." Regina grinned and took Thea's hand for a firm shake. "Deal. And no problem. We all know he's a pain in the ass when he's not gagged or tied up. So out there, he's all yours. If you ever need any tips on how to give him a good beating, let me know."

Then, more seriously, she'd squeezed the woman's hand. "We'll take good care of him. And if ever you're not comfortable with this, you don't need to worry. He loves you more than what happens here."

"I know." Thea met her gaze squarely, showing her a woman who did know her man, who didn't need another woman to tell her any damn thing about him. "He was going to give it up for me. That was why he was gone for a couple months. It took me a while to understand. But I know...when he comes home from this, he's more relaxed, more attentive, more...him. I trust him. I trust his love." She'd looked up at him and caressed his jaw. As she did, Rob dipped his head and kissed her palm.

Regina came back to the present as Rob approached. Taking her friendly, casual nod as a cue that he shouldn't kneel and enter a more formal sub protocol, he came to her as an equal. But he was dressed for play in a utilitarian collar and a pair of jeans only, hanging low on his slim hips so she knew he wore nothing under them. He wasn't built like Marius, but Rob took good care of himself. He was a jogger who worked out at the gym several times a week.

"What's Thea up to tonight?" she asked.

"Girl movie with her friends. She's going to come home ready to jump me because she'll have been ogling some half-dressed movie star for a couple hours."

"Well, fair's fair." Regina grinned. "How many times do you come home from here and ravish her until she can't walk because we hardly ever let you come? Our thanks to her for her donation to our cause."

He flushed a little, though he grinned. "You're right, Mistress. On that note..." He lowered his gaze. "Is there any way I can serve you tonight?"

"It depends. I was waiting for someone." A glance at her watch showed it was one minute after nine. Well, then. "He's late, so he's missed his chance. But he may show. If he does, I want to be involved with someone. If you've no objection to me shamelessly using you to prove a point, I promise to pay for your and Thea's next dinner out as thanks."

Rob lifted his head, giving her a speculative look, but properly refrained from asking more penetrating questions. "No need for that. I'm happy to serve. What do you have in mind?"

Her gaze coursed over him. "I want you wearing a lot less. And Rob..." She paused until he met her gaze, another equal-to-equal communication. "This could get ugly, but it's between me and him. If things escalate, I need you to step back and trust my lead. No testosterone displays. That's a red flag to this bull. I'm not trying to placate him. I'm trying to teach him something, and that requires me to have total control over all reactions to his behavior, mine or yours. Understood? You can still back out, if you're not comfortable."

Rob considered that. "Sounds interesting. Short of him throwing a punch at you, I think I can sit on my powder keg of testosterone."

She chuckled, appreciating him. "Great. Well then?" She put a hand on her hip and quirked an imperious brow, feeling the pleasure of her Mistress side taking the upper hand as Rob picked up on it. He immediately stripped, set aside the clothes and dropped to one knee before her. Then all the way to his elbows as she propped a high heel on his back and applied pressure. She'd worn skin-tight thin leggings under a micro skirt that clung to her ass, and a snug, crisp button-down shirt loose over it. Schoolmistress meets school girl. The slick red heels added a touch of blatant sex to the ensemble.

She heard the little catch in his breath when she dug one of the sharp stiletto points into his side. She loved her challenges, but

Goddess, a willing sub was like a free piece of birthday cake. Nothing anyone with brain cells would pass up the chance to eat.

She bent and ran a hand over his thick, sandy blond hair. "Go kneel before the throne. I need a footrest."

"Yes, Mistress."

~

He showed at 9:40. One of the first things she noticed was he hadn't shaved, because the shadow of his beard was dark on his jutting jaw. He wore jeans and a snug white T-shirt that had no embellishment except the impressive muscle beneath it. Given the cut and fit of the jeans, he also intended a Mistress to know exactly what she could have. If she played his game.

She'd slipped off her shoes some time ago and had her soles pressed against Rob, one on his side, the other on the curve of his ass because he knelt before her in profile. Thanks to Marius being so late, she'd had time to entertain herself. Rob was currently stroking his cock in time to the music coming over the speakers. He'd almost gone over the edge with a couple faster pieces, but the ballads disrupted him, earning her amusement and his affable frustration. But he was a pleasure to watch. So obedient and sexy at once, his cock hard and thick in his hand, his buttock and side flexing under her foot. He was breathing fast now, so close.

She lifted her gaze to Marius only when he approached and stood on the other side of Rob, so that his tempting lower body molded by denim was in her line of sight. He could have seen that she was engaged and blown her off right then, but he would have had to leave, since he was here as her guest. She expected he would have done it, regardless. He would have let her see him, then left the club as if it didn't mean a damn thing to him, with his lips curled in that sneer. But he hadn't.

Though she didn't expect tonight was going to be a smooth road, she took that as a step in the right direction. When her attention moved to his face, his expression suggested he was about to unwisely toss off some smart assed quip.

He showed a modicum of good sense and suppressed it. Instead, he stood still and stared at her defiantly, waiting to be acknowledged.

Thanks to the past forty minutes, during which Rob had eased her deep into that liquid pool where she could feel every ripple through the waters from her chosen submissive, the vibrations of energy off Marius were as detailed to her as a polygraph.

"Yeah, I'm late," Marius said abruptly. "But I'm here now. Ready to serve, Mistress."

She noted he'd barely looked at Rob. He seemed to be actively avoiding any acknowledgement of his existence. Interesting.

"Do you have an excuse?" she asked.

"Would it matter?"

"No. Come now," she said gently.

His gaze snapped to her, Marius visibly caught off guard when he realized she wasn't speaking to him. Rob jetted into the condom he was wearing, his body jerking, hair falling attractively over his brow and eye as he let the orgasm have him. Regina kneaded him with her toes, crooning, giving him her approval and encouragement. She ignored Marius. No matter that she'd chosen Rob to help her teach him a lesson, she wouldn't deny the man her full focus as Mistress during his release.

Regina had negotiated an orgasm from him, but before she cut him loose, she'd make sure he was sufficiently revived and hurting for pussy. He would be required to properly care for his wife after her "girl movie," and Regina wouldn't be the one causing him to fall down on the job, so to speak.

When Rob finished, she eased him to his elbows and knees facing her, his forehead touching the ground, and let him get his breath back. She sat back, sliding her feet into her heels so she could brace those against Rob and let him feel the pleasurable dig into his shoulder and flank again. Marius remained motionless, one hand hooked in his pocket, the other loose, fingers curled in a half fist.

"Take off the shirt," she said, making eye contact so this time there was no doubt she was addressing him.

He obeyed. As he stretched his upper torso, she saw the slide of one hip bone below firm flesh as he twisted and pulled the shirt loose. His bruises had healed some more, now yellowish and fading, rather than purple and dark.

"Throw it over here," she said, lifting her hand.

"I can bring it."

"No. Rob has that spot right now. Toss it."

He balled it up and complied, probably with more force than required, but she caught it on her outstretched fingers. Spreading it out over both hands, she lifted it to her face, inhaling the scent. He might not have shaved, but he'd showered. His scent differed from encounter to encounter, as if he changed out soap brands often. Curious. Most men stuck with one preference. She had no objection to this one, a spicy citrus. She could feel the lingering heat of his body through the cloth.

"This is the price of being late," she said, settling the shirt on the chair arm. "How do you think I'll look when I go to bed tonight, wearing just it and a pair of panties?" Lifting her hand, she caressed her breast and ran her thumb over the nipple, which grew more erect against the fabric of her button-down shirt as she stroked it. Rob's performance had aroused her, and it didn't take much to send a ripple of response arrowing between her legs. Marius's hot gray gaze sped it along. His jaw was tight.

Not sure how to respond to me, are you, angry boy? Not used to dealing with someone who not only doesn't cater to your shit, but doesn't get worked up over it.

He stepped forward, so close the toes of his shoes pressed rudely against the side of Rob's curved body. The man stiffened, but he kept his head down, in the position Regina had dictated. Yeah, he was going to test his testosterone against Rob's, just as Regina had anticipated. She didn't want to go too far down that road, though she wasn't going to back away from it, either, if Marius pushed it. She trusted Rob to follow her direction.

"I think it won't fit over your tits," Marius said, his eyes coursing over them in insolent appraisal.

"Think not? Hmm." She straightened and flicked open the buttons of her shirt before shrugging it off her shoulders. Her red lace bra had a front fastener that she handled just as easily, lifting away from the back of the throne chair enough to slide it off. Rob's head lifted.

In an instant, Marius had his thick tread shoe on the back of the man's neck. "She didn't say you could look at her," he growled.

"I didn't say he couldn't either," she said coolly. "Step back, Marius."

His expressive lips were capable of a wide variety of snarls and grimaces. This one tried to convey a *fuck it, who cares* sneer, but it was closer to a predatory snarl. He did step back, however. Not far, one shoe tip still against Rob's knee, the other under his body. She could tell Rob's temper had sparked, but the man was holding, his body language still mostly relaxed.

She put on the T-shirt. It was snug over her D-cup breasts, but the effect was everything she wanted. Her taut nipples strained against the fabric so that the areolas were visible dark smudges. "Looks like a perfect fit to me," she observed, sitting back. "Go get me a Coke Zero with lemon. And a bottle of water for Rob. Tell the bartender to run a tab for me."

She cupped both her breasts, pleasing herself with the way they looked in Marius's T-shirt. She'd enjoy using a vibrator on herself tonight when she was home in bed. She'd inhale his scent, look down at her body and imagine his eyes flashing with the fire she saw when she gave him the drink order. He seemed caught between murder and lust...and stark need. The last could derail her, so she set that aside. She couldn't give him what they both wanted until he knew how to ask for it the right way.

She heard Rob mutter a soft curse, telling her he was seeing enough in his peripheral vision that his engines were re-starting. Good. She was a generous Mistress that way. On other things, she was a hardass bitch.

Marius returned with the drinks. He set the bottled water next to Rob when she pointed, and offered her the Coke Zero.

"Rob, drink some of the water. I'll need your mouth wet shortly." Rising as the sub moved to do her bidding, she took her drink from Marius's hand, limiting the contact between their fingers. As she sipped, she studied his face, not bothering to hide her frank assessment. His bored expression said he thought he knew the game she was playing, and he wasn't impressed with her attempt to punish him for his attitude and lateness. Yet when she handed the drink back to him, she felt tension in his fingers.

"I changed my mind. I want a Diet Coke instead. Over ice, no lemon."

Marius stared at her, but she turned away from him. Taking off the leggings beneath her micro skirt meant she gave both men a brief glimpse of red satin creasing over her ass before she readjusted the micro skirt and settled back on the throne. Hooking one of the stools with her shoe, she drew it close so that she could prop one foot on it, tilting her other knee back against the arm of the throne to spread her thighs.

"You pleased me, Rob. Come closer to get your reward."

The man immediately moved into a kneeling position where he'd be able to put his mouth on her cunt over the panties. Being the good sub he was, he didn't make contact. He stopped close enough his breath touched her through the fabric, but his mouth didn't.

If it had been Marius between her legs, he would have taken *Come closer* as the starting gun. He would devour, bite and demand. He'd grip her thighs, shoving them wider. There would be growling.

She suppressed a hard shiver of lust. If only she could achieve the connection they needed with a snap of her fingers, where she could unleash his animal instincts for their mutual pleasure without worry that he would twist it to fuck with both their heads. But he'd shown up late and his attitude so far sucked. She couldn't let any of that go.

She could have allowed Marius to see that shiver of reaction but let him think she was responding to Rob. It wouldn't be difficult, since she'd had Rob's mouth between her legs before and he gave damn good oral. But while jealousy and competition would add a kick to the mix, it wasn't the right bait for Marius. Plus, dishonest manipulation wasn't her style.

"Get my drink or take off, Marius. You're either here to be a sub or you're not." She stroked her long fingers through Rob's hair as he remained still, waiting on her, his gaze focused on her cunt with the gratifying eagerness of a quivering Labrador ready to lunge into action. Slipping off her shoe, she placed her bare foot on his shoulder, curling her toes into the muscle. "Or maybe we're approaching this all wrong."

She tilted her head, ignoring the flash of puzzled surprise in Marius's gaze. "Are you sure you're not a top playing the wrong side of the fence? You seem to fight this pretty hard. If you think that's the case, we can knock off the Mistress and sub shit between us right now. Grab yourself a drink, pull up a chair and we'll talk about it. There are some good topping opportunities here tonight."

She nodded toward a trio of female subs. They were sitting on the floor, playing jacks. All three were dressed in ruffles, simple cotton panties under the short skirts, their hair done in pigtails. "Daddy's girls are always fun and playful, a good way to start. A little slap and tickle, some spanking. But Liza over there is a jack-of-all-kink. Likes bondage, impact play, electrical…"

"Not interested." His expression had gone cold.

"Not interested in either preference? Or topping?"

If Marius had a drop of topping blood in him, she'd go jump in the bay in the dead of winter, but maybe it wasn't her who needed to be convinced. Trying to figure out where one fit in the BDSM world wasn't unusual. Some men came into it trying to be Masters, not realizing that what had drawn them to it was the desire to submit. It took time to set aside societal expectations and tap into a soul's true needs.

Once most people were in it long enough, they felt more comfortable trying on the different roles until they found the one that fit the best. Maybe he hadn't found that comfort zone, for whatever reason. Did he need a reset, to remind him where he really wanted to be?

"Have you ever done it before?" she asked. "Topping?"

His steel gaze was on Rob's head, particularly her fingers, stroking the submissive's hair. Was he thinking of how her fingers had stroked him last night, when he'd become her mount?

She expected his palm was starting to ache from gripping the ice-cold glass of her first drink order.

"I'll come back when you're done with him and we'll talk." His voice was wooden.

"Okay." She spoke to him as an equal, as if it was already a done deal, any pressure on him to behave as a submissive removed. "Feel free to wander around. As my guest, you're not authorized to play with anyone but me, but if you see something you want to do, come back and hang out at the bar until I'm done and we'll figure it out. This won't take long."

She said the last four words in a sultry tease to Rob, letting him know how fine a job he'd done prior to this, pleasing and arousing her. She settled back and cupped the back of his head, a mute command to proceed. A smile curved her mouth at the first touch of his lips against the crotch of her panties. This was going to be relaxing and therapeutic, easing the burn higher in her gut the proximity to Marius was causing. So what if Rob wasn't the demanding beast she wanted between her legs? She'd never been one to trade out Mr. Right Now for the elusive Mr. Right.

Even if the sullen cloud four feet away from her was Mr. Right, he wasn't offering to be Mr. Right Now, and her pussy wanted a release.

Marius stepped forward and threw the drink in her face.

She'd told Rob things might get ugly. She'd known there was a lot brewing under the surface, but she'd underestimated how close to that point Marius had been. But that didn't piss her off nearly as much as him ruining the olfactory pleasure of the shirt she'd wanted to take home with his scent firmly imprinted upon it.

Rob leaped to his feet. Anger suffused his features as he planted himself between Regina and Marius. To an honorable male like him, this was probably equivalent to Marius punching her. She gave him credit for self-control, however, because he limited himself to providing a human barricade between Marius and his Mistress.

She'd never had anyone dash a drink full of ice in her face before. It had stung and was cold, but it was hardly catastrophic. He'd soaked the front of the T-shirt, so her nipples were even more noticeable dark points against the translucent fabric. Rob had been splattered, because the drops ran down his back and his hair was sprayed with a light dew. She laid a hand on his tense shoulder, the pressure of her grip a mute command to move to her right and clear the field between her and Marius. While he was initially unresponsive, his desire to protect her struggling with the promise he'd made, eventually he complied. He remained close, a vibrating current of electricity at her elbow.

She wasn't surprised that Marius hadn't moved an inch. Until Rob shifted, Marius had been almost eye to eye with him. His fists were clenched, his gaze pinned on her chosen sub for the evening, but she reached out and tapped Marius's jaw, making his eyes snap to her.

"Your fight begins and ends with me, not him," she said coolly. "And that's not because he wouldn't like to deck you. It's because he knows how to respect a Mistress."

Energy rippled through Marius. "He respects her by being a pussy and letting her be attacked?" he spat.

Rob made an aggressive noise. When Regina shot him a quelling glance, he subsided with effort, but she kept her pointed gaze on him until he backed up another couple of steps, giving them all more breathing room. Regina brought her attention back to Marius.

"He's not the bastard who attacked me," she said mildly.

"You know what you were doing," Marius gritted out. "Fucking with my head."

"A thief always thinks he's being robbed," she observed. Schooling her expression to dispassion, a far cry from how she was feeling, she turned her back to him and faced Rob. "Get me a towel to dry off. Then you can finish what you started."

"With pleasure, Mistress."

No more scathing looks were sent toward Marius, though from his expression, Rob vehemently disapproved of Marius's behavior. But he'd picked up on her dismissive cues, proceeding as if the drink had appeared upon her magically, as if Marius didn't exist. As if his act was as insignificant to adult matters as a naughty child's.

Rob retrieved a towel from the bar, speaking a low word to Leonard that she knew would assure the staff member everything was under control. It wasn't a lie, though she didn't exactly know how this was going to go.

Marius was standing behind her still. As she turned, she saw his fists remained half curled. But he wasn't moving. Was he waiting to see what she would do next, what switch she would flip, what string she'd pull? Or was he uncertain what to do next, caught in some kind of stasis, an internal loop?

The scene with Siren had built into a disaster. This time he'd taken it to DEFCON level with almost no build up at all, which confirmed what she already knew. He'd been on slow burn ever since their pony play scene, and come spoiling for a fight.

Rob returned with two towels and offered one to her. As she patted her face and throat, ignoring the tower of quivering heat that was Marius, Rob dried the throne and the floor around it. He gestured her politely back toward her seat, though she saw the spark as he anticipated getting his mouth between her legs again. And this time there would be a component of *fuck you* to Marius as he did it. She'd let that pass, since a man had to be a man, after all. Keep a stranglehold on a male sub and he became too much of a pet for her liking.

The important part was that he could follow her direction and take care of her. As she took the throne once more, she lifted her chin. "I have some soda here. On my throat. I'd like you to use your mouth to handle that, Rob."

She had enough multi-tasking ability to anticipate the pleasurable sensation of Rob's mouth *and* keep Marius on her radar. Rob put his heated lips to her throat, sucking off beads of moisture. As she made a noise of encouragement, he moved down toward the rise of her breasts, a man's literal wet dream under the cling of the soaked T-shirt.

Marius still hadn't moved. It was unsettling, if she allowed herself to feel that way, which she didn't. He put off vibrations like a ticking time bomb, but he'd be reviewing his options in his mind, stewing in the vacuum where she'd left him, because she'd provided him no further direction.

He wasn't a newbie sub. She didn't need to handhold him through the different options to resolve a self-inflicted fuck-up. She projected nothing but indifference to his presence. However, since inside she was far too curious about what he'd attempt next, Rob provided a very pleasant and creative distraction with his lips and tongue.

He'd only reached her cleavage, his tongue sliding in to enjoy the deep valley the damp T-shirt molded, when she heard something very much like a snarl come from the densely-packed zone of heat and muscle to her left.

"I still have some water on my arms," she said casually. "Dry that with the towel, Rob."

As he straightened to do so, Marius at last moved. He muscled in, hauling Rob to his feet and putting a palm on his chest to press him back. One step, two step, taking him out of her personal space and putting Marius squarely before her. He did it with such brutal effi-ciency, Rob had no time to resist until the second step. He bristled and pushed forward against Marius's straight arm, but he fortunately shot her a glance at the same time. She shook her head, quelling the spike of alarm. Rob was capable enough, but she'd seen firsthand that Marius was a street fighter, a violent brute.

A good club was worth its membership fee. She noticed Leonard was bussing a nearby table, a strategic decision that put him closer to the situation. The Dungeon Master that patrolled the several public spaces of the club also had his eye upon them.

She wasn't going to let this get any further, but she appreciated the backup. She didn't usually bring problems into her chosen clubs, so she'd have some latitude in this situation.

She'd noted something else important. The moves Marius had used were not what he'd employ in the ring, but the quelling, neutralizing moves she'd use as a C.O. Or that he used as Zone security.

Yes, there was violence vibrating off him, which had contributed to her alarm, but his choice of that tactic helped keep her voice steady, her posture relaxed. She rose from the throne.

"Rob," she said. Just one word, the command implied.

The man's jaw flexed hard enough to crack at Marius's transgression, but he inclined his head in a respectful nod and gave way. She really was going to owe him and Thea dinner. An expensive one.

What was vibrating off Marius was a web of anger and confusion, but she wouldn't get snared in it. Instead, she rested on the strands like an alert spider, anticipating what the vibrations through the threads might mean.

As he lifted the towel to press it against her skin, she didn't move, except to lock gazes with him before he made contact. "If you touch me," she said coldly, "You will not touch me again. This will be over."

Not a dare, not a taunt. She meant it. She had to. No matter the clamor of her Domme senses that told her this was the sub who could kneel in the hidden depths behind her heart and stay there indefinitely, she would walk away if he defied her in this key moment. This was a game where every move could be the final move, and she couldn't back away from that. The question was, would he unwisely assume she was bluffing?

If he could get enough space from his emotions, he was smart enough to figure it out. But she knew it was equally possible the demons inside him might say fuck it, make him reach out and rudely tweak her breast like some stupid frat boy playing a prank. Was he stronger than his demons? Could he leash them before they took him past the point of no return? They hadn't the other night with Siren. Had he regretted or learned anything since then?

Don't do it, Marius. Take control. You know you need a Mistress. No matter how fucked up your head is, somewhere in your heart, you know it.

She was in a hard battle of her own, not to betray any tells of anticipation, like a held breath or an increased pulse.

He still had the towel lifted between them, his arrested movement when she'd warned him not to touch her. She'd told him he had no leave to touch her, but she had no such prohibition. She closed her hand over his, clenching the towel with a white-knuckled grip.

She'd had her growth spurt in middle school, her tall, big-boned body suddenly endowed with high, proud breasts and an impressive ass. It had inspired more than one high school boy to think that grabbing the booty just because it was out there looking like it needed palm support was the right way to go. Until she'd laid out one of those horny good Samaritans with a solid blow to the nuts, using the handle of a PE class hockey stick.

She didn't need to be petite or act helpless to feel womanly. Yet she noticed he had a big hand. Long, thick fingers, wide palm, scarred knuckles. He'd have a strong grip, like he had on the towel.

She curled her fingers over his. "Release it," she said quietly. "Kneel at my feet."

She wasn't a negotiator. She didn't caress his fingers as she wished to do. She merely held him, reading the energy pulsing through the scarred knuckles. No new scrapes on them, so at least he hadn't been back in the fighting ring since last she'd seen him. Though maybe he would have come here more settled if he had, that was a defusing tactic she didn't want him utilizing.

She slid her hand to his wrist and held it as she took the towel from his loosened grip and handed it to the tense Rob. "On your knees," she said softly to Marius. "Or get out of my sight."

When she'd touched his hand, he'd adjusted his attention. He was staring down, at her breasts, at the taut nipples and rounded curves etched out by his wet T-shirt, her dark skin turning the white fabric a gray color, like a dove. Or like his eyes, which were fixated on them. Not in a lecherous way, but as if he was trying to understand something by holding his mind there, maybe following the rhythmic rise and fall of her breath.

He lifted a hand, his fingers half curled. For a moment, she thought he was going to brush his knuckles against one of her curves, or even her face, but he didn't.

The switch flipped and the lights went off behind his eyes. Her heart sank three or four floors.

He stepped back from her. Took a couple steps, his eyes remaining on her face until he pivoted and left the sitting area. He headed toward the exit, not looking left or right. The abrupt decision and departure sent a hard jolt into her chest, which suddenly felt so empty her legs almost buckled from weakness.

Fuck. The ultimatum had been necessary, no question, but where did that leave them now?

Finished. It was done.

CHAPTER SIX

or better or worse, that was the end of it. So there was no reason for her to contact Marguerite and request a meet with her. But Regina had and here she was, at Tea Leaves on an early afternoon. The sun was sending shards of mellow light through the branches of the oak trees canopying the porch at the café's entrance.

She'd been here plenty of times before, and not just because the tea selection and the baked treats were incomparable. Once a year, Marguerite threw a card party for her Domme friends. Dress code was "dressed-up," but the chosen outfit had to come from a time other than the present decade. Regina had worn a 1940s peach-colored dress with lots of gauzy fabric over figure molding satin, coupled with a white hat festooned by flowers and feathers. Donning elbow-length white gloves had made her realize just how erotic they felt, clinging to wrists and finger tips, a feeling increased by the plethora of rhinestone bracelets she'd worn.

Tea service had been handled by a small team of female submissives hired from The Zone staff. Gen had pitched in to coordinate their efforts. Gen had worked for Marguerite for some time, but when she became Lyda's, she'd left full time employment with the café, with Marguerite's blessings. She handled the books and other administrative duties at Lyda's landscaping business.

Until she'd found her current subs, Noah and Gen, Lyda had been much like Regina, enjoying her submissives but not pursuing much with them outside the club-type environments. Perhaps one of the main reasons she and Lyda were friends was that they held the same viewpoint on relationships. When Lyda found the right one, she'd act on it, but until then she'd made it clear there was too damn much to do and enjoy to spend a lot of time on romantic pining. If she'd had any patience for such nonsense.

Lyda was even farther on the pragmatic end of the scale than Regina was. But Lyda had revealed a woman's desire to love and commit when she'd found the two submissives she wanted above all others. She was still a hardass and a tough Mistress, but now the extreme end of that manifested itself only toward anyone who didn't understand Noah and Gen belonged to her.

At the tea party, Regina had teased Lyda about leaving Noah at home. Lyda had promptly responded that Marguerite had said no pets. That bitch. Which was a shame, because looking at a collared Noah, kneeling at Lyda's feet, was never a hardship on the eyes.

Regina imagined Marius doing that. When she'd ordered him to kneel, he'd wanted to obey her. She'd felt it.

After their two encounters, she had an even better understanding of why a lot of Mistresses didn't go any further with him. Who would bother, even if they had caught that glimmer inside him she had? Most Mistresses would rightly decide he could take his precious dysfunctionality and go jump in a lake with it. *Get over yourself already, dude.*

But she was dealing with more than some narcissistic, self-pitying, the-world-doesn't-understand me crap. She went back to that moment when he'd stared at her breasts in a way that wasn't entirely sexual.

As a woman, she'd responded to the desire of the fully grown, powerful man. But her inner spirit, that deep Goddess Mother that every woman carried, had felt the yearning of the child, his need. She thought he was trying to find his way to her through alligators and monsters, things so twisted in his own head they were blinding him. His only hope was that she would hear his silent scream with something that went far beyond hearing or sight.

What had happened to this man? The abyss within him was deep and dangerous, and she knew she was too close to the edge. But she wasn't stepping away. Which was the crux of why she was here, trying to find out more. Even though she'd told him they were over and had meant it.

Yeah, it didn't have to make sense.

There were Mistresses who had the damsel-in-distress problem, only the damsel was male. However, no different from their male counterparts who embraced the surface role of hero, they lost interest once the "damsel" was seemingly "saved."

It was a dysfunctionality she recognized and disliked. It had no more substance than falling in and out of love every six months to enjoy that euphoric high of the connection.

Up until now, she'd set clear lines with the troubled subs she'd taken on. She was up front about what the relationship would and wouldn't be. But she *wasn't* clear about what this relationship would and wouldn't be. Which meant she wasn't done with it yet.

As she entered Tea Leaves, Regina felt the spurt of warmth she always did at seeing Chloe, Marguerite's full time employee. The young woman was working the mostly occupied tables with the help of another girl, perhaps a part-time hire from the local college. Marguerite would take her time choosing a second fulltime person to replace Gen. She didn't enter into any relationship lightly.

Chloe was unique in the BDSM world. She was self-admittedly vanilla yet sexually adventurous, enough to have won the interest of Brendan, a delicious and fully committed submissive male who thought the sun rose and set behind Chloe. When she looked up and saw Regina, she beamed and waved with such infectious pleasure in her brown eyes, Regina couldn't argue with Brendan's assessment.

Chloe could top Brendan when needed. Dominance and submission were traits as well as an orientation, and everyone had a reservoir of either one. Fortunately, it seemed Chloe could call on her Dominant qualities in ways Brendan needed. He served her with all the devotion and care that any worthy man in love did, regardless of his sexual interests.

It was yet another example of why Regina loved the BDSM world. No relationship was predictable, though the undercurrent was something as familiar and stable to those in it as the foundation of a home.

Chloe straightened and pushed back a lock of her curly hair. She had it bobbed right now and it was tousled in a series of chaotic ringlets, some of them dyed blue. Her purple T-shirt had a Tree of Life on it with the gentle declaration *"And it harm none, do as you will."*

"She's in the back garden, Regina. Just go behind the counter and out the side door. She's expecting you. I made you those little strawberry cakes you like."

"Bless you. Just right for my mood." Regina didn't hesitate to give the girl a quick hug. Chloe responded with a strong return squeeze and a girlish, breathy laugh.

"Marguerite insists that Tyler stays with her only for my baking skills. I told her if that was really true, I'd kill her off and he could sample my goods anytime he wants."

Regina laughed. "Don't you have a man, you insatiable midget?"

"The best man in the whole universe," Chloe agreed without hesitation. "But it's *Tyler*. He's a god, not a man. Those amber tiger eyes, the trace of sexy silver in his hair... Brendan understands."

"Too true. But let's not remind Tyler of that too often. He already thinks too highly of himself." Regina ran an affectionate hand down the young woman's arm and moved toward the counter.

No matter the suggestive banter about Tyler being the top of the pyramid in man candy land, Chloe knew the same truth that anyone else did who'd ever seen Tyler and Marguerite Winterman together. Those two souls had been forged in the fires at the beginning of time and would always be the only one for the other.

Regina initially had been dismayed when she'd heard that Marguerite switched for Tyler. Most Dommes' hackles rose over that kind of thing, because way too often Dommes were interpreted one of two ways by an ignorant world. Either they were a pro-Domme, whose dominance was tied to professional services offered, or they weren't really a Domme at all; just a strong-willed woman waiting for the right man to top her. *Give me a fucking break.* She'd like to break the first person who'd planted that seed. Probably from the same family of inbreeds who suggested a raped woman was asking for it.

Marguerite's Domme skills had been legendary at The Zone, and they still were. Yet before meeting Tyler, Marguerite had been closed off, reserved, sitting on something in her past that had given her Dominance a different form. Powerful and amazing, yes, but... detached. Regina realized abruptly it might be a different form of what she felt in Marius, a wall between himself and sincere submission.

Remaining a Mistress yet submitting to Tyler, Marguerite had found a whole new level. She'd needed that ability to switch to tap into something she needed, both as a Domme and as a woman. If that worked for her, it wasn't Regina's place to pass judgment. And Tyler had clearly found the woman he'd been wanting all his life.

So again—there was nothing like the BDSM world. A carnival of possibilities, and nothing was written in stone. There was no one path, which was what kept it a maze of interesting adventures.

Marguerite was sitting at a wrought iron table beside a large pot of overflowing flowers and vines. A whimsical sculpture of a rabbit sat in the middle of it, matching the smaller one sitting on the table between two place settings. A pot of tea was waiting on the table, along with an assortment of small sandwiches, fruit, cookies and Chloe's cakes. The cloth napkins at the place settings were in a triangle tent design on the matching china. Showing her usual style, Marguerite had created a lovely setting and props for their conversation. The relaxed environment eased something in Regina she hadn't realized was tense.

Even with the changes due to her relationship with Tyler, there was still a reserve to Marguerite that set her apart from everyone. Frankly, it made her intimidating at times, and Regina didn't get intimidated by much of anyone. So that coil of loosening tension suggested she'd been a little concerned about what Marguerite would think of the situation.

Well, she was looking for some genuine guidance, even if she was told some things she might not want to hear. She considered the woman a friend and amazing Domme, her opinion highly respected.

A semi-serious curve of lips was Marguerite's version of a smile, but her gaze was warm as she rose to take Regina's hand in a brief grip. "It's so rare we get time for a one-on-one visit," she observed. "I'm glad you called."

"If you'd come to my place, I would have cracked open a bottle of wine and dusted the cobwebs off the porch chairs. This is beautiful." Regina sat down, smoothing the table cloth. "You make a visitor feel like a VIP."

"I've been to your place, and your back porch is a gorgeous

outdoor living space. It needs no embellishment, and a glass of wine sounds like the perfect way to enjoy it. From your message, this felt like a meeting of import, and it's been my experience that requires the right kind of headspace. An intimate tea, done correctly, gives us a quiet space to do that."

"No arguments, though I may wolf down all Chloe's cakes and get a sugar crash." Regina chuckled and indicated assent as Marguerite gestured to her tea cup. Marguerite was elegant and graceful in all she did, but there was a ritual to the way she did tea that enhanced it. It created a calmness in the recipient, as well as a respectful silence as she poured and prepared the tea with spare movements. She'd remembered Regina liked mint-flavored tea, and the amount of sugar and milk she preferred, which didn't surprise Regina.

After Marguerite was done, Regina sat back and sipped. A hanging planter festooned with dozens of tube-like lavender blossoms was being mined by a hummingbird. The creature dipped its long, sharp bill into each bloom, drinking the nectar. His wings were a blur of motion over his glossy green and purple body.

"I'm betting you never brought a sub to this inner sanctum." Regina smiled.

"No. This isn't a place for that. It's a good place to think and plan about it, though." A glimmer of humor went through Marguerite's gaze before it was replaced by something more serious. "Or consider big decisions like the one you're facing."

"Well, technically, there are no more decisions to be made. I drew a line in the sand and he crossed it, so I kicked him loose. I told him we were done. It wasn't a bluff. It can't be." She sighed and put down the cup. "But I'm here, Domme to Domme, because I know it's not finished. And I'd like some insight in how to reconcile those two truths."

Marguerite pursed her soft lips. "There's a difference between a bluff and changing your mind in the face of new information. Which is, I suspect, also why you're here. You know I've had a successful session with him, and you want to know more about how that went."

When she didn't say anything further and the pause drew out, her expression remaining closed, it prompted Regina to ask the question. "Is there a Dom and sub confidentiality clause?"

"If the Dominant feels it's necessary," Marguerite said.

"Is it necessary, in this case?"

Marguerite gave her a long look over the tea cup, this one more Domme than friend. Regina held the pale blue gaze, giving as good as she was getting. Not a wise idea to let Marguerite Winterman see you flinch.

"Tell me the most important thing you've learned so far about him, in session," the woman said.

Regina ate one of Chloe's cakes, gathering her thoughts. "Most Mistresses think he's a pain slut or uber-brat, craving physical punishment. But he absorbs that like a bottomless cup. Pain fuels the twisted part of him and shores up his defenses, so the last thing he should be given is extremes of physical pain."

"Hmm." Marguerite's body adopted an eerie stillness when she was listening. Regina forced herself to say nothing further, to wait her out and not fill in the silence with pointless information. A few breaths later, Marguerite decided that confidentiality clause didn't apply to Regina, revealing it through her most common method of communication. Minimalist and to the point.

"Stay away from his childhood."

Regina's brow creased. "But if that's where the root of the problem is..."

Marguerite shook her head. "I'm not saying overlook or ignore it in the decisions you make. Stay away from it in scene. It's a place that holds no safety for him. The submission he knew there was forced, cold and dark, the kind no one wishes to experience. Introduce him to the pleasures of submission and safety in the here and now to get to the treasure beneath. There's a trove there."

Regina felt an absurd push of jealousy. "Oh? What kind of treasure?"

"It wasn't mine to plunder or enjoy. Just as he wasn't mine to heal." Marguerite met Regina's gaze. "I felt that cold, dark place from him, but I didn't compel him to speak of it, nor did I push past it. The details I provided are the details I have."

"So how did you know it was there?"

"Intuition. You stand outside an abandoned building in a bad part of town, you feel the opposite of what you feel when you enter the gates of a spring carnival. Energy has its own language that can be read without the details." There was a faint note of rebuke in Marguerite's tone. "You've done enough sessions to know that."

"Yeah, but you're putting it into context for me. Don't do the Morpheus Matrix thing. I know you're like a Domme guru, but it's annoying."

Humor flitted through Marguerite's gaze, but she inclined her head in gracious apology. "You're correct. You're a formidable Mistress, and I was reacting to what I know of that, rather than being sensitive to your own energy. When someone gets into our heart or soul, it circumvents our knowledge and experience, and plays havoc with that logic."

"But he hasn't gotten into my head, fucking me up the way he's done the other Mistresses," Regina mused. "He's trying hard to do that, and he gets points for effort, but it's something beyond that. Something I feel from him. Something I recognize that I don't think anyone else has. Except maybe you. It's an ego stroke, I don't deny it, but it's also a challenge."

"A challenge can also be a warning."

"Is that from your husband?"

Marguerite's lips curved again. "He is concerned about his role in this, but I told him he made the right call."

"Thank you." Regina lifted her tea cup to take another sip. "Okay, stay away from his childhood in session. Got it. But you said 'introduce him to submission.' He's already an experienced sub, and I know you know that, so what did you mean?"

"He knows how to act like a sub. I'm not sure he's ever allowed himself to embrace it as his true nature. I expect that would be a wondrous thing to see. The Mistress who can get him there will receive a gift, but it will be a hard-earned one."

Marguerite broke a cookie into three parts and put them in a line on her plate. She wiped her fingers on a napkin and rested her hand on the table.

"Marius is an accomplished, self-aware split personality. At one time, he excelled in any structured role that didn't challenge what lies deep inside him. It allowed many Mistresses to enjoy him. In turn, they likely provided him an outlet that kept the darker things managed. But at a certain point..."

"A switch flipped." Regina nodded. "He couldn't do it in session anymore. But he also couldn't submit, so he started to push back harder and harder, until it went into the unhealthy area. He can't stay on the surface of his submissive cravings anymore, but he can't let go enough to do the deep end, which is really where he wants to be."

She blew out a delicate breath. "I was trying to narrow down when it happened. The first time I noticed it was the session he did with Lyda. That was what, about seven or eight months ago?"

"Yes." Marguerite appeared to be running through the timeframe in her head. "Soon after that was when he started coming to work with more injuries from his fights."

"So you knew about that?"

"Not at first. As long as we've known him, Marius has trained in different fighting styles. He's also competed, but they've been events through his local gym, well-monitored and legal amateur sports. When Tyler realized he was starting to participate in the underground circuit, he confronted Marius about it. Marius explained it was to make extra money and refused Tyler's offer to help him find additional work, less hazardous to his health. He is proud, as most men are. He also told Tyler it helped him manage aggression. As I said, he is self-aware, and likely realized his sessions were turning sour."

Marguerite sighed. "Since it is illegal, Tyler debated whether he should terminate his employment then, but decided not to do so, if it did not negatively affect his work performance at The Zone."

"Tyler realized if he fired him, Marius might turn to it as his sole income and he'd end up with his brains as soup."

"Yes." Wrapping both hands around her tea cup, Marguerite dipped her head without drinking, as if inhaling the aroma deeply. She was quiet a moment before she continued. "Tyler has a particular soft spot for...lost souls. It was difficult for him to make that decision. While it was far harder to fire Marius, the decision was more clear-cut. Endangering members of The Zone is something Tyler won't tolerate."

"Nor should he," Regina agreed. "He did the right thing, both in making that decision and in giving me the choice to get involved."

"I'll tell him you think so, and perhaps he'll realize he's not expected to be God."

"If you'd stop calling him that during sex, he wouldn't be such a megalomaniac."

Marguerite chuckled dryly. "You are very inappropriate, Lady Regina."

"But I am right." Regina grinned. "It's one of the few ways we other Dommes confirm you're human. You blush when you're teased about him. Not lobster or anything. More like light pink roses in your cheeks." She paused. "I followed him to one of his fights. Marius, that is."

"Oh?" Marguerite's gaze lighted with interest. "And how was that?"

"It was terrible, horrifying. Marius was both train and wreck. I've never seen anyone fight like that. In movies and professional sports, it's so choreographed. This was like watching a snuff film." Regina offered a grim smile. "Though my primal female side didn't care about my moral outrage. I was so turned on, I had a marathon evening with my Hitachi. Just imagining that amazing, powerful body wrestling, flexing, pounding..."

"We've had several members propose gladiator events at The Zone for just that reason." Marguerite's eyes gleamed. "The suggestion is still under review, but is receiving favorable reaction, so don't be too hard on yourself."

Regina sighed. "I've grilled myself as hard as any interrogation scene I've ever done, trying to figure out why I have my eyes wide open and I'm still walking right into a mine field. I've told myself I'm not in deep enough to worry about it yet, that I can stop it at any time, but I did stop, didn't I? And yet here I am." She drummed her fingers on the table. "Give me a sanity check. Am I addicted or on a mission? Even if it's a mission, is that the right reason to pursue this?"

"Perhaps it's neither. Perhaps it's something even more unsettling." Marguerite gestured with her tea cup. "When I said you're formidable, it's not because you are a formidable Mistress, though you are. You are a formidable woman, probably the most balanced one I've met within The Zone walls. You said yourself you're going into this with your eyes open. You won't allow anyone to destroy your sense of self. If that becomes a danger, you will drop him immediately. But someone that can add to your sense of self, that challenges you to grow and welcome a man into your heart? You'll embrace that, and not fear the cost or the fight to make it happen. You also won't mistake the conflict for something negative."

"Wow." Putting another cake on her plate, Regina stepped off the subject long enough to scowl at the three pieces of cookie on Marguerite's, still untouched. "Will you please put that in your skinny body before I jump over there and force feed you? It's rude not to eat with a guest. What is it with white girls and being thin? Don't you know how much men like having an actual ass to grab?"

Marguerite's expression flickered with surprise, then amusement again. Picking up one of the pieces, she put it in her mouth, chewed and swallowed. "Better?"

"Tons," Regina said dryly, then returned to topic. "You're right. That is a scarier proposition than drug or calling. But I think there's an interim step before I get all googly-eyed. He's a puzzle I haven't been able to solve, and that drives me crazy. I know there's something more there, and it interests the hell out of me. When it doesn't, I'll back off, but right now it's in that nice zone of physical attraction, emotional interest and simple, 'man, I'd like to crack that fine ass and fuck him up until he begs for more.'"

"A goal understood and approved by Dommes everywhere," Marguerite agreed. Two more bites of the cookie had disappeared.

Regina looked beneath the table. "Do you have a dog that snuck through here so you could feed the rest of that cookie to him?"

"The hummingbird is trained to take morsels from my fingertips without being detected by the human eye."

Regina snorted. "Wise-ass." She settled back with a fond look at Marguerite. "Okay. So what do I do about that line in the sand I've drawn?"

"Erase it with the toe of one of your magnificent thigh high red boots. Then put that same boot up the orifice where it will do him the most good."

Regina appreciated the visual. "I don't feel approaching him again is the right thing. So he has to come to me, but it may take him a while. Tyler forbid him to do it, which won't stop Marius, but he'll need time to fight with himself over it."

"Maybe. But I think he will approach you for another chance, sooner rather than later. If he would with anyone, it would be with you."

That surprised Regina. "Why?"

Marguerite blinked. "I'm not in the habit of answering questions another Mistress already knows."

"Unless it's a request for a sanity check," Regina reminded her. "Which we've already established is why I'm here. And for the company and sweets."

Marguerite acknowledged that with an amiable nod. "You already understand him better than other Mistresses who have reached this stage. They figured out his game, and discarded him. You figured out his game, but you looked beyond the game to the reason he's playing it. He interests you, and not for the reasons he has interested others, which gives him no frame of reference for dealing with you. That's probably good, because he has no time to come up with a suave new routine. The broken part might be able to take the lead, which will be ugly, but honest."

Regina thought of the way he'd acted at Safe Word. Belligerent, petulant, angry. Very little evidence of the charm he used as his mask.

"Okay. That tracks for me."

"I should ask a different question, one that I'm sure you don't get asked any more often than I do, given the type of women we are, the personalities we project. What do you fear, Lady Regina?"

Regina cocked her head. "What do you mean?"

"To work with difficult subs, a Domme must have the right blend of self-confidence, creativity and arrogance. And the arrogance is a potent part of the recipe. Too much and you blind yourself to warning signs. Too little, and you won't risk enough to change anything. You'll question yourself, wonder if that's your role at all. It's a tough call, and it gets more difficult when your heart gets involved."

Marguerite adjusted the pot further to the right of her elbow and then folded her arms anew to square off with Regina. "You are not as in control as you wish to be. Not as detached."

"Yeah." The woman was good at hitting the nail on the head, Regina gave her that. "I've always been reasonably sure of who a sub is, and what I want from him." She shook her head. "With him? Soon as that energy starts to spin, I don't want to play it safe. I want to push, I want to challenge, I want to tear into him...and I want to let him tear into me. That's new."

She grimaced. "Good old-fashioned fear, that's what it is. Maybe he's drawing me into his fucked-up self deeper than I realize, but I'm usually not an easy mark. The alternative is I'm taking this path knowing it's going to get dark and twisty, and I'm worried about getting so carried away by it that I misstep...and he turns me into the final straw. The agent of his destruction. He gets pissed, out of control, runs off to one of his fights and ends up dead."

The silence drew out between them. Regina finished her cake, mentally computing how much she'd have to add to today's workout. It was a good distraction, helping her rein in the uneasiness that her own words had caused her, or handle how Marguerite was looking at her now.

"I think Tyler might be the better person to discuss that fear."

That surprised Regina. She saw the other Domme's eyes had become even more somber. "He has walked that path with a submissive, and had to take extreme measures to save her soul," Marguerite said. "Measures that could just as easily have resulted in her being immolated by her path."

Regina expected it would take a big measure of arrogance—which yes, Tyler had in copious quantities—for a Dominant to tell him or herself that unearthing a person's darkest needs and exposing them to the light of day was worth the risk of the potential consequences.

In Regina's estimation, Marius was a man on a cliff, half of him wanting to fall to the sharp rocks below, while the other part grimly hung on, hoping someone would come by to pull him back to solid land. A wrong step could make the former a tragic reality. She could end up being the boot that stepped on his hand.

Marguerite's hand covered hers, startling Regina. The woman rarely indulged in casual touch. In her eyes, Regina saw equal parts disturbing shadow and reassuring light. Suddenly the world was just the two of them. The intensity in Marguerite's gaze reflected what Regina had glimpsed in Marius's a few times, so similar it startled her.

"I will tell you what I have told Tyler," Marguerite said quietly. "Sometimes a person needs to be destroyed. For some people, that's the only path to love, walking out of the ashes of a fire that consumes us. But if that fire happens, it will be set by Marius himself. Even if it's from so down deep in his soul he can't acknowledge it, that choice is his. You protect yourself enough to move out of the way if it's too late."

Regina locked gazes with Marguerite. "That's not the choice Tyler made. He would have burned in hell with you for an eternity rather than leave you there."

Marguerite went still. Regret jolted through Regina. She couldn't set aside the Domme intuition, but sometimes it was better to keep that shit contained. There was a code, and she didn't want to disrespect that with anyone she considered a friend, or respected as a Domme, the way she did Marguerite.

Before she could form an apology, Marguerite's expression altered. The million emotions it reflected tied Regina's heart strings in a knot, connecting to that indefinable pit-of-her-stomach feeling about Marius.

"Sometimes, deciding there is only one choice is a choice, too." Marguerite lifted the pot. "More tea, Lady Regina?"

They didn't talk much more about the topic of Marius, but not because things were strained. Regina had what she needed and, apparently sensing it, Marguerite turned the flow of conversation to shared interests. BDSM practices they both enjoyed, new techniques they'd observed in recent sessions, and a smattering of fun, not mean-spirited, gossip about other Dommes. That part of the dialogue was initiated by Regina, but Marguerite's dry wit proved she could keep up when the subject was lighter fare.

At the conclusion of the tea, Marguerite walked her back up front. Chloe was ready with a package of more cakes and another hug. In true Southern fashion, the leave-taking took another quarter hour as Regina chatted with the women and several of the regular customers. Marguerite's clientele were mostly women, so the environment had that pleasant women-bonding, hen-house feel. The soothing cadence of cluck-cluck-cluck from multiple feminine conversations was punctuated by the occasional cackle of laughter or squawk of surprise at an unexpected reveal.

Marguerite bid her good-bye with a curious gleam in her eyes. "When he does come your way again," she said, "you'll be ready for him."

"Probably because I'll have had months to think about my strategy," Regina said. "Though I retain some slim hope he'll try sooner, just because his Zone membership is so important to him."

"That will be his excuse for approaching you again. Not the real reason."

Regina eyed her. "Do you have to practice that, saying things like they're indisputable fact, when it's really speculative bullshit?"

Marguerite assumed a demure expression. "You'll have your answer when you confirm it as indisputable fact."

"It's obvious as a brick in the face why you and Tyler are together," Regina noted wryly, but she touched the woman's arm. "Whichever it is, thanks for the vote of confidence. And for the tea."

"Your company is a pleasure. Good luck. Not that I think you'll need it."

As she emerged from Tea Leaves, Regina puzzled over the emphasis on those final words, but she didn't have long to wonder. Marius was across the street.

"That crafty bitch."

Regina looked through the screen door, but Marguerite was giving instruction to Chloe and the new girl, to all appearances oblivious to what was happening outside the door.

"Yeah, right," Regina muttered, but moved down the steps and walkway, toward where she'd parked her car on the street. She kept her peripheral eye on him, though.

He was sitting on a low brick wall, keeping company with an elderly woman sitting on her porch and a trio of young men playing a card game on her stoop. A little girl rode a bike carefully up and down the sidewalk.

Tea Leaves operated out of a restored historic home surrounded but not overcome by a low-income district that had had its battles with drugs, gangs and petty crime. Marguerite was part of the community watch group taking it back house by house. The elderly woman looked like another active member, if her protective demeanor toward both the young men and the little girl were any indication. Her property was well-tended, despite the age and small size of the simple box of a house.

The young men wore tanks and tees over beltless pants that hung way off their asses. A fashion decision that always made Regina roll her eyes, not just because it was so idiotic-looking, but also since she knew better than most that it had likely been co-opted from gang styles in prisons. Exactly what every young man should aspire to be—a felon. Though at least it did have one benefit. The police loved the style because it made the criminals far easier to catch during foot chases.

Fortunately, these young men sported no gang markers. The fondness with which she overheard one of them call the elderly woman Grandma, and how the others emulated his respect to her, suggested they wouldn't dare come to her door with any evidence of gang involvement. She probably gave them hell regularly about pulling their damn pants up. It made Regina smile. She'd seen firsthand too many young men destroy their lives before they'd barely started. Evidence that those at-risk had some sharp-eyed guardian angels trying to keep them on the right path was always encouraging.

And speaking of at-risk souls... She only had time for those quick impressions before Marius saw her, proving he'd been keeping his eye on the entrance to Tea Leaves. Saying something to one of the men in apparent farewell, he crossed the street to where she was unlocking her car.

She'd been surprised to see him, but was even more bemused by the effect his presence had on her. She wouldn't have chased him down, not in a million years. If he wouldn't come to her, she would have considered it done, no matter how interested she was in pursuing it further. This couldn't go in the right direction if he wouldn't make the effort, regardless of his motives. But now that he'd made that step, she let herself savor the possibilities. And him.

He was wearing a pair of blue jeans with a brown belt, worn to soft gray edges. A black button-down shirt was tucked into the pants. His hair was a bit rumpled, as if by the wind tousling it as he drove, since it was a warm day and he'd probably had the windows down. He had his sleeves rolled up so her gaze was drawn to the points of his wrists and length of his forearms, sprinkled with dark hair.

With time and some discipline, a man could develop a body that met all the physical measurements for hotness, but that didn't translate to sexy. Sexy meant that he could make a woman think of sex just by moving and breathing, because his sexuality was bone deep, a vital part of his masculinity.

It was in their gait, their attitude. Regina had seen overweight, middle-aged men with receding hairlines at The Zone who possessed the quality, and muscle heads with tight asses and big dicks completely lacking it.

A sexy man understood what aroused a woman. He knew because he paid attention, and because getting that response was what he craved to drive his own arousal. It was a trait all sexy men had, be they Doms, subs or vanilla.

Most importantly, it couldn't be contrived, even by someone like Marius. He might be able to exaggerate it in a deliberate way, but the substance had to be there for the exaggeration to work. *You might be able to fool yourself, boy, but you can't fool me. I know you want me to be turned on by you, not because you're a conceited ass, but because you want to give me pleasure.*

It might be wishful thinking, but she thought if he could let himself, he'd approach sex the way she reached for a good book. With the intent of making it a slow experience to savor, pulling her into it so the outside world became far less real than what was in the pages. A place she'd never want to leave, but when she did, it would stay with her like a memory she never wanted to lose.

Such thoughts allowed her not only to enjoy the view, but imagine all the ways such a body could move in service to her.

He stopped a few feet away as Regina turned and leaned against the car door, looping her keys around her fingers to clasp them in her palm. She could ask him what he was doing here, but that would assume his presence had to do with her, and he'd have to work a little harder for that opening. Instead, she nodded across the street. "Friends?"

"Just met them. I walked over from Marguerite's to see what the game was. And because the lady, that's Mrs. Grant, she wanted to know what I was doing loitering around Marguerite's place without going in. She wanted to know if I had un-Christian thoughts in mind."

"What did you tell her?"

"Probably." His lips tugged. "But not the kind that would cause Marguerite or anyone here any problems."

"Even me?" She tilted her head and watched his eyes follow the ropes of her hair where they tumbled back over her shoulder.

He tucked a hand in one pocket, drumming the outside fingers against his upper thigh. Nervousness or pondering, she couldn't discern. He covered his emotions well. But he looked as if he might be trying to figure out the answer himself.

Regina gestured toward Tea Leaves. "Marguerite's inside."

"I'm here to see you." Marius met her gaze, though his tone stayed neutral. "She got a message to me. Told me you were coming here at one o'clock and, if I wanted a chance to talk to you about things, I could wait outside and see if you were willing to talk to me when you came out. If you say no, I'm supposed to walk away, get in my car and not bother you further."

"Have you ever obeyed someone that cleanly and decisively?"

He considered the question. "Not in recent memory. I get hit in the head a lot, though, so I could have lost a few instances."

Regina glanced at her watch, telling herself she wouldn't smile. The curious thing was he hadn't, as if he hadn't meant it as a joke. Did he know how to have a sense of humor when it wasn't a deliberate attempt to charm? It was almost three, just as she'd estimated. "You've been here since one?"

"About one-fifteen. Didn't want to interfere with your meeting, and Marguerite said not to disrupt your good mood by letting you see me on the way in." His tone was brittle at the recitation, but Regina could imagine Marguerite saying it in her acerbic way. Her lips twitched again.

"So she ordered you to be here?"

He shook his head. "She told me it was up to me, and you, if you wanted to talk to me. As I said."

"You came by your own choice. That's a good step. But the rest depends on what you have to say."

She settled against the door and leveled a cool stare on him. "You here to beg or bullshit?"

His lips tightened. "I'm sorry about throwing the drink at you. I shouldn't have lost it like that."

"Actually, that was the first honest response I've seen from you in some time. Though it pissed me off that you ruined the shirt. I'd looked forward to wearing it to bed that night and smelling your scent on my skin."

He blinked. She understood his confusion. Her words suggested something far different than her distant body language. Both messages were true, however. She played no games with her subs. Men required clear-as-damn-Windex communication. Since they were used to women being confusing, though, brutal honesty from one had the added benefit of sometimes throwing them off balance. But she liked his recovery.

"I'd have liked thinking about that. It didn't look all that ruined." He tucked both hands in his pockets and rocked, heel to toe. "Don't think it's ever looked that damn good."

For once, it wasn't a line. He said it with an unguarded look, his wry smile almost...shy. Wasn't he a puzzle?

"What is it you're here for, Marius?"

He cleared his throat. "To answer your question. Duncan. You asked me if that was my real name. It is. Duncan Marius Walczek."

"Okay. It suits you. Though you hold yourself a different way when you say it. It's not a familiar fit, but more honest, maybe. Why meet me here to tell me that?"

"I want to get back into The Zone. I like the work. I need it. And I'd..." He sighed. "I'm sorry for how I acted. I can do better for you, if you'll give me another chance."

"So your primary motive is getting restored to The Zone's good graces and employment." She lifted a finger before he could answer. "Fortunately, I'm interested in you, Marius. Duncan." She purred the name, intrigued when he shifted. It made him less confident, more uncomfortable. Her evaluation was correct. It was his truer name.

"It's a self-serving relationship," she continued. "But I have no desire to cater to your side of that equation. I'll take this where I want it to go."

He came a step closer, but at her stare, he moved back. "So does that mean we can try again, whatever it is you're willing to try?"

A little edge to his tone. He was sure he was getting a victory, though she sensed some surprise...maybe even a little disappointment that the challenge hadn't been as difficult as he'd expected.

"Maybe." She slid a thorough perusal over him, head to toe. "First, you take me on a normal date."

If she'd told him to lie down in the street and pretend to be road-kill, she couldn't have surprised him more. "Excuse me?" he asked, brow furrowing.

"You're a man, I'm a woman. You do know how to take a woman

on a date? You didn't hit puberty, walk into a BDSM club and that was the sum of your hookup experiences?"

"No." He didn't smile. "It's been awhile, though."

"For me, too." She met his troubled gaze. Interesting. This did kind of freak him out. "I've seen the sub. I want to see the man, how he treats a woman outside of a club. So I want a normal date."

He crossed his arms over his chest and frowned. "I don't get it."

"Is there a question there?" She leveled cool eyes on his arms. The muscle in his jaw twitched, but he uncrossed them.

"Why do you want a normal date, Mistress?"

An extra bonus. She hadn't required him to call her that, but it had a nice sound to it, sliding down her spine like his fingertips.

"It's too easy for you to weaponize yourself inside the BDSM world," she said evenly. "It may be what you crave, but you've poisoned it, and I don't think you know how to purify the waters. Show me who you are outside of the scene, why you'd be worth the risk to go inside it with you again. I'm going to give you a clue, so you have a slim chance of not fucking it up. No over-the-top grand gestures that mask the man behind a show. You're limited to a fifty-dollar budget."

His scowl deepened. "Teenagers spend more than that just to go out to the movies."

"Yeah, they probably do."

"I can afford—"

"Your income is not the issue. Fifty dollars. Save receipts."

"No."

She'd turned to open the car door but stopped, brows raised. His jaw set in a stubborn line, he stepped forward. Closing his hand over the car door handle, he opened it for her and stepped back. "If it's a real date, no guy would show a woman his receipts. If you say fifty, that's what I'll do. I assume you can take my word on that at least."

"I can." She'd laid her hand on the window frame, and his other hand was resting just above it. Their smallest fingers were touching, a brush of contact. He withdrew, his touch sliding over hers, and then he thrust his hand back into his pocket, as if he might be burned.

"A real date," he said. "Next Friday, at six? I'll pick you up."

"In front of Safe Word," she said.

He scowled. "You can trust me to pick you up at your place."

"That may or may not be true, but I'm not letting you into that part of my life."

"Right." He watched her get into the car. "Because this is just about getting back into The Zone for me, and trying out a new sub for you, because you like new flavors."

"Maybe. It doesn't bother me that you're using me as a means to an end, Marius. Why should it bother you, unless it isn't just about that?"

She'd put the keys in the ignition and lowered the window before letting him close the door. Reaching through the opening, she pinched up a small section of his shirt over his abdomen, tugging on it lightly, both a tease and a gentle rebuke. He stilled under her touch.

"Don't calculate or measure," she said. "Just answer my question, first thing that pops into your head. Do you know what you want?"

"Yeah. And no." His gaze flickered as if he hadn't meant to speak so baldly, revealing a confusion of feelings.

"That's okay, because I know what I want." Her grip on his shirt telegraphed her demand. As he bent toward her, she leaned far enough out the window to meet him partway and nibble on his bottom lip. Nice and full, a heated cushion, just the right kind of firmness.

When he would have responded in kind, she made an admonishing noise. "I'm the one doing the tasting here," she said. "Be still."

She was aware of his hands landing on the window frame, the resulting tension rippling through his biceps.

"Sweet. So many wicked, sweet things I could do with that mouth." She drew back, and met blue-gray eyes heated with desire, and conflict. Would he try to seize her, use physical force to make more of the kiss? She could feel that energy shuddering off him, but his eyes had that wary look. He'd talked himself out of it, for his own reasons. Maybe not the right ones, but that was all right. She'd take home some good fantasy material from her side of the kiss.

"I look forward to our date," she said, letting go and starting the engine. "How do I reach you if my schedule changes? Tyler didn't have a number on file for you; just your message inbox on The Zone private forum."

He nodded. "I have a pay-as-you-go phone for Tal to contact me about fights, but that's all I use it for. Tyler agreed to let me keep The

Zone account for now, just to send and receive messages. I can check it at the library."

Interesting. She was sure Tyler had allowed that specifically to ensure she could communicate with Marius. And so Tyler could hack in and track what was going on between them, the protective control freak. She bit back a smile at the thought.

"Be sure and check that inbox, at least once daily," she said. "See you Friday. Oh, and Duncan?"

That little ripple again as she used his given name. She met his stormy eyes, letting him see the heat and intent in her own. "I'm not unhappy with the choice you made, coming to see me today at Marguerite's direction. But while you're under my command, no other Mistress gives you orders. I don't share my toys. Got it?"

A nice flare of heat among gray clouds, like heat lightning. He moistened those tempting lips. "Yes, Mistress."

CHAPTER SEVEN

*S*everal days felt far longer than she expected, waiting to see him again. In between the demands of her job, her busy social life and the usual weekly home chores, she couldn't keep her mind away from what he was doing with his daylight hours. Did he have a job other than The Zone and his fighting? Where did he live? Did he have a pet?

Had he lain in his bed this week and closed his hand over his substantial cock, thinking of her? She had a couple nice sessions with her vibrator, imagining his muscular body naked and straining, hips lifting off the bed to shove his cock into his grip, his eyes fixed on her. Waiting for her to give him permission to come. Waiting and waiting, until he was quivering, his lips peeled back in a snarl, eyes wild.

"You can't come in your hand. But you can come inside my pussy."

Her own climax had surged through her as she imagined the way he'd bolt up from the mattress, seize her around the waist and take her up against the wall, pounding inside her, all that strength hers to command and call. Could he put his head on her breast afterward, defenses drained away? She wanted to have him sleeping in her arms, his body heavy against hers, damp with their combined heat.

She was aware her fantasies and questions were where a woman went in her head when she was interested in a man. She could be fully infatuated without being led around by her heart or pussy. Women put too many obstacles in their own way. It was her heart to risk, and if it

133

got burned, she much preferred it to happen because she chose the path she took, no regrets.

She admitted she was worried about him being in the ring again. She kept thinking about that scar under the Aussie man's eye. Or Marius's disturbingly flat statement about losing moments thanks to repetitive head injuries.

She couldn't control any of that, though. And as the day of the date dawned, she let herself enjoy curiosity and anticipation about what he'd planned for their night. She had no expectations. He might blow it, surprise her, or come up with something that passed muster but wasn't memorable. But she'd walk away with more information about him, no matter what.

On principle, she was five minutes late. When she arrived at Safe Word's parking lot, he was leaning against his car, watching for her. He was shaved, wearing his white dress shirt and jeans again. He wasn't diverse in the fashion department, but that was fine by her. It was a good look for him. He had two shirt buttons open, straddling the line between exceptionally modest and disco-era. The decision showed enough of his chest to help her imagine her fingertips sliding into the opening. She'd stroke the crisp hair and muscled chest, feeling his heat and heartbeat.

The tails of the shirt and the crossing of his ankles drew her gaze to the packaging beneath the jeans. That, too, earned her approval. She was in the mood to get hot and sweaty tonight, aroused and wet. She'd said a normal date, and she had no intention of having sex with the man, but there was a lot of playing room between chaste distance and sexual penetration.

He jogged over to her car, holding up a hand to keep her from getting out. When he reached her, he opened the door and leaned on the outside of it. "Full service date, right? Door opening and everything."

"Did you go onto the Internet and brush up on your top 100 dating tips?"

"A man doesn't reveal his sources," he said, poker-faced, then the expression relaxed into a smile. "Fuck, you look good."

She was sure that wasn't in the dating handbook, but it worked for her. She liked it when his roughness slipped through. Until he figured that out, it told her when he wasn't acting.

She'd left him a message in his Zone inbox, asking what dress the night would require, and he'd responded "casual sparkly, but comfortable shoes. Sexy always works."

He wasn't much of an online chatter, but that worked fine for her, too.

She'd chosen a pair of jeans that fit her the way she and any straight male with a pulse liked, and combined it with a shirt that stopped just above her navel and had a halter-style back. The length allowed him to see a strip of smooth skin and the delicate silver spiral charm she wore on her navel piercing. The top also revealed a provocative amount of cleavage between full breasts held high in her lace bra. The back was a series of thin straps that crisscrossed her bared flesh, one thicker strap masking the bra line.

A spider-shaped pendant rested in the pocket of her collar bone, the jewelry a sparkling array of onyx and rhinestones. The boots she wore under the jeans were comfortable but gave her ass a nice swing.

As Marius offered her a hand out of the car, his grip heated and firm, their bodies brushed. The contact set off the expected sparks along her skin. He registered it, because he started to draw her closer. She held fast. "The kiss attempt happens at the end of the night, not the beginning."

"Not a woman who eats dessert before the meal. Check." He released her hand and closed her door when she moved out of the opening. As his back had to face her while he accomplished that, she allowed herself to brush it with her fingertips. "You look nice, too. And you smell good."

He looked over his shoulder at her. She leaned against the rear passenger door of the car, her hands folded behind her hips. "A brushing of mouths, a brief greeting of sorts, *is* acceptable. Can you handle that?"

He braced a hand against the top of the car, by her head, and leaned in, sliding a hand along her waist. As he closed the distance, she spoke again. "Like your mouth is a feather, stroking lightly across my lips."

His fingers twitched on her waist, his gray eyes flickering. He wanted to take more, to coax and seduce. By her instructions, this was a "normal date," but she wanted to start with this subtle reminder that she was the Mistress. What was deep inside of him needed that, too, a tug on the sub part of his nature.

Their mouths were very close. The solid wall of his chest pressed against the give of her breasts, another hint of deeper pleasures. His eyes slid to her mouth, but as he came so close contact was only a breath away, his lashes lifted so they were looking directly into each other's eyes.

A lot of subs would avert their gazes at half this proximity. It didn't have to be a requirement of the Mistress. Something instinctive in the sub defaulted to deference.

But there was another kind of sub. One who would lock onto his Mistress's gaze with near violent tenacity, as if knowing the survival of some critical part of him depended on it. Sometimes there was another layer under the desperation. Simple, lovely need. To serve, protect, hold fast.

She saw a glimpse of it, a light in his eyes, in the dark pupils, and her heartstrings tightened.

"Hello there, Duncan," she said softly.

He stilled. She used the blink of uncertainty, where he stood between the decision to fight or retreat, to caress his jaw. And remind him he had a higher priority than his reaction. Her command.

"My kiss," she said. "Light as a feather."

She reminded herself how badly this man could fuck up a woman who eased up too soon, trusted him prematurely. Right now, she would treat him as she would a wild animal. Just because he took food from her hand didn't mean he'd stopped seeing her as prey.

He nodded, a barely perceptible movement, and closed the distance. She kept her hand on his jaw in case he decided to disobey and devour her, but she didn't expect that. The hand was mainly to keep that whisper of contact between them as long as she damn well wanted it.

He had firm lips, a little chapped. His breath was cinnamon and mint, his jaw smooth under her hand. He was a furnace. She'd noticed that before. Her bad boy had all the fires of hell burning inside him, twenty-four seven. A shiver ran through her as his shoulder and arm muscles flexed, his hand molding in tighter contour to her waist and hip. That indication of rising desire matched what unfolded inside her at the teasing contact between their mouths.

She'd leaned forward. So had he, his chest more firmly pressed against her breasts. His hand left her hip so his arm could slide farther around her waist. Yet he still obeyed, keeping that same light, provocative touch between their lips. Tendrils of desire glided up her inner thighs like a painter's brush, only she imagined it as his mouth. What a beautiful mouth he had. That twist at the corner gave his kiss a different pattern of friction, less uniform and more pleasing.

She broke the contact, easing back and rubbing her thumb over his lips, a lingering touch. He'd been perfectly restrained, but had offered so much erotic potential her lower belly had become a butterfly garden. She moved out of the shelter between him and the car.

"So," she said, aware that her voice was a throaty purr. "Where are we going?"

He cleared his throat. "Would you prefer to take your car? Mine—"

"Is perfect. It reminds me of the car my prom date drove."

She adjusted so she had her hand in the crook of his elbow, showing him how she wished to be escorted. "Though hopefully you will not have a bag of weed and giant can of Icehouse under the seat, my date's master strategy to get me so mellow I'd melt out of my clothes."

"Did it work?"

"What do you think?"

He gave her a shrewd perusal. "You came out of the womb in control, Mistress."

"You're saying it to charm me," she said mildly. "But rumor is I told the doctor how to cut the umbilical cord. I'm kind of fuzzy on those details, but it sounds like something I'd do, particularly if I thought he wasn't doing it right. You still haven't answered my question. Where are we going?"

He paused at the passenger door of his car and reached in his back pocket. The shirt stretched over his chest and shoulders. When he noticed her noticing, she arched a brow.

"I don't pretend not to enjoy what's mine to look at," she said. "You have a problem with that?"

"No, ma'am," he said with that wry smile she liked. In prison, inmates were required to be formal with the C.O.'s. Always "yes, ma'am," or "no, sir." Hearing those two words on Marius's lips was a pleasant distraction and pure fantasy material combined.

She shifted closer and touched his mouth, this time in a more functional way, punctuation to her question. "How did you do that? The crooked lip."

"Guy with brass knuckles. I kept clear of them for most of the fight, but had to risk them up close and personal one time to get in a solid shot to his gut and drop him. It doubled him over and I finished him off with a knee to his face that broke his nose, so we both got bloody."

"It does seem so." She took her touch away, quelling her irritation with his disregard for his own life. He was so matter-of-fact, reminding her of her high school years, being around boys who boasted about carrying guns and dealing drugs. Thank God, that world hadn't been directly part of her middle-class suburban one, but it wasn't as far from that of her closest friends, so she'd had exposure. Still, thinking of how Marius jeopardized himself bugged her, probably more than it should at this point in their relationship.

Proving it, she realized he'd pulled something out of his pocket for her to see and she was looking down at it without seeing it. She was caught up in visions of him with his face torn up and bloody, no hands to wipe the blood away and tend to him, other than his own. He'd become quiet and tense, deducing from her silence she wasn't pleased. Then she saw what he was holding. She seized his wrist in a death grip, making him jump as if she'd sprung out at him from behind a door.

"No fucking way. Oh my God. Seriously?" She practically squealed like a teenager. Laughter at herself took over, warmth rushing through her body. "All right, who told you? How did you find out I love Boyz II Men?"

He shrugged with his usual cocky assurance, but his eyes were twinkling in an unguarded way, a surprised reaction to her ebullience. "Didn't I say a guy never revealed his sources?" Handing her the tickets to hold, he opened the passenger door with a flourish. "First, we'll get dinner at a great Lebanese place I know, then we'll hit the concert. Polish off things with a stroll on the Riverwalk before I drop you back off at your car."

"Okay. Sounds good." Actually, the Lebanese place gave her pause, since she was a Southern comfort food kind of girl, but she'd charged him with planning the date, and she'd see where it went. He'd pretty much already put it over the top with the tickets. She could handle a little foreign food.

"One more 'this is awesome' reaction." She did an impromptu hip hop dance that surprised another grin out of him. "Fair warning, I may throw my underwear up on stage."

He held up both hands. "Just don't expect me to do it. I'm not wearing any."

She snorted on another laugh and put a hand on his arm, letting her palm slide along it as she folded her long body into the seat. The car was still as clean as she'd noted at The Zone, and he'd put a flat black cushion over the duct tape repair on her side so she was comfortable. Unlike in a lot of older cars, the door didn't squeak when he closed it. Clean and well-maintained.

She appreciated that combination. As he moved around the hood, all snug jeans, obvious muscles and steely gray eyes, strong chin and a fantastic ass, she decided she liked it a lot.

～

The Lebanese place was a cross between deli and diner, with a large horseshoe display case in the center of the room displaying a sampling of all their foods, desserts and carryout options. The hostess showed them to a corner table in the back and Marius held Regina's chair for her. As she perused the menu with a faint frown between her brows, he touched the top of it. "Have you eaten Lebanese food before?"

She shook her head. "This will be a first."

"May I order for both of us?"

Her gaze slid to his and she set her menu aside, folding her arms on the table. "Yes. Since you asked so prettily. But I don't like a lot of weird flavors, and I fall on the mild to medium end of hot and spicy."

His lips quirked. "I'd argue with that."

She made a face at him. "Order my food."

"Your wish is my command." He gestured to the waiter. As she watched, he ordered a selection of what sounded like mostly appetizers. Should she tell him to knock it off, the flirty D/s references? Maybe not. It was a part of who they were. Maybe he was treating it like that because he was nervous. She saw signs of that, in the way he put his hand on the table, down below it, then back up again to tap a finger against the table top, an unconscious tic. The intent of the date was to take him out of his comfort zone. So far it appeared to be working. Though he might not see that as an appealing thing, it wasn't his wishes that would matter tonight. Hers would take care of both of them.

After the waiter left them, he flattened his palm against the table, as if realizing the reveal. "So is it okay to ask questions like we would on a normal date?"

She took a sip of the ice water the waiter had left her. She might have ordered a beer or wine, but she wanted her head sharp and clear tonight. Marius had stuck with water, but he was on a fifty-dollar budget. When he had that occasional beer he'd mentioned, she expected he was a Budweiser guy. "Why wouldn't it be?"

"Privacy is an issue for most folks at the club. We don't usually ask what anyone does for a living, or about family or where we live, unless someone volunteers the information."

"True." She leaned against her crossed arms again. His gaze slid over her breasts and the interesting effect on them under the sparkling shirt. When he noticed her noticing, his smile became even more male.

"Like you said, no reason not to look. I want the woman I'm with to know she's appreciated."

"Well, her tits at least," Regina said dryly. He toasted her with the water, not denying it, and she shook her head at him. "So are those the kind of things you want to know about me? What I do for a living?"

He shrugged. "Small talk. It's what you do on a date, right? Figure out more about each other, the surface stuff that breaks the ice and gets us that much closer to sex."

She chuckled, though he didn't appear to mean it as a joke. "You think that's all it's about?"

"Mostly. Some people want to get to know one another ahead of time, but you can watch them and see the hope for sex is in the driver's seat."

"They could be interested in each other *and* want to have sex. They're not mutually exclusive."

He looked doubtful. "Even if that's true, until the sex is out of the way, it's hard to get to that."

"Sounds like they're rushing instead of savoring. We may have childlike impulses, but we're not children. Weaving deeper things into the sexual slows things down, while holding onto the promise of more intimacy, making it better when it's finally the right time." She let her attention course over his face and shoulders, the set of his hands on the table. How he wore his clothes, the things happening in his face. "I look at you and imagine a whole list of things I'd order you to do for me, in bed and out. Lay out the nightgown I want to wear, turn down the bed. Kneel by it while I read. Climb in between my legs when I'm ready, burrow under the covers and eat my pussy until I come."

Her itemizing commanded his full attention, and what pleased her was that the entire list drew his interest, confirming her suspicions about his desire to provide both service and pleasure to his Mistress. Leaning forward farther, she ran a thumb over his bottom lip. When he started to part them, she shook her head, pleased when he listened and remained still under her hand. The man had such a mouth. She indulged herself a heartbeat before she sat back and continued. "But a whole lot more than that interests me. Else I wouldn't be here tonight. Anticipation and savoring tell us things about one another, so when sex does happen, it's even better."

He took a swallow of his water and set it down. Rotated it with his fingers tented on the top of the glass, as if he had too much nervous energy to stay still. "You're not bad at delivering a line yourself, Mistress."

She blinked once. "I think it's easier for it to be about the sex for you, Marius. You spend a lot of energy not being straight with others, but you won't assume the same about me."

His eyes went to that quick frost, which he quickly masked behind indifference and a placating spread of his hands. He sat back in the chair, hooking his arm over the empty one next to him. "All I'm saying is a fun fuck has its place. It can get you through the week, with none of the emotional stuff dragging you down. Will he call, will she call, what's the relationship going to be..."

"You've had experience with that?" But he sounded so detached from the process, she wasn't surprised when he shook his head.

"I watch other guys go through it. It's kind of pointless if all they want is to give their dick a workout. I think they figure it's just part of the burden of dealing with women. Though sometimes they find a woman that feels the same way a guy does about it."

"Maybe some of us start out wanting to give our gonads a work out, but then we stumble over something deeper we like," she pointed out. "That's why we go back for more, with future dates."

"Yeah, it happens that way for some guys. It even works out for some of them."

"But not you?"

"I haven't really gone down that path." He shifted forward and started rotating the water glass again.

She dropped her hand over his. "Stay still," she said quietly. "Keep your eyes on the table."

His thick lashes had started to flick upwards, but at her command, he kept them fanned over his cheeks. She moved her foot so the toe of her boot pressed on his shoe, where his leg was bouncing in a staccato against the table base, making it vibrate. "Still. No fidgeting with your Mistress."

The leg stopped, but his voice took on that flat tone that she was starting to realize was the lid on a simmering cauldron. "I thought this was a normal date." His fingers half curled beneath hers, knuckles pressing up into her palm.

"It is. But as you aptly pointed out, there are things that run beneath the surface of every conversation, no matter how we dress them up. You're a fulltime sub, Marius. And you know I don't ever stop being a Mistress. So when I notice something that needs adjustment to help your 'normal date' skills, I won't let it pass. Be. Still."

The leg had started to move again, but it stopped with a jerk. She closed her eyes and tuned in to the rise and fall of his breath, uneven, erratic, and the steady cadence of her own, though her heart might be tripping an extra beat as he responded to her.

Did he realize what a step that was? He could have set her back with another quip, but instead, he'd reacted to the command automatically. It had been a long time since he'd interacted with a woman outside the scene. A man made such a decision intentionally, with the result that his social skill set diminished. She could integrate some of the structure he understood to help him stay out of trouble. Mostly.

She hid a smile at the thought. Even if the boy wasn't fucked up in the head, he'd be a handful. He wanted a Mistress who could hand him his ass whenever he needed it. Whether he realized it or not.

He was a lot of wild, chaotic energy. She'd always liked standing in the middle of a storm.

"You can look up now." She took her hand away and picked up the previous thread of the conversation. "You asked what I do for a living. I consult for engineers and tech people. Sometimes it's guidance for a current project, but lately it's been free form thinking."

"Free form thinking?"

She smiled. He wanted to sound sullen, but she could tell he was curious. He was also calmer, less twitchy. "Engineers and tech people have very rigid thinking processes. It comes from how they're trained in college. They might be able to write programs or design systems that would boggle our minds, but they can't break it down for lay people. And they have very little mechanical or improvisational skills, unless they had them before they went through their formal education. I reintroduce them to those concepts and how to apply them to their work and interacting with clients and non-engineer coworkers."

He nodded, his expression becoming more closed. "Were you one of them? Engineer?"

"Still am. I have a mechanical engineering degree from Georgia Tech. I also have a teaching degree. I went to work out of college for a big corporation, but then I was hired away by a consulting firm they'd brought in to teach what I do now. Usually I travel a lot to do my job, but I've agreed to a two-year contract with the community college as part of their corporate resource program."

His fingers crumpled the napkin, though he stilled again at her look. "Sounds like you're used to the corner office set. Good thing this is all about using one another. Otherwise I'd say you get off on slumming."

She lifted a brow. "You think you're being insulting, but if all that mattered to you was using me to get back into The Zone, our class differences wouldn't bother you."

Unrolling her fork from her napkin, she twirled it in her fingertips, and then brought it down in a swift movement against the top of his hand, still flat on the table. She didn't stab him; merely pressed the tines against the series of veins running from his knuckles to his wrist.

She increased the pressure while holding his gaze, which had gone steely gray. He could reach over with his other hand and remove the utensil, brush her away, but he didn't. His acting out against her seemed to have self-imposed boundaries, which also interested her.

"You know what I want in a man, Marius? It's a short list. One who's honest, and who uses his head and follows his heart when it comes to caring for and serving me."

"That's not a long list."

"It has the only things that matter on it." Setting aside the fork, she laced her fingers on the table. "Any other questions?"

His jaw flexed. "Any kids, husband, exes?"

"No. None of those. I'm very particular about who shares my space. While I haven't ruled out the idea of children, a husband is a far harder choice, and I won't have one without the other. I'm a traditionalist that way. You?"

"No." He scoffed, taking a swallow of his water. She tilted her head. "Do I seem like the type of guy interested in offering anything to a woman other than my dick? And a guy they call 'Rabid' isn't at the top of a list to play father to a kid."

"I'd argue just the opposite. I think you're very interested in offering your heart and life to a woman. You just have a lot of crap piled on top of the desire. And you'd use those 'rabid' instincts of yours to tear apart anyone who hurt her or any of your children."

She'd hit a serious nerve. His gaze flicked to her, showing her an odd flash of vulnerability before something far harder replaced it.

"Give the floor to Dr. Phil," he said. "Turning something that isn't a problem into one. What I want from a woman is an even shorter list. Want to hear it?"

She pinned him with a cold expression. "Resort to crudeness, and I'll slap your ear through your head. If you think Mommy won't spank your ass in front of everyone in this restaurant, I'd think again."

His lips parted, a baring of teeth. While his eyes fired in challenge, she let him see nothing in her own but resolve. After a weighted moment, he shut his mouth, his jaw flexing before he spoke.

"I only want one thing from a woman. That she doesn't ask for more than I'm willing to give. It's only when she does she gets herself into trouble."

"Kind of like the person who sticks their hand into a tiger's cage and then gets outraged that she gets bitten?"

"Got it in one." He attempted a casual shrug with tense shoulders. "Maybe we should stick with talking about you."

She extended her palm. "Let me see your hand."

His visage turned wary, but he put his hand palm-to-palm with hers and then deliberately moved farther up to clasp her wrist in a firm hold. It allowed her to do the same with his, so she ignored the impertinence for now.

"You're as mercurial as a bulb with a short," she observed. She stroked her fingertips over his pulse. It was pounding, a hard current. "But you know what I could be for you, Marius? The sun. Doesn't matter what kind of clouds your bullshit kicks up. My job is to bring light. Make things grow, keep you warm, tell you there's something more than darkness."

Her gaze held his. "You're not quite being the asshole you think you are, because most of what's coming out of your mouth is honest. And that's what I want. But if you want to keep pushing toward the asshole side to make this date be over, you can save the effort and say so."

"What about the concert?" he asked.

"You'll let me keep the tickets so I can find someone else to go with me tonight. I know that, because you want to be good to me. You just can't get out of your own head. So what about it? You want it to be over?"

She didn't bring up The Zone ultimatum. He wanted back into The Zone, but that night in Tyler's office, he'd shown he would set fire to his own interests to protect deeper things. While him getting back into The Zone wasn't the main reason she was doing this, she knew whatever they were confronting now was one of the big hurdles to it.

The waiter arrived as the decision hung in the balance. From the picture hanging at the entrance, she identified the handsome Lebanese man as one of the owner's sons. In the way of a well-run family restaurant, he was proprietary and proud of the food he arranged between her and Marius. Spinach puffs and spicy potatoes, a bowl of soup, a basket of fresh pita and a trio of shawarma meats on small steel spits.

"If anything isn't excellent," he declared, "you let us know and we'll fix it."

"Thank you." As she smiled at him, her focus lingered for an extra second on olive skin, broad shoulders and dark, dark eyes.

The waiter hesitated but then nodded, backing away. He bumped the table behind him, fortunately empty, before he recovered his balance and strode away.

She brought her gaze to their food. "So where do I start?" she asked. "And do we ask for a to-go bag for you?"

"Maybe you'd like to take *him* to the concert?" Marius asked in a tone that brought to mind an ill-tempered wolf.

Regina propped her elbows on the table and rested her chin on her hands. "Would you like to know what I saw when I was looking at him?"

"No."

She ignored him. "When a man catches my eye outside the club scene, it's rarely because I'm interested in pursuing him. He's another page in a book of inspirations when I imagine what I want to do to my subs. For instance, in that blink of contact with him, I imagined myself stretched out on a white sand beach on Cyprus. You're one of my slaves captured from foreign lands. You come to me and kneel beside my lounge chair, holding a tray of dried fruits, nuts and candies over your head so I can pick what I want to eat. I enjoy all your bare skin, because my slaves wear only a short tunic. Nothing under it, of course."

Reaching out, she slid a fingertip along Marius's neck. "I take my time making my choices, and your arms start to quiver. You say nothing, so determined to please your Mistress. But I know when enough is enough and tell you to put it down beside you. I tie your hands behind your back and order you to pick up each piece of food I want in your mouth. You must come and drop it into my hand, or place it between my lips, without getting yourself in trouble by trying to make that close contact into an actual kiss." Her gaze coursed over him. "I expect you'd try very hard to get into trouble, though."

Those eyes of his were like a mood barometer. Silver for anger, defiance, confusion. When he was aroused, like now, the blue in his eyes became more pronounced, the pupils even more dark in contrast.

His lips firmed. She sensed something in him had both relaxed and become more tense at once.

"That's my purpose in appreciating our waiter," she said. "I like who I'm with tonight, Marius."

She noticed he'd shifted his hand closer. "What do you want to touch, Marius? One thing."

"Your hair." The response was instant, surprising her. When she nodded, he lifted his callused palm to her shoulder, and closed his grip around the fall of slender locs there, fingers stroking, testing the way they felt before he released them, and drew his hand back to his side of the table.

"I'd suggest the potatoes first," he said abruptly. "You can use your fingers if you like. Sometimes it's better that way."

"All right. I like my idea of you using your mouth better." She shot him a look. "But we'd probably scandalize the family diners."

Her playfulness seemed to take him off guard. As she proceeded per his direction, she braced herself, since she didn't care for a lot of unfamiliar spices or textures. Instead her taste buds instantly approved the crispiness of the potato, and the mild blend of herbs flavoring it. Before long she was sampling from all the offerings and folding the shawarma into a piece of fresh pita from the basket on the table.

"This is amazing. I love these little spiced potato things. What's the soup?"

"Lentil." He spooned up some and started to offer it, then rethought that. Before he could return the spoon to the soup and push the bowl her way, she touched his wrist, telling him it was okay. She leaned over to let him put the spoon in her mouth. His hand was steady but the energy bouncing off him was not, his attention on her so intently. She sat back, touching her lips with her napkin.

"Good stuff. I'll take some more of that."

Pushing the bowl in between them, he picked up the second spoon, nudging the handle of the other to point toward her side of the table. "Lebanese food is better shared. Try the spinach puff."

He hadn't answered her question about wanting the date to be over. She'd let that go, crisis averted. He seemed to like watching her share the soup. As she tried the spinach puff, licking the delicate flakes off her lips, she went the casual conversation route again. "Okay, your turn to spill. Tell me how you knew about the tickets. Seriously."

He leaned back. His leg brushed hers under the table when he braced his foot against the bottom slats of the chair next to her at the four-chair table. She didn't move away. The incidental touch created heat, something she was sure he felt as much as she did.

"One night at The Zone, you and some of the other Dommes were hanging out in the lounge. You, Mistress Violet, Marguerite, Lyda, Lisette... Violet jabbed you with a finger and said she wasn't taking any shit about Taylor Swift from someone who owned every Boys II Men song ever performed." His gaze lit with careful amusement. "You started singing one of their songs at the top of your lungs. She covered her ears and howled."

Regina laughed. "I don't recall seeing you. You must have been lurking."

"I was covering the bar. You all were caught up in the girl talk thing."

"Girl talk." Regina snorted, but pulled the concert tickets from her back pocket and looked at them. They'd printed a photograph of the current band trio on the face of the stubs. "Originally they started out as four guys, with Michael McCary singing bass in his wonderful deep voice." She offered a half smile. "He'd already left the band when I discovered them in middle school, but I'd put on my head phones and go to sleep with his voice and the rest of them crooning their ballads. My music tastes are pretty eclectic now, but like most people, the songs you loved in your teens are your touchstone of good memory and nostalgia."

She noticed his face went blank as an empty page. It was a look she wasn't sure how to interpret, but it sent an uneasy tingle through her stomach. Trying to defuse it, she offered the tickets back to him. He shook his head, the expression disappearing.

"You're right, they're yours. If I piss you off before we get there, you can still go."

"Are you anticipating or planning for it, to get out of going to a Boys II Men concert?"

He chuckled. While it was reserved, it was the first true laugh she'd heard from him. She expected an unleashed one would be rolling and deep, and stroke a woman's nerves in the right direction. "Too obvious a strategy," he said. "I can handle one boy band concert if the company is worth it."

"I don't know. You've already told me sex is the point of all this, and you're not getting sex tonight."

"It's an investment in the future."

Shaking her head at him, she put the tickets back into her pocket and took another bite of meat-filled pita. "So who was your favorite band in your teens?"

He spooned up more soup, lifting a shoulder. "Don't really remember. Probably same as most guys."

He kept his eyes on the food, the set of his body language saying it wasn't a topic he wanted to pursue. With a shock to her system, the meaning of the blank look clicked, along with why it had made her uneasy, as if her subconscious had understood it before the rest of her had.

He had no frame of reference for teenage rites of passage like favorite rock bands. What kind of childhood wouldn't have included music?

She thought of Marguerite's words. *It's a place that holds no safety for him.*

Maybe there had been music, but darkness covered that and the rest of the memories. He clearly kept them locked away, inaccessible.

She'd made a vow to keep this a normal date. But since D/s sessions had different goals, she filed the information away as a key that might get her further into his head during one of those. She gestured to their surroundings.

"How long has this little place been here? It looks like a hole in the wall from the outside. But most good restaurants do."

He nodded. "About fifteen years."

She'd glanced at the menu and found the prices unexpectedly low. Which raised another thought. "There's no way you bought those two concert tickets plus my dinner here for fifty dollars."

"Nope." He shook his head. "Got the tickets in trade. Did some work for a guy at the Amalie Arena and he owed me a favor. You never said I couldn't work it out in trade," he reminded her.

She hadn't, but then she hadn't expected him to go the extra mile that way. His charm routine had never struck her as a long con. She was impressed, not just by him doing it, but by doing what most men wouldn't. Paying attention and giving her a gift she wasn't expecting but truly wanted. Another thing that interested her was how long ago that night with the other Dommes had been, and yet he'd remembered that one key detail.

Men didn't remember such things about women who didn't interest them. They barely remembered those kinds of details even when they did. As Marius had pointed out, they often did have one-track minds, at least during the dating phase.

"So have you ever taught regular school?" he asked. "With your teaching degree."

"I did some substitute work and helped out in my mother's daycare. And I offered GED coursework in the prison system when I was working as a correctional officer. I did that for a few years while finishing up my engineering schooling."

His gaze snapped up to her and she smiled. "In my current job, I teach people to think outside the box. Nobody thinks outside the box quite like a convict or a preschooler. There's always a way around things, which means you have to teach them to integrate morals and judgment into those decisions, without hampering the positive sides of creativity and survival skills. I'm sure you can figure out how the skills apply to a Dom/sub dynamic."

He bit into a pita he'd stuffed with the shawarma and potato, chewed and swallowed. "A prison guard?"

"We prefer correctional officer, though prison guard evokes more Dom/sub fantasies. So you can use either term." She smiled faintly. "Got a few images teasing your cock now, right?"

She bumped her leg against his under the table and stayed there, knee pressed to his thigh. She liked the smile he gave her, a little sheepish and a lot of heat. Naughty boy and aroused man intertwined. If she sat next to him, she could put her hand beneath the cloth-covered table and stroke his cock through his jeans, feeling the evidence of those fantasies swelling its size.

A normal date could be chock full of sexual innuendo, couldn't it? But she liked the sweet pleasures of anticipation, so she reined it back. He helped by teasing her, too.

"Has it ever been difficult to keep it straight? Solitary for prisoners, time-out for kids, and full head mask on your sub?"

She chuckled. "Fortunately, the subjects have significant differences. Though all of them could use a good paddling on occasion, I was only allowed that option on the subs. Here, have some more of this. Take it from my hand with your mouth."

She gave him a warm look, proffering a spinach puff. He leaned in and bit, but clasped her wrist to steady the contact. He holding her as they brought their elbows down to rest on the table. She rocked inside the grip, turning her fingers around to trace his knuckles. He watched her touch him, his eyes shadowed.

"You're interesting," he said gruffly. "Even if you are fucking with my head."

"Hey." She touched his chin. "There's a difference between that and making it clear you're not going to fuck with mine. I want you to do one thing for me. Think you can?"

"Depends on what it is." His lips had that rueful twist. "I can't stand on my head or buy you diamonds."

"Well, damn, that was exactly what I was going to ask you to do." She waved her bare fingers and motioned to the sparkling bangles on her ears, costume jewelry. "Because obviously expensive baubles are my thing."

She sobered. "I want you to stop worrying about screwing up this date. I'm not going to let you do it, okay? Whether you realize it or not, I know that would hurt you as much as it would disappoint me."

"So you think you know what I want and need." He made it a flat statement.

"No. Not everything. But some things, yes. Whether you accept that, or go in an opposite direction just to prove me wrong, is up to you. But I'm having a good time. I hope you'll decide to have one with me."

He hadn't let go of her wrist, but his grip wasn't antagonistic. She wondered if he might need the connection, and so she left herself stay there. Myriad emotions brewed behind his eyes.

He stroked her pulse, and then he let go. "Okay," he said.

"Good." She let out the mental breath she'd been holding and gestured with her fork. "Now finish your meal, because you have to get me to my concert on time."

CHAPTER EIGHT

*N*athan Morris had taken Michael McCary's place with Boys II Men, and he held his own, even if it wasn't the same voice as the one from her youthful fantasies. Regina noticed there were quite a few women her age here, as well as younger ones. Some had patient boyfriends or husbands in tow, though most had come in female packs to fully immerse themselves in the sensual crooning that wove its spell over the darkened arena. The notes vibrated in the heated air, increasing the sense of insulation from the outside world so the audience could cut themselves adrift in the experience.

Their seats were ten rows from the front. Close enough for Nathan to amble right by her aisle seat when, just before his solo monologue in "On Bended Knee," he left the stage.

A ring of security prevented him from being swallowed by a mob of enthusiastic women. But as he met her eyes through his tinted glasses and held out his hand, the guards adjusted into a cone formation to give him access to her. When she put her hand in his and he dropped to a knee, her own almost gave out. All the women started screaming.

Regina laughed out loud, tears dotting her eyes for some crazy reason as he grinned up at her. She was as fluttery as the teen she'd once been. After he concluded his entreaty for her to come back to him, with the far-too-tempting words "I'm begging you," he rose to his feet, leaned in and brushed her cheek with warm lips, his trim goatee rasping against her jaw. Her heart pounded right up into her throat.

He gave Marius a "what's up, man, all's cool" nod before he let her go and wandered back to the stage, the rest of the band kicking in as the monologue gave way to syncopated singing once more.

She'd drifted back to her seat, only realizing after the fact she'd done it with the help of Marius's hands on her waist. Turning in his arms, she planted a hard, fierce kiss on his mouth. "Best date *ever*," she shouted, since it was the only way to be heard.

She liked the smile on his face, the grip of his hands on her hips, the shape of his mouth and heat in his eyes that said he wanted her to keep kissing him. She wanted that, too.

She also wanted to climb onto and take him in every conceivable way. She'd use every ounce of his considerable strength to satisfy her lust, which was boundless. In her ebullience, the desire came not just from her body, but from the crimson swirl of heat inside her heart and soul.

Fortunately, she restrained herself so she could enjoy the rest of the concert rather than being arrested. She channeled her energy into clapping, whistling and seat dancing, until everyone stood up on the final song and danced in the aisles as much as security would allow. Marius didn't dance, but he stayed in his seat and watched the enthusiastic shaking of her ass with a man's unabashed appreciation, until she tugged him to his feet and made him at least do some hip bumping and swaying to the music next to her.

She was still riding that high when he drove her to Tampa's Riverwalk. She gushed about the history of the band, everything she knew about the members, what she loved about their songs...and he simply listened. Not like he was tuned out and waiting for the topic to change to something he found more interesting. He was really listening, with a peculiar look on his face, like he was experiencing something unfamiliar and wasn't sure if it was good or bad. She didn't want to see it turn to the latter, so she slowed herself down and sat back, giving him a shrewd and droll look.

"So the whole Nathan singing to me thing? Within budget or not, I said I didn't want any grand gestures. That surely broke that rule, if the tickets themselves didn't do it. The Amalie guy apparently owed you the mother of all favors."

"Yeah." He parked the car. When he turned to look at her, his practiced smile had returned, which she expected he'd follow with some feigned modesty that would skirt the borders of that charm she kept discouraging. Then abruptly the smile disappeared, with no prompting or warning from her. Instead, he stared out the windshield.

"I didn't do that," he said.

"What?"

He shook his head. "That was spontaneous. Well, in a way. When you're doing the Mistress thing, you realize what you do to a man's senses. Like to the waiter at KeBob's. But other times, you don't seem to realize it. There was no one else who shone the way you did in the first few rows. He saw you right off. You're impossible to miss."

Without another word, he exited the car and circled around the front, leaving her startled by the candid observation. When he reached her door, his expression was back to being the same, that unreadable cocktail that could go in any direction. As he handed her out of the car, she held on, making it clear she didn't want him to drop the contact, unless that was his choice. He laced his fingers with hers, glancing at their link. But he didn't let her go.

The Riverwalk was a good place to meander with a date, stretching along the Hillsborough River and following the bend to Garrison Channel. While it did have more crowded tourist spots, it was long enough that residents like the two of them knew some of the quieter areas, where the mix of tourists and local transplants enjoying the views of the water and passing boats weren't elbow to elbow.

Regina liked all the lights at dark. The blue tinted glow of the bridge over to Harbour Island, the dotting of lights on the cylindrical Rivergate Tower—fondly known as the Tampa "beer can" building— and the warm yellow lights marking the railings along this section of the Riverwalk. There was a mix of hotels, restaurants, and clusters of shops. While the restaurants and bars were still open, she had no interest in any of those when Marius asked if she wanted a drink.

"Let's just walk," she said.

There were other couples on dates, walking hand-in-hand like them. More sat on benches or hung out in groups, laughing and chatting. After walking them a little farther down from the noisier ones, Marius drew her to the rail at the water's edge. "Ever stood on the other side of it, on that ledge?"

"No. I'm a proper citizen who obeys all laws."

"I don't think you're proper in any way, Mistress. One of the most likeable things about you." He nodded. "I bet way back when, they didn't have railings at all."

"They also didn't have to protect themselves from lawsuits, because people took responsibility for their own stupidity," she added dryly.

"I try to accept responsibility for my own stupidity, even if it's way past due. It's the one thing that's all mine, after all." Flashing a smile at her, he put his hands on the rail, hoisted his hips onto the top piece and swung his legs over in one swift, athletic move that had her biting back a sound of alarm. He brought his feet down on the narrow concrete ledge on the other side.

"It can't be okay to do that," she observed. As he leaned against the rail in a standing position, nothing was between him and the water below but a breeze ruffling his hair.

"If a cop sees you, he just tells you to get back on the other side. They won't arrest you or anything." He looked over his shoulder at the other people strolling along the Riverwalk. "And everyone thinks you're a badass for doing what they'd like to do."

"Or they think you're an idiot who's going to show up on tomorrow's news as a drowning, swept away by the current." But after a moment of pondering her sanity, she emulated him, though more carefully. She straddled the rail and sat down on it, swinging the other leg over from a sitting position before easing down to stand next to him. As she came down, he put his arms around her in a loose hold until she was settled. It was surprisingly respectful, a steadying gesture only. When he took it away, she was tempted to hold onto him, keep her hands curled around the arm that had been braced in front of her waist and then above her chest as she slid off the rail onto her feet. Maybe later. She didn't want the gesture to be construed as her being girly and needing support.

The ledge was narrow, not more than a few inches, but she felt secure enough with the rail supporting her from behind. She braced her hands on either side, which allowed her to brush her knuckles against his back. Looking down, she studied the dark water, frothing up phosphorescent white foam where it lapped against the wall.

"Be pretty easy to give your date a nudge and be done with her."

"Yeah, but I don't have enough money to buy two scoops of Dreamy Time ice cream." He pointed to the cart, within a stone's throw from their position. "But to get the two-for-one scoop special, all you have to do is tell the ice cream guy I'm dreamy. If I push you into the water, I don't have anyone to do that."

"What if the girl's buying the ice cream?"

"Then her guy has to say it to her. They're equal opportunity at Dreamy Time."

She shot him an imperious look. "What if I refuse to say it? Going to push me?"

He lifted a shoulder. "I'll still buy you the one scoop. And hope you'll share a bite with me."

She'd pressed the point of her chin to her shoulder to check out the ice cream cart. As she brushed her locs out of her line of sight, her weight shifted and her balance teetered. She told herself she wasn't in danger of falling, but it made her realize how easy it really might be to fall off such a narrow ledge, her grip on the rail notwithstanding. Unless her date suddenly had his arm around her waist, fingers wrapped over her hip and caught in her belt loops, his other hand firmly locked on the rail.

"You know what?" he said. "Let's be badass on that bench over there."

"Tired of breaking the rules?" she asked, a glint in her eyes.

His lips twisted. "You know the answer to that better than I ever could, Mistress," he said. "Hold onto the rail with both hands until I'm back over and then I'll help you. You can do it on your own, I know, but humor me."

Common sense told her he was right, so she waited until he was ready before she climbed the rail. She swung one leg back over and then the other so she was sitting on top of it again, only this time facing the Riverwalk. It wasn't a big hop to the ground, but he set his hands to her waist and lifted her down, a stirring sense of non-gravity she didn't get to experience that often. The man was breathtakingly strong.

When he set her on her feet, he let her go, though she could feel the reluctance in the loosening of his grip. She would have been fine with prolonged contact. He gestured to the bench, and they strolled over, taking a seat. Fortunately, he stretched out his arm behind her, giving her a comfortable rest for her back, instead of the top edge digging into her shoulder blades. Not necessarily a come-on, but decidedly a gallant gesture.

"You treat me like a girl."

He gifted her with a warm look that swept over her. "You are a girl. Woman. Female, from head to toe. Is that a problem?"

"No. I'm tall and strong, and I put off a don't-fuck-with- me vibe that seems to neutralize the chivalrous, protective side a man automatically shows to a daintier woman. Then there's the Mistress thing."

"Does it bug you?"

"No. I don't think about it as a pro or con. It pleases me, though, that you treat me with that kind of care and respect. Even as it makes me curious. I've watched you DM and work security. You watch out for everyone and keep them safe, with an unflappable courtesy that gives them confidence you'll protect them. Yet when a Mistress crosses the line you don't want her to cross, it all disappears. She becomes prey. The enemy."

"Thanks for the recap. We covered that in Tyler's office, didn't we?" He removed his arm and leaned forward, linking his hands to dangle loosely between his spread knees as he stared out at the water. "Maybe you're right and I'm not all that cut out to be a sub. But you said you wanted a normal date. I know what you said about the Dom/sub stuff still being part of this, but first dates don't usually delve into that other shit." He shot her a look, remote and closed-down. "Right?"

"No, they don't. I'll leave it alone, but I am going to say one thing. Come back up here." She met his gaze with an unflinching one of her own and tapped his shoulder, a reinforcement of the command. Barely suppressing a sigh, he sat up.

"You know a great deal about women, Marius. There are Masters like Tyler who have that gift. Because he watches a sub so carefully on the Dom side of the equation, he can pick up any change in her mood or thinking. He works with that to connect with her, both as a woman and a submissive."

She let a faint smile touch her lips. "Now all that artistry is directed toward one woman. But my point is that it happens because he's a man who loves and adores women. There's another kind of man like that. One who worships a woman, drinking in every detail, learning all he can so he can be what she needs. That's a male sub. Add an alpha personality to it, and there's a protectiveness over and above what a normal male sub shows, and even a beta can be pretty damn protective, like Rob."

He grimaced. He obviously didn't want her mentioning Rob. She propped her head on her hand, her elbow on the back of the bench as she turned onto her hip toward him. Since he was still leaning forward some, she smoothed her hand down his back, curling her hand so she stroked his spine with her knuckles. He tilted his head toward his shoulder, watching her out of his peripheral vision. She drew a circle and feather-caressed everything in the center of it.

"A good man is a good man, and that is an innate part of him, whether alpha, beta, or something else entirely. So, tell me a story of how my boy learned how to see a woman as a woman, no matter her physical appearance or how tough she seems. I know it won't be just one story that helped you get there, but tell me the first one that comes to mind."

"Does it matter?" He turned his face back toward the water so only his voice revealed his state of mind. "You said I use it the wrong way."

"Do you think you use it the right way?"

"I think they want too much."

"Well, you could tell them that. Negotiate it so everyone knows you just want a light, fluffy fuck, a little *Yes, ma'am, No, ma'am* role play. Then no one would ever cross the lines. All it takes is clear communication. But you keep getting yourself in situations where you say you want one thing, but you go after another, and something goes wrong."

His fist curled on his knee, but she kept stroking his back, another calming circle. "You figure out what's going on in your head, you'll be able to be what you've always wanted to be for a woman." *You might be everything she wants, too.* But she kept that to herself.

"I don't need a therapist."

"No. You probably need a team of them." She tempered it with a smile and a friendly nudge of her shoulder that seemed to take him off balance as he glanced back at her again. "So sit back up, put your arm around me like a proper, *normal* date and tell me a story."

"Does it have to be true?"

"I'll leave that up to you."

When he sat up and stretched his arm behind her again, she put her back against his side and her boot soles on the seat, her knees bent. Dropping her head on his shoulder, she looked up at the sky. She brought his arm across her chest, curling her hands around his forearm as his palm molded against her shoulder. Then she waited for him to speak. As she did, she felt the rise and fall of his body from his breath, the heat of his flesh penetrating her thin shirt. His jaw brushed the top of her head as he adjusted. She closed her eyes, enjoying the position, and his cautious acceptance of it.

"There was this girl in middle school," he said at last. "Eloise. She weighed about two hundred pounds and was tall. Short hair, and average-looking. Not pretty. She was mean. She got suspended a lot for fighting, bullying. I hadn't really hit a growth spurt, so she tried to take my lunch money one day. I didn't have any, but I didn't tell her that. I busted her nose instead, set her down on her ass, hard."

"You were already honing your fighting skills."

"Yeah." But there was no humor in his voice. "Later that day, I went to the place I hung out at lunch, this spot between two of the buildings where they had a bunch of old desks stacked up. It was quiet. A lot of times I took a nap beneath them instead of going back to class. It was like a tree fort. Eloise was there. I'd never seen her there before, so I figured she must have found it when looking for a place to be by herself. She was crying."

Regina played with his fingers, stroking the rough knuckles, her gaze still on the stars. "What did you do, tough guy?"

He paused, and his lips were closer to her head, breath moist on her scalp. She thought he was inhaling her scent and wondered if he was looking at the stars, the Riverwalk, or if he had his eyes closed. He was still, no fidgeting now.

"I sat down next to her. She was sitting on this pallet, and I was on an old chair, so it made me taller than her. Maybe that's why I did what I did. I felt bigger, like I could protect her and make her feel better, so I hugged her. Held her. Said I was sorry and it was going to be okay."

Regina could see it, a gawky adolescent boy and a hulking, overweight girl, giving and receiving comfort. One of those not-so-Hallmark moments.

"When she stopped crying, she said she was sorry, too. I noticed how soft her mouth looked, so I leaned down and kissed her. She socked me in the gut and left me wheezing."

Regina chuckled. "Another lesson in the capriciousness of women —and the cluelessness of the hormonal male."

"Yeah, yeah." He flicked her knuckles with his captured hand. "But she was never mean to me again. When she'd see me in the halls, sometimes she'd nod to me. I guess I figured some of it out, then. That it didn't matter that she was so much bigger and stronger physically than I was, or the way she acted... All of us have vulnerable moments, but there's this special quality to a strong woman's, in that rare second when she'll let a guy...help. Make it better. I liked being the guy who helped. It's there even when the woman's not so obviously vulnerable. The diamond in the center of a ring, if that makes sense. A gift."

Yet he regularly shit on that gift in his sessions with Mistresses, the puzzle she had yet to figure out. She could have probed, but she'd told him she'd leave it there. Even though she knew as well as he did they were walking a tightrope over that pool.

He was silent, and she honored that for a time. A whole conversation was going on between their fingers, tangling and untangling, stroking.

"Do you have an opinion about me, Marius?" she asked at last.

She adjusted her head so she was gazing into his face. It made having his arm around her closer to an embrace, increasing her awareness of the press of his biceps against the side of her throat. The flicker in his gaze said he'd noticed, but the crease in his brow said he was puzzling over her question. She explained further.

"I'm not fishing for a canned answer or compliments. It's an exercise I do with my engineers to help them step out of their heads and evaluate human behavior. When we meet someone, we form an opinion. In every subsequent encounter, that opinion is reinforced or changed. However, at any point in time, you'll have one opinion that defines that person for you, like a label or tag. It's how we classify and structure our relationships. Well, not entirely, but engineers can be such linear thinkers, it's a good way to help them learn how to integrate social skills with tech-speak."

She gestured to the people walking by. "Like that man over there with the cigar and the beer belly? Statement: Health crisis waiting to happen and doesn't give a shit, because he's at the age he wants to enjoy his pleasures in life—until a heart attack happens. Then he'll clean up his act for a few months before going right back to the same behavior because he wants what he wants."

She nodded in a different direction. "That teenager at the smoothie vendor? Pretty but doesn't know it. Insecure but stronger in her individuality than she realizes."

She glanced at Marius. "So, what's your opinion of me? Good or bad; doesn't matter."

He shook his head. "That's a female trap if ever I heard one. If you don't like what you hear, you'll pitch me over the rail."

She chuckled. "I'm not like most women. Your opinion of me isn't going to change mine about myself. You don't have that kind of power over me. It's an exercise. So tell me."

He settled back more, a sprawled pose that made letting her hand fall into a resting position on his thigh a natural decision. His fingertips curled against her shoulder, an arrested caress.

"Could I ever have that kind of power?" He spoke quietly, keeping his gaze on her hand.

He wasn't as concerned about her question as the qualifier. It touched her. Even as she warned herself to stay on topic, she had to give him an honest answer. "When you stop abusing it, anything's possible."

"I think you're attracted to lost souls." His gray eyes became more opaque, and she sensed tension in his leg. "That's my opinion."

"Does that bug you?" she asked.

He lifted his shoulder, a non-answer, but he dropped his head back and looked up at the sky. "Angels are attracted to lost souls. To guide them. Guess that's their job, if you believe in angels."

She was amused. "Honey, I'm no angel. And with no aspirations in that direction."

His eyes swiveled to her, his head still resting in its recumbent position. "Lucifer is an angel. And he does take care of lost souls."

She faced him again, her hip on the bench and her cross-legged position allowing her to run her foot teasingly down his shin. Because she propped her elbow on the back of the bench, inside the span of his stretched-out arm, she felt his biceps flex against her when he captured some of her locs in his hand. "I think Mrs. Grant was right about those un-Christian thoughts of yours," she said.

"Maybe." He did something with a small handful of her locs, released them, then did it again. She realized he was winding them around his wrist. Her Domme cravings, already on low simmer with such an intriguing submissive under her fingertips, sparked to flame.

"Sometimes I wonder if it's not as bad as people think," he said. "Maybe Hell's for those who feel good stuff is too bright. They couldn't figure out how to let that kind of light in during their lives, so Lucifer's job is to help them out. In Hell, they can let in light a little at a time, until it doesn't hurt so much or make them angry. Then it can burn all the bad stuff away."

His brow still had that thoughtful crease she wanted to tease with her lips. She let her fingertips slide across it, under the strands of his dark hair. "Why would good things make people angry?"

His opposite knee, the one she wasn't touching, twitched as if tapped by a doctor's mallet. "I don't know. But it does. Maybe because they can see it but not feel it. The sun is like fluorescent light, no heat or substance to it. They don't feel the qualities everyone else says are there. So those people need hellfire for light to seem real, and to finally feel warm." His lips tugged. "Even if it hurts like hell."

"You don't feel any heat from the sun, hmm?" Despite the emotions his words raised inside her, she said it teasingly, reminding him with the pointed comment what she'd said about being the sun.

"You're different. I did compare you to Lucifer, after all," he said. Removing his arm from behind her, he grasped her hand on his thigh. A well-trained sub like Rob would have waited for her to approve contact each time, unless she gave him a specific, open-ended directive. Whereas once encouraged to do so, Marius hadn't hesitated to continue to make that kind of contact.

She'd given him tacit permission to treat this like a date. Yet she didn't think it would have mattered. It was a core difference in the type of subs they each were, and it didn't displease her. She appreciated Rob, but was admittedly quite drawn to some of Marius's less disciplined qualities. Except when they led to him being more self-destructive.

She also noticed Marius either hadn't caught or had let pass her decision to make his analogy more personal, referencing him as one of those who had trouble feeling the light...and dealing with anger.

As their fingers interlaced, she felt the coarseness of his knuckles and palm, the heat and strength of his grip. He nodded to the ice cream stand. "Ready to tell me I'm dreamy?"

"With fluttering lashes, clasped hands and everything." Managing the wiseass remark was an effort, given how much was going through her head. He hadn't been bullshitting her with his unexpected evaluation of Hell. Yes, he was clever and manipulative, but when he was giving her total honesty, he spoke slower, in a more measured way.

Truth wasn't easy or quick for him.

She chose a scoop of chocolate. He went with root beer, a hideous combination in her opinion. Until he put the two flavors together on a spoon and convinced her to taste. Then she was sure of it.

She ate every bit of hers, avoiding the connecting point between the two scoops so he could have that distasteful part. She noticed his amusement when she licked the spoon clean.

"I have to pay for every calorie with blood and sweat in Lyda's insane fitness class. Which should be called the You-Are-Paying-Me-To-Kill-You work out. I torture myself there three times a week."

"Yeah, I've heard about it." He took cup and spoons from her and threw it all away before they wandered back toward the rail. "She doesn't like me much."

"Can you blame her?"

"No. Not really. What I said that day, in Tyler's office, about it not being my fault that Mistresses get in over their heads. She's not one of those. But I shouldn't have said that anyway."

It was an unexpected admission, but she accepted it with a neutral expression. "No, you shouldn't have. But you were still pretty wound up from the scene. Makes a person stupid. You needed more aftercare to calm you down."

He picked up on the direction of her thoughts with unsettling accuracy. "It wasn't your fault."

"No. But if I could do it again, I would have stepped in and told Alex that you needed more defusing time before seeing Tyler."

"You would have had to be my Mistress to have that authority."

"Yes, I would have," she agreed, meeting and holding his gaze.

"I don't know if that would have made any difference," he said, looking back out at the water. A shrimp trawler was trundling past, coming in from a late night out on the ocean. "I don't really need a lot of aftercare. Just toss me a towel and a bottle of water. Not really into the cuddling, nurturing shit."

"That night, hair of the dog would have been my choice," she said. "Tie you down to a spanking bench, take you with a strap-on. Give you a brisk rub down after you'd come a couple times. Your testosterone was running way too high and you still had too many knots inside you. Just because you put off the tough guy vibes doesn't mean you don't need extensive after-care. It probably means you need more, when the session's done right."

She made the words casual, matter-of-fact, but felt his intent stare come back to her as they leaned against the rail together, hip to hip, shoulder to shoulder. When he didn't say anything, she turned to look at him. He didn't smile, studying her hard enough to pierce blood and bone. His eyes reflected a need so strong she wanted to reach out and touch him, but she quelled it, especially when he straightened, his expression shuttering.

"I don't want to be put under a microscope, by you or anyone else."

He pivoted and walked away from her. He didn't seem in a hurry; he just needed to be away. Even though it was an effort, she let him go. She went back to studying the movement of light on the water, crossing her arms on the rail and propping her upper body against them to make her viewing more comfortable.

He might leave her there. She had a phone and knew how to call a cab, so that didn't concern her. She wouldn't get in a car with him if he was making a shift to a more volatile mood anyhow. Disappointment lurked in her lower belly, but she pushed it away. Whatever happened, happened.

It took him about five minutes. As he'd progressed down the Riverwalk, his movements became more jerky and angry, as if he was having a fight with himself. She didn't watch him for long, preferring instead to enjoy the night scenery and listen to the brief snatches of conversation from people strolling along behind her.

She'd closed her eyes and lifted her face to the touch of the breeze, when she felt the rail vibrate from his weight settling against it.

"I can't be what you want," he said, his voice wooden.

"Yes, you can." Opening her eyes, she lowered her chin. This time she put every bit of a Mistress's challenge in her expression and voice. "I can prove it. Give me something real, Marius. Tell me something you want, from your gut, your balls and your heart. Better yet, show me. Put all the bullshit aside and just show me."

She saw the flash in his irises, a storm lit by lightning. Then he straightened, pinning her against the rail. She closed her hands over the metal bar on either side of her; he locked his hands over her wrists, holding her there. Her eyes never left his as the two of them stayed motionless a few charged moments. His groin pressed against her pelvis, his erection growing harder with every breath she took.

Since she hadn't worn heels, she had to raise her chin about an inch. It made her aware of how close their mouths were. She didn't flinch or retreat, letting the energy build. His gaze swept down, where her breasts were against his chest, the position giving him a more revealing look down into the lace cups of her bra.

As he studied the flesh cradled there, something flashed across his expression. For a second, she was almost sure he would bend and put his head there, nuzzle and lick. If she'd been sitting, he would have knelt between her spread thighs to do it, cradling the curves, handling them with gentle fingers and a relentless grip.

But he lifted his gaze and fastened his attention on her mouth. Her lips would be full and wet-looking, thanks to her gloss.

"Something real, Marius," she said, a husky whisper. "Don't drag your ass."

"I'm not even kissing or fucking you, but I feel like I am." His voice was husky. As if he expected her to fight him, his hands slid up to her biceps and gripped. He used his strength to bring her up on her toes and his mouth to hers. He did it like an avalanche, deceptively slow and ponderous, and then all that brutal power, the ability to bury everything in its path with its weight, was upon her.

Careful what you wish for. Wasn't that the saying?

This embrace was raw, animalistic, like the night of the fight. It was as if he was locked in combat with her, though she was giving herself to his embrace, her hands sliding up his abdomen to his chest, pressing against the hold on her biceps until he let her reach his neck. She gripped and held on, feeling his pulse hammering against her palm. He didn't let go of her upper arms, though. If anything, his grip became more bruising.

Hard, hungry, painful. He needed to make it hurt, because he was hurting. It was too much light for a denizen of hell, as he'd said. When she parted her lips under the demand of his, his tongue slid in as he tried to dominate the kiss. She evaded him with slippery, wet heat, tangling and embracing his mouth instead of letting him fight with hers. His body was pressed as insistently against her as was possible with them both clothed. He hiked her up on the rail, her feet leaving the ground as he pushed himself between her legs, grinding against her core and banding his arms around her, one hand gripping her ass and the other flat against her back.

Her back was to the water and they were in a brace of shadows, but there was no mistaking this was over the line of socially acceptable PDA.

He didn't care. She could feel it, and a reaction shuddered low in her belly, strumming through her upper thighs. He wanted to take her down and fuck her right here. The thing that lay at the core of Duncan Marius Walczek was untamed and uncivilized. Rabid.

The night of the fight, she'd seen a lot of men don personas to add to the drama. He had unmasked himself. By doing so now, he resurrected a primal throb she'd been carrying deep inside her, ever since seeing him fight.

He wanted her to fight him. She refused, for entirely selfish reasons. She was too busy enjoying all that male heat, unleashed and uncontrolled. Not practiced or charming at all, praise God and Goddess both.

But in time, she did start to soothe the beast with a quiet noise against his mouth, with the stroke of her fingertips along his neck and shoulders, and by easing her body off the rail so she stood against him. She wasn't sure what helped him power down, but if she had to make an educated guess, she'd say the unbelievable potency of that kiss had freaked him out.

Gradually, control of the kiss moved back into her court, though the weakness of her knees and a million feathers brushing inside her thighs and stomach said his aggression hadn't been unwelcome. When she broke the kiss, she kept her mouth close, brushing it against the corner of his, along his cheekbone. His fingers flexed on her hips.

"Let me take you somewhere and fuck you." He said it in a hoarse growl. "That's as real as I know how to be."

"This is enough. This is everything." She stroked his jaw and drew his eyes to hers. Still wild and filled with animal heat, but he was getting a grip on himself.

She'd like to take a grip—of the hard, impressive shaft pressed against her pelvis. She'd guide it into her cunt and let him pleasure them both, but it was all too soon. She had to rein herself back as much as he did.

"I want you to know something, something that might trigger your asshole reflex," she said softly. "But I'm saying it anyway so you can think about it later. I wasn't kidding at the concert. This is the best date I've ever had."

He stared at her with that searching look that was confusion and anger, and so many mixed up things. He parted his lips to speak, but he was interrupted.

"Some spare change for a flower, son?" A wizened, dark-skinned man carrying an old fishing bucket had stopped behind them. The flowers in the bucket were created from the type of reeds used to make baskets. He'd twisted them into spiral roses. "You can have two if you want," he added. "They're not hard to make."

He wore clothing in a nondescript meshing of colors and which had a loose fit on his aged frame. His thin face was cloaked by a shaggy beard, and his fishing cap had seen many better days. If he wasn't homeless, he was close to it.

"Live flowers are pretty," he told Regina. "But they fade. These never do."

Regina managed a smile. Marius dropped the rest of his change into the man's hand, chose a flower and nodded. "Thanks, old timer," he said.

"Hang onto her," the man said, moving on down the Riverwalk, the bucket clasped in one hand. "Else you'll be like me, even if you're in a fancy suit and office somewhere. Alone is alone, no matter where it is." He turned the last comment into a blues riff and scatted it out, earning smiles from other people as he passed them doing soft shoe.

"Curious bastard," Marius commented. Meeting her gaze, he offered the flower. "I had a good time tonight, too."

Regina smiled and took the offering. "He's right. As pretty as a real rose might be, I like this one better."

"Of course you do. It was made by a lost soul."

And offered to me by one.

A decision formed in her mind. It would take things deeper than she'd intended tonight, but it felt right and she was going to run with it. It wasn't a late-night booty call craving. She knew the difference between that and this.

She put her hand on his face. "Normal date is over. We'll pick up my car, and then you'll follow me back to my place."

The look she gave him told him what she wanted. His own reflected heat and more confusion, mixed with some residual anger he hadn't been able to let go. But she knew he received the message from how he responded.

"Yes, Mistress."

CHAPTER NINE

*R*egina lived in a waterfront bay community near the Tampa airport. She told him the address in case they were separated, but he kept pace with her car, pulling into her driveway after a fifteen-minute drive. During that time, she caught glimpses of his face at stoplights, but couldn't read much from it. From the neck up, the boy was a hell of a poker player. Other body language gave her far more insights into what was happening in his head.

"This is probably stupid," she told herself for the second time. Or maybe the third. She'd been technically alone with him at the stables, but she knew that was a rationalization. A pair of security guards monitored cameras throughout the grounds from an office in the clubhouse, where they stayed discreet and invisible. They didn't disrupt scenes in process unless it looked necessary.

She didn't have that safety net in her home. But there was a reason it was called Risk Aware Consensual Kink, right? Yep, they could put that on her tombstone when she pushed him too far and he was in prison for murdering her in a fit of rage.

Stop it. If you're really worried about it, call it off. If not, keep following your gut.

Getting out of her car, she motioned him to follow her inside as she unlocked the door and left it open behind her.

The two-story sand-colored stucco home butted up to the deep-water canal that led to the bay. The water views made the sun porch and back patio endlessly enjoyable for relaxation. Inside, it had all the amenities she wanted. The four bedrooms and three baths had given her an adult playroom, spacious enough to host the occasional small party with kink friends. Her upstairs home office offered her an impressive view of the bay beyond the canal. Her bedroom was a first-floor nest on the western side of the house, where morning sun wouldn't wake her. When she'd traveled more often, her hours had often been irregular.

She dropped her keys on the granite countertop in her kitchen. She enjoyed cooking, though living alone, she didn't always take the time to do it. That made the conveniences of the modern kitchen a nice-to-have, but not as important as the features offered by other spaces. Like her playroom and the outdoor living areas.

Unzipping her ankle boots, she pulled them off and the stockings beneath, sighing with her usual contentment as she stepped onto the living room carpet and let her toes curl into the softness. One lamp was on, a golden glow contrast to the silvery illumination coming through the bank of living room windows, thanks to the lights lining the canal boardwalk.

She was aware Marius had come into the kitchen and stood behind her, saying nothing. As she pivoted, the lack of light in the kitchen put him in the shadows.

"Take off your shoes. Socks, too." Her gaze slid over him. "Actually, take it all off."

"Sure you want the normal date to be over?" His expression might not reflect his thoughts on the matter, but his words offered her the chance to keep this a simple late night fuck, rather than complicating it with the Dom/sub stuff. That would keep it easy for him. Easy for them both.

She wasn't in the mood for easy.

Moving to him, she cupped his nape. He was more than ready for her, meeting her mouth with an abundance of banked hunger. She braced her feet when he would have pushed her against the counter, instead holding him with one hand on his neck and the other against his chest. His fingers curled into her waist and hips like talons, holding her belt loops. She teased and tangled with his tongue, slowed them down. Putting a palm flat on his chest, she broke the kiss.

"Take all of it off and stay here until I come back."

She would have enjoyed watching him remove his clothes, but she gave up that pleasure to invest in another form of indulgence. Going to her playroom, she set out what she wanted and covered the items with a towel so he couldn't immediately see them when she brought him there.

Returning to her kitchen, she found he hadn't obeyed her. He stood fully dressed on the tile, fingers half curled at his sides, his eyes broody and mouth set. The expression coupled with the darkness in the kitchen caused a ripple in her vitals and took her back to her internal debate in the car.

Yes, he wasn't entirely safe to bring home. Tyler would have snarled at her for it, but sometimes a Mistress or Master had to follow instincts and rely on emergency services to do their job if the worst happened.

The spurt of grim humor came with the memory of the night Tyler had agreed to let Marguerite top him in a semi-public session. He'd tapped a bad internal trigger, one that made her lose control and beat the hell out of him. But whatever breakthrough they'd had that night had made him say, more than once, that it was the best error of judgment he'd ever made. So if he wanted to lecture her, she'd just remind him of that. Though Tyler being Tyler, an old school Southern male, he'd say without an ounce of shame that it was different, because he was male and Regina was female. *Yeah, right.*

"Problem?" she asked, her tone neutral.

Marius shook his head. "I think I'm going to go. Shifting gears like this. I wasn't expecting it." He stopped, obviously struggling with what he was really trying to say. Or how to escape without actually saying it.

"Okay. Fair enough. You want to split some of the spinach puffs I had them box up, and take them home with you?"

His gaze lifted to hers, slowly. "I'm not invited into a woman's house often." He moved another step toward her, fingers flexing at his sides. The shadows cloaked his eyes now, making them impossible to read. "Not alone, like this."

The alarm tingle got a lot stronger. She moved forward, so she could see his eyes. He had a cool, detached stare, but a lot was happening behind it. He was fighting on a battleground far from here, and this golem left in his stead might still spill blood in her kitchen. If she left him here, and walked calmly into her living room, she could make it to the rear patio door and be outside in a blink, within calling distance of plenty of help. And—

Stop. Fuck that.

She went a step closer to him, within reach of his powerful hands that had broken three strong men in one night. A raw energy gathered, prepared to leap. He was going to reach out, grab her, make her startle or flinch, which was what that demon inside him wanted. It wanted to make her afraid. That's how it would take control. So...

She slapped him, then caught his shirt collar and yanked him back to her mouth for a violent kiss. When his arms went around her, she ripped open his shirt in one pull, summoning a snarl from him. His hands clamped on her hips and she countered, raking her nails down his chest, drawing blood. She'd had the occasional hardcore sub who craved bloodplay, and she knew how to deliver that when needed.

Gray eyes went back to lightning storm, but she'd startled him enough to get a split-second of advantage. She ducked under his arm, gripped the back of the shirt collar and yanked the whole garment off his broad shoulders to his forearms, restricting their movement. She hit the small of his back with the heel of her hand, pulled him back to his heels and put him on the ground while his balance was off. Shoving him face-forward to the tile, she changed her grip to his neck and planted her knee in his back, digging her nails into his flesh.

He wasn't the first grown man she'd had to take down.

"You're under the mistaken impression that there's a rabbit in this room, boy," she said sharply. "And you think you're the big, bad wolf. That may be true, but I'm the she-wolf here, the bitch in charge. If you want to turn this into an all-out fight, you might win the physical side. You're a strong beast. But if you want me to show fear, cower or startle when you whip out all that badness, you've picked the wrong fucking female."

She backed off him in one lithe move and spoke in the same ruthless tone. "Your hands should still be able to reach your buckle. Strip off your belt and hand it to me. Then open your jeans and push them down to your knees. If you can't handle that, if you're afraid of me, if you just want to be done with this, you can leave. I won't stop you. But if you stay, you do as you're fucking told."

Slowly, he maneuvered himself to his knees, head bowed. She

could see his profile in silhouette, the rise and fall of his shoulders, the way his fists were clenched at his hips, beneath the folds of the tangled shirt.

Reaching out, she feathered her fingers over his bare shoulder, the point of his neck, an easy stroke. She kept doing it, a casual gesture at odds with her hard demand and the violence of the past moment. At length, she took the shirt off of him, helping him slide the sleeves over his hands, and stepped back. She masked her held breath and tense center, which didn't release until he unbuckled the belt. Stripping it from his lean waist, he held it out to his side for her. His jeans slid down to his hips.

"Good." She took it from him and watched the ripple of movement across his shoulders as he unzipped the pants and pushed them to his knees. He wasn't wearing underwear, as he'd said, and his ass was fine and tight, muscles flexing, the neat seam between his buttocks making her want to tease and probe.

"Rise." She put her hand under his elbow to steady him. "Take off the shoes and socks, then get rid of the jeans."

When he complied, Marius was naked in her kitchen. As she circled him, she noticed with satisfaction and a nice spear of lust his cock was high and stiff. She looped the belt around the base, cinched it, then brought the tongue up to her shoulder so she could see his reaction as she pulled, so insistently he lurched a step forward. It wouldn't stop the strap from biting into tender flesh.

He showed his teeth at the pain, but she ignored that. Instead, she dropped her free hand and gripped his cock, stroking the smooth but hard erection with light fingertips. When at last she allowed the belt to loosen and slip away, she replaced it fully with her hand. As his gaze went opaque and lips parted, she gave the belt to him, pressing it into his half-curled palm. "Put it behind your back, and wind it around both your wrists," she said. "Restrain yourself. We're going to take a walk together."

His brow furrowed but his shoulders twitched as he began to comply. She didn't let herself indulge the victory. She kept stroking his shaft, investigating the glans and slit with a probing thumb, noting the quiver through his muscles as his arousal started to build and pre-come dampened her skin. He was getting thicker and bigger in her grasp, a temptation to which she wasn't immune. Her own body tightened, loosened and liquefied in all the right ways.

She was also getting warm. She let go of him long enough to strip off her halter top. As she stood before him in jeans and a demi-cup bra that barely held her breasts in a frame of lace and sheer mesh, his gaze tracked the sparkling spider pendant resting in her cleavage. He moistened his firm lips and she could feel them there, along with the tip of his clever, teasing tongue.

She increased her grip on his cock, emitting a purr as it convulsed under her touch. "Walk with me," she said. "One step back for me, one step forward for you." She put pressure on his cock to help him understand, and he did. He moved with her as she brought her other hand to rest on his chest, controlling their pace. He had his hands wrapped in his belt so his chest was open terrain for her to explore. Stroke, play with a taut nipple with her thumb, tug on his chest hair, scratch him with her nails. He missed a stride and stepped on her foot, but they were both barefoot. Her quick smile seemed to knock something loose, his intensity lessening, lips quirking. He took a breath, chest expanding under her touch.

"So this is being led around by the cock?"

"The literal interpretation, yes. Much better than the pejorative meaning. You're your own man, Marius. I don't make any choices for you. Not even the choice to stay here."

They were moving down the hallway, nearly at her playroom. She stopped, letting go of his cock with a caressing touch, and gestured into it. "Go stand in the center of the room."

He moved into the space, filling it up with his size and the energy vibrating from him. She let him look his fill, see the spanking bench, the several pieces of BDSM furniture she'd splurged upon over the years. The walls were extra insulated oak paneling to muffle noise, the floor covered with a bold, dark red throw rug.

Rising on her toes, she unhooked a pair of steel cuffs from the doubled over chains embedded in the ceiling beams. The doubling over was a practical measure to keep her from banging into them when she was doing other things in the room.

"Drop the belt to the floor."

She'd picked up his shirt, and now shimmied out of her jeans, leaving her in her bra and panties, a matching mesh and lace. Shrugging into his shirt, she left it open over the set, and freed her hair from the collar. She wrapped herself in his scent, enjoying the touch of the cloth still holding the heat of him. His face might be hard to read right now, but the way he had his gaze locked on her sent its own message.

She stepped closer to run a hand down the valley of his spine, slow, molding her palm to his lower back and hip. "Put on the cuffs. Do you trust me enough to do that?"

In answer, he locked them onto his wrists.

~

So she was going with soft play. Surprising, since his reputation was for more hardcore stuff, but so far, even in pony play, she'd gone a different way. Well, yes and no. He'd expected the pony play to be undemanding, but she'd used the trappings to mindfuck him pretty damn well, taking him somewhere he hadn't been before. So maybe he shouldn't assume he knew where she was going with this. Thinking he did kept him in a comfort zone that might not last very long.

This, his hands in cuffs, he'd done this before. It was like a Domme staple. When she pulled them up, taking the slack out of the chain so his arms were over his head, she didn't put any strain on his shoulders. She even double-checked that with the welcome grip of her smooth hand on those muscle groups. Was he disappointed? No...not necessarily. But her going the well-worn track with him was unexpected. She'd probably do a little flogging or spanking, maybe take him with a strap-on, have him come.

What he wanted to compel her to do was fuck him herself, her tight, wet pussy sliding down the full length of his cock, her ass pressed against his upper thighs as she seated herself there. She'd denied him direct participation in her last climax, denied him the right to fuck her. It was starting to piss him off. Or maybe that was the cuffs, this whole soft approach. He wanted a fight. He wanted her to push, to hurt.

Hell, what was she fucking planning to do? She'd asked if he trusted her enough to let her cuff him. He did. But alarm bells still went off. Especially when she put a blindfold on him, an eye mask she seated securely so he was kept in darkness.

But why did it bug him? He'd been blindfolded before. Hell, full head mask, gagged, hog-tied and immobilized. That didn't put him out of control. He still knew how to work a Mistress, even when it seemed all senses were hampered. Body language was almost impossible to completely silence and Mistresses looked for the responses they wanted to see. He could give her a good time. Why wouldn't she give him the freedom to do that?

Why was he having a fucking two-way argument with himself that was threatening to burn out the hamsters turning the wheels of his brain?

"I don't want a blindfold. I want to see you in my shirt." *Longer. More.* He never wanted her to wear anything else.

He'd said it like a demand and knew it. Wouldn't apologize for it.

"There'll be time for that. You're a little too bossy right now. Let's take care of that." Her fingers were at his mouth, easing in a ball gag. He locked his jaw, but she merely slid her finger into the hinge and wrenched it open the way she had with the bit, strapping it in before he could force it loose. It had a handkerchief wrapped around it. When the scent hit his nostrils, it stilled him.

"I rubbed that between my legs," she said. "I want you to know how much I liked thinking about doing this to you. And how much I liked that kiss at the Riverwalk." Her knuckles slid along his sides, to his hips, down over his upper thighs.

Her voice thickened, giving him an unexpected glimpse of emotion. She stayed in such control, was she playing him now? But her words hit him in a way that didn't leave room for him to analyze.

"I don't know if any sub can truly understand what it does to a Master or Mistress, seeing you helpless, surrendering your will to us. It takes the mind some interesting places."

She pressed against his back, her hands sliding along his bound arms. "You think you can scare me, big bad wolf? You don't know all the uncivilized things I want to do with you, here, trapped in my house, bound and helpless. It's you who should be worried."

He could get out by tearing the hook out of the ceiling. He knew it, she knew it. But the teasing caress of her breath on his neck had him quivering, his cock getting stiffer.

She'd moved away from him and was doing something, perhaps at the table he'd seen when he first came into the room, the one that had items concealed by a cloth on one end.

When she returned, the clatter of metal suggested she'd set a bucket next to him. Next, she ran her hand down his left leg. "Lift," she ordered. When he did, she slid a cushioned mat under one foot, then the other as he shifted.

"Some people use plastic, but I like to have my sub stand on something soft and warm. It has a rubber backing to absorb liquid, though. Remember the other night? You became a horse, and it was an amazing thing to watch. Tonight, we create something different."

He started as she smeared a handful of clay-like substance along one shoulder. It was crazy, how he was more skittish about the unknown things she might do than the harshest punishments he could see coming from the frustrated Mistresses at The Zone.

The clay was warm. As she packed it on, it stayed where she put it. It also seemed to be hardening fast, like wax. She applied it to his chest, back, abdomen, buttocks. It smelled like earth and cocoa butter. He'd used cocoa butter lotion on his tattoo to keep it supple while healing, per the artist's direction.

Regina had left that shoulder bare and was stroking the design. "This is a good symbol for you, Marius. I think you're the skin over the armor, being ripped away. Duncan is the armor and the man beneath."

He tensed. He didn't want her going down that road, but fortunately she returned to working with the clay. She spread it over his ass, tracing the seam between his cheeks, the sensitive lines where buttocks and thighs met. Her touch was meditative, like she was detached from his reaction as she savored her own.

"It's different for you, isn't it?" she mused. "Whether intentional or not, you chose Mistresses who think the way women are expected to do. How is he doing? Is he engaged? Is he thinking about me? What is he feeling?"

She chuckled, a husky sound that stirred his nerves like a hot summer breeze. "I prefer to think about what *I'm* feeling and thinking. What *I'm* doing. Am *I* engaged? You can only touch my heart and mind if I allow it, and right now I'm busy pleasing and engaging myself. I've blindfolded and gagged you so I can watch your reactions and feed off the pleasure of those. No interruptions except those I want."

His breath had slowed while she spoke, but his heart had compensated threefold. Her fingertips glided over his upper thighs, back along his sides. His cock was throbbing, aching and stiff, and she was ignoring it. His hands were clenched in fists above his head.

"I told you my thoughts go to some interesting places when I do this. I think of a goddess, at the dawn of creation, sculpting life. I imagine this is the way she did it, spending days, maybe years, to create every curve, angle and feature of a male body like yours. She wants to know exactly what she'll have the joy of gazing upon when the babe grows to manhood."

A blade slid through the clay on his shoulder, a curved edge that scraped him as clean as a razor and left a tingling burn behind. Her voice was a sensual current, carrying him away from the shore he knew.

"When a baby is born, we think that's perfection. New, pure, unsullied. But a goddess looks into our future and uses our experiences to sculpt her vision of our adult selves. That's what makes the results interesting, how those experiences affect our bodies, our faces. Our soul and heart inside. The soul is as visible to her as our bodies."

A smile entered her voice. "Despite her interest in our souls, I imagine she'd linger over a body as fine as yours. I would if I were her. She'd also weep at some of the damage you've done to her work." The blade slid down his back, over the upper curve of his buttock, her fingers following and stroking, lingering over various scars. The chain clanked as he shifted. Her touch stilled, her voice dropping.

"And here's where I imagine myself stepping into that goddess's bare feet, for she never wears shoes. Perhaps on occasion there's a soul, a sculpture, so fascinating to her she decides to keep him for herself for a while. She hasn't yet given him eyes or a tongue, just a powerful, yearning, virile body, and what goddess wouldn't want to take full advantage of that? She wants to see if he can serve her as she desires."

She was doing it again, transforming him. Suddenly he was a faceless entity in a goddess's workshop, with no existence beyond the molding and sculpting of her hands, the direction of her voice.

The part of him that stayed in this reality became acutely aware of not being able to control any of this, not without destroying it. He stilled as she set the blade to the base of his cock, her thumb against the top of it to control the movement as she scraped a long smooth line along the turgid flesh. She hooked the curved edge under the glans and pressed metal against him. His thighs quivered.

If she'd left him unbound, merely ordered him to keep his hands curled around the chains, his eyes closed and mouth shut, would he have obeyed, simply to please her?

The thought startled him.

She removed the blade from his genitals and gripped his hair, pulling his head back. She patted more clay onto his exposed throat, then skinned it off once again with the blade. Slow, letting him feel the pounding of his pulse beneath the press of the knife.

"She'd need to fuck him before she sent him off into the world, to leave her mark upon him, wouldn't she?"

He nodded vigorously. God, he wanted that. Wanted to ram into her soft, wet cunt, feel her grip him with those strong, internal muscles.

He let out a groan and snarl of frustration when the tip of the strap-on nudged his rear entry. No. He wanted—

Her fingers wrapped around his throat, holding him fast, restricting his breathing.

"You belong to this goddess. You submit to her will. She can keep you a slave forever, make you crawl on your hands and knees, make you climax over and over. You control nothing, because your loss of control is what pleases her, what turns her on so much. You want to fuck her, bring her to climax, but no. You haven't earned, learned, or accepted, what that desire is. You tell yourself you're taking, but only a goddess takes. A servant serves, gives, submits. He cuts himself open and lets her take it all. That's how he finds his salvation."

She drove in, hard, and he strangled on a curse. She chuckled, a sound of lust and heat. "So tight. Lucky for you, this goddess believes in lubrication. She's going to bring her newest creation to life, over and over, until he understands. Even when she at last cuts him loose to wander the earth, he belongs to her."

"Want inside you..." The words were muffled by the gag and she disregarded him anyway. She thrust, teased him, brought him to the cusp of climax, took it away and started again. The clay dried on his skin where she hadn't scraped it free. She stayed buried deep within him when she used her blade on it and pressed harder, both within and without, making him flinch. His body was twisting in the chains, hers moving with him. He was groaning against the gag, the cloth saturated with his saliva.

She took him up and nearly over, such that he snarled like a crazed animal when she pulled out. Yet she'd aroused him so much, he didn't have time to rally and strike back before she'd set him off balance again. She gripped his cock in a blissfully firm grip.

"Stay very still so I don't hurt you. Can you stay still for me, Marius?"

He nodded, though he had second thoughts when a hard, thin rod began to slide into the slit of his cock. She paused.

"Okay. Nod again for me. Tell me you're going to stay still or I'll remove it."

She had an implacable, stern voice in this mode, yet the way she mixed care with it messed him up. He found himself nodding again.

She slowly let the rod invade him, sending tendrils of that weird not-good/good mix of arousal and trepidation through him. He'd done sounding once or twice with mediocre results, but submitting to it with her had him stiffening further in her gentle hands.

"Lovely. To bring a creation to life, one needs lightning. Electricity."

Christ. He jumped at a crackle of sound, right next to his ear. A fucking violet wand. But she wasn't done. Something cool and sharp slid along his shoulder, a prick in the pocket of his collarbones.

"It's amazing, what putting together a knife blade, electrode pads and a cock stuffed with a urethral sound will do. At a certain point a man will feel like he's having a climax even when he's not. Wave after wave, pounding him against a brick wall that never gives way, never relents a bit. And then, when the climax does come, it's overwhelming."

Her breath was against his ear, her body against his back. "It destroys his fucking mind. All his walls are knocked down, so there's nothing between him and his Mistress but his overwhelming need to do everything for her."

She applied the electrode pads with tantalizing touches on his genitalia, and then ran the wand along his cock before he could figure out any kind of defense. It was an invasive, crazy feeling, impossible to describe.

His groans had words, lost against the gag, but Christ, this was... He bucked and convulsed as the wand danced over his cock, again and again. She lifted it away to alternate the sensation with the grip of her hand. Sometimes she played with the sound, sliding it out an inch and then back in. She rubbed her pussy, clad in satin, against his ass. Then she was back to using the wand on him. Not just on his cock. Nipples, a tingling path over his abdomen, then back to his dick. Oh fuck. Fuck, fuck...

She was right. Suddenly it was like he was coming, only he wasn't, and the feeling was going on and on, like a torture that he wanted to stop yet didn't.

He was thrashing in his bonds, crying out, kicking, but she was too nimble, moving around him and keeping the wand going over his cock as he screamed for release, for mercy. He was enraged, needing to do violence. Yet he also wanted to beg. To do anything for her.

"Please, please...fuck..."

She took the wand away, though it felt like the metal rod was still vibrating. Probably the throbbing of his cock. He hoped like a lost man in the desert when she removed the electrodes, but then groaned in despair as she pushed the strap-on inside him again. She'd put everything else aside to wrap her arm around his waist and hip to give her more leverage. Christ, she fucked like a man, shoving into him so he was pushed up onto his toes. She didn't touch his cock, and it was slapping against his abdomen from the force of her thrusts, giving a whole new meaning to the term beating off.

Her breath rasped and he suspected there was a clitoral stimulator on the strap-on to get her off. But she didn't go over either, pulling out and stroking his chest, his sides again. She loved playing with him this way, and nothing he did swayed her from her course or rushed her. She would not be moved. She was the wall itself.

Like a goddess who had all eternity to play with her creation in her workshop.

He was panting, his body quivering. He'd stopped trying to tell her what he wanted to do to her. She removed the gag, her fingers deftly slipping the strap and plucking out the ball wrapped in the soaked kerchief.

"What do you want?" she asked in a voice that gave nothing away. It was full of emotion, but he couldn't latch onto a single one to identify and use it.

"Please. Let me give you pleasure. Please." He couldn't handle her doing it as she'd done it before, driving him to climax and then handling her own needs, denying him the right...the privilege.

A privilege. "Please," he said with a dry throat and tongue.

She moved away from him and he thought she was going to turn him down again. He would deserve it. He hadn't done enough to prove he wouldn't be a total shit to her at the first opportunity. Because he would be. It was the desolate truth.

The chains holding his arms above his head loosened enough he could drop them to his sides, but he was still bound. A scraping, a chair moving across the room. The noise stopped behind him, and he heard her body settling into it.

"Turn around, get on your knees and come to me."

He dropped. She'd given his arms enough slack to be at his sides when standing, but when kneeling, they were raised to shoulder height again, just enough freedom to be frustrating. But he wrapped his hands around the chains and used the anchor to move forward on his knees. He bumped into her leg.

"Stop there," she said.

Leaning forward, she ran a strap around his throat, buckling it securely. She hooked his wrist cuffs to the back of it, the chains swaying above him. Now his hands were denied the ability to participate.

"Use your mouth to figure out how I'm sitting. You don't touch my pussy with it until I command you. And I won't forgive an 'accidental' contact."

He started with her knee. He had to suppress a quiet oath as his lips trailed over her inner thigh and he realized she was sitting in a chair with arms, and she'd draped her thighs over them, spreading them out like Rod Stewart's double entendre reference to angel wings. He wanted to touch her with his hands, his body, with every fucking inch of himself, but she'd taken away everything but his mouth with which to worship her.

He stopped over her pussy, and hovered there, breathing hard to inhale her arousal. His head was bowed, his fists clenched. An ache was in the center of his chest, hard enough to clog his throat. What was the matter with him? He could play with her now, soon as she did what he was sure she would, have him go down on her. He would be able to prove how good he was at that. Way better than goddamned Rob.

Yet when she molded a hand around the back of his skull and drew him to the center of that flower of soft, glistening flesh, all he wanted to do was eat her out like a starving animal, suck on the petals of her labia, bite them, thrust his tongue into her deep. Fuck her with no control, no finesse, just pure hunger, a driving need for her that was riding the edge of violence. He wanted her to gush, to grind herself against his face, scream her pleasure as she suffocated him with her sex.

He wanted that because he knew his uncontrolled, raw response was what she wanted. His wants didn't matter, and understanding that was such a relief, such a release of weight, he swayed. He didn't want to have a name. He didn't want to be created and released from this goddess's presence to make his way in the world. He didn't want to be Duncan or Marius; he wanted to be the marionette in a goddess's workshop, serving her however she desired, no other demands or expectations on him.

Not because he wanted to escape his life, but because for the first time, he felt like he'd been given one. Something that mattered. Someone that mattered.

And that terrified him, awakening the blackest parts of his soul.

Before she'd pulled the chair over, she'd ditched her bra and panties and shrugged back into his shirt, liking the feel of it but not wanting any barrier between her flesh and his mouth. It was working on her like he'd never want anything but pussy again. She came in a matter of minutes, though she'd intended to hold out longer. Regina arched up, rubbing her cunt against his face, his clever tongue, the firm lips, the roughness of his jaw.

The chains clanked as he strained against her. He made animal noises of need as savage as her cries. He kept going as long as she needed, and modulated his strokes to a hungry yet gentle licking so she could keep him there, enjoying the aftershocks.

She was a little amazed at the force of the shudders still coursing through her. God. Goddess. Everything in between. If that was what a little visualization could become between them, coupled with strap-on and oral play, then actual sex might realign the planets.

She gripped his hair, stroking, pulling. She permitted him to keep nuzzling her. When she finally put enough pressure on him to make him stop, he braced his jaw against her inner thigh, his breath bathing her soaked labia. Her heartstrings tightened at the evidence he didn't want to be pushed away.

She studied him, the flushed skin below the eye mask, the set of his jaw, the way his body was quivering, his muscles all tight. Intuition told her not to unchain him. He was resting between her legs, but he was not at rest. She could almost feel those demons howling, telling him he needed to get his shit together, take charge of this bitch. Yet she didn't think they had the upper hand yet. From the way his skin was creased around the outside of the blindfold, she suspected his eyes were closed tightly, as if warding off their battle roars. When she stroked his hair off his forehead, he leaned into her touch.

"Introduce him to the pleasures of submission and safety in the here and now to get to the treasure beneath. There's a trove there." Marguerite's words. Had they gotten there?

Maybe not, but they'd taken some steps in the right direction.

He still had some of her "clay" on him. A mix of heated wax, lotion and some other ingredients she'd tailored from a spa treatment she thought could have intriguing applications on a sub. As she'd painted it on him, drawn shapes in it to tease and caress him, she'd enjoyed every reaction of his fine body.

He probably hadn't realized when he finally started to climax, since the beauty of the wand and sound combo was that the climax had no beginning, middle or end. It was just endless. But her eyes had drunk in the gushing fountain from his cock, the way it had splattered his thighs, the slender rod plinking to the floor, expelled by the force of his ejaculation. That cream still marked him, drying like the remains of the lotion-clay mixture.

Gentleness could be administered with every bit of ruthlessness as the bite of a single tail. Each sub was different in what could break him down. The key wasn't the degree of pain administered. It was about consistency; not relenting until whatever strategy was employed unlocked what was inside of him. Sometimes that door got blasted off its hinges. She hadn't made it that far, but she was pretty sure she'd made it harder to close.

Now for the next step. He needed aftercare, but the question was what kind. His chest was rising and falling more rapidly, and the press of his forehead against her was getting more insistent, like he wanted to drive his head through something far harder than her palm.

In a few moments, he'd be as ready for cuddling as a dangerous animal coiled in the back of a cage. "Sit back on your heels," she said quietly, when she could trust her voice. She had to reinforce it with touch, putting her palm to his chest and pushing him into position. When she rose from the chair, the tail of the open shirt she was wearing—his shirt—brushed his face. He caught the hem between two of his fingers, though his hands were still bound behind his head.

"Let me go," he said, his voice hoarse and raw.

"In time. Let's get you settled down first." She unhooked his cuffs from the collar, but left the chains attached. "Sit all the way down on the floor."

He started to comply; she began to walk away. And then everything happened so fast, even in hindsight, she wasn't sure how he'd done it.

She'd seen him fight three men in the ring with brutal ferocity, and still she'd underestimated how he could use those skills.

He was on his feet, had spun her around toward him. With one loop and a shriek of metal, he had the slack of the chain wrapped around her throat. One hand held it taut, his other in her hair, holding her fast against his body.

He had her in mass and power, which was clear from the unshakable strength of the hold, his mouth a twisted slash beneath the blindfold.

The most dangerous situation involving a prisoner was when he invaded an officer's personal space like this, leaving very little maneuvering room to strike back.

"I said"—his voice wasn't steady—"let me go." His body twitched, which meant his fist did as well, twisting the links of chain on her throat. They bit into her flesh, pinching, and the blood vessels started to constrict.

He could kill her. The idea jumped from surreal to real in a heartbeat. She'd fucked up, not realizing how close to the top she'd brought his darkness. Aftercare for him should have been her cutting a wide swathe around him, turning off the light and leaving him to lie here for about half an hour, working through a mass of emotions far blacker than a dark room. But she didn't want to leave him alone with that. She didn't want him alone in the dark.

"Duncan," she said, trying to ignore the break in her voice from restricted air flow. "You're hurting me. Scaring me some, too. Please let me go."

A split-second calculation and risk, which name to use. She didn't overthink it.

"Doesn't matter. It's over. Right?"

He didn't sound as if he was talking to her, but she answered anyway, forcing her fear at bay. It just fed devils; it wouldn't help her at all. "I don't know. I've never had a sub try to strangle me, so I don't have a protocol for it. I could try to knee you in the balls, but I think you're ready for violence." She swallowed and it was painful against the unrelenting steel links. "I think you'd rather lie down and let me curl around you, stroke your hair and hold you."

His lips became a straight line. "That's what you do to a child. I'm not a fucking child. I was never a fucking child. I want to fuck you. I'm tired of you holding it out of reach like a fucking carrot."

She realized his cock was starting to stir again, the violence fueling his arousal. "Bringing me to climax wasn't enough?" She softened her voice with the query, kept it calm. "You didn't like that?"

Something flickered over his expression, at least what she could see of it around the blindfold. "Yeah, I did. I wanted...to do that."

"Yes. And you did it. Honestly, purely, and with a hunger that took my breath away. The kind of sub any Mistress would want."

His grip hadn't increased, but it was tight enough. As her lungs tried to expand, she forced herself to take shallow breaths.

His lip curled. "Don't want to be any kind of sub, faceless...only faceless for you. But don't want you to care...want you to stay apart. Above me. Don't get down on the ground with me."

The words didn't make sense, but she thought she picked up

enough of the underlying meaning that it heartened her. It was like he was trapped in worse-than-usual sub-drop, a post-session state of mind where a sub floundered in dark places, often thanks to triggers inadvertently tripped during the session.

"Then let me go." Carefully, she lifted her hand to his on the chain and lightly stroked his knuckles. Blood was pounding in her ears, but she pushed past the roar to move her hand to his nape, her other to his biceps, caressing. A soothing touch. "Right now."

Clamping down on his neck, she slammed her elbow into the side of his head, twisting her torso to knee him in his side. When he staggered, she shoved him back, breaking his hold. There was a terrifying yank on the chain that bit into her throat like a dog's teeth, but then he'd let go and it loosened. She ducked out of the loop and backpedaled out of his range.

He didn't pursue, though he looked as if he was about to blindly charge her. If he did, depending on how fast he came at her, he'd dislocate his shoulders when the chains went taut. Training kicked in and she was prepared to move forward, strike against his biceps with all her strength to shove him back again. The tactic could prevent him doing himself that kind of damage.

Though never mind what he'll do to you if he gets hold of you again, girlfriend.

"Prison guard." He breathed through the pain, bending over to brace his hands on his thighs. His breath was short from the shot to the midriff. The side of his face was red from the impact of her elbow. "Fucking forgot that."

"Correctional officer, and yeah, you did." She took a breath. "You got a little lost all the way around. You back?"

He shook his head, and dropped to his knees. "Stay away. Just leave me here. I'm sorry. Fucking sorry. That wasn't how I wanted that to go." His voice broke, startling her, but he'd turned away. As his fists clenched, every muscle in his back tensing, she reached for the wall, because another wave of lightheadedness hit her. This one came from the cold, hard realization of what could have happened. Her throat hurt. Those chain links were going to leave marks.

Don't be a fucking child right now. Be the woman and badass Mistress you know you are.

She went to her cabinet as he spoke dully. "I'll go. I won't bug you again. Tyler was right about me."

"Of course he was," she said briskly. "The man is right about everything. But what you're thinking he's right about is the wrong thing. Don't start with the self-pity crap or you'll piss me off worse. You tried to choke me. You fucked up. We'll deal with it."

He removed the blindfold. She saw a flashing, dangerous eye as he tilted his head her way, but there was desperation there, too. She quelled her gut reaction, which was still trying to get her to run far, far away from an imminent threat.

She tossed a new set of steel manacles on the floor in front of him with a sharp clank and thud. "Ankles."

They were combination locked, so once latched, the only way out was with the combination. She crossed her arms.

He stared at them. He wasn't meeting her eyes. Shame or something else? "What if I tell you I'm done? Safe word and all that, let me the fuck out of here."

"I'd say you're a chickenshit. In addition to being a poor date. Choking me, then taking off."

His jaw set. "This isn't a fucking joke. I could have hurt you. I would have hurt you." His fists clenched anew. She wondered if he had permanent crescent scars on his palms from how often he fought himself with that physical tell. "I don't want to hurt you."

"So don't." She hardened her heart against the anguish she heard behind the harsh words and pointed to the manacles. "Trust me to make sure you don't get a second chance. You feel like shit right now about what you did, right?"

He nodded, wariness in the gesture. "So do I," she said bluntly. "You scared me, and I don't like that feeling. I won't let you make me afraid of you, Marius. You go now, I think about how you scared me and the way things could have turned out, until I paralyze myself with what ifs. For your part, you'll do something stupid, like go to a fight to punish yourself, and end up in a coma or dead. I'm not going to permit you to do that."

"How're you going to stop me?"

She blinked. "Those chains are looped over a load bearing beam. I reel them back in, and you'll only have as much slack as I want to give you. I could turn out the lights and leave you here for a week with a couple jugs of water. I'd throw food in once a day."

She met his furious, confused gray eyes. "If I think it will save your life, I'll do it and won't think twice. Or, you could put on the goddamned manacles."

He stared at her. Slowly, almost like an old man, he turned toward the restraints.

"Before you put them on, use this." She moved to the far wall, making sure her stride was confident. Drawing back a curtain, she revealed a small bathroom with a pedestal sink and commode. "I won't have you getting an infection from the sound. After you're done, I expect you to put on the ankle cuffs, then put your arms behind your back and roll onto your stomach. Keep the chains untangled."

She turned her back on him to move to a cabinet and peruse additional supplies she intended to use. She gave him visual privacy, but was pleased when she heard him use the sink to wash his hands afterward, the chains clinking against the ceramic bowl. As she heard him move back toward the center of the floor, she paid out more slack on the chains so he could lower himself to a seated position. She moved to the back wall to lean against it and watch him with a dispassionate expression. It also prudently kept her out of range.

He locked the cuffs on his ankles. His expression was stone, eyes cold, but he did it, then rolled on his stomach, adjusting his arms so his knuckles rested against the small of his back. The chains to the wrist cuffs swayed above him.

Picking up a baton, she telescoped it with a snap, so he'd know she was prepared to use it if he tried anything. She locked the ankle cuffs to one another with a combination clip, and did the same to his wrists. Then she pulled up his ankles and latched them to the wrist cuffs so he was in a hog tie. She used two rolled-up hand towels between his ankles and knees to cushion the joints.

As she did that, she was squatting next to him. Since she was only wearing his shirt, she noted his gaze coursing over her breasts, full and firm beneath the open garment, and then down to her pussy. The folds were soft and still damp, thanks to his beautiful mouth. After she finished securing him, she ran her fingertips down over her labia and dipped between, collecting the residual moisture and tasting herself.

He swallowed, his body tensing in an appealing way, muscles hardening. From the shift of his hips, she expected his erection was reviving again. Extremes of emotion tended to arouse a male, and she fully expected the shaft would stay stiff and jutting until he calmed down. She could use the former to help the latter.

She'd brought one other item with her, and she picked it up now, fitting it over his head with a short, firm tug. A head mask, followed by a scold harness that she buckled over his skull, fitting the metal piece in his mouth that held down his tongue and was kept in place by the straps around the jaw and back of the neck.

The head mask was of a thin fabric that would allow him to see through it, though more shapes than details. Which meant he could see her silhouette. Standing, she used her foot to shove him to his side and pressed her sole against it, letting him feel her weight, the psychological advantage of her standing over him. Dominant, in control.

"Look at that naughty cock, getting all messy at the tip. It may fuck up your radar, but a woman taking complete control gets you off like nothing else. The problem is, every time you find joy and quiet in it, you fuck it up, Marius. It's a pattern."

Her tone went from sensual, biting tease to stern and uncompromising. "You've always been a pain in the ass and arrogant motherfucker, but now you're just looking to burn your whole life down, aren't you?"

He said something against the metal piece that couldn't be understood and she was sure hurt, because the metal had barbs that dug into tender flesh if the wearer didn't keep his mouth still.

"You don't get to talk anymore tonight, so you might as well stop trying." She came back down to his level, stretching out on her hip in front of him. Her brief hesitation at getting closer to him, even with him bound where he couldn't hurt her, pissed her off. So she slid right up against him, caressing his stretched lips and moving her touch down to his chin and throat. Then over his chest and nipples, pinching and scraping hard so he quivered.

"Looks like I have you at my mercy for the rest of the night." She trapped his cock between her bare thighs. As anticipated, the organ was a hot, thick bar of steel beneath her flexing muscles. It wasn't just because of the violence of the past few moments. As she'd known, true to his sub nature, he responded to her taking the upper hand, binding him, rendering him helpless. He fought the things that were so good for him, poor boy.

His body was vibrating with a self-imposed stillness, laden with all the emotional energy churning inside him.

"You wanted to fuck me?" Reaching down, she gripped his balls, digging her nails into their heavy weight and rough texture so he sucked in a breath and pushed against her touch.

"You don't fuck me. I fuck you. When and how I say I will. Try that intimidation shit with me ever again, there won't be enough of your body left to find."

She thought of his broken words about wanting to be faceless. There was a risk in going down a path she wasn't sure she fully understood yet, but hell, she'd already chosen territory tonight most Mistresses wouldn't have. "You're my creation, my slave. Mine. You wear a face for the whole world, but not for me. You get to take it off here and be faceless. You're nothing here. Only mine."

He made a noise, a sound that was desolation, relief and need at once. She gripped the back of his neck, this time in a firm, caressing hand. "Tyler gave you a chance to come back. Through me. He wouldn't have done that if he thought you were a lost cause."

He shook his head, as if to deny it, but she dug her nails in deeper. He strangled on a sound caught between rage and pain. He could handle the latter. She'd seen him take much worse.

"You fucked up at the club with Siren on purpose. What happened just now was because you lost control and you had no idea how to deal with it. There may be fucking demons hiding deep inside you, Marius. But you don't have to be one. We're not done. We're just beginning."

She let him go to stroke his testicles and caress his cock, rubbing her pussy over it. He made another noise, this one more of a growl. He was straining against her. She could detect the flick of his lashes against the fabric of the mask.

"Would it help if I let you loose, bad boy?" she whispered. "You could overpower me, fuck me however you wish. You'd believe you've taken away my choices and given yourself up to that darkness once and for all. Is that really what you want? You stand on one side of that line and you do everything you can to push up against it, to convince everyone you'll make that step. But you won't fool me again. You can't get yourself to step across. Because it's not you. The monster isn't you, Marius."

She caught his face in both hands, fingers hooking the straps of the harness, nails digging through the thin covering on his face. "You remember what I told you, the story of the goddess in her workshop? She's not going to step out of your way so you can throw her creation into hell. Not on her watch."

He tried to shake her off, tried to move away. She knew how to deal with that.

Hooking a leg over his hip, she pressed her calf against his buttock. Drawing out the packet she'd slipped into his shirt pocket when she'd visited the cabinet, she tore open the condom. The sound had him freezing again, and a groaning protest escaped him as she rolled it upon his erect member, her fingers caressing. She brought her lips to his ear.

"You want to be punished, but I don't deal in pain. That only feeds your demons. I demand you give me pleasure, serve me as a sub should. The way I know deep down you want to do it, even when it causes those demons to turn on you, and try to tear *you* apart. I don't yet know why, but when you trust me enough, we'll figure it out together. Then I will kick their asses and tell those fuckers to back off. Because you're mine."

He might be protesting, but his cock wasn't. Emitting a pleased little noise at his impressive size, she pushed herself down on him one laborious inch at a time. Even at a somewhat awkward angle, it felt good. He felt good.

His body flexed but he was moving with her, adjusting, so she could get him all the way in. When she was seated to the hilt, she tightened her leg further over him. She wished she'd tied him a different way so she could roll over and ride him, but this would work for now. While it took time for a climax to build in this position, he was utterly helpless to whatever she wanted to do, which suited her overriding goal.

"There you are," she crooned, tipping her head back on her shoulders. "Goddess, what a cock you have. I may keep you locked up here as my sex slave for a few weeks anyway. Make you use up all that fighting energy serving me." She stroked his flank, his taut buttock, which pleased her even more.

She pushed up, then back down. It caused a slow, slow rub of his pelvis against her clit, the friction of his cock on the inside keeping her sighing and moaning out her pleasure in little bursts. She watched his face, the pressing of his lips against the metal piece, the twitch of his facial features beneath the molded texture of the mask. She ran her thumbs over the curves of his eyes, down his cheeks to his jaw, hooking back into the collar and holding him there to aid her up and down movements.

"Like riding on the waves," she purred, breathless. "Oh, fuck, you feel good. And you're so hard...I know you want to come, but you take care of me first. Yeah, you're nodding. That's what you want, Marius. Not because you want to screw with my head. But because it brings you peace. Pleasing a Mistress. You've been denying yourself that for so long...punishing yourself. That's not your job. Only a Mistress can punish you the way you need."

The climax rose high and she took that wave, surfing it with long cries and undulations of her body against the wall of his. It was a good, solid orgasm, more surface and purely physical than she desired, but it still shuddered through her with power. She gripped Marius's chest with her nails, digging into the crisp layer of hair, her leg flexing along his ass.

"Now, baby," she murmured. He came at the command, groaning against the barbs of the scold. His hips bucked back and forth with no rhythm. He was just a mindless, big, strong animal, responding to her demands.

She'd had plenty of hookup sessions with subs, satisfying physical and emotional experiences always preloaded with mutual respect and regard. Some of them, like Rob, evolved into genuine friendships.

This didn't fall anywhere in that realm. They'd brushed into some serious territory in previous sessions, but tonight, she'd invaded it. This was do or die time. Either she was all in or out, because she couldn't fuck with this kind of hot mess if she didn't have long term hopes and dreams. If she wasn't willing to let her heart get broken.

From experience, she knew having her heart broken was a worse feeling than being choked to death with chains. But it didn't matter. She was all in.

"That's my sweet boy," she breathed, feeling him fighting it all the way to the end. When he couldn't fight anymore, the climax draining him, he relaxed in her arms. She stroked his back, his face, his side. Gripped and kneaded his ass, holding him inside of her, because she could and it felt so damn good. Her boy had a beautiful, tight ass.

At long last, she pulled off him, pleased at the little sound he made that might have been a grumbling protest. Rising, she went to the bathroom and dampened a cloth with warm water to clean herself. She rinsed it and returned to him, pausing to look down at him. Lying bound at her feet, every line of his hard, scarred body exposed, the replete cock limp against the mass of his testicles. He had his head resting on the ground, a position that would give him a crick in his neck if she kept him that way too long.

Kneeling, she removed the condom and disposed of it, then cleaned him thoroughly, handling his testicles and cock with efficient familiarity.

Some tension was returning to his body, to the parts of his face she could see. What she wanted to do was unroll a padded mat and put him on it. She'd release his ankles from his wrists, run a tether between the front of his collar and his knees to keep him in the proper position so she could spoon up behind him. Cosset and comfort.

It was automatic to want to calm a submissive with childhood ideals of mothering comfort, yet Marguerite's warning and his own behavior told Regina he resisted nurturing aftercare. Even so, the need she felt from him, a yearning, felt like it drew from that realm. She couldn't pick up a strong enough signal to act on it, though, and she'd pushed him out of his comfort zone enough tonight. Hell, even outside her own.

Retrieving and unrolling the mat, she released his ankles from his wrists and then pushed the edge of the mat right up behind him. When he was ready, he could use it for his own comfort.

She said nothing, letting him breathe while contemplating her next course. If she hooked his collar to his knees to hold him in a half-fetal position, but left his hands bound behind his back, she could spoon up behind him and guide his fingers between her legs, cup them right up against her pussy. If he was good, she'd let him play with her, bring her to climax again while she stroked his head.

She'd like to know what he felt like inside her without the condom. The idle thought gave her pause, since it was something she rarely sought with her subs. Trust, yes. Surrender, and a range of lovely emotions between them. Commitment, not so much. At least not beyond the scene or the schedule of sessions they set up.

It figured she'd have that urge toward a sub so difficult it was possible she'd never win that kind of commitment from him. And one so messed up he'd threatened her with serious physical harm.

Sitting down on the mat, she put her palm in the center of his back, the other on his hip. "Just keep breathing," she said, low. "No thought. Just breathe. Slow it all down."

He did, relaxing a little when he realized that would be the full extent of her aftercare. She wanted to remove the mask, stroke his hair, close both her arms around him. In short, she wanted to be a fool. It was time to put some distance between them.

She rose and changed positions, squatting before his face. Removing the scold harness freed his mouth to speak, but she left on the head mask to keep his vision limited to light and shadows. She didn't remove the clip between the wrist cuffs, though she did between his ankles. Attaching a fixed length of chain to one of the ankle cuffs, she ran the chain across the floor and around the pedestal of the bathroom sink. She adjusted the sturdy combination-locked clip to include both ankle cuff and attached chain, to keep him from removing either. He had enough slack on the chains from the ceiling to his wrists that he could lie down, stand up, or reach the bathroom. However, unless he did serious structural damage to her playroom, he couldn't get loose or reach the doorway to the hall.

She felt his eyes tracking her as she went to the cabinet and pulled out a blanket and pillow. When she returned, she set the bedding on the mat. Next, she went to the kitchen and came back with a bottle of cranberry juice. Though typically she had her subs drink it before sound play, a preventive measure against harmful bacteria, she sterilized her toys carefully and felt comfortable having him administer it afterward. She also brought him a bottle of water, and a couple protein and carb snacks.

"I'm headed to bed," she said. "There's a webcam and mic in here, so you can call out if there's a problem."

His jaw hardened, then relaxed. The reaction swept his body, giving it a weary slump. He was done fighting for tonight. "I can leave," he said. But he didn't try to get up.

She dropped to her heels before her naked and bound man, running her fingers over his lips. They moved as if they wanted to nuzzle or kiss her fingers, but he was still too zoned out to coordinate it. Even if she had been willing to let him leave, he'd be in no condition to drive right now.

"No. You stay here tonight. Rest. Sleep. No forward or back. Just here."

A little sigh left him, a heave of his considerable shoulders and broad chest, and he nodded.

"Yes, Mistress."

She smiled, though it cracked her heart. Not just the words. All of it. Before bedtime, she was treating herself to a hefty glass of wine.

She teased his throat beneath the edge of the head mask. "Tomorrow, I'll feed you breakfast and give you a shave before I kick you out. If you use the bathroom again, I expect you to leave things neat. You miss that bowl and I'll have you licking the floor around it clean."

Rising, she moved toward the door. As she did, she heard a painful chuckle and he mumbled something. She paused. "What was that?"

"I said you're a real nurturer, Lady Regina." He didn't sound unhappy about it, but thinking of how she'd really wanted to care for him, the observation turned screws tighter in her heart.

"I'm what you need, Marius," she said. "You might want to think about that before you try to throw it away again. Good night."

CHAPTER TEN

*H*e slept some. The pillow smelled like a not-unpleasant flowery herbal thing. As much as he'd liked a lot of things that had happened between them, he tried to push all of it out of his mind, because it would circle him back to the thing that he didn't want to think about. It didn't matter. It wouldn't leave him alone anyway.

When he'd had the chain around her neck, a screaming voice in his head had told him to do it, to keep going, finish it. Damn it, he'd resisted that, but all he'd wanted to do after that was get the hell out of here. It never occurred to him that she wouldn't be in complete agreement.

She'd acted like it wasn't a big deal, a guy threatening her life. And not because she was some twisted up, self-destructive bitch. She'd sounded in control the whole time. He knew he'd rattled her, and she'd admitted it. But she hadn't backed down. She'd defused him, backed *him* down. While that should piss him off, instead, the violence had drained out of him, leaving nothing. He slept on her floor like a stray dog grateful that she'd taken him in, no matter that he'd tried to bite her hand off when she fed him.

Stop thinking. Or give it up and think about better shit. Easier shit. Like her body against him, that unexpected move when she'd fucked him while he was hog-tied and on his side. God, that had felt like heaven. He kept waking up hard, just reimagining it. He needed to be back inside her, like now. Like an hour ago. Or maybe he never wanted to stop. Just wanted to stay inside her until he was hard again and keep doing the cycle, over and over again.

Was she watching him through the webcam, or was she asleep? What would it be like to sleep in her bedroom? He wouldn't need to be in her bed. He'd be fine on the floor, merely positioned where he could see her. Where he could guard the door. Guard her.

He pressed his face into the pillow. Who would protect her from him? Truth, she'd done a damn good job of that herself. But he was good at adapting. When that darkness rose again, he would know what to anticipate. He'd screwed with the other Mistresses until they kicked him loose, before that side of him could cause damage. He'd come close to it tonight, and next time he'd succeed.

If he wanted to protect her, he needed to end this himself. He would. He'd sleep, and have the breakfast she'd offered in the morning, because he didn't pass up free food. Then he'd be on his way, done with all this. Under the mask, he closed his eyes, increasing the darkness so he could imagine smelling her hair, her skin, nuzzling them. Holding her so close, her body moving against his, things spinning around them, a cocoon taking away everything else.

She'd come out of that cocoon a butterfly. What would he be? Was it better to come out as something terrible, or just as a caterpillar, failing to have transformed, unable to move on?

He'd fallen asleep. He drifted, vaguely and then completely aware of where he ended up as he opened his eyes and saw the basement of his childhood. Inhaled the scent of blood, and heard the cries start, his father's laughter, his demand that he obey. *Come here, shit for brains. Take it. Goddamn you, take the knife.*

The thud of blows, the aching pain, but that was okay. The cries stopped. He could beat Marius to death, as long as he never had to hear those cries again.

Marius started awake. He was a light sleeper, but he'd gone under much deeper here. Way deeper. Blinking, he realized the head mask was gone, as were his bindings. He was curled on the mat, the blanket he hadn't unfolded now over him. A steaming cup of coffee was near enough the smell had woken him, driving back the darkness of his dreams. A note was by the cup.

I'm doing my workout. Towels in guest bathroom. Also a fresh toothbrush.

Get a shower, then meet me in the kitchen for breakfast and the shave I promised.

He rose, finding himself stiff. That was normal, but typically it was from a night of fighting, not a workout with a Mistress, Siren's justified beating notwithstanding.

He folded the blanket and put it on one of her tables. His clothes, including his shirt, were there. The shirt had been mended and ironed, buttons back in place. All evidence of the things she'd used last night were gone, including the serviceable collar she'd strapped around his throat. He ran his hands over that spot, feeling its absence. He closed his eyes and tried to call up a memory of her removing it, her fingers slipping over his skin, then unlatching the cuff from his ankle. He couldn't tell if it was true memory or what he imagined, but he supposed it didn't matter.

Though he figured they were alone in the house, a compulsion for some type of shielding had him pulling on the jeans before picking up the rest of his clothes and stepping out into the hallway. She had a neat, well-ordered house with decorations that reflected her personality and made it a home. Things with bold colors and broad strokes. There was a set of wire frames hooked together in a puzzle design on the hallway wall. Family pictures, he guessed, from all the similar facial features to her own. Maybe parents, siblings, nieces and nephews.

When he looked behind him, the big hallway tree with a mirror startled him with his reflection. He looked like a guy who'd broken into her house, with his wary eyes and disheveled appearance. He ran a hand over his coarse jaw. Fuck, he should just go. But he could smell...cinnamon buns?

Yeah, he was a selfish shit. He'd eat her food, then take off. Irritable with himself and not sure what to do with it, he went into the bathroom. She'd left little sample shampoos and soaps with the fresh toothbrush. Did she entertain guys so often she was stocked like a Holiday Inn Express?

The growly thought was a little too uncomfortably possessive. The quick surge of relief he felt when he remembered her saying she'd done a lot of traveling before the community college job didn't make him less uneasy with himself.

Shoving anything away related to why he was having such an idiotic train of thought, he got into the shower. The hot water was sheer bliss and, though he knew he should keep it short, he had to indulge it. He soaped everything up good, though when the friction brought the scent of her climax to his nose, his hand slowed and gripped his cock. It had hardened instantly when his brain identified what he was inhaling. The memory of her pussy required that he stroke, and he did, for about half a minute, long enough for his breath to start catching, but then he stopped. He didn't jerk off in a Mistress's shower if she...if she hadn't said it was okay.

It wasn't a sub thing, he told himself. He wasn't thinking of her as *his* Mistress. He just owed her that courtesy.

Yeah, he was a twisted, screwed-up fuck. He needed to leave. Really, really, really needed to leave.

Finishing the shower, he toweled off fast and put on his clothes, which were still reasonably clean. He finger-combed his hair, brushed his teeth, and gave himself a look in the mirror. He wished she'd left him a razor. She was probably joking about shaving him herself. He wanted to look a little better for her than this. But it was all he could do.

He heard movement in the kitchen. That was where they'd come in last night, so he'd missed his margin for escape, unless he just told her he had to go and left it at that.

She'd let him go. He knew she would. She didn't overindulge in sentiment, but she was ruthless in her determination to have what she did want. It was a combination he wasn't used to handling.

If he was being brutally honest, he didn't want to leave yet. But lying to himself was his preferred coping mechanism, so he decided to stay because it wasn't worth the hassle of figuring out an escape strategy. Plus the cinnamon buns smelled really good.

When he reached the kitchen doorway, he had to pause to look at her. Take in as much as he could, another form of hunger, before she told him to stop staring.

She stood before the stove. She was wearing a sports bra and bike shorts. It wasn't a woman's most attractive look, everything held way too tight in his opinion. Her in his open shirt and nothing else... Thinking of it did odd things to him. Not just arousal, which was a given around her. It made him feel things that had him wishing she was wearing it now. He'd strip it off his back and give it to her.

Another part of him never wanted her to wear it again, since he didn't know what to do with that feeling.

The woman had a superb body, no question on that. Smooth muscle layers on her abdomen, biceps and thighs, but still feminine. A sheen of sweat limned her neck, her locs coiled in a thick twist above it. As his gaze went to the delicate column of her throat—because it was the part of her that always made him feel things he shouldn't feel but wanted to—things came to a full, bone-jarring stop.

He had no right to be looking at her. No right to her at all. The dark purple-red bruising, clearly marks left from links of chain, said so.

Yet his feet were moving. They took him to her, one step, one painful breath at a time. When he stopped beside her, he could tell she was aware of his presence, but she didn't seem tense or worried. That didn't erase what he'd done last night.

Eyes closing, he leaned forward and put his lips against them. Then stayed there, eyes closing. She made a quiet noise and turned her head, her lips brushing his cheek as she lifted her other hand to his jaw.

Forgiveness. She didn't have to say a word for him to feel it, because it was something he'd always wanted...and never deserved.

Pain ripped through his chest, down into his belly and made his balls draw up against him like a wild animal facing the crosshairs of a rifle. It startled him enough he snapped up straight and stepped back.

"I've got to go."

"I know," she said agreeably. "I have things to get done today. But first you're going to help me eat these cinnamon buns so they don't all end up on my ass, and I'm going to give you a shave. Sit down, shut up and eat. You burned off everything last night. You look gaunt."

She pointed him toward a table that had two black, green and white striped place settings. A sparkling pitcher of orange juice was surrounded by bacon, eggs, fresh cut fruit and granola.

His stomach gurgled, betraying his resolve.

When she turned back to the stove, he saw she was spreading cream cheese icing on the hot cinnamon buns. She tossed him another quick but distracted smile and set the case knife aside. As she lifted the tray with one hand and took it to the table, he noticed her holding the other hand out to her side, fingers upraised because they were dotted with icing. She probably intended to clean them off in the sink after she put down the platter.

He intercepted her.

What was going on with him this morning? He didn't know. There was no calculation to this, no ultimate objective, to bring her closer or push her away. He just wanted what he wanted.

He'd caught her by the waist, stopping her at the sink. As she lifted a quizzical brow, he brought her fingers to his mouth and began to suck the icing off of them. Her eyes got darker and more intent, and she moved closer. He gave way to prop himself against the counter and bring her between his knees, holding her waist with one hand. But when she took the lead, feeding him her fingers one by one, his hunger increased. His touch dropped to her ass as he followed her direction. He gripped her like he thought letting go of her would result in a fall.

She made a pleased little humming noise and leaned into him, her mound brushing his pelvis. She was allowing him to hold her and he felt...grateful.

Recalling himself, he straightened, but she'd already anticipated his retreat and eased back, tossing him a smile as she nudged him away from the sink. "Pretty good icing, right?" she asked, washing her hands. "I could eat a whole vat of it myself. Did it once and made myself completely sick. Now I avoid overindulgence in the things I find irresistible."

She gave him a pointed look and took a seat at the table, gesturing him into the other one before she spooned out a generous amount of eggs, fruit and bacon for herself. "Take as much as you want and don't hold back. I let myself have as much as I can pile on after a workout, but the rule is I can only have the one plate. And I use a mid-size plate." She winked. "The games we play with ourselves."

He slid into the chair and surveyed the food before him. At her encouraging nod, he admonished himself to pull his head out of his ass and get a grip on whatever the hell was going on with him. He put double bacon on his plate; no need to tell him twice to help himself.

As he loaded up, she watched him, eating her eggs in small, polite bites. "Ask me a question," she said at length.

He grunted, consuming food like a high-powered vacuum. "What do you want me to ask?"

"Something to start a conversation. You're practiced at getting a woman to talk about herself, so she'll think you're interested in her. Something should come to mind."

"I am interested in them," he said shortly. "I remember everything they tell me, and lots of stuff they don't but I pick up."

"Hmm." Her gaze became more thoughtful. "Like my attraction to lost souls?"

"Yeah." He bit into a cinnamon bun, and died a little death. He could hardly stop himself from shoveling in the eggs like a backhoe. He loved her voice, so he wished she'd just talk and not ask him to do so.

Fortunately, she seemed to pick up on that. She didn't ask him to talk again. Eating was serious business, so when he got a chance at a spread like this, he didn't like to split focus. Though he didn't mind that he was sharing the meal with a beautiful, hot Domme who smelled like clean sweat, cinnamon and sugar. And bacon.

As he scraped the last of the eggs from the bowl onto his plate, he realized the bacon was gone, and he'd mowed through half the cinnamon buns. She was still working on her first one, pulling the soft, fresh sweet bread into pieces to put them in her mouth, licking icing off her fingers after each bite and making him want to do that for her all over again.

However, her scrutiny distracted him. She'd been watching him closely.

"When was the last time you ate, Marius?" she asked.

"Last night. With you."

"I meant before that. I get the feeling you're used to feeding yourself on the cheap."

"It's not hard. McDonald's has a dollar menu." *Christ, shut up,* he told himself.

"You made money working security, and you make money on those fights, I hope. Where's your money going?" She leaned forward. "Marius, your only contact info is a Zone email account and a burner phone just for Tal. Where do you live?"

He pushed back from the table. "I got to go. I have to go."

"Nice grammar correction, but it's not the first time you've slipped. I know you're a rough man. That you have to work at it to sound educated. But you can do it, because you're also a smart man.

That's different from an educated man, but valued far less than it should be. I'd hire a smart man over an educated one any day."

She rose and went to the counter. "I'm giving you a shave. Then you can go."

"I'm going now."

"That would be poor manners for a full breakfast. Or are you scared to let a woman shave you?"

She pivoted and he saw she was holding a hunting knife. Perhaps five inches in length, the blade flashed, catching the overhead light over the kitchen table.

The look in her eyes was pure Mistress, and it did something to him, he couldn't deny it. He felt rooted to the chair.

"I'd think twice before letting anyone shave me with that," he said, to buy himself some time.

She grinned, and something loosened in his gut at the relaxed gesture. She was going to let the other topic go. For now.

"See? Smart man. But am I just anyone?" Setting the knife aside, she pulled off the sports bra, freeing her generous breasts. Beneath the sports bra, she had on a scrap of a bra that engaged the male senses far more provocatively. It seemed to be nothing more than a transparent, shimmering black mesh. She shimmied out of the exercise shorts, revealing a matching pair of panties which showed the cleft of her sex. Tiny red bows were at the strap on either hip, which he found absurdly sexy and delicate at once.

Picking up the knife again, she gestured. "Pull the chair back and straddle it, facing away from the table."

He swallowed. She had him, she knew it. If she'd kept it casual, just "fine, leave, and have a nice day," he would have left. But she'd shown him the knife and pulled out her Mistress side. She knew how to bait a hook. She was registering his triggers, learning how to stay a step ahead of him. That could get her hurt again, and he needed to go. Needed to go...

"Duncan." The edge of her voice cut into him like the physical blade. His lip twisted, an automatic reaction of rebellion and defense, but the rest of his body betrayed him, already turning to straddle the chair as she'd commanded. Her gaze slid along the denim creased over his thighs.

"See something you like, Mistress?" he said, trying to work up the energy for the taunt.

Her dark gaze lifted to his. "You're the one with a hard-on. Seems I should ask you that question."

He shifted his gaze to the wall before him without answering.

"Shirt off," she said. "I don't want to get it wet."

He removed and laid it aside. He wanted her to keep it anyway. Wanted to think of her wearing it like she had last night.

She brought a bar of soap and a bowl of warm water to the table. Putting the knife to the far side of them, she cleaned her hands, adding a froth of bubbles to the water, then dried her fingers on a towel. When she moved in front of him, everything inside went on alert, gravitating toward her. Her breasts, the nipples barely contained by the translucent fabric, were before his face. Her fingertips caressed his stubbled jaw, his chest. When he reached for her, this time she evaded his touch. "Just sit there, or I'll cuff you to the chair. Once I start this, don't talk or move unless I say so. Don't want to cut you by accident."

"How about on purpose?"

She pulled his face up with enough force to spark things in his lower belly and cock. "Maybe. We'll see."

He closed his eyes as her thigh brushed his. Moving behind him, she put a knee on the chair, against the seam of his ass and leaned into him. Gripping his throat anew, she tilted his head back. Her nearly bare body was brushing his, her breasts against his shoulder blades. But she hadn't started yet, and he wanted to ask a question.

"How did you figure out the Domme thing? That you liked being a Mistress, that is."

"Ah. I knew you'd eventually be curious about how I discovered my super power."

The dry quip surprised him into smiling. She saw it, her fingertips brushing the curve of his mouth before she started lathering the right side of his face with the soap. "High school. I was dating a football player. I was into sports myself. Basketball, track. Wanted to join the wrestling team and they didn't have one for girls, so I created my own and learned from watching the boys do it. The boys started coming to the matches because, well, girls wrestling."

Marius chuckled and she clucked. "Remember not to do that when I pick up the knife."

"Believe me, I won't be laughing then."

"Don't be a wimp. You'll be fine. I've only had a couple people bleed out when I did this, and it was before I learned how to properly sharpen a knife. That's the key to doing it right. Having a knife sharp enough for the job."

"Well, if it's only been a couple people..."

She tugged his hair. "Anyhow, the football player, Clarence, came to one of my matches. We started talking after it and then started dating. He was in line for full scholarships to major schools because he was a tank on the field. Unstoppable. But in the bedroom, it was a different story. He'd do all the right things, show me a good time, but I kept having this feeling something wasn't quite right. He didn't hook up with many girls, despite there always being a million after him. I'd heard that the rest of his teammates were getting nonstop pussy, and they teased him about saving himself for marriage, even though he wasn't a virgin. But he liked me, liked what he saw when I wrestled, the way I talked to him.

"So one night, just following an instinct I didn't yet fully understand, I told him to get on his knees, put his arms behind his back like they were tied, and go down on me. He turned into a freaking sexual beast." She paused, fondness in her voice. "It was like I'd unlocked something deep inside him. Taking away his control, making him subject to my commands, we both discovered a drug we couldn't get enough of. Didn't know shit about what we were doing, and so of course we had some near misses as we got deeper and deeper into it with each other."

Her lathering fingertips were a firm stroke that made his cock harder, but also had him closing his eyes just to enjoy the sensation. He didn't like the warm affection in her voice as she talked about the previous lover, though. Which was stupid. He tried to ignore it.

"He got his scholarship and I had other college plans, so the relationship went the way most relationships do between high school to college. But we've stayed in touch over the years. He went pro, did several years in the NFL and then became an assistant coach. He married a Domme he met out in a dungeon in California and they have two kids."

"All thanks to you."

"Not hardly, but I played a part. Don't be an ass because it bugs you that I'm talking about another man."

"I'm not," he said reflexively. She picked up the knife and gazed down at him, a faint smile on her mouth, though her eyes were serious.

"Yeah, you are. Possessive isn't a bad look for you, but keep the sarcasm on a leash. Now be still."

She gripped his jaw and he saw the blade in his peripheral vision as she brought it to his cheek. Her gaze was intent, her hold on his face firm and steady.

His eyes closed again, and not because he feared the blade. It did something to him, her holding him still and running that lethal blade so close to his jugular. He could hear his heart pounding in his ears, a slow thud. He realized her leg was pressed against his knee and he curved his hand around her thigh, needing more contact. He stroked her warm, firm skin, and thought about her pussy beneath the sheer panties, only a few inches above his touch.

He wouldn't go there, because it would be idiotic to try and arouse her when she had a knife to his throat. She also hadn't said he could touch her like that. She hadn't given him permission to touch her at all, but she hadn't rejected him sucking on her fingers or kissing her neck, and she wasn't objecting to how he was touching her now. She wasn't that kind of Mistress.

He'd studied her as hard as he'd studied any of them, but he'd done that to figure out advantages, weaknesses. Now he thought about it in terms of the things she liked. When out of scene, she didn't discourage physical affection from her subs, and seemed to enjoy it as much as they did. She was an unexpected combination of hardass Mistress and a softer Domme side.

She tipped his head up, holding his chin as she worked the blade over his jaw and upper neck, following it with her thumb to ensure she'd left it smooth. Then she turned to rinse off the clippings in the bowl of water. As she continued the cycle, he slid his arm farther around her thigh. When she finished and patted his face with a towel, he circled both her thighs, and pressed his mouth to her abdomen.

She threaded her hand through his hair, and he sighed, letting out a breath he hadn't realized he'd been holding. He didn't want to go forward or backward, think about his mistakes or missteps, how fucked up he was or what he needed to do to stay on guard against the whole world, and especially against all the flammable shit inside himself. He just wanted to be held in her arms.

He couldn't ask, because he had no right to do so, and he wouldn't know how to ask anyway. But she kept stroking his hair, and let him put his head there on her abdomen, her soft breasts brushing his crown. He had his arms coiled around her hips and upper thighs, the thin panties and her excellent ass.

She eased him back, but her hands moved to his forearms to maintain the connection between them. "Come," she said quietly. As she tugged him to his feet, she caressed his now smooth jaw critically. "Good. No missed spots."

Interlacing their fingers, she led him out of the kitchen and down the hall. They passed the guest bathroom. At the end of the corridor there were two doors, one closed and one open. The open one was the playroom. This time, he noted the mirrored hallway tree had a dried flower arrangement and some knickknacks on the two raised flat surfaces that framed it like miniature tables.

Regina drew him to the closed door and turned the knob. As she pushed it inward, uneasiness spiked in him. It was her bedroom. Through the doorway, he could view the clothes she'd worn last night, draped on an easy chair. A set of notebooks and a closed laptop were on the seat. The bed was unmade and inviting, lots of blue and green linens and pillows.

Her room, her life, separate or integrated into who she was as a Domme, it didn't matter. He couldn't go in there. It was like a vampire not being invited into a house, to protect the inhabitants. He wouldn't, couldn't bring what he was into an area where she might not have as many safeguards against something like him as she obviously did as a Domme.

He banded an arm around her waist from behind and pushed her up against the wall, next to the door, his erection grinding against her ass. "Here," he said hoarsely. "Right here."

He spun her around, seeing the dark flash of surprise in her gaze, and lifted her, putting his mouth to her budded nipple in the sheer, thin bra cup. She spoke, but he didn't hear her. He had his cock against her pussy and rubbed. The denim and sheer mesh could only delay—not deny—the build to climax he could give her from just the friction. He wanted inside her, wanted it badly, but he didn't want to take his hands from her to search for a condom. He wished he could be inside her without it, but he'd keep her safe this way, at least.

He was exciting her. Her breath was accelerating and she was pushing her core against him, her back arching so more of her breast was accessible to the heated wetness of his mouth, the sucking and nipping he was doing to it and the nipple. He had her. She was giving in to him.

No. Some part of him roared it. *Stop. Don't ruin this. Don't...*

But it was too late. She'd shown she was just like the others. He could get her off, and that was all he'd need to give her to remain in control. She was aware of the tide turning, however, because she'd started to push against his shoulders. She was telling him to let her go. He wouldn't. He couldn't.

He turned and brought them to the floor, holding her there with the weight of his body. She was strong, she knew how to defend herself, but he knew all that now, knew how to hold her down and keep her there. He wouldn't bruise her, but he wouldn't let her go. "Condom's in my pocket," he said. "Put it on me. I'm fucking you no matter what, so protected or not, that's your only choice."

She stared up at him. Somewhere in the twisted labyrinth of his mind, he knew she could do all sorts of things, whether or not he thought he had her pinned. Hell, when she put the condom on him, she could tear his dick off. She'd do it. It made him grin, in a demonic sort of way. He was fire and ice. Heart of ice, cock on fire, needing her pussy to ease everything.

He could see into her room from here so, as she reached for the condom and tore open the packet, he leaned over, caught the edge of the door and closed it with a decisive slam. Now he wouldn't have to see inside her life like that. Just two doors and a wall, the end of a hallway.

She opened his jeans, pushing the zipper and fabric out of her way to roll the condom on him and grip his cock. From the tightness of her hold, he thought he might be right about what she was going to do, but she released him to push his jeans off his hips and grip his ass in both hands. He tore through the mesh of the panties and plunged his fingers into her wet heat, savage pleasure twisting through him at her soft moan, the way she responded to his touch. Her dark, glittering eyes speared him to his worthless soul. She was letting him take her. Letting him have this.

"Fuck, you're everything," he muttered. "Beautiful tits and cunt, long legs, face of an angel, heart of a stone-cold bitch."

She didn't respond to that. She kept watching him with those angel eyes. Measuring, judging. He pulled his hand free and replaced it with his cock, thrusting into her with one hard shove that felt like heaven and hell combined. She was slick and hot. As he braced his hands on either side of her, he jostled the hallway tree. He heard something wobble above him and instinctively covered her face with his back and shoulders. The falling object bounced off him and shattered on the floor next to his braced hand. He saw it was the vase that had held the small dried flower arrangement, but he didn't care as long as the broken glass was clear of her body. Soon as it settled, he started thrusting, keeping his gaze fastened to her face.

She would come. He would make her come first. No way was he giving himself an orgasm before then. He wanted to feel her pussy ripple around him, the fullness of her clit, the sharp points of her nipples. He definitely wanted another taste of those. He ripped one cup free, shredding mesh, and curved his back over her like a beast to suckle. Hell, he wanted to spend a day of doing nothing but enjoying her gorgeous tits. Then another day for her ass. Maybe a week for her cunt and months for all the rest of her. Every inch of warm, brown skin with that faint luster like gold dust.

He braced himself back up on his arms and pumped into her, slowing down, watching her expression, every signal of her body that would tell him he was giving her pleasure. He could do that. He could give her physical pleasure, if she didn't ask for any of the rest of it.

"You're going to come when I say," he told her. "And it will be good."

She lifted her hand to his face. When he caught her wrist, he realized he was bleeding. The glass had cut his fingers, his palm. It didn't matter, but he couldn't put her hand back in the glass, so he put it against his side, molded his bloody palm to it so she knew to keep it there. Her breasts wobbled as he pushed in harder, deeper, pulled out, tried to balance between how much he needed to just rut on her and how much he wanted to give her pleasure. Stroke and stimulate, tease and drive her higher and higher. He wanted her to see stars and galaxies. That was what he could give her, if she'd just stop asking for anything else, like wanting to bring him into her fucking bedroom.

She squeezed down on him, and he caught the little set to her lush mouth. She was going to try and make him come first? Yeah, that wasn't happening, but oh Christ, she was good at that. Fuck...

She'd started to meet him thrust for thrust. Her eyes glittered, her hand lifting to grip his nape, a hold that centered him in an unexpected way. Last time she'd done it right before she'd cold-cocked him with her elbow, but that wasn't her intent now. She was doing it to hold that pinpoint laser focus between their gazes.

"My only choice, hmm?" she said breathlessly. "I told you last night, Marius. You don't fuck me. I fuck you. Serve me. Bring me pleasure. Work your fine ass off to satisfy me."

Just like that, she'd turned the tables on him. Her legs adjusted high on his back, clamping down. She stretched her arms up above her head like a queen waiting to be serviced, her lips in a half curve, her eyes heavy lidded. It pissed him off, made him harder and yet he wanted to please her. She was turning him into a fucking split personality, both sides vying for control of his mind. He focused on the easiest route.

He dug in, pressing his knees harder into the floor to give him better leverage and make every stroke count. Her nipples became harder, darker tips as she built toward climax. Her lips parted, her tongue touching them, her eyes closing then opening, chin lifting to expose her throat as she gave herself fully to what he was offering her. Her leg was silk under his hand as he gripped her thigh to add to his efforts. His cock was ready to spew, but he wouldn't...couldn't. He had to serve her first. She'd said so.

He knew she was seeing how long he could manage to hold out, her control intended to school him on just who had the reins. Sweat gathered in his back. He knew he was doing it right and she was wildly excited, just as close to climax as he was, but somehow she managed to revel in those feelings, balance on that precipice and prolong it even further while he moved inside her endlessly.

Somewhere along the way, he got caught in that same torrent, enraptured by the feel of it, her cunt squeezing down on him rhythmically, her heels tattooing against his ass and thighs, her soft words of encouragement and pleasure, praising him. He didn't remember when that started, but he was suddenly willing to work for her pleasure until his heart burst in his chest.

"Now, sweet boy," she whispered. "Together."

The climax was prolonged and intense, because they'd delayed and denied themselves. *She'd* made that happen. She'd taken back control. He groaned through the overwhelming sensations, closing his eyes in savage male bliss at her cries, the two of them together in a cyclone so powerful it was almost frightening. Like a roller coaster ride with no brakes, just a precipitous, open-ended fall into the unknown.

Her arms came down during the climax, hands gripping his back and then tearing into his flesh as she pulled him closer. He set his teeth to her shoulder, closing his eyes when he saw he was marking her beneath those other, earlier marks. She turned her face against his, not allowing him to get distracted by that, making him hold fast through the full, rocking experience. And when it finally ebbed, he was cradled in her arms, just as he'd imagined. But he was also holding her tight about the waist with one arm, the other braced so he didn't have his full weight on her.

"Fucking hell," he said against her skin.

"Mmm." She pressed her face against the side of his head. "You owe me a vase."

"Regina..." Had he ever said her name? He wasn't sure, but he didn't think he'd ever said it without the honorific of Lady in front of it. The familiarity startled him enough that it caught on his tongue.

She didn't notice his disquiet, because she'd noticed something else, something he'd realized some time ago. Her reaction to it was far different from his, though.

"Oh, Marius. Here, sit up slow. Pick your hand straight up off the floor."

He'd been vaguely aware of the burning sensation, his hand in the broken glass throughout the build-up to climax. His hand was a bloody mess, as was the floor, the shards glittering with crimson.

"It's okay," he told her absently. "Probably just some splinters and shit."

"Up," she said, easing him back so he'd sit on his heels. He pulled out of her body reluctantly, gratified to see her bite her bottom lip and hear a little moan catching in her throat at the friction. But as she started to lift herself up without using her hands, he realized the hazard the glass posed to her. She wasn't wearing shoes, her exercise shoes and socks neatly placed on the linoleum in the kitchen.

"Hey, don't move," he told her. Pulling up and fastening his jeans, he rose to his feet, bending to slide his arms beneath her. She shot him a bemused look and started on a halfhearted protest, likely bullshit about her being too heavy or maybe it conflicted with some independent woman feminist shit. He didn't care. She wasn't walking barefoot in glass, and he could carry her.

He lifted her free, moving a few steps back up the hallway where any scattered pieces wouldn't be a danger to her bare soles. She was a tall woman, so he had to turn so her feet wouldn't hit the wall, and he had to adjust his balance to distribute her weight a little better, but she wasn't difficult to carry. It seemed to bemuse the hell out of her, which was a plus since he couldn't seem to get anything past the damn woman.

Why that made him want to smile and helped that constant ache in his gut, he didn't really care to examine.

"Put me down, Tarzan," she instructed.

He did, but in the kitchen, where he was certain the glass couldn't have traveled. Regina pushed him into a chair and went to the sink, taking the shaving bowl and rinsing it out to refill it with water and bring it back. "Put your hand in that so we can get the blood off and see what's what. Don't move or I swear I will put my foot up your ass."

"Little soon after fucking for more foreplay."

She swatted him upside the head, a slap hard enough to make his ear ring, but she didn't seem to mean it with malice as she went back down the hallway, muttering about the stupidity of men. When she returned with a first aid kit, she'd donned a short, silken robe, loosely tied so he could see a good length of thigh when she moved. She'd removed the remains of her underwear, so it was all her beneath the clinging fabric.

Blood swirled in the water, turning it a pale crimson. When he lifted his hand out, he showed her what he'd suspected. "See? Just a few cuts on the fingers and one on my palm. A couple splinters I can get out later."

In answer, she produced a spot light from a utility closet and clamped it on the edge of the kitchen table before directing the light toward his hand. Then she donned a pair of reading glasses and lifted a pair of tweezers out of the first aid kit. "Which cuts have the splinters?"

She refused to be dissuaded, so for the next few minutes, he subsided and watched her concentrate on the task. His fingers were playing with the hem of her robe and touching her thigh. She glanced down at the contact, but didn't object.

Instead, she poured peroxide over his cuts. The burn was something he was used to feeling, so he didn't react to it beyond a brief tightening of his grip. She dried the wounds and wrapped three Band-Aids around his affected fingers. They were Snoopy Band-Aids, the famous beagle and his yellow bird pal cavorting across a cheerful blue background.

He closed his hand around them. He got lost in his head for several moments before he realized she'd dumped the water, rinsed the bowl and was setting it in the dish drainer. Turning, she leaned against the counter, her arms stretched out and braced to either side of her as she studied him.

Her face was so inscrutable; the tightness came back to his gut. It was better that way. He was used to that feeling. The rest just messed him up. He cleared his throat.

"Thanks for breakfast. I'll uh, head out now. I um..." He shrugged and rose, pushing the chair in and picking up his shirt. "I get it. I know this is it. And that's...well, I'm sorry if I acted... You're pretty damn awesome, Mistress. You deserve far better. I appreciate you trying."

He went to the playroom to retrieve his keys. Once there, he paused, thinking about it only a few seconds before he left the shirt. He was being a sentimental dumbass. She'd probably tear it up and use it for cleaning rags.

He lingered, thinking about what had happened in here last night, what had happened in the kitchen, the hallway. And before that, their date, her reaction to the concert. She'd laughed and smiled, and made him do the same, sometimes giving him a lightness of feeling that scared him.

It was the most thorough experience and connection with another human being he'd had in some time. The words he'd said to her just now were a pathetic thanks for that. But the best thing he could do was leave. As bad as things had gone this week, what would happen next week would make him even more of a menace to be around.

It was the event that had been building into dead weight on his gut for weeks, making it harder and harder to shake. He shouldn't be around anyone after it was done. Not for a while. Tyler's edict had been great timing, the hand of fate.

He came back up the hallway. She was still in the kitchen, her back to him as she did something at the counter. He should go straight to the door and keep going, but his feet took him right up behind her, a foot between them. He stared at her slim shoulders. She was a strong woman, yes, but he was a male fighter, and he saw all the signs of female fragility that he cherished, along with her strength. Slim shoulders, a graceful back, a delicate neck. She'd unbound her locs, so he could no longer see the marks he'd shamefully left on her, but he knew they were there. He wanted to press his lips there again, inhale her scent straight from heated flesh. But he didn't. He was about to backpedal for the door when she turned.

She handed him a paper bag. "The extra cinnamon rolls are in there, as well as a couple ham and cheese sandwiches. I don't have a guest room, but I have a pallet I'll put on the floor of my bedroom. You're not welcome in my bed without an invitation, but you can come sleep on that when you don't have a better place."

He stopped her, his hand closing over hers. His heart was hammering in his ears again, the floor dropping out beneath him. *Please don't trust me this much. Don't let her trust you this much.*

"I haven't earned that, Mistress."

"Good boy. Smart man. No. You haven't." She placed a hand on his face. This was a different kind of touch. Part Mistress and part something else, her eyes assessing and kind. "My sub may not have earned it, but you need a friend, Marius. Probably more than you need a Mistress. For the moment, you have both. But I'm no more gullible a friend than I am a Mistress. You watch your ass, or I'll kick it for you. If you're going to fight for money, I have no say on that. But fighting to get rid of demons is a dangerous road for you. Will you promise me not to do that?"

He didn't know how, and that inner anger raised its head, saying she had no fucking right to require that kind of promise from him. But it mattered that she cared, enough that he almost said yes. In the end, he stayed silent. She stroked his cheek.

"Asshole. Okay. I'll be in touch."

"I..." He shook his head, biting it back, but it came out anyway. "I've got to visit my dad, so I won't be around next week."

"Okay." She digested the unexpected turn of the conversation. "The college is on break next week, and I can shuffle some of my consulting projects. Want some company?"

The idea was so outlandish he choked on a harsh laugh before he could stifle it. And immediately panicked at the curious look in her eye, because it made him want to say yes. Hell, what better way to end this? Since he lacked the will to do it with words, he could drive her away—in a manner that wouldn't risk her life, but with something even she couldn't see coming.

She was right. He was a chickenshit.

"Yeah," he said. "Why the hell not?" Moving to the counter, he picked up a pen and wrote down the address on a pad there. She gave money to St. Jude's, because the pad had their logo on it, and a crayon drawing print of a girl, a dog and a bright sun, done by one of the sick kids, he supposed. "You'll have to meet me there, because it may take longer than you want to hang around."

She was giving him that scrutiny that said she sensed something wasn't as it seemed. It wouldn't matter. Not in a million years would she guess this. He felt sick. It was stupid.

In a day or so, when he had his head clear, he'd leave a note on her door, tell her not to come. Then he'd disappear. Maybe drive to the beach for a few days. It was warm enough to sleep in his car and hang out at the shore. It was quiet there. He might even pick up some work and stay awhile. Get hooked in to the Daytona Beach scene, though the BDSM community was close knit. Tyler would have already sent out word that he was bad news, nixing his reciprocal privileges that membership to The Zone had given him.

"Duncan." She must have said his other name a few times, because she spoke his given name emphatically, snapping him out of his head. Her hand had fallen on his arm. "Are you okay?"

"Yeah. Probably better if you don't come." He shook his head, stepped to the counter and ripped off the note, stuffing it in his pocket. "Definitely. We'll get together another time. Thanks for the food, Mistress. Thanks for everything. See you sometime."

Brave asshole that he was, he grabbed the care package she'd put together for him and fled.

CHAPTER ELEVEN

*A*fter she heard his car start up and pull out of the driveway, Regina dropped into her kitchen chair. The shakes she'd locked down broke loose, making her fingertips resting on the table surface tremble. What the hell was...all of that?

First, there'd been his transformation in the hallway. It had been so abrupt, the quiet sensuality in the kitchen suddenly replaced by a maelstrom. It was as if he'd viewed the door to her bedroom as the gateway to Hell.

A different kind of shudder gripped her as she closed her eyes and remembered how he'd pinned her to the floor. Pure alpha animal. He'd told her he would take her body without her express consent. Yet, belying that, in the very next second, he'd shielded her from the falling vase and obeyed her commands to take them both to an incredible climax. All while the glass ground into his flesh as if he couldn't feel it.

She'd navigated the dark maze in his mind, and brought them to a different place, but one neither of them had expected to be equally so intense. The man was exhausting, exhilarating...and a danger to himself.

She didn't kid herself. Being a correctional officer had taught her that overconfidence was a sure way to getting in trouble, but when she'd told him he needed a friend, his shields had dropped enough to show her that quick view into his soul once more. It was there, a light inside all those thorns. He wouldn't appreciate the analogy, but she really was starting to feel like the prince in Sleeping Beauty, hacking through the briar wall to reach the sleeping princess.

Her fingertips went to the bruises on her throat. At his core, he understood violence better than he understood tenderness, but he craved tenderness so much it was impossible to miss. Somewhere along the way, he'd learned to be charming and sexy, irresistible to women for his own purposes. But the reason it worked so well was, in his unguarded moments, he *was* that sexy and irresistible. How he'd touched her while she was shaving him, that questing caress, had conveyed that he wanted to give and receive pleasure, unselfishly. She could feel how much he enjoyed touching her, the feel of her skin, the press of her body. He desired her for himself, not just as a game or a competition.

The feeling was mutual. But fuck, what a mess the boy was. Last night when she'd left him on the playroom floor, she'd done a serious reality check. After brushing her teeth and getting ready for bed, she'd taken out that scary moment and given it a close, hard look. How she'd handled it, how he'd reacted on the front and back end.

She knew a lot of women would have ended it right there. Hell, if they'd understood half of what she had known last night, they wouldn't have risked bringing him home for a scene.

She didn't consider herself stupid or reckless. But she did have a different well of experience from which to draw. She'd done extreme interrogation scenes where the sub had completely lost it, been a risk to himself or her. At the prison, she'd routinely handled violent offenders. Both those things were why she'd taken the incident in stride and not freaked out. She'd slept well, even though she'd woken with her fingertips stroking the marks on her throat, a subconscious way to soothe the early morning uneasy feelings chasing her out of dreams.

Everyone, even someone who grew up in Sunshine Suburbs with Suzy Perfect Parents, could be goaded toward their animal nature, though it took extreme circumstances. Some people's triggers for uncivilized behavior were far closer to the surface. It didn't take a Domme with her intuition to know where Marius fell on that spectrum.

Yes, she had experience with violent males. But she didn't have experience with violent males with whom she was sexually and emotionally involved. Since she *was* a smart woman, she knew she needed perspective, and she needed it badly. Regina needed a Dominant who'd dealt with a soul as damaged as Marius.

Tyler? He'd react with typical male overprotectiveness. Much as she respected and admired the man, after the mine field she'd just navigated, she didn't feel like cutting a swathe through the testosterone. If he'd been dealing with what she had last night, he wouldn't have backed down or cut Marius loose, either. Alpha male thinking was to confront and overcome a problem, not retreat. But it was hard for an alpha male like Tyler to realize an alpha female saw a volatile problem the same way. A smile touched her lips. Though perhaps being married to Marguerite had adjusted his thinking on it.

Still, she realized she'd prefer to talk to a woman, one more like herself. Ah. The obvious light dawned. Regina knew exactly the right woman, one who'd dealt with a damaged male and successfully brought him out of the darkness. And she had a ruthlessness akin to Regina's own. She picked up her cell and sent a text.

Need the face-to-face opinion of a heartless bitch. Have some time?
For you? Always. I'm at work. Stop by anytime this morning.

The Growing Things Nursery was both residence and business. When Regina bumped up the gravel road, she paused at the fork between the company parking lot and the driveway to the house. Lyda's home was a 1920s clapboard farmhouse, her nursery contained on the acreage behind it and within several large greenhouses.

Since she'd said she was at work, that meant the greenhouses, so Regina turned toward the parking lot. It was populated by several company vehicles, including a flatbed loader, a couple pickup trucks, a bobcat and a small dump truck painted M&M green with yellow daisies under the Growing Things logo. Everything that belonged to Lyda was well-tended, from plants to equipment. And submissives.

Regina's attention went to the man currently loading bags of mulch into the back of a pickup truck. His long hair was tied in a tail that fell down his tattooed back. Stripped to nothing but a pair of faded jeans that hung low on his hips, he had a tanned muscularity and lean appeal sure to catch a woman's eye. Plus an ass that just screamed to be squeezed, strapped, marked...the list was endless.

As she parked her car and propped her elbow on her open window, she indulged in a long, enjoyable look. It wasn't hard to imagine what he could do on his knees with his clever mouth, which Regina happened to know contained a tongue stud with versatile uses. While she was aware of approaching footsteps, she didn't stop her perusal.

"Enjoying the view, bitch?"

"Absolutely," Regina said. "You're interrupting a good fantasy. It'd be selfish of you to begrudge me that, since you have two of what I have none."

"That's because I am so much Mistress, it takes two amazing people to satisfy all my needs."

Regina chuckled and pulled her gaze away from Noah to give Lyda a friendly look. The nursery owner was in jeans, work shoes, and a baby doll T-shirt that showed off her fit body. Beneath her cap, the gold highlights of her dark red braided hair glinted from the sun. She had gray eyes like Marius, only Lyda's were gunmetal where his were that slate-to-silver color. Plus he had those dark, expressive brows and thick lashes. Lyda's lashes matched her hair and brows, the same golden-red color against her milk-white skin that refused to tan, despite her outdoor job.

"So is this a flyby, or you want to go inside the greenhouse and talk to me while I work?" the Domme asked.

"Let's do that." Regina emerged from the car. Since the day was warm, she'd worn a vee neck T-shirt over jeans herself. Lyda enjoyed both men and women—pretty obvious since her two subs were one of each gender—so Regina took it as a compliment when she gave her a frank appraisal. Back when she was in her twenties, Regina had competed in fitness competitions. Lyda's intense workout classes three times a week were a barometer for how well she was keeping herself in shape.

She supposed she owed the woman a silent thanks for that, because physical strength had played a role in her handling of Marius, more than once now, though she had no illusions that she could do that indefinitely. She'd had the element of surprise, both times.

Lyda stopped her with a hand on her arm, eyes suddenly far more serious. She touched the bruising on Regina's neck. "Is that what it looks like?"

"Only if it looks like a sub tried to choke me with the chains I put on him."

Lyda scowled. "Marius. I'd heard Tyler kicked his ass out. Apparently about fucking time."

"This happened after that. That's what I'm here to talk about. He's become my project." Regina took a breath. If she wanted good information, she couldn't bullshit. "I came to you because I didn't want to deal with the testosterone display I'd have to handle with Tyler about it, some lecture about getting in over my head in a situation he would have handled in exactly the same damn way. Am I in the wrong place? Did you have an operation I don't know about?"

Lyda's eyes narrowed. "You think only men can be protective?"

Regina snorted. "No. But we don't transform into cavewomen over it and become entirely unreasonable. And this is about helping someone damaged figure out the best path to healing." Regina's attention shifted meaningfully to Noah. "Which sometimes means doing some things that look wrong from the outside but are the right course."

Lyda snorted. "Using my own history against me?"

"Nope. Just proving a point. You think I'd let a man abuse me? I'm far more likely to carve off his testicles with a grapefruit spoon. I keep one in a kitchen drawer, just in case. I don't even like grapefruit."

Lyda's expression eased, her sensual lips curving ruefully. "Point taken."

Noah had at last noticed their presence, and lifted a hand in greeting, but kept working as the women made their way to the greenhouse. Regina studied him. "He's pretty deep in his head for a guy not even listening to an iPod. I could have come up behind him and groped his fine ass before he saw me coming."

"After which I would have shoved a planting stake up *your* fine ass," Lyda observed.

Regina snorted. "Think you're so bad. Poor guy. Are you one of those strict employers who doesn't let their employees listen to music while doing tedious manual labor?"

Lyda shook her head. "I'm strict, but that's not why. He doesn't handle electronic noise well. TV, music players, even radio in the truck. He gets twitchy and irritable. He's better with nature and quiet. So I forbid it, except when he's watching TV or a movie with me or Gen, in limited blocks."

The interesting tidbit reinforced why Regina was here. Lyda had had her own challenges with Noah. The strong bonds and contentment that emanated between them like an ever-present energy field said they'd surmounted them.

"Where's Gen today?" Regina asked.

"She's running some errands and then I told her to take the afternoon off to do some girl shopping with Chloe. Not sure how I ran the administrative side of this place half as well without her help, but I have to make her take some time for herself now and again."

"Says her workaholic boss and Mistress."

"Yeah, but I'm different." Lyda winked. "Before you ask why, I'll tell you the same thing I tell her. Because I said so."

"Ah. The universal response of parents, workaholics and Doms of either gender." Lyda had the greenhouse doors rolled open to allow in the breeze coming off the fields behind it. It reduced the normal humidity inside the enclosed space. At Lyda's gesture, Regina took a seat on a stool. When Lyda started digging into an open bag of soil and scooping the contents into flats, the motion sent a pleasant aroma of moist earth and green things her way.

Regina needed a couple moments to gather her thoughts, and Lyda apparently picked up on that. The woman finished filling the flats and stripped off her work gloves to handle the fragile plants she was transplanting. It revealed her slim, elegant hands, which could wield a single tail whip with fascinating precision.

Ironically, Noah was even more expert with it than his Mistress, so much so that Lyda sometimes loaned his skills to another Domme. Never with sex attached, however. Since Gen had come into their lives, Lyda and Noah's attentions usually were focused on her. Or Gen and Lyda's on Noah. Lyda was the head bitch in charge, but Noah was more than capable of topping Gen in very intriguing ways, under Lyda's direction. On other delightful occasions, she turned those tables and she and Gen topped Noah together.

"It's not bad to have employees you can play with at the end of the day," Regina observed. "And wake up with in the morning."

"It doesn't suck," Lyda agreed, a smile softening her sharply sculpted features. "Started the day by pushing my rabbit down between my legs and putting her to work first thing. Gen's got a lovely, lovely mouth. Made Noah fuck her while she was doing it, so I watched the two of them with the sunrise coming through the window. Came twice before I let them finally go over. Day can't start better than that."

Regina thought of shaving Marius at her table. He'd been so still under her hand, his attention riveted on her. "Yeah. You got that right."

"Hmm. No comment about me rubbing it in, so you must have started the day well yourself. Before things went to shit."

"They didn't go to shit. We had some ups and downs this morning, but left it on a good note. Sort of." She frowned, thinking of his weird behavior about meeting his father. He'd ripped up the note, but she'd looked at the pad and found the impression of the address still on the sheet below it. She'd traced it in, so she could join him if she damn well wanted to do so.

The address was Raiford, Florida, nearly three hours from Tampa. Maybe that was why he'd decided it was stupid. But during that blink of time between when he'd asked her to go then decided against it, she'd picked up a mix of desperation, resignation, and a longing that seemed like a desire not to leave her house at all.

"Going to sit there and run over everything in your head, or use your words? I'm pretty good at reading subs' minds, but Dommes are a little harder," Lyda said. "Not impossible, but I'm working here and don't want to pull a muscle. Spill."

Regina rolled her eyes but proceeded. She gave Lyda the full rundown on the situation, and the tactics she'd employed thus far, including the "normal date." She always liked talking shop with another experienced Domme. It cut out the need for a lot of explanation, since Lyda picked up on the nuances and strategies quickly.

She was only halfway through transplanting the plants when Regina concluded. Despite her concise delivery, Regina had dredged up more emotions than she'd expected, especially when she offered full disclosure on both the chain incident and what had happened in the hallway. She realized her hands were a little shaky and moving too much, and placed them on her knees, gripping there until she finished.

Lyda picked up a two-way radio and pressed a button. A second later it beeped and Regina heard Noah's voice. "Yes, Mistress?"

"Come to the greenhouse."

Lyda studied one plant critically and readjusted it. Apparently the slender stem hadn't been as straight as she'd wanted.

"What will they be?" Regina ventured. She knew the other Mistress was thinking and would give her opinion once she'd chewed over Regina's words.

"Tomatoes." Lyda stepped over to Regina, holding up her palm so she could sniff. The aroma of tomato plant leaves made Regina think of lazy summer days in her childhood backyard. Her mother still gardened at her assisted living community in Florida. Regina visited her frequently.

What would her mom think of Marius? Since hitting her thirties, Regina hadn't brought a man home, such that her mother had once asked her flat out if she was a lesbian. *"If you are, honey, that's okay. You've always been so sure of yourself. Scares most men off, but if they can't handle a strong woman, that's their loss. I just want you to be happy. If you find yourself someone special, I want to meet them."*

She'd never brought one home because she didn't keep them. Not long enough to justify an introduction to the family. But she was starting to get in so deep with Marius, she wasn't sure if she was going to be able to climb out of that hole so easily this time.

Sure, Mom. I'll bring him to meet you. Soon as I'm sure he's housetrained enough you don't have to lock up the breakables.

"How can I help you ladies?" Noah took the two steps up into the greenhouse in one stride. Sadly, he'd put on his Growing Things Nursery T-shirt, but he was still a welcome sight.

Lyda nodded toward Regina, her gaze still on her task. "She needs one of your hugs. The kind that Gen talks about."

Regina sent her a surprised look. The woman's shrewd eyes glinted with amusement. "Trust me. It's a gift. Dommes need aftercare, too. You forgot that, and it shows."

"I didn't forget," Regina grumbled. "Just had other priorities at the time."

"Well, you have time now." Lyda turned her attention back to her plants, considering the matter settled.

Noah was one of those remarkable submissives, so comfortable in the role he rarely broke out of it. He was Lyda's in every way, and watched over her and Gen with all the protectiveness that Tyler demonstrated on the Dom side of the fence. But there was a gentle beta quality to Noah, an energy to him that cocooned her as he drew closer. Even without touching her, he projected what Lyda was offering. And since the damn bitch was right, Regina gave him a nod, telling him it was okay. He closed the distance between them and slid strong arms around her.

In a seamless blink, she was immersed in that energy, held with a mental and physical strength that felt tireless, endlessly patient. The embrace came with no expectations except to give her comfort and a sense of reassurance, safety, steadiness. He'd keep doing it, with the same total focus and care, concentrated in the peaceful strokes over her back and arms, until she or his Mistress said stop.

Lyda was right. She hadn't realized how much she needed it until it was happening. Regina had invested herself deeply in Marius, and last night's encounter would have hit max red zone on anyone's stress meter. But she was such a powerhouse of Type A and get-it-done, she rarely noticed such a drain until it hit her in the face like a brick wall. This was a much nicer way to become aware of it, and replenish that energy.

She took a deep breath, inhaling a welcome combination of sweaty male and earth, and let her head rest on his shoulder. In time, she slid her arms around him to give him some of the same energy back as thanks. His body was solid, a lot of firm muscle, all the best of what the human male animal was supposed to be.

"Grab his ass and I will cut your hands off at the wrists."

With her usual insight, Lyda knew exactly when Regina had what she needed and the melding of spirits could separate into two people again. Regina smiled at Noah as he stepped back, sliding his hands down her arms with affection. She noted he assessed her state much as Lyda had. While it was from a different perspective, he didn't miss the marks either.

"Anybody I need to kill?" he asked lightly, though his eyes said he wasn't joking.

"Maybe Marius," his Mistress responded, taking a seat on another stool while she sipped from a bottle of water. "But we'll see. He's a work-in-progress."

Noah's fingertips touched Regina's neck, a gentle and unsanctioned contact, but the concern in his eyes eliminated those boundaries and made it allowable. "Hmm."

Lyda arched a brow. "Some thoughts about him you want to share, Noah?"

"He's messed up. More than usual if he did this. Normally, if you stay within his boundaries, he gives a hundred percent."

The dual stare from two formidable Mistresses, apparently warned Noah that his words had sounded like an admonishment. Regina bit back a smile as he spread out his hands in a placating gesture. "I didn't mean that you should have stayed in those boundaries. I meant that he used to give a hundred percent within them. He's changed."

Regina lifted a shoulder. "His boundaries played it safe, kept him from being the sub he really wants to be. The strain of that is starting to collapse inward on him. I want to change that."

Noah glanced toward his Mistress. "Must be a thing with uber-Dommes."

"Any complaints?" Lyda asked, a gleam in her eye.

"No, Mistress," he said, and dropped to one knee beside her, touching the leg of her jeans. "But it's not playing it safe."

"Safe is boring."

A smile touched his lips. Noah shifted his gaze back to Regina.

"Marius is the kind of friend who'd help move a couch or give someone a ride across the state to visit their sick mom," he added. "Without asking for anything in return. But sometimes I think that's because he doesn't want anyone to have a road inside of him, and letting people help you does that."

Lyda slid the tail of his thick hair through her fingers, tugging. He glanced up at her, a rueful look crossing his face, then brought his attention to Regina again.

"He's been interested in you for some time, Lady Regina. But it wasn't until about eight months ago he asked me about you. I think he wanted to see if I knew more than what he'd picked up from watching you before then."

Well, didn't that just make her pulse flutter?

Lyda dipped inside the collar of Noah's T-shirt to caress damp flesh. "Did I tell you that you could put your shirt back on?" she asked.

"No, Mistress." Staying on his knees, he stripped the garment off with a pleasurable flow of rippling muscle, folded it and handed it to her. Lyda set it next to the flat of plants. "Though I didn't want to get Lady Regina's clothes damp from my sweat," he offered politely.

"A courteous thought, but hindsight, since you didn't know you'd be hugging her. You were anticipating, being modest with what belongs to me. You know I've gotten irritable when some of our customers enjoy looking at you too much."

"Yes." His gaze swept down, a light smile on his firm lips. "My Mistress isn't always in a sharing mood."

Regina grinned as Lyda shot her an oh-shut-up face.

"And who could blame her?" Regina said. "If it's all right with your Mistress, I'd like to know what you told Marius, Noah. When he asked about me."

Noah's body gravitated toward his Mistress as she stroked his bare shoulder, a tacit approval for him to speak. "Not in these exact words, but I warned him if he tried to fuck with your head, you'd grind him into hamburger. That you didn't give an inch in letting a sub play with your emotions. I've never seen you lose control of a scene or not stay a couple steps ahead of your submissives. Ever."

Pleased by the compliment and, because she knew Lyda would be okay with it, Regina leaned forward and squeezed Noah's other shoulder. Lyda dipped down to brush her lips over Noah's while cradling his jaw. His sun-browned hand rose and closed gently over her wrist, stroking her knuckles.

His attitude toward Regina was respectful and affectionate. What shone from the dark brown irises he fixed upon Lyda was adoration. Love. He saw Lyda's dark and light corners, and embraced all of them, as she had his.

Seeing it, Regina ached, and that ache conjured a series of pictures in her mind of Marius. She missed him. Maybe she should have kept him chained in her playroom.

"That'll be all, Noah," Lyda said. "Get back to work."

"Sure thing, Mistress." He grinned at her, teasing her knee with long fingers before obeying, earning a swat. The two women watched him jump the two steps back to the ground and stride back toward the truck.

228

"He's a treasure," Regina observed. "I should have groped his ass. You wouldn't have cut off my hands."

"Try me," Lyda said dryly. "So, feel better?"

"I do." Regina tossed her an amused look. "I'd keep him around for the hugs alone. The great ass, energetic cock and irresistible banquet of submissive traits are just bonuses."

Lyda took another swallow of water, studying her. "I think you were wrong, what you said earlier about me having two of what you have none. I think you do have a sub."

"Yeah, maybe." Regina sobered. "You're my sanity check, Lyda. Anything sending up flags?"

"Oh, hell yeah. But they're the same flags you're seeing clearly enough." Lyda shook her head. "You're one of the steadiest, strongest and most responsible Dommes I know. You're also a balanced, independent woman with no self-esteem issues, a freaking miracle in this world. You don't let anyone fuck with your compass. If it tells you that you're on the right track, I have to believe you are. Though I admit, I'm worried about you. And ticked at him for screwing with what could be the best thing that ever happened to him."

Having two of the Dommes she most respected give her an almost identical vote of confidence bolstered her as much as Noah's hug. Lyda wiped her hands on a towel and rose to stand before Regina, surprising her when she gripped both Regina's hands. Lyda didn't normally indulge sentimental gestures, any more than Marguerite did.

"I'm also pissed at him for hurting my friend and upsetting her," the woman added.

Regina shook her head. "You know I'll be fine. All part of the process. It's hard to break me."

"Yes, it is. Impossible. But scars are a different matter." She touched Regina's neck and stroked the bruising, a caress that conveyed her awareness of a woman's sexual potential as well as comfort. "If there's anything I'd ping you about, it was taking him home last night without a spotter. That's where your emotions took the upper hand on your good sense. You knew better."

"Yeah, I did. But sometimes you take a chance on the emotions. I got my foot in the door, Lyda. Booby-trapped and damn heavy as it was, I got in."

Lyda pursed her attractive lips. "I know the rush of that. But next time he puts a finger on you that you haven't sanctioned, you put his ass down, hard. You make it clear you have a zero-tolerance policy for that bullshit."

"Yes, ma'am," Regina said soberly, then let a smile break through. "I did that, both times. Whereas you just think you're a badass, I actually *am* one. I might even be enough Mistress to need two subs one day. If you ever get tired of Noah."

"Yeah. Said no woman ever." Lyda let her own smile show, a baring of fangs.

"Well, he's safe from me for now. Marius is two handfuls."

"It's more than that. You're a one-sub woman. I know you've been keeping an eye out for the right one, on that subconscious level that sends up an alarm when a potential candidate comes along. And Marius is ringing all those bells."

"Yeah. Hell of a bell ringer."

Lyda chuckled. "It's never easy when it's worth it. But it's been a long time coming. I hope he doesn't break your heart."

"You and me both. But I've had my heart broken before. It mends." Regina recaptured one of Lyda's elegant hands and laced fingers with the other Domme, indulging in a flirty rock back and forth of contact. "And now I know where to go to get the kind of hugs and friends that help with that."

❧

When she left Lyda's, she saw she had a message from Tyler. *Call me.*

Frowning, she dialed his cell and turned out onto the rural highway leading away from Lyda's corner of the world. "Were your ears burning?" she asked when he answered. "Lyda and I were just talking about your overabundance of testosterone."

"I count myself fortunate not to be present for any discussion between two Dommes that involve my testicles." He chuckled. The sound eased her mind about the purpose of his call, though that reaction reversed course when he got right to his reason for calling.

"Thanks to some of the fallout on this thing with Siren, I had to do some more digging on Marius, but you can't share the info with anyone else, even him. It came from a sealed juvie file and I don't want my source's ass in the fire. Can you agree to that?"

"If you think I need to hear it, of course." Anticipating the gravity of what he had, she pulled into a convenience store and parked facing a field. Her attention was caught by a cluster of starlings swooping in formation amid the long grasses. She made herself loosen her grip on the wheel.

"He was arrested on nine counts of animal cruelty when he was eleven."

"What?" Based on what she knew of him thus far, she'd been expecting an assault charge. Her mind darted through possibilities as quickly as the starlings' movements. She didn't want an answer to her next question, but she asked it. "What did he do to them?"

"The police report said they were mutilated, likely tortured to death. They caught him burying one of the bodies, and dug up eight others in the same location. Cats and kittens mostly. A couple dogs."

His voice had gotten tight as he relayed the information. She understood why. On one thing, Tyler wasn't hard to read. How seriously he took his responsibility to protect those who were his.

"No. It doesn't make sense." She shook her head. "What he did to Siren and the others...he didn't lift a finger against them. It was vicious mindfucking, yes, but still mindfucking. He didn't physically hurt anyone."

He fought other fully grown men for money, and to spill off aggression with likeminded parties. She'd tripped his triggers, such that things had become a little crazy during an intense session. Both of those things, no matter how inadvisable or over the top, were a far cry from goddamn hurting a puppy. The man who'd shielded her face from a falling vase and carried her out of the hallway to protect her feet from broken glass didn't have that in him.

"Did he plead guilty to it?" she asked.

"According to the report, he was mute through the entire process. The court attorney assigned to him got him mandatory counseling sessions and community service. The counselor reports say he did the same thing for the first couple sessions. Nothing. Not a word. Then he spouted all the usual teenage rhetoric. How he often felt different, frustrated by his differences, and he felt really badly about the animals and wanted to do better."

"He started learning how to use the charm early."

"Yeah. They cut him loose. Nothing after that point."

A headache was starting, stabbing behind her eyes like tiny daggers. "Tyler, I promise you, it's wrong. I don't know what happened, or why, but it doesn't fit. You have nothing to feel guilty about, hiring him for The Zone. The file was sealed, anyway."

"Yeah." He sighed. "My source had to relay it to me from memory, so I couldn't get any details on parentage or other clues. Maybe the answer's there."

"So you believe me?"

"Yes." And the more relaxed tone in his voice confirmed it, though she remembered Marguerite's gentle teasing about his God complex and knew he'd probably still rake himself over the coals for it. "My source agreed with you, which also helps," he continued. "She thought whoever harmed the animals had all the marks of a serial killer in training. Marius is good at masking, but not that good. And he's smart, but he's not a genius. I can anticipate and outthink him, and so can you."

Yes. But he still could surprise her. And had, several times, in both tender and sensual ways. "Okay. Thanks for the info. It may not have a matching piece in the puzzle yet, but it's another piece, and that's something."

"How's it going? Or would you prefer not to share yet?"

"Well, he invited me to meet his dad. Then promptly rescinded the invitation. Probably because his dad lives up in Raiford. But I'm thinking of taking a couple days off and going." Especially now.

"Raiford?" Tyler's tone sharpened. "That's where Florida State Prison is. The town would pretty much disappear if it wasn't there."

Eleven years old... The picture that formed in her mind was ugly, which summoned Marguerite's words about his childhood. *It's a place that holds no safety for him.*

"Okay." Her nails drummed the steering wheel. Tap, tap, tap. Tap, tap, tap. "Since we're violating his privacy, I have another question about him. Where does he live, Tyler?"

"I can give you the last address we had on file. He's moved several times in recent months. When Alex told me Marius was living at a Salvation Army men's shelter, I offered to help him find a better place to live, but around that time, he told me he'd found a new place. That's where he is now, far as I know. A basement room rented by a woman supplementing her social security."

"Care to share that address?"

"Thought you'd never ask." After he gave it to her, he paused. It made her smile a little, knowing what was coming and hearing it in the same breath. "You being safe, Mistress?"

"Not entirely. He'll only hurt me in the ways I allow to happen, though. Trust me."

"I do. But I also know you. Have you talked to Lyda?"

"Are you freaking psychic?"

He chuckled, a warm, masculine sound. "Sometimes, according to Marguerite. Glad to hear you ladies touched base. Let me know if you need my help in any way."

"You know it. And same to you." The BDSM community was tight-knit and supportive. One of the many things she liked about it.

Learning the flavor and shape of a new sub had always been another favorite part of her life in the BDSM world. With Marius, it had gone beyond that. She didn't want just those elements. She wanted the very soul of why he was as he was. She wanted to bring that soul into her service.

She just hoped she was prepared to handle what the core problem was and turn it into something that would work, for her and Marius both.

"Duncan's not there. He's gone for the next few days."

At the sound of a reedy voice, Regina looked up the concrete steps that had brought her from street level to the basement apartment door. At the top of a second set of stairs, the ones to the stoop of the house's front porch, a desiccated-looking black woman stood in a lavender house coat and fleecy thick knee socks. Her steel wool hair was tucked beneath a shower cap.

"Oh. Thank you. Are you his landlady?"

"I am. Volula Jones. He's not in any trouble, is he? I know they always say this kind of thing, but Duncan is a very good boy. A sweet boy. Does all sorts of things here I never asked him to do. Brings in my mail, rolls out the trash, keeps the hedges trimmed. Even does repairs. He keeps to himself, doesn't bring in any loud friends or loose women."

Her wrinkled expression creased even more deeply as she looked Regina up and down. "He's a good boy, but you look way out of his league, honey."

"That may be true, but the best players always start in the minors, don't they?" Regina smiled up at her when the woman cackled. "Do you know when he'll be back?"

"He didn't say. Which is kind of strange for him. He usually lets me know. Just said he had to go out of town for a few days and might be a little while coming back. Left me money for this month's rent, though, so I'm sure he'll be back before the next payment's due. He's never been late."

A rippling of the housecoat hem heralded the appearance of two cats, one black and one calico. They peered at Regina curiously before the calico started winding between the woman's legs and her cane. The black one moved down several steps to sit and wash his paws.

"That's Orlando and this here is Patches," the woman said. "They're friendly. Even though they've never taken to Duncan. Give him a wide berth, and he seems almost afraid of them. Says he doesn't mind them, but I can tell they make him so uncomfortable."

She offered a grimace laced with fond puzzlement. "About the only thing I can't ask him to do is take care of them when I go see my brother up in Gainesville. He says, 'I'm so sorry, Miss Volula. I can't take care of pets. Ask me anything else to help out, and I will.' And he does, so that's a small thing. Long as he's not mean to them, and he never is. They just stay out of each other's way. It's odd. So many good things about that boy, except that."

As Regina came up the stairs, Orlando obligingly bumped her hand to be stroked by her long nails, then started winding around Regina's legs. "Ah, look at that. He took right to you. He's been neutered for a long time, but he still appreciates a fine-looking woman."

Volula laughed at her own joke before turning to spit an impressive stream of tobacco over the edge of the stoop and cough. She had a spit bottle in her hand, but Regina supposed she didn't think it necessary to use it outside. "It's about time for Judge Judy, honey. You need me to leave a message for Duncan? He doesn't have a phone."

"You can tell him Regina came looking for him, but I expect I'll find him before then."

"Hope you do. You seem nice. He deserves something nice, I think. Such a good boy. Awfully good body, too. Can keep even an old crone like me thinking sinful thoughts."

With another wink and cackle, Volula shuffled back into her house, Orlando trotting up the stairs and following her, slipping past the threshold a breath before she closed the door. Patches remained lying on the stoop, giving her an indifferent look before turning her face up to bask in the sun.

Smiling, Regina returned to the sidewalk. As she moved along it toward her car, she paused. There were several narrow windows that provided a view to the basement room. Taking the chance Miss Volula would wonder if she was snooping, Regina squatted next to one, peering inside since there were no curtains.

She saw a bed, a chair. An older model TV, not a flat screen. Some books piled up on the chair next to the bed. Small fridge and possibly a microwave in a kitchenette set-up, but that was about all she could discern through the dirty glass and security bars. She wondered what kind of books he read.

She wondered, period. A day of data gathering had resulted in more questions than answers.

Well, she knew who could answer them. It looked like she was going to Raiford next week.

CHAPTER TWELVE

*S*ure enough, the address he'd left imprinted on her note pad was Florida State Prison. Since inmate visitation was approved by 30-day advance application, it left her wondering if she was wrong in thinking his father was an inmate. Marius wouldn't have invited her to visit his dad, only to have her wait in the parking lot. Maybe Marius's father worked for FSP.

But Marius didn't always do the socially appropriate thing. Maybe his father *was* a prisoner, and it was only when the words had left his mouth that he realized it wasn't the most optimal date. He hadn't asked her to join him for social reasons, though. All she had to do was remember that unusual amalgamation of emotions—desperation, anger, regret, retreat—to know that.

She could have used some of her former contacts in the correctional system to help her find out more than the online prison database could provide, but Marius had initially invited her to join him, opening this door. Digging deeper behind his back instead of simply broaching the topic with him didn't make sense, not if she wanted to build trust with him.

If she reached her destination and he'd changed the time he'd written down, she might be in for quite a wait. But she'd find his car, and pass the time working on her laptop. She had lectures to prepare for upcoming classes and two consulting projects requiring status reports and evaluations. She could stay busy.

If his car wasn't there...well, it was a nice day for a round-trip drive to the state's maximum-security prison.

Upon arrival, she entered the main parking lot near the multi-building complex. When she found Marius's car, next to a giant, shiny blue Hummer pimped out with lots of chrome, she pulled into a spot a few spaces down, backing in so she was looking at the rear of the Civic. When she'd passed, it looked like he was still in the vehicle. He'd written down two o'clock, and it was one-thirty.

She hadn't given much thought to her approach, because she'd decided it was best not to overthink it. Picking up the insulated tote she'd brought, she emerged from her Mercedes and locked it. For this outing, she'd chosen her block heeled boots, black leggings and a wine-colored tunic top with a slash neckline that revealed the red jasper stone pendant she wore, with matching gold and jasper bracelets and earrings. The right mix of business casual with hints of Mistress and sexy woman, all to telegraph a variety of necessary messages.

As she reached the rear of his car, she saw both driver and passenger side windows were down, so she chose the passenger side approach. She'd expected he'd hear her heels on the pavement, but when she reached the window, she realized why he hadn't moved. He was asleep, his head tilted to the right on the headrest, one hand on the wheel, the other on the console. He'd pushed the seat back so his legs were sprawled, stretched out.

She dropped to her heels, laying an arm on the window sill, and studied him. He wasn't a peaceful sleeper, his expression concentrated even in repose, as if he were solving problems or slogging through disturbing dreams. But as she quietly opened the door, his breathing didn't change. With a frown, she noticed fresh scrapes on his knuckles and the shadow of a bruise on his jaw. He'd been fighting again. That might explain him sleeping so soundly in public and broad daylight, since the fights went on into the early hours of the morning. He'd probably driven here shortly after that, though he looked as if he'd showered and shaved.

She slid into the seat and clicked the door shut. Putting the tote between her feet, she sat back and watched him some more. Indulging herself, she laid her hand on his on the console. Leaning in, she began to stroke his hair back from his brow. His forehead creased, but then relaxed, as did his mouth. He murmured something and settled into the seat more deeply, his legs adjusting.

Regina turned on her hip, propping her head on the headrest to look at him. Then jumped when his hand jerked out from beneath hers and clutched, fingers digging in. "No," he said. *"No."*

It was rage and resignation in a single syllable. But his grip conveyed the opposite, as if she were a lifeline of hope to which he was grimly clinging. She put her other hand over his and held on while she made quiet noises of comfort. His grip and expression eased, but he maintained the hold. She didn't pull away.

After a time, she reached down with her free hand and opened the tote, allowing the aromas contained within to escape. It amused her to see them penetrate his slumber minutes later. His nostrils flared and his dark-lashed eyes lifted, his gaze disoriented.

"I brought snacks," she said. "Or a late lunch, depending on how much you want to eat."

Marius sat up, disengaging his hand to run it over his face, comb it through his hair in a charmingly self-conscious way. "No drool," she informed him. "You're a very polite sleeper. You don't even snore."

He blinked at her. "I told you not to come."

"No. You said it was probably better if I didn't. That's different from saying you don't want me to be here. You invited me to visit your father. So I decided I wanted to be here."

"Okay," he said at last. "I usually sleep lighter than that."

"Maybe your subconscious knew that I could be trusted."

"Yeah. Maybe." He cleared his throat. "What food did you bring?"

She smiled. "Should we wait for your dad? I brought enough for all three of us. Unless you were planning to take him to dinner."

Marius studied her a long, unreadable moment, then shook his head. He adjusted the seat so he was in a less reclined position. "This is how I visit my dad. I don't go in to see him. I just sit in the parking lot."

"Oh. Okay." So his father was a prisoner. And even if Marius had been going in to see him, food wouldn't have been allowed. But she'd seen Marius's appetite. He'd be happy to have the extra.

When he didn't seem to want to say more, she decided to leave it alone for now. He snaked his hand down to fish around in the tote and she smacked his wrist. "Out of there, rude boy. I have it arranged and you'll mess it up."

He didn't smile, but he looked like he wanted to do so. His gaze roved over her mouth and eyes, her hair and body. "You look nice," he said.

Reaching over the console, he gripped her collar and pulled her to him, meeting halfway to kiss her mouth, hard, his hands digging into fabric and her firm flesh beneath. She put her hands on his face, holding him, trying to hold onto control. An impossible task, because that kiss had her swimming in a sea of hormones and emotions tangled together as his own tempest of them came through. His grip moved to her neck, fingers threading through her hair, clutching handfuls of it.

He broke the kiss and her heart tripped over itself, because he moved his face into her locs, rubbing against their softness.

When he was calculating or manipulative, she could see him coming from a mile off and remain unaffected. When he acted with simple raw honesty and brutal need? He could strike her heart with the targeted force of lightning.

She cupped the back of his head, stroking, letting him take as much time as he wished. His hands had dropped to grip her hips. There was a restrained sexual urgency to it, the need for simple contact uppermost. Then he seemed to recall himself and eased back.

"Did you bring cookies?"

She chuckled, caressing his jaw and hoping he didn't notice the little tremor that went through her fingers. "There's a white cake with powdered sugar. It's my grandmother's recipe. I also brought a vegetable stew that is excellent at sun-warmed car temperatures, and roast beef sandwiches."

"You're a goddess," he said. "Are you going to hand me some of that, or do I have to be rude again?"

Smiling, she offered him a sandwich, a container of stew and a spoon, with a napkin. She also pulled out a bottle of water and a can of Coke from the cooler portion of the tote and gave him the choice. He chose the Coke. "You can have the cake after you eat your meal," she said.

"Yes, ma'am," he said dutifully, a glint in his eye. As he sat back and dug in, he passed his gaze over her again. "I saw a lady at the gas station who had hair like yours, only they were in corkscrews. Like yours at The Zone. Do you do that a lot?"

He meant the night with Siren. It was interesting, that he'd remembered that detail with so much else happening. "When I have the time and patience," she said. "A couple times I've thought of just shaving myself bald and having an elaborate tattoo put on my skull."

He swallowed a mouthful of stew, started to wipe his mouth with the back of his hand and reconsidered, using the napkin. "That's what Skullface did. Before the face tattoo and head shave, he had curly red hair and freckles."

"No kidding."

"Yeah. They called him Opie before that. Skullface was more intimidating."

"I can imagine."

He touched her crown with unexpectedly gentle fingers, tracing her scalp between a parting of locs. "I could see you with a real sexy tribal tat that curved under your ears, and right above your neck. Then again..." His gaze shifted. "I wouldn't cover any of your skin with a tattoo. You wouldn't need it anyway. Your eyes and your mouth hit a guy dead center."

Turning his eyes back to the prison, he fell silent, continuing his meal. Ignoring the tingle along her flesh where he'd touched it, she unwrapped half a sandwich and started eating it. "The prison entrance took me by surprise," she commented. "The wire archway with the letters on it reminds me of when you enter a family campground. And that white building over there with the top that looks like a lighthouse? Looks as if it belongs on a Florida resort."

"Yeah. It's pretty. Guess there's no rule against having pretty things at prison. You're here, right?" He smiled at her, though it didn't reach his eyes.

"Charmer." She didn't mean it as an accusation, which his behavior usually required. Not this time. To reinforce it, she touched his hand. "So your dad's an inmate?"

"For a few more hours. He's going to be executed today."

Marius delivered the comment in such a matter-of-fact manner, the significance didn't sink in for several breaths. When she snapped herself out of the shock, he'd set the sandwich on the napkin she'd draped over his thigh and unscrewed the Coke, letting the fizz die back before he raised it to his lips. He didn't look at her as he picked up the sandwich again, but he stopped short of taking another bite. Instead he seemed to get lost in his thoughts. He was staring at the prison again. She suspected he knew where his father was in the complex, because he kept looking in the same direction when he looked at the buildings.

"Kind of sick, right?" he said abruptly. "A guy asking a girl to come to his dad's execution?"

"It's unorthodox." She tried to pull a variety of thoughts together to handle the unprecedented turn of events, but when he parted his lips as if to say more, the brittle look in his eye made her lead with instinct. She stopped him, curling her fingers around his wrist.

"Eat your food. You're about to say stupid things. We'll talk about it when it's time, but right now we're going to talk about other things."

"Issuing orders, Mistress?" His look became more challenging.

"When you need it, yeah. And you need it right now, big time."

He'd triggered the Mistress side that came forth when called, and she let him see it when he finally locked gazes with her. She tapped his knuckles. "You've been fighting again."

"Winning again," he said after a weighted pause. "Picked up about five hundred on a street fight before the cops were called and we had to take off. Not a bad take for fifteen minutes."

He returned to eating, merely adjusting his elbows so he didn't impede her when she lifted his shirt. The bruising along his ribs and abdomen had her wincing. And made her mad. But she sat on it. He noticed the tight set to her lips, though.

"Don't worry about it," he said, no belligerence in his tone now. He seemed to have an earnest desire to reassure her and get her to move on from the subject. "Pain doesn't really hurt anymore, Mistress."

"Well, that's good." Picking up a napkin, she blotted a small smear of mustard away from the corner of his mouth. "It's not like pain serves a vital purpose, such as telling you when a bone is broken or an organ has ruptured."

His unrepentant grin made her want to slap him, as much as she wanted to do other things to him. "I didn't fight angry, so I didn't break my promise."

"I'm so relieved." She blew out a sigh and put a hand to the side of his head, shoving it. He ducked away from the resigned admonishment and used the movement to reach for another sandwich.

She'd worried that he wasn't eating enough because of limited finances, but since then she'd developed a more logical theory, given his muscle mass and fighting energy. Seeing him attack the homemade food she'd brought proved it. No one cooked for him, including himself. He must eat out all the time, so that the breakfast she'd cooked him, the sandwiches and cookies she'd brought him now, were as welcome to him as a meal in a five-star restaurant might be to her.

She was a Domme, but she was also her mother's daughter and a good Southern girl. She liked cooking for a man, liked seeing him enjoy the food. It made her think about cooking for him as a regular thing.

Every once in a while, she thought about what it would be like to have a husband who was also her dedicated submissive. Of all the inappropriate times to be remembering that Cinderella kind of wish, this one rated at the top. But so far, very little of her and Marius's trek together had fit between the lines.

She pushed away the unsettling thoughts and the emotions that came upon her, watching him eat her food at such a strange and terrible moment in his life.

"I've never had a man more eager to reach between my knees for food than pussy," she observed.

"Well, there are cameras and perimeter checks. This seemed like my second-best option." His gray eyes slid over to hers and held. "Believe me, Mistress. I never stop thinking about pussy. Particularly yours."

He glanced at the Hummer next to them. "If I had a ride like that, there'd be enough leg room you could roll the seat way back. I'd kneel between your legs, eat you until you came."

"If I said you could."

He paused. Swallowed the bite of sandwich. "If you said I could. But I hope you would. I wish I could do it right now. I'd like to at least touch you, feel if what I'm saying is getting you hot."

She cocked her head. "Then ask me, Marius."

His expression flickered, lips pressing together as if he was struggling with something. "Could you...would you call me..."

He couldn't finish it, but she could. "Ask me, Duncan," she said softly.

"May I touch your pussy, Mistress?" His voice went rough and growly, but his gaze dropped to stare at the console between them. He had lowered his eyes, a submissive instinct, but it kept what he wanted in the range of his hungry glance. "I want to stroke it. Put my fingers inside of you so I can taste how wet you are. Can I?"

Her throat was dry. "Yes, you may."

He stuffed in the last bite of sandwich, swallowed. His urgency proved his desire, but he remembered courtesy to his Mistress, stopping in the act of reaching for her to wipe his fingers thoroughly on the napkin. Only then did he slide his hand up her thigh, palm pressed against the thin legging fabric that covered her flesh. He went up under the tunic, found the waistband of the leggings and dipped beneath, adjusting toward her so the front of his shoulder pressed against the side of hers, their bodies forming a corner. His face was so close to hers, making her lips part as his gaze latched onto her mouth.

He found out fast she was wet. He muttered a reverent oath as his fingertips stroked through the moisture and eased in. Her hips lifted to accommodate the penetration, her other hand falling on his biceps. His gaze became fierce, and gloriously possessive. "For me?" he said, in a near whisper.

"For you," she confirmed, threading her fingers through his hair, caressing his bruised cheekbone with her thumb. He pressed his face into her palm and bit, his eyes sliding to her face to watch her reaction, a spear of arousal that had her breath elevating. He left a mark he traced with his tongue as his fingers pressed in deeper, knuckles feathering along the base of her clit.

"I need you to come. I need to see that, feel that. I need to do something for you, and I don't want you to let me come. I want you to be selfish, demanding, and take everything you want from me until I'm dying and my cock's so hard I can't walk, and I need you to still tell me no."

As he spoke, he became even more urgent. His tone, his body language, the energy filling the small car. To calm him, she put her hands on his face, framing it, holding his feverish look. She saw a man driven mad by whatever was going on inside him, grasping one possible thread of sanity...her demands. He wasn't topping, he was telling her what he needed. She wished the circumstances were different, that they weren't in a prison parking lot, his soul besieged by whatever crazy things knowing his father was about to be executed would cause.

However, according to evolution, man had started as a princely frog worming his way out of primordial muck. Good things had to start somewhere. If a prison parking lot was the first place he'd let her see his soul naked and bare, she would take it as the victory it was, for both of them.

Digging her nails into his scalp, she dropped her other hand to his chest, taking as tight a hold on his shirt as he had on her collar when he'd kissed her. "You're going to make me come, Duncan, with those callused fingers of yours. And you're not going to get to come for a long, long, long time. Not until I say so. I plan on being unbelievably cruel about that."

His gaze lighted with fire, and overwhelming relief.

"You come without my say-so," she managed to say in a steady voice, "and I will twist your misbehaving dick off with this hand." She caressed his cheek with it, scratching his bruise lightly with her nails. "You understand?"

"Yes, Mistress."

"Good. One more thing." She tapped his misshapen mouth. "You said you don't go in to see him. But will you today? Are you one of the witnesses?"

Slowly, he nodded. His jaw flexed, but she shook her head to keep him from feeling like he had to say anything more.

"Okay. When you come back out, I'll be here. You will leave me your keys, because you won't be driving yourself anywhere."

Before the darkness could rise in his eyes, she leaned in closer, spoke against his ear, her breath caressing him. She put all her energy into drawing him into a sensual web, even as her heart hurt for him. "We'll take my car to a hotel, and you're going to make me come again and again. As rough and fast or soft and slow as I demand, and everywhere in between. We'll start with you eating my pussy, because just thinking about you doing that, and knowing we can't do it here, is enough to make me want to have you do that first. A good, long time."

Just as she'd hoped, he'd become caught up in her words, enough he started to bend over the console, his knee sliding forward as if he intended to position himself to do just that. She stopped him with a firm grip on his shoulder. "No. That's not what I want right now. Fingers. Close your eyes. I want you to focus only on my pussy, and I'm going to look at you without you getting to look at me."

"No. I want to watch you come." His fingers pressed deeper. She caught his wrist, giving him a hard look. His dangerous expression slipped, showing that raw need again. Though he had to bite back what she expected were harsher words, she couldn't find it in her to be too hardhearted. Especially when her bad boy made a sincere effort to behave.

"Please, Mistress," he said again. "I...just let me watch you."

"Very well." She relented and settled back, releasing him. Bracing her knee against the door, she spread her thighs as she slid her other hand to his back to stroke.

Marius changed the angle of his penetration as she moved with him. The result was pleasurable, the stroke hitting the right spot inside. He added a finger, so he was using three, folded together. The man could fuck with his Mistresses' heads, but when he wasn't doing that kind of bullshit, he knew how to fuck them the right way, no matter what part of his anatomy he was using. She appreciated that in any man, but particularly this one, right now.

He went at it with intense concentration, such that she felt like he was aware of every nerve ending in that channel, the ripples of sensation through her clit and labia, the quivering inside as he hit those wonderful erogenous zones. Her body lifted and fell, her head tipping back, though she made an effort to appear like she was just sitting in a car having a conversation with someone, not being finger-fucked into total bliss.

She could hear the wetness of her cunt sucking on him, and a little moan broke from her as his thumb played music with her taut clit. If he'd only focused on the mechanics, he wouldn't have tipped her over so fast, but his gaze clung to her expression, swept over her body, so obviously savoring her every reaction it took her even higher.

"Your nipples are hard," he muttered. "I want to bite them."

She could imagine him doing it, the edge of his teeth like they'd felt on her palm, his tongue following behind to ease the sting. What would it be like to remove all restraint with him, let him be as wild and uninhibited as his lust could drive him to be? To trust that it wouldn't take them crashing into a brick wall like a fatal car wreck.

She brought him closer with the hand gripping his neck as she pushed up harder into his touch, her gaze holding his, a breathy moan coming from her. His cock was a bar of steel against his jeans, and her cunt throbbed as if it could feel him there.

"Please come for me, Mistress," he whispered.

"Kiss..." She didn't get the rest of it out, but he understood. He dove on her mouth, his own restless, violent and demanding. Her climax surged forth, wresting a scream from her throat. Hot fluid gushed against his fingers. Putting her hand on his face again, she prolonged the kiss, her body dancing with his hand, rocking together in a slow, tight waltz as she drifted back down to earth.

He laid his head on the seat back, his fingers still gliding inside of her in ways that had her shuddering with aftershocks. He greedily drank in every one of them with his intent expression.

At last, her body settled. His hand went still but his fingers remained inside of her, a place she didn't mind him being. She watched him, pleased with him, her body on a low simmer. His erection was still prominent against his jeans, registering his tension as he managed his own arousal. Holding it back at her command.

He rested the heel of his hand on her bare stomach. He used his thumb to play with the tiny silver spiral dangling from the curved barbell of her navel piercing.

"I love the way you feel," he said, his voice hoarse. "I just want to stay like this."

"Taking you to work like that might be awkward," she said. "Though I wouldn't mind bringing you to class on a collar and leash and letting you curl up under my desk. Keep me entertained with that beautiful mouth when my students are taking a test." The hot flash in his eyes gave her a wicked shot of pleasure. Brushing a short strand of hair along his forehead, she glanced down at his lap. A groan tore from him as she dropped her touch to give his engorged cock several firm strokes. "You keep it in for your Mistress," she reminded him.

"If she keeps doing that, it might prove difficult."

"Depends on how much you don't want your dick twisted off," she said, a threat and a tease at once. "Time to keep your hands to yourself, young man. I see the security check turning into the parking lot. The cameras probably told them there might be a couple out here exercising un-Christian thoughts."

He eased out of her. Though his erect state made him move with intriguing caution, he opened the glove compartment, producing a packet of damp wipes. "You can use these or, if you want, I can clean you with my mouth after he passes by. It shouldn't take long enough to land us in trouble."

The idea sent one more hard shudder through her, but she took the wet wipes from him with an arch look. "You underestimate how long I plan to keep you down there once I have you between my legs, boy. You might be living on a diet of pussy until dawn."

"Sounds like I better fortify myself with some other nutrition then," he said, plucking out one of the individually wrapped pieces of cake before she could stop him. She snatched for it and he tried to hold it out of reach in the small space, fending her off as she wrestled him for it. She would have tried a punch in his side to get him to lower his arm, but she was conscious of that bruising along his ribs and wouldn't add to it. She rethought that when he resorted to tickling to defend his pillaging.

"What...ah! Quit...asshole..." She was laughing, and he was grinning, the cake juggling between them as they both tried to secure it without crushing it. She snatched it back and tossed him a glare. "You are the rudest man I've ever met. Ask nicely."

"Please, Mistress, may I have some cake?" He said it with a straight face, a betraying hint of mischief in his smile. She sighed and handed it over.

"Pain in my ass. That's what you are." She stroked his hair again as he settled in to eat the cake, and watched his strong profile.

He was built like a man, top to bottom, thank the Goddess. But inside, there was so much little boy. She didn't say that, but it puzzled her, and she really did want to ask some questions. She couldn't ask about the animal cruelty charge, but thought she could find the truth a different way.

"When did your father go to prison?"

"When I was twelve. It took several years for his trial, and then he's been on death row a long time while some anti-death penalty lawyers tried to appeal his case. A few months back, they told me it was a pretty sure thing the last appeal was going to fail. Like I should be sorry about that." He scoffed.

"Can I ask what he did?"

"He raped and killed a woman. Stabbed her, strangled her, tortured her. Not in that order."

The comment came out flat, though he'd obviously intended to sound flippant. She gave him points for not being able to pull it off. Marius looked as if the cake had become particle board. He picked up his Coke and took a swallow. "At the end of the trial, he told reporters he would have been a bigger serial killer in Florida than Collins or Dahmer. Said it like it was the world's loss he was too stupid to avoid getting caught on his first kill."

She remembered realizing he had no frame of reference for having a favorite band as a teenager. In much the same way, she had no frame of reference for this. Not as his Mistress, nor as a lover, or even a friend. As he spoke, he was becoming more remote, drawing back into himself again. He wrapped up the rest of the cake and set it aside on the dash, returning to a broody stare at the structure.

"What time do you go in?"

"In about ten minutes. I go in that way, over there." He nodded. "They'll take me to the witness gallery when it's time."

He didn't want to be touched now. He was slouched against the other side of the car, elbow propped on his knee, Coke dangling from his fingers. Regina turned toward him on her hip again, drawing her legs up farther onto the seat.

"Did he call you Marius or Duncan?"

Surprise flickered in Marius's eyes, but he answered her. "Neither. Called me boy. Not like you do it. Sounds like a different word when you say it." He tilted his head and looked at her, a small victory, though his eyes seemed distant. "I like how you use it. The shadow called me Duncan. She was scared of him."

"The shadow?"

"Yeah. She was scared of everything. If the house was clean and I had the basics, she stayed in her room, with all the lights off, in the bed. I thought she was a live-in maid or nanny, hired help going through the motions. One time when I was five, I asked my dad who my mom was, where she was. I asked that in the kitchen, in front of her. He thought that was hilarious."

He jammed the Coke in a plastic cup holder. "This is fucked up. Go home, Regina. Please."

All of it dropped. The submissive, the charmer; every layer she'd seen covering him since this had begun between them. What she saw was a tired man whose eyes looked like they belonged to an eighty-year-old. "Really. I need you to go."

"I think that's the last thing you need. I'll go sit in my car if you want, but I'm not going." She spoke firmly, calmly. Not aggressive. Not right now. Just resolute. "When you come out, I'm going to be here, as I said. I'll be anything you need then, even if it's someone to sit with you without saying a word."

He stared back through the windshield, and she saw his throat work. "Ok. But...do me a favor."

"Anything, sweet boy. Except leave."

He closed his eyes and was silent a long moment. Then he opened them. "Will you make me breakfast again sometime? With those cinnamon buns?"

"Yeah." Reaching across the console, she ran her knuckles along his biceps, up to his short shirt sleeve. She caressed beneath it, knowing she was touching the armor tattoo. The cinnamon buns were the canned kind she broke open on the counter, peeled apart and put in the oven, with a packet of icing to melt over them when they came out, but she agreed, they were good. "On one condition."

"What's that?"

She pulled his keys out of the ignition and tucked them away into her bra. "I keep these for now. All right?"

He eyed her. "Putting them there only makes me want to take them back."

She squeezed his arm. "Anytime you feel lucky."

He sighed and shook his head, pulling away as he opened his car door. "Not today."

She thought he'd walk toward the prison entrance without another word, but he circled around to her window, dropped to his heels and folded his arms on the sill.

"If we'd gotten together a couple months ago, there'd have been time for me to add you to the guest list," he said thoughtfully. "They did say I could bring a date. Though not in those exact words."

She didn't rise to the bait, twisting her fingers into the collar of his shirt as a warning, and to touch him. "You don't have to do this. Nothing says you have to watch him die."

"I know. But I need to know he's dead. I need..." He put his forehead down against the side of the car. She laid her hand over the back of his skull and kissed the top of it.

"It's okay. Even totally-not-okay situations like this can be okay, once you get through them. It's just the getting through."

"Yeah. I don't want to feel anything. But I'm afraid I'm going to feel too much, and it's going to spill over onto you. Don't let me use this against you," he added, vehemently.

"Let me worry about me."

"Doesn't work that way, does it? You're worrying about me, and I'm not worth it."

She lifted his face to meet her gaze. "Yes, you goddamn, fucking are," she said softly. "When you're not being a total asshole."

He offered her a ghost of a smile. "Which is most the time."

"Even so. It may be a small window, but during those five minutes a day, you are very much worth it."

He clasped her wrist and kissed her palm, holding his face against it for a brief second. "When I kissed you before, your hand was trembling. I liked that. It made me feel like a far better person than I am."

He rose and let her go. "See you in a while."

Now that she had more information, it wasn't difficult to find news articles on his father. Marius had changed his last name, or perhaps he'd used his mother's, not an uncommon decision for the offspring of a well-publicized death row inmate. Donald Eric Larabee had been caught within a day of murdering Sally Montrose, a convenience store clerk he kidnapped and tortured for two days in a storage facility before strangling and stabbing her to death.

A little more digging turned up a reference to him in a book on Florida serial killers. Because of Larabee's boast Marius had mentioned, the author, Mel Wilham, had used Larabee as a dramatic footnote to hint at how many serial killers were perhaps first-time murderers caught before they could "actualize" themselves.

Her lip curled at the corporate buzzword. She'd bought and downloaded the book, and made herself read the chapter based on the interview Wilham had done with Larabee. One key and chilling paragraph held her, turning the cold knot in her stomach into jagged rock.

"Yeah, I had a kid. He never had the stomach for it. Made him watch when I practiced on stray cats, their kittens, the occasional dog, but the little shit couldn't even get it up for that. Preferred me to beat him rather than cause a squeak out of something else."

The book had been published about a decade ago, after Marius's cruelty charge. She wanted a marker in that sealed juvie file, because this confirmed Marius had done nothing to any of those animals. He'd been found burying them, that was all. Had that been his father's mandate, or had Marius done it himself, expressing the remorse his father never would?

She wished she could go in there and administer the injection herself. Or set aside the ridiculous notion of humane execution and just use a baseball bat with nails driven through it. She noticed Wilham had added that Larabee's son had disappeared off the grid years before and could not be located to contribute to the work. Larabee's wife was living with her sister in Arizona somewhere and had likewise refused any comment.

So at the time of the book's publication, "the shadow" was alive. The detached way Marius referred to her, as if he'd never had the experience of a mother, even though she was living in the same house, was as disturbing as the rest. Not only did he have no obvious emotional connection to her, his mother hadn't expended any apparent effort toward creating one.

There was a picture of Larabee. He had Marius's beautiful eyes, his strong jaw and good looks. She hated that for Marius. How often did he look in the mirror and see this monster?

She closed her laptop. The driver of the Hummer had emerged not too long ago and departed. He looked like some drug dealer's right hand guy, all decked out in gangster wear. He'd made kissy noises at her as he got into the vehicle. She'd given him a steely gaze and her middle finger, been called a cunt, and he'd peeled off. She'd moved her car next to Marius's, but had preferred to stay here, in his vehicle.

Smoothing her hand over the head rest and his seat back, she thought of his body pressed there.

She had a reputation as a practical and unsentimental Mistress, but that didn't mean her heart couldn't bleed. She thought about what he'd said. *Don't let me use this against you.* He was self-aware enough to know that he might twist any sympathy or pity against her in a vulnerable moment. She had more faith in him than that. And in herself. The more she knew, the less opportunities she was giving him to take those shots. The less opportunities he had, the less he would try, and who he really was, really wanted to be, would start to come through. She had faith in it, because she was already seeing evidence of it. Those five minutes a day were expanding.

The armor beneath the skin. She smiled, thinking of his firm flesh. That tattoo really was more appropriate than he realized.

Leaning her head back against the seat, she closed her eyes. She'd take a short power nap, because she had a feeling it was going to be a long night.

She woke a few minutes before he emerged, as if some second sense had warned her it was time. As he moved across the parking lot and drew close enough for her to see his face, she could feel it almost before he reached her. A miasma around him, so potent it was like an impenetrable fog, or a sucking mud that would pull in everyone who got too close.

"Well then. We have our work cut out for us, don't we?" she mused. "Get to it, girlfriend."

She emerged from his car, locking it, and pocketed the keys. As he reached the driver's door, he put one hand on the handle, and started fishing for keys in his jeans pocket with the other.

"Duncan," she said firmly. He looked up, startled. He hadn't remembered she was going to stay. Or maybe he hadn't expected her to do so. "I'm fine," he said, his voice hollowed out. "I'm just going to drive home."

"I'm glad you're fine. But no, you're not. Get in my car."

She went to her Mercedes and waited him out. As she did, she put his keys under her seat, a hard to reach spot and not the first place he'd look.

She tapped out a song on the steering wheel, humming to herself. He might refuse to get in her car. Hitchhike his way home. If he tried, she debated the merits of knocking him on his ass with a glancing blow of the bumper to get him in the car, but ruled it out. It might scratch the car's paint.

About five minutes later, he opened the passenger door and got into the car. He gazed forward, as expressive as a crash test dummy. No anger, no sadness. Just blank.

She leaned over him, pressing her breast into his chest to pull his seatbelt across him and latch it. As she drew back, she caressed his thigh. His eyes swiveled to her, flickering with something. Signs of life. She wanted to kiss him, hold him, but that wasn't what he needed.

She'd already programmed the GPS for the hotel where she'd made reservations for the night. It was about thirty minutes away, because she wanted to put a decent amount of distance between him and the energy of this place, even though they'd have to return to retrieve his car in the morning.

She didn't ask him questions, didn't speak at all. His gaze had returned to the windshield and he stayed in that position, not moving, his hands loose on his thighs. A couple times she saw them clench in reaction to whatever thoughts were going through his mind. Energy was getting denser around him, a feeling of impending detonation. He was locked down, likely strapped to a powder keg of emotions too strong and conflicting to let loose.

She remembered the night he'd been kicked out of The Zone. He'd gone straight to the fighting ring. Everyone had their coping mechanisms. Belatedly, she realized she should have made a reservation at a fleabag hotel where broken sheetrock and scarred furniture was part of the décor.

Yes, maybe he needed to do violence. But when violence wasn't an option, men would sometimes choose the closest thing to it. She'd see if she could channel that violence toward a different kind of passion. She'd already opened that door, with the earlier directive she was sure he'd forgotten. She'd be happy to remind him of it.

When it finally came into view, the Marriott was a welcome sight, because that vibration had become so strong she was starting to wonder if they'd make it before everything blew. She put her laptop bag and food tote on his shoulder, threading his arm through the straps. She tugged on them to catch his attention. "Carry those and come with me."

He stood mutely in the lobby while she handled check-in. From the surreptitious looks of the desk staff, she expected they were picking up the unstable vibes, his stillness too peculiar not to be noted. She gave the clerk a reassuring smile as she handed over her credit card. When she moved toward the elevator, she made an imperious motion toward Marius that fairly screamed *"Come, boy."* It pulled him out of his head enough to earn her a narrowed glance from the steely gray eyes. His mouth set in a flat line, and he started to look a little mean.

Yeah, triggering him out of his stupor wasn't going to be the problem. The challenge was going to be channeling it in the right direction. He was like an animal in a cage.

It was unsettling, how often he inspired that analogy from those around him. He'd been dubbed "Rabid" as a fighter. Tyler had told Regina she had the key to his cage. *"It's up to you whether to unlock it or not."* Now here she was, using the same imagery. But though he might think he was trapped, she knew Marius himself clutched the key to that lock. She just had to help him realize that.

They were on the fifth floor, a corner suite where they'd have plenty of room and lots of privacy on this weekday night. "Put them down there," she said, pointing to the desk. The bed was a king with a heavy wood headboard bolted to the wall. The jacuzzi tub and bathroom were equally spacious.

She moved back to the center of the room. He stood a few feet away in the lamplight, his hands loose at his sides, but nothing about his body loose. He was rigid as a corpse, except for his eyes, which were tracking her movements. Good. Grasping the hem of the tunic top, she removed it, standing before him in black leggings, boots and burgundy satin bra. She removed her jewelry, placing it on the nightstand.

"Want me to service you now, Mistress?" He spoke at last, a cutting edge to his voice. He thought he was as far away from her as the moon. She was about to prove him wrong. They were so close together they were sharing the same still, explosive point of the universe. His eyes had latched onto the quiver of her breasts, held up high in the satin. If he was a beast in truth, saliva would be gathering around his fangs. He wasn't sure if he wanted to fuck or eat her, but both weren't out of the question.

"As a matter of fact, I do." She cocked her head. "You remember the night I transformed you into my stallion? You could have freed yourself from the ropes I had on you. But where you went in your mind, you didn't have hands to untie them, did you? Only hooves."

Taking a step closer, she let her hand drift over the top of her breast, down her abdomen to play with her navel piercing. He tracked the movement, a quiver going through him. She wanted to see that tension play over his muscles.

"Take off the shirt."

He did it with impatient jerks, an aggressive shrug of his shoulders. His muscles were so unyielding they stood out in stark relief from the play of light and shadows in the room.

"You've tried a lot of things to throw me, Marius, but none of them work, because I see past the bullshit. I see you."

Tonight, she'd call forth another kind of animal. The human male, at his most primitive. Her pulse elevated, recognizing the signs that the hunt had started and she was walking the fine line between being huntress and prey.

"I know you're a violent man. I also know you're a good man, maybe sometimes even a gentle man. I'm not as physically strong as you are. I know how to defend myself, but you've learned that, and the darkness inside you is ready for it. If you want to hurt me, you'll be able to do me real damage. Maybe even finish the job you started the other night."

His attention snapped to her face. She'd startled him. "Is that what you want, Marius?"

Another ripple through his upper body, his jaw setting. "No." His gaze latched onto hers, and she saw the pain flash through it, jagged crimson. "I need to leave."

"You don't have my permission to leave. You're not going to damage me, Marius. I'm not physically stronger than you are, but I am stronger in another way. Here." She tapped her temple. "And that's what you need the most."

The meanness resurfaced. "No." He growled it, eyes roving over her with glittering avarice. "Not the most."

She bared her teeth. "If pussy and a pair of tits were all you needed, you wouldn't have asked me to be here, before all your shields kicked in and you ripped up the note."

His lip curled, that broken sneer, but she saw the flash of dangerous desperation in his gray eyes, almost dominated by dark pupil.

"Before you went into the prison, what did I tell you was going to be your first job when we came here tonight?" she asked.

"I don't care. I don't remember."

"Hmm. Okay." She slid her fingers into the waist band of the leggings, pushing them down far enough he'd see the lace edge of her burgundy panties as she dipped below it to stroke herself. "Too bad. Guess I'll take care of this myself. I'll think about Noah, Lyda's boy. How accommodating he is, how willing to please."

She tipped her head back with a little hum. "He can put his mouth between a woman's thighs and get her worked up in no time with that tongue stud of his. He turns a woman's pussy into a feast and makes her feel like a seven-course meal he's going to enjoy one tiny nip, lick and suck at a time."

"I won't be gentle," he said harshly.

She brought her head back up, sharpening her gaze. He'd shifted forward, but she was all too aware he hadn't closed the distance between them yet.

"Earlier today, your Mistress gave you permission to be rough," she said evenly. "Or did you miss it, because your head was too far up your ass?"

He was on her within the next breath. His forward momentum slammed them into the wall, his hip hitting the side table and lamp. The items toppled, the lamp tumbling over the easy chair next to it. Her shoulder blades made bruising contact with the wall, and she hoped the people next door didn't think they were coming through, if there were any tenants there. But then she had no more thoughts except for the here and now, and the male whose rage and need overflowed, commanding her absolute attention.

He pulled the right cup of her bra down and seized her breast in a calloused palm. He clamped his mouth on it, sucking, pulling, biting.

She writhed away and yanked at his hair, scratching his back hard enough to draw blood. "Do what you were told," she commanded. "I want your mouth between my legs."

He snarled against her flesh but swung them around, bringing her to the bed with his heart-stopping strength. He flipped and shoved her face down, her knees braced against the side of the bed, her feet planted on the floor. "First I'm fucking your ass. Your beautiful, round ass."

"No, you're not." She hooked his leg, twisted and tangled them into a heap that slid them both to the floor. Now she was on her back, and she pushed the leggings and panties to her thighs, stroking herself again as he reared up over her. "Do as you're told," she repeated.

He clamped his hands on her thighs, his lips curled in a snarl, but his eyes were riveted on her glistening labia. His cock was a mouthwatering thickness against his jeans, the violence driving him to an even more potent erection. Her pussy contracted against her fingers in reaction.

"Everything you're getting, I'm allowing you to take," she said through gritted teeth. "You're still not doing a damn thing without my permission. I won't let you. What's more, you won't let you. You need your Mistress, and that's the deal."

He stripped off his belt and bent over her, grabbing her hands and wrapping the strap around her wrists, cinching it up in the middle before linking it to one foot of the heavy dresser beside her. "Now I can do anything I want."

She laughed. "That's the point. What you want is your Mistress to command you. So stop talking and fuck me with your mouth already."

He stared down at her. She held his gaze without flinching, her body lifted and exposed by the restraint. They both knew the belt wasn't impossible for her to shake. He'd just been making a point. So had she.

The air conditioning unit cut off, leaving the room in total silence except for his rasping breath and her heart, pounding in her ears.

It was a slow-motion moment, everything focused on what might happen next. He swallowed, his gaze sliding down her body again. "My Mistress."

His voice still held darkness, but it had transformed, now hoarse and hollow.

"Yes, your Mistress," she said, low. "Your mouth, Duncan. I demand your mouth. Rough, hard, soft or gentle, just as we discussed. You'll stop when I tell you to stop and not a minute before, even if I make you do it until the sun rises."

She heard her heart beat a dozen times, still thundering in her ears, her throat, the pit of her stomach. When they'd knocked the lamp over, the bulb must have blown, because there was barely any light in the room, except for the hellfire in his gaze and the parking lot lights penetrating the sheer window panels. His lips tightened and then so did his hands on her hips.

With a deep, shuddering sigh that seemed to ripple through him like a desert hot wind, he bent and put his mouth on her.

CHAPTER THIRTEEN

She was ready for his anger. She hadn't calculated what everything this day had brought would pull from her. Finally getting the missing pieces—the traumatized boy who'd become a tormented man—had driven the emotional tide within her to overflowing. Especially when those emotions came face to face with what she already felt for him.

As a correctional officer, she knew there were bad men. But even in the worst of the worst, she occasionally glimpsed who they might have been if they'd chosen that different fork in the road. When she saw those flashes, she also sometimes caught the rare instance when the spark remained, the wish for what they could have been. Astronaut, firefighter, dragon slayer, the hero of the story instead of the villain. Instead of the dregs of society, relegated to a prison jumpsuit and locked away to be forgotten.

There were exceptions. The psychopaths like Don Larabee, born bad, coughed up from Hell. She couldn't fathom the divine power that would allow a child to be born to such a creature, a helpless victim from his first breath outside the womb. But in this room, on this night, she'd be the avenging goddess who would provide him her fury, her sex, her passion and fearlessness, to give him a safe haven for the full range of his feelings between grief and rage.

Or, in simpler terms, she was pissed, she cared about him, and if she couldn't bash his sperm-donor's brains out with a bat, she'd fuck the son senseless, until he let it all go inside the safety of her arms and body.

He pulled off her leggings and panties, leaving her naked. He didn't stop to savor or look, but dove on her as if he were jumping off a cliff into a welcoming tropical sea. When he buried his face between her legs, she wrapped them over his back. His hands came up and gripped, held on to her thighs and ass as he dedicated himself to pleasuring her, following her command. He started out forceful, impatient, but after that first wave, something settled and he was moaning with a painful relief, a vibration against her pussy as he immersed himself in the task she'd imposed on him.

He thought he needed violence, when what he really needed was something that made sense. This made sense.

"That's my boy," she crooned. She freed her hands from the loose hold of the belt and stroked his head, her breath catching. God he was good at this, his tongue and lips working so well together. "Oh, baby, keep doing that. Your gorgeous mouth. That's it..."

It didn't take long, this first time. The violence, the need in them both, shot her right into a powerful climax. She let herself go up and over, and made sure he heard it, what he could do to her. She grabbed his shoulders, clawing at him, and brought him up her body, her palms spreading out on his chest, gaze dropping to the jeans.

"Off. All of it."

He stood up and obeyed, standing over her. In that position, the tide could change back to him and his demons, but she didn't allow it. She gazed up the length of his body, letting him see how much she liked what she saw. How she owned him, head to toe. When their gazes met, she spoke. "Put me on the bed."

Setting aside his clothes, he bent and lifted her. She looped her arms around his shoulders, put her face in the curve of his throat and bit him lightly. He swayed, and she flattened her palm on his back, sweeping over the broad expanse. "Put me on the bed," she repeated.

Moving to it, he slid a knee onto the mattress, and lowered her. When he released her, he did so reluctantly, but he straightened and moved back, standing at the foot of the bed, between her feet, as if he didn't trust himself to be too close. Or as if he were waiting for his

Mistress to take further control. Direct his actions, because he didn't know where to go from here.

His vision had gone bright and hazy at once. Like his eyes were full of unshed tears, though they were dry. He kept staring at her, not moving. Except for one hand, slightly twitching against the foot she'd propped onto the bed, her knee bent.

She slid down to the end of the mattress and sat up, her legs flanking him, dangling on either side. Enclosing him in her arms, she slid her hands up over his ass, the small of his back. Using the pressure of that embrace, she bumped him a step closer and put her lips against his upper abdomen. His cock was pressed between her breasts and his stomach. It was temptingly close to her mouth.

He cupped the back of her head, oddly tentative. But what was moving inside him wasn't ready to let him be gentle. His hand dropped to her hair, clutched and then jerked, making her look up at him. His mouth had become a hard line, eyes cold.

"I want to try topping, like you said."

"Oh?" She tugged against his grip to prop her chin on his abs and blinked, wide-eyed. "So what do you want...Master?"

His lips curled. "Suck my cock. On your knees."

She shook her head. "No." And went back to kissing his stomach, ignoring the steel shaft nestled in her cleavage, the testicles pressed below her rib cage.

His biceps bunched into a knot against her temple. She added a teasing trail of her tongue along the ridges of muscle. Stretching up to his nipple, she closed her lips over it for a tiny nip. He shuddered, and let out a noise, half snarl, half groan. "You said I should try topping."

"I said that when I was letting you figure out your way, figure out your own bullshit. Not tonight. Tonight you need a light in the storm. You're all darkness, baby. Let me lead the way."

As she tipped her head back to look into his face, she gripped his wrist and squeezed. "Duncan," she said with soft firmness. "Obey your Mistress. Trust her, if only for this."

His grip loosened. She let him go too, using elbows, ass and feet to sensually slither back toward the head of the bed. As she stretched out, she spread her thighs, drifting fingertips along the inner track to caress the damp arousal he'd already left there. "Bring that fine mouth back to my cunt. I want you there again. Soft and easy, because I'm still sensitive. Show me that you can build me back up again. Then I'm going to want you inside me."

He pressed his lips together. From the obvious struggle with his emotions, she expected more fencing with words. She didn't expect what he said next, especially when he spoke out of stiff lips, his eyes still brittle and not particularly kind. "I wish I could do that without a condom."

"So do I." She cocked her head. "There've been hookups at the fight, right? Women all worked up, watching strong men being violent with one another. They'd come on to you afterward, fucking you in your car or theirs, right? Sometimes you didn't even make it to the parking lot. Just did it in the alley. It worked for you because they were hot and demanding, like a Mistress would be. Telling Rabid to fuck them. Fuck them hard."

His gaze lifted from her body to her eyes. "Don't ever call me that."

He'd intended to make it sound like a threat, a warning. But she heard the plea beneath it. "I never will," she said softly.

"I always wore protection." His jaw flexed. "I wouldn't lie about that."

"No. I didn't expect you would. But something has you hesitating to be inside me without a condom. Maybe because that's a big step. It says a whole lot."

"Yeah." But that wasn't entirely it, or maybe he just hadn't gotten to that concern, because another was in line in front of it. She could tell from the shift of his gaze. Moving her hand onto her pussy, she began to stroke and play. Most men couldn't be led around by their cocks unless they wanted to be, no matter popular notions to the contrary. But there were men closer to their animal instincts than others, and Marius was one of those, particularly right now. She couldn't lead him by the cock, but she could use it to distract and unbalance him. A form of truth serum, so to speak. A serious smile touched her lips, her heart aching at how his gaze clung to her hand, what she was offering him behind it.

"Tell me, sweet boy," she said. "Then you can come have as much of this as you want."

"I want to be sure." The fist clenching thing, evidence he was fighting something inside himself. "I want...to keep you safe."

"Okay." It was an effort to keep her voice even, to not betray how the honest admission moved her. "Go get tested next week and be sure. But if you do that, there will be one more condition to being inside me, nothing between us."

She paused, because she wanted to make sure he heard her next words, branded them inside his head. "You're mine exclusively. Until I say otherwise."

The gray irises flickered with heat. It was that same hunger, but with a different quality to it. Settling her head back on the pillow, she tossed him a heavy-lidded look. "You're making me wait for what I want, sweet boy. You do that another second and I'll make *you* wait three times as long to fuck my pussy with your bare cock, whether you get clean test results or not."

A properly motivated man could be deliciously obedient. Putting his knee on the bed again, he went to all fours over her legs, his muscled arms spread out over her, elbows bending. In the semi-darkness he looked like a beast in a feral crouch. But as she gazed into his eyes this time, she didn't see a predator poised over prey. It was more like a man-wolf crouched over a mate, ready to tear apart anything that tried to take her from him. Or cause her harm. It caused an odd little tremor in her belly.

He doesn't know you're almost as scared shitless as he is by where this is going.

Or maybe he did. He didn't immediately return to going down on her. Instead, he slid forward, reaching out to touch her throat with one questing finger. She lifted her chin, enjoying the sensation as he traced her jugular, moving down between the collar bones, caressing that soft pocket of flesh. He stayed there a bit, gaze trained on her pulse, on her reaction to how he was touching her. His expression had been unreadable before, but the energy was different. Something strong, not violent or angry, was moving through him, guiding his touch in a way that had her holding her breath.

His fingertips glided down her sternum, detouring to follow the curve of one breast all the way around, then the other. He bent, still on all fours and leaning over her so his hips were higher than his shoulders, his thighs spread and braced as he nuzzled her breast. He rubbed his face against it, teasing her nipple with the friction of his jaw. He did it to both breasts, to the area in between, like an animal marking another. There was a potent stillness to him, and she stroked his shoulder, the side of his throat, his hair and face, letting the connection speak the words they both needed to hear.

He pressed his mouth to her navel, teeth catching her piercing briefly before he continued downward, scattering kisses over her flesh. She kept coiling and uncoiling her fingers in his hair, tugging, her body moving in sensual choreography with his.

Together. For the first time, they were moving together, no barriers between them. The feeling of it was like coming home to a place she'd never been, but had been waiting for her all along.

He pressed his lips to her clit, an easy tease, his tongue slipping into her to curl and explore as if it was all new treasure to him. She moaned, a low sound as her body rose to his mouth like steam drifting up from a hot spring. He curled his arms under her thighs, clutching her ass to bring her hips up farther, give him more angles and depths to penetrate. His thumb stroked through her folds, gathering the wetness, and came back to her ass, dipping between her buttocks to trace her rim. It sent tiny shocks of pleasure through her, her cunt contracting in response.

"Such a small, tight pussy," he muttered against her. "When I first fucked you, it took me by surprise, because you're..."

He'd muffled the next words against her, so she didn't know what he said, but she knew what he meant. Not petite. Built like Xena, not Gabrielle.

"I'm normal size. You're just a well-hung man, Duncan Marius Walczak."

Her humor didn't dilute the feelings she was having. They could ride the waves of gentle teasing to serious intensity and back again without changing course or the overriding feelings that had them in their grip.

He smiled against her flesh, shook his head, and then put his mouth all the way over her, thrusting his tongue in deep and driving other thoughts away. She spiraled up, and up farther. He took his time, showing he knew what he was doing as her sensitive tissues warmed back up again. Much sooner than she would have expected, she was pressing herself more insistently against his mouth, which took on a rhythmic licking, sucking and penetrating pattern. Her hips answered him with a coital cadence until she was gasping.

"Now," she ordered. "I want you inside me."

"I want to feel you come like this, against my mouth again."

"You will. Several times tonight. But first this."

He obeyed, dipping off the bed to pull out his wallet and retrieve a condom. He slid up her body, his lips glistening from her response. When he would have opened the packet, she held out her hand for it with a commanding look. She gave herself the pleasure of rolling the protection on his turgid cock herself. Caressing it and the testicles beneath, she tangled her fingers in the light coating of coarse hair over the heated weight of them. She looked up to see his eyes close at her touch.

"Come back down here," she whispered, bringing him between her thighs. Her grip telegraphed what she wanted, what she was going to do. He held her in place a bated second, a wolfish look crossing his face. A feline smile curled her lips in response. Then he rolled them as she'd intended, helping her so she was straddling him.

"Just proving I can't push you around?" she asked, sliding her cunt along his cock, a heated, wet track that had his grip tightening on her hips and a breath catching in his throat.

"Maybe just letting you know how much strength is at your command, Mistress," he said.

"Charmer." Curling her fingers around him, she brought his cock inside her. She closed her eyes, bracing her hand on his chest to control the pace as she slowly, slowly descended, his thick member impaling her in a way that brought her an even deeper shudder of pleasure.

Putting both hands on his chest, she started to ride, clasping him inside on both the upward and downward strokes. He held her in sure hands, his gaze coursing over her quivering breasts, the arch of her body, the joining point between their sexes. His lips were parted, his eyes heated and jaw firm, intent on what she was feeling, and feeding off it for his own arousal.

"Goddess," she breathed, dropping her head back and digging in with her nails. "Want to do this forever."

His grip tightened, a silent agreement. She pulled them further and further up, until his hold was bruising and her nails might be drawing blood, but neither of them were complaining.

His emotions weren't predictable when he was this close to his primal nature. Especially tonight, with all else he'd experienced. So it wasn't unexpected when he went for a change of course. With a sudden ripple and flexing of muscle, he rolled them, putting her beneath him again, one arm clamped beneath her thigh to hold it high on his side. He planted his knees to give him harder thrusts, as if he wanted to get deeper inside her than anatomically possible. She met his ferocity, wrapping her arms around his shoulders and setting her teeth to one, next to the pulsing artery in his throat.

She'd told him she'd make him wait for his climax. He'd wanted her to be cruel to him, had begged to be denied. But she sensed he needed something else now. There would be time to be cruel later.

"Now," she whispered, as she went over the edge and gave herself to the orgasm. Responding to her command, spoken as much through her body as her lips, he groaned and bucked, his release jetting into the condom.

In a week she could have him this way, nothing between them. She wanted that, vehemently enough that if they'd rewound to the decision, she might have pushed him to go without it tonight. But he wanted to protect her, and she wouldn't take that significant turning point away from him.

That more gentle moment wasn't in command now. He was rutting on her like a bull, grunting, his eyes holding hers in an intense lock, his hands hard on her body, demanding. But she could feel the difference. He was on top not to resist her control, but to show her he could bring her pleasure this way. He was hers to command from the top or bottom. He knew she liked his strength; was aroused, fascinated and wanted to be immersed by it.

With her, he didn't have to use it to fight. He could use it to serve. It might be fleeting, but in this moment, she saw he understood.

Coming down was like being on the tail end of a summer storm, the air still crackling with electricity and distant rumbles of thunder. He was braced on his arms, but she brought him down to his elbows, cupping both hands over his skull and pressing a kiss to his forehead, then to his lips when he raised his head. His own hand curled around the back of her neck, holding her as the kiss deepened, as he adjusted his hips to make another firm push inside her. She offered a soft moan against his lips that had his eyes sparking.

"Like that, do you?" He did it again, and she met him with

squeezes of her internal muscles, a mutual giving that kept those quiet spasms coming, their bodies rocking together as if they'd always known how to move with that synchronicity.

She slid her hands around to his face, thumbs caressing his lips. He kissed her fingers, then he dropped his head, pressing his face hard into her neck. The shudder that ran through him now was something different. She stroked his back, his wide shoulders. "What is it?"

He shook his head and eased out of her, moving back up to his knees. He gazed down at her, much as he had in that portentous turning point at the beginning. Shadows were gathering, reminding him of what had brought them here. She could see their grasping hands trying to pull him away, and they were faster than hers. Before she could hold him, he rolled off the bed and moved away from her, disappearing into the bathroom.

Cold without him, she pulled the blanket over herself, a dissatisfying substitute for his body. She reminded herself it wasn't a setback. He'd just gone farther with her than he ever had before. She pillowed her head on her hands and studied the bathroom door. He hadn't turned on a light, but she heard running water. When he emerged, he picked up his jeans and pulled them on. He righted the lamp and side table before taking a seat in the easy chair. She studied his shadowed features.

"I miss your heat," she said. "Come back to bed."

He didn't say anything. Despite the darkness, she sensed he was drilling her with that trying-to-figure-you-out stare, which was fine, but she was concerned other energies were closing in on him.

"Why did you ask me to join you at the prison?" she said.

"I had a weak moment."

She didn't respond to that, and kept her gaze leveled on him. He slouched down in the chair, stretching his legs out, his hands resting on the arms. Now she could see his moody eyes were fixed on her, but on no particular point. "I asked because of the way you are with me," he said gruffly. "How I feel when I'm with you...I thought you'd come, and I wouldn't feel so alone with it. Stupid."

"No," she said. "No, it wasn't. I wish I could have gone inside with you."

He shook his head. "That was the last place I would want you to be. It didn't matter anyway. He didn't look at me. Didn't even seem aware of any of it. Stoned, or his mind's all gone now. He didn't want to say anything. They just did it, and it was done."

She thought he might fracture the polished arm of the chair with his grip. Rising from the bed, she picked up his shirt, donning it, and came to him. A hand on one of his knees, her foot against his, and she'd pushed his feet apart. Under his brooding gaze, she sank to the floor, drawing her knees up as she used one of his legs for a back brace and laced her fingers over her bent knees. She didn't ask for anything. Just waited and looked at him in the darkness, only broken by that filtered light through the drapes. With it, she could see the shape of his forehead, the strands of hair over it. The broken line of his nose. The roundness of one broad shoulder.

"He wanted me to be like him. He'd bring in animals he'd caught and…" He paused, and his voice became so flat and dead she thought he'd had to go somewhere far beyond where his personality and soul resided, the things that made him Marius, or Duncan. "He'd torture them, make me watch. I wouldn't help, so he'd beat me."

His gaze came back to her, and so did the full force of his personality, so fast it was as if he'd slammed back into his own body. Seizing her by the shoulders, he dragged her up to her knees, bringing her eye to blazing eye with him. "I never helped. *Never.* He'd throw them in this dumpster, and I'd sneak out at night, go get them, bury them."

"Okay," she said softly, putting her hands on both his knees. "It's okay. I know you didn't help him."

He stared at her, and something in him crumpled up like paper. "How could you know?"

"I've been inside you, remember? You can tell me as much or as little as you like, but I know who you are. What you are…and aren't… capable of doing."

He nodded, a quick jerk. He didn't let her go, his touch still bruising, as if he didn't realize how hard he was holding her. "Every time, I hoped he'd kill me so I wouldn't wake up, so he couldn't do it again. Thought that maybe if I was dead, he'd stop. He didn't want a partner. It was never about that. I was just one more way to torture something weaker than himself. There was no sense to it, no reason for why he was the way he was."

His voice was raw, but strong, unbroken, like he was being beaten now and defying the one hammering him to break him. He would never break. She had a flashback to him in the fight ring and suddenly all of it made sense. And if she hadn't caught up, he added to it with his next words.

"He didn't get it. I'd take the pain, take the beating a hundred times, just so I didn't have to hear their cries or watch him do what he did to them." He released her, dropping back into the chair with a dull thud.

"I learned to fight. Even after he was put away, I kept learning, getting better and better at it. I needed to be ready to fight, to not be helpless, if ever he tried to do that to me again, tried to do that to anyone." He chuckled harshly. "My dad was never getting out, even if he beat the death penalty, so it didn't make sense. It didn't get through my thick skull until the lawyers told me the final appeal was likely to fail. Then it hit me, how futile it was. He was going to be beyond any retaliation, beyond anything, and I'd be left here with all of it in my head, inside me. The way it had always been. I'd been kidding myself, thinking there was a way to get past that."

He'd been forced to face all the feelings he'd been bottling away, instead of focusing on being prepared to fight. *That was your trigger, baby.* That was what had switched up the game for him, made him start to act out with the Mistresses far more aggressively. The more the truth had sunk in, the worse it had become. Regina would bet on it.

"It didn't make any difference. It didn't…"

"Yes, it did." She gripped his face in gentle but inexorable hands, making him look at her. "You never let him win, Marius. He was after your soul, and you never gave it to him. You were a child, and you let him beat on you instead of doing more harm to innocents. There are grown men who don't have that kind of courage. You weren't weaker than him at all."

"It wasn't courage." His face folded up in anguish. "I couldn't stand to hear them cry. I still can't, it tears things loose in me…"

Volula Jones thought he didn't like cats. Animals picked up distress signals, and those that came off him when he was around them were probably so strong they sent up alarm flags. Particularly when the cats started to plaintively meow for food or attention.

It wasn't that he disliked animals. Far from it.

He was shaking, but no tears came. So much was bottled up, the pressure was threatening to shatter him. He was bending forward into her, not seeking an embrace, but folding up over the pain in his midriff. She scrambled out of the way, catching him around his waist and shoulders to ease him to the ground as he toppled there, shaking so hard she felt a spurt of fear.

Grabbing the blanket off the bed, she used it to cover them as she curved up behind him, wrapping as much of her body around him as she could.

"I'm here," she said. And kept saying it.

She'd stayed away from his childhood, yet now that she knew the root of the problem, it was time to follow her gut. He was hurting, spiraling down into a dark, lonely place, and she could feel his pain. She'd handle it the way he needed.

She started to rock them, holding him to her. "Ssh, ssh, easy..." She rubbed her hand over his chest, his stomach, pressing her mouth between his shoulder blades. "Hush...sweet boy. So sweet. So brave. So strong..."

Closing her eyes, she began to hum. It was a formless tune until it wasn't, until she realized she was humming a lullaby to him, the mockingbird lullaby they'd all heard at one time or another in their lives.

"Hush, sweet boy, don't say a word. Mama's gonna buy you a mockingbird..."

He shuddered, but he gripped her hand on his chest like he'd never let go. And he was letting her rock him, rocking with her. She kept going, telling him if the mockingbird didn't sing, then she'd get him a diamond ring. Lyric after lyric, saying that no matter what thing didn't work out, mama was going to make it okay. And no matter what happened, she was going to always think he was the sweetest boy that had ever been born.

She wasn't his mother, but there was a serious, deep purpose to Mommy/boy play that wasn't play at all. She had maternal instincts, and he needed them. He was plunged deep into the abyss of his childhood, where his mother hadn't protected him, hadn't been capable of thinking of anything but her own survival, the two of them merely random strangers trapped in the same prison with a monster.

He didn't cry. He never even spoke or made a sound at all, but he held onto her. Slowly, his heart's racing started to slow, and his body relaxed into a more natural position, rather than the tight fetal coil.

She kept singing, kept rocking, kept stroking. After a long, long time, a little sigh lifted his shoulders. Then he was still.

They lay like that for a while. She thought he slept some while she hummed to him. Eventually, she curled an arm all the way around his chest and squeezed, a way to partially wake him. "Let's move to the bed."

He nodded and rose. Though he helped her up, he moved as if in a groggy dream state, collapsing onto the mattress after they reached it. Removing the shirt she'd taken from him so she could press her bare skin against his back, she pulled the blankets over them and curled back around him. She also resumed her singing, taking him back to dreams.

She went there herself, but it was a slumber populated with some dark and disturbing shadows. That was okay. If they were his nightmares, she'd hold them off as long as he needed.

Tonight, she would make sure he had peace.

When the shadows dissipated and her eyes opened, there was only him. Early morning sunlight filtered in through the panel, outlining his upper body. He was facing her, his head propped on his hand, elbow pressed to the mattress.

She stroked his jaw with light fingertips. He looked tired still, but not as haunted. Not right now. Just pensive.

"If you're a proper sub," she said, "you know how to make your Mistress coffee."

His eyes were more blue-gray this morning, becoming even more blue when they warmed and he agreeably left the bed. She watched him. He'd slept in the jeans, though they were unbuttoned, riding so low it hinted at the crease between his buttocks. As he stood in front of the coffee maker, he had one hip cocked, upper body curved in an easy slouch he made look appetizing. But she enjoyed the simmering effect of the lust, keeping it in check while she considered other things. He had the first question of the morning, though. He delivered it with his back to her.

"I guess you figured out why I asked you to come, even if I'm not sure of it myself," he said quietly. "But I don't know why you did. Or why you stayed after you found out you'd come to a freak show."

She frowned at his choice of words, but decided to not start the day with contentiousness.

"I wanted to give you a safe place." When he turned his head to look over his shoulder, she swept a hand up and down to signify her entire body. "This is it."

His weary expression showed amusement. "That's a hell of a padded cell."

"Watch it, boy," she warned.

He grinned and returned to the bed while the coffee brewed. Sliding in under the covers when she gestured, he came into her arms and rolled her to her back. His heat and weight were welcome. She was a Domme who held control on the top or the bottom, so she enjoyed either position equally. Her leg hooked around his hip, and his hand closed over her wrist, holding it pinned at her side, his gray eyes measuring her response. She cocked her head, gazing up at him. "What, baby?"

His gaze flickered. "You do that. You bring up the anger and then, you take it away. I don't want to hurt you and be angry, but I am, and I can't stop it. You make me stop it. I can't figure it out. That makes me feel..."

"Out of control. Which makes you mad again. You're trapping yourself in a cycle." She lifted her other hand and traced his shoulder, the one with the armor tattoo. "How about for now, you not try so hard to figure it out? Just ride the ride for a little bit."

His gaze sparked. "Was that an invitation?"

She chuckled. "Only if you're always thinking about sex. Oh, wait, you're male. That answers the question."

"Well, I am lying on a hot, naked woman. Kind of hard not to think about it."

"Kind of hard, period." She undulated against his morning erection and purred as he answered in kind, rubbing himself against her mound. "That's nice." She curled her fingers in the short hair at his neck. "When you're ready, I want you back inside of me."

His fingers constricted on her wrist, telling her he was all for that, but regret flashed through his eyes. "I'll have to make a trip across the street to that Quikstop we passed."

"No, you won't. You had a box of condoms in your glove compartment. I put it in my purse. Aren't you glad I'm nosy?" She tilted her head toward her pinned arm. "You going to keep holding onto me like that?"

"Maybe." He bent and put his mouth to her throat. As she turned her face away to expose her neck even more to him, he bit, making her draw in a shuddering breath. She pressed up against him, breasts and taut nipples rubbing against the coarse hair on his chest. He gripped her other wrist, holding her pinned on both sides.

"Trying that topping thing this morning?" she asked in a deceptively lazy tone, though her pulse kicked up, a warning.

He shook his head. She wasn't sure he knew what he was doing or why, but she waited him out. He was staring at the way his fingers looked curled around her wrists.

"You're so delicate."

She snorted. "That's the last thing I am. I..." She stopped as he looked down at her, his expression switching to something else.

"Don't be afraid," he said.

In a heartbeat, he'd moved and flipped her. He had her arm behind her back, holding her firmly in place. His knee was pressed firmly between her legs, his thigh against her buttocks. His other hand was on her wrist, which he'd angled to make it impossible for her to move unless she wanted to break bone, similar to how she'd put him on his knees the night with Siren. When she tested it, the sharp stab of pain made her suck in a breath and him speak.

"Don't move. It only hurts if you move." He bent and kissed her between her shoulder blades, moving up to her nape, his mouth dwelling there to nip and caress, suck. She wasn't liking the hold, but she tried to relax, enjoy the sensations he was giving her while she figured out what the hell he was doing.

His grip tightened. "It's that easy," he said. "I could break your wrist with little effort. One punch to the face, and I could break your neck." He stretched out on her full length, some of his weight held on his knees, but his cock beneath the jeans pressed against her buttocks. He shifted to hold her wrists in a normal way, extending her arms out to either side like wings. He pressed his chest to her back. His breath was heated on her neck. "But you can break me with a word, or a look. It makes me not trust myself with you. But you do."

"Yes." Relaxing, she closed her eyes as he nuzzled her cheek, kissed her neck again. "Be inside me like this. Take off the jeans, get the condom out of my purse."

He obeyed, the mattress depressing under his movements as he left the bed. She drew a deep, calming breath, listening to the rustle of clothing, the tear of foil, as he complied. She'd left her hands where they were intentionally. When he returned, he clasped her wrists again. She lifted her hips, accommodating him, and he slid into her slick tissues. He let out a soft oath. "I wasn't expecting you to be that wet."

"I woke up and saw you. That was enough to get me started. But don't get too used to that. I'll still expect foreplay."

His chuckle vibrated against her, a heavy rumble, as if it were still weighed down by his thoughts. "Yes, Mistress."

He stroked inside her, slow, easy, the two of them in no hurry. Somewhere along the way his grip became a hold, not a pin, his fingers caressing her pulse points and forearms. When the climax came upon him, he held himself back, sliding a hand beneath her to stroke her clit. "Come first," he urged. "I want to hear you. I love hearing you."

Since it sounded more like a request than a demand, she obliged, and he followed behind her, a spinning, dizzying, intense but soft, morning lovemaking.

They breathed slow and deep together in the aftermath. He turned them to spoon, only he was behind her this time, his arms wrapped around her, breath on her neck. A couple of times last night she'd woken to find him in that position, a possessive arm around her waist, his body curled as protectively around her as she'd been around him when they first went to sleep. Yeah, he did have some of that in him. A sign that he wanted something for himself. It was a good sign.

They indulged another short doze until the smell of the coffee teased her senses. But she wasn't ready for him to move yet.

"I want to adopt a dog," he said. "But I don't want to screw it up."

She tilted her head toward him, her temple brushing his jaw. "You're such a puzzle," she said, but she put a smile in her voice. "Have you been thinking about this for a while, or just now?"

"Yes and no." He buried his face in her hair, inhaling deep and giving a pleased growl when she stretched against him, rubbing her backside against his cock. "Fuck, that feels good. Will you do it again?"

"Since you asked so nicely..." She savored her own reaction when he fondled her breasts, stroked the nipples. Just a pleasurable, playful aftermath. "Tell me about the dog."

He curved his arms back around her, one over her breasts and one around her waist, holding her so close to him, like he didn't want to let her go, even for an inch of space. She didn't deny him, not right now. But he was going to get his ass out of bed and bring her coffee soon.

"When I was little, I wanted a pet, but he said no. I didn't know why...until. Then, after he went to jail, the shadow went to be with her sister. She handed me over to her second cousin in Miami for a few years. He had a spare bedroom and said if I helped with household chores, I could stay there until I was old enough to be on my own without social services coming after him."

If his best relative was a cousin who grudgingly took in an adolescent for the free labor, Regina needed to have a talk with the powers-that-be about letting a kid be born under such an unlucky star. But she put that aside to hear the rest of the story.

"He had a dog, a chocolate lab named Ricky. I didn't ever pet him, because...animals just don't take to me. But sometimes he'd come lie outside my room at night when Fisher went to work second shift. It was cool. I'd watch him and think about touching him. His ears looked so soft. I liked how he'd pile on the couch with Fisher and they'd hang out together."

He propped up on an elbow as she turned onto her back. Sliding a finger along the outside of her breast, he cupped it, seeming to like the act of simply holding it, his fingers moving in a slow knead that sent tendrils of arousal back down between her legs. They'd be having sex again before they left the room, she was sure of that. At this rate, they'd probably fuck themselves to death by noon checkout.

"Well, boys and dogs are a lot like girls and horses," she observed. "They naturally gravitate together. Maybe you need to ease into the adoption thing, see what your options are in the right environment. Ever been to New Orleans?"

"No. I've barely been outside Florida."

"Good. I can show you something you haven't seen." She smiled at him. "I'm giving a workshop there next week. If you don't have anything pressing, why don't you come with me? It'd be a three-day trip. There's a guy there, a retired Navy SEAL and a Dom. He runs a unique kind of animal shelter. You could check it out if you want. No pressure. We can enjoy the food and a couple tourist attractions, then come on back home. NOLA also has a great club, Progeny, and The Zone has reciprocal guest privileges there. If I get in the mood to use some fancy equipment on a sub, we might go there."

"Would you be using the equipment on 'a sub' or me?" He said it as if he were teasing, but his gaze became a little more challenging. "You'd pick someone out and I'd watch with my thumb up my ass?"

"That would depend on you," she said. He behaved better if she didn't let him get away with being too pushy. But she wanted to test the ground some, so she asked him straight out. "How would you feel about me working out another sub?"

"I wouldn't like it."

"Then I suggest you stay on your best behavior," she said, concealing the little trip to her pulse. Possessiveness wasn't always a good thing in a sub, and could go too far. But in Marius, it was progress, wanting something enough to show it, work at it, rather than sabotaging it. She wanted him to embrace the idea that he could choose, could desire a Mistress instead of playing her. He could have something for himself. "Does that mean the trip interests you?"

"Yeah. I can chip in for gas, because my car's not reliable for a distance that far. Not if I'm chauffeuring a lady."

His considerateness pleased her. "We'd be flying. I have a friend who private jets it between New Orleans, Tampa and Miami, because he and his wife like The Zone and he's the plant operations manager for a bunch of Central American facilities. I checked with him a couple weeks ago to see if I could hook up with his latest flight schedule, and it worked out. His wife will be with him on this trip. You'll like her."

"Okay." He looked a little taken aback by the idea of a private plane, and she expected the jolt was giving him some other second thoughts. It was a pretty big step from where he'd been only a week ago. She tapped his cheek.

"If you change your mind, all you need to do is let me know so I'm not waiting around for you. But I hope you decide to go. I'd enjoy your company. Now where's my coffee? Two sugars, one cream."

He left the bed without saying anything more, though his thoughts were loud enough. When he started to pull his jeans back on, she cleared her throat to command his attention.

"Did I say you could get dressed?"

He stopped. She'd dialed down her usual Mistress level this morning, instinct telling her a lower tone had been needed, but those same instincts told her now might be a good time to raise it up again, to help his focus.

As he met her gaze, she sharpened hers, a rebuke. It was amazing how responsive and intuitive a sub he was. But then again, he knew all the rules—thoroughly and bone deep. It was why he was so accomplished at breaking them. Not right now, though. Indescribable pleasure unfurled in her belly when he pointedly dropped his gaze toward the floor.

"No, ma'am."

"We'll call that one infraction, then. Bring me my coffee."

He left the jeans and moved across the room, all flexing ass and thigh muscles, and mixed the brew according to her specs. When he brought it back to her—another pleasing view—she sat up and took the cup with both hands, inhaling the scent with gratitude and sipping. "Not bad for hotel coffee." She pointed to the chair, where he'd draped the belt that had been in his jeans. "Bring that to me."

That intriguing muscle in his jaw jumped again, but he complied. She gestured. "Stretch out across the bed, your chest against the edge of the mattress, hands gripping the side rail. Spread your legs out."

She slid out of the bed as he complied. Setting the coffee aside, she threaded the belt through her fingers. "Mistresses in the past punished you because they thought you were asking for pain, and you were, but to hide what you really wanted. When I strap your ass, Duncan, I'm not after your pain, though that will be an intriguing side effect. I'm reminding you that you did something wrong, and you've disappointed me. Watching a powerful ass react to being strapped, watching you hold all that strength in check and submitting to discipline...that eases my disappointment while reinforcing the lesson. You understand?"

He had wrapped his hands around the rail, his head bowed so she could see his concentrated profile. Slowly, he nodded.

Part of the build for her, the anticipation, was taking a long, drawn out pause to speculate on what might be going through a strong sub's mind before he was punished. Right now the kick of it was so powerful she felt a tremor go through her. Circling the bed, she squatted in front of him, stroking her fingers through the hair over his brow. It was quickly becoming a favorite caress, running those spiky, soft strands through her knuckles, tugging on them like a horse's forelock. Could he feel the faint quiver through her fingers, like he had yesterday? Wasn't it amazing that, for once, she wanted a man to feel that reaction?

As he started to lift his lashes, she tsked, and he kept them down. "You have no idea what your obedience does to me," she said, low. "Makes me want to care for you, protect you, fuck you until your legs shake. Wrap your throat and your dick in a collar with my name stamped on them. Not just on the collar, but into your very flesh." She watched his fingers whiten on the rail. A lovely reaction.

"Do you know why I'm feeling that way, Duncan? I can see—truly see—how hearing it breaks things open inside you. The truth of it makes your cock hard, makes your heart hurt and pound. Now, tell me why I'm punishing you."

He had to sort through a maze of emotions to find it, and when she saw the brief flash of panic at not having the answer ready to hand, she adored it. That panic came when a sub truly wanted to please his Mistress, and was afraid of that disappointment she'd mentioned.

"I started to put on my clothes without permission."

"A gold star for the right answer, though delivery time needs work." Rising, she circled back around him, trailing her fingertips over his shoulder.

"Spread your thighs wider. I want to see those big, badass balls of yours. Make you worry I might include them in your punishment."

His thighs spread, and she scraped her nails down one buttock, pleased with the light fur and muscled flesh. "Beautiful."

Doubling up the belt in her hand, she struck, hard. She was satisfied to see he hadn't been expecting the force and flinched, a breath whistling out between his teeth. "I may have my fragile moments," she said with amusement, "but am I weak, sweet boy?"

"No, ma'am." The red mark was already showing on his ass. His biceps bunched as he constricted his grip on the rail.

She put a knee on the bed and slid her hand between the mattress and his genitals, gripping his testicles. "Lift your ass for me," she said with menace. "Don't you tuck down."

"I won't."

"Sassing me now? This isn't a fight. This is you giving me what I want. Isn't it?"

"Yes."

"Yes, what?"

"Yes, Mistress."

She struck again, keeping her grip on his testicles, so when he jerked, he felt the pull. She maintained that hold as she doled out a dozen stinging strokes. They were less powerful than the first one, but plenty hard enough to keep his attention.

"Turn over and get on your back. Swivel around and put your head over the edge of the mattress on my side. I know you're not going to make your Mistress walk around the bed."

She stepped back to watch him comply. His erection was at full mast. The punishment had aroused him. His hands were in half curls on the mattress. Not fist clenching anger, or evidence of him fighting himself. Anticipation and need were keeping him caught between erotic tension and emotional upheaval.

"More," she instructed, giving his hair a tug. "I want you looking at the wall."

After he adjusted his body so he could tilt his head farther over the mattress, she threaded the belt under the base of his skull and wrapped her wrists in the slack on either side. Since she'd been administering his punishment in nothing but her skin, his gaze flicked to the view of her bare pussy she was giving him, standing so close.

Then, miracle of miracles, he shut his eyes tight. A soft smile crossed her face.

"I didn't tell you that you could look, did I?"

He shook his head. "No, Mistress."

"You might have the makings of a good boy yet." *Though not too good, thank Goddess.* She straddled his head, bringing his treat right up against his nose and lips. "I told you yesterday you'd be eating pussy over and over. You're not done with that. Get back to work."

He put himself into it a hundred percent. Watching his cock get higher against his belly, the slit oozing with pre-come, goaded her own arousal to higher levels than she'd experienced with any other submissive in recent memory.

Fucking divine angels in heaven. His mouth sucked, tongue licked, teeth nipped, and he did patterns on her flesh, swirls and stabs that had her gasping, her hands clenching the belt. What nearly pushed her over was when he started vocalizing against her, groans and grunts of pleasure, savoring his meal, encouraging her own gasps.

As her stomach coiled up, warning her the orgasm was imminent, she stepped back, taking a forever-keeper snapshot of that first second, his mouth smeared with her juices, hair rumpled, eyes glazed with lust and the total concentration he'd given to the task she demanded.

"Turn around so you're stretched out the usual way, toward the headboard, but far enough down your legs are bent over the bottom of the mattress."

As soon as he did, she straddled his face again, only now her knees were on the bed and she was facing his feet. She set the belt to the side, her thighs spread over his face but knees clamped against his head to reinforce her pussy was out of bounds now, no matter that it was close enough he could smell her arousal, see it trickling over her flesh.

She bent forward to take him in her mouth, all the way to the root. His breath stuttered, puffs of air against her engorged tissues. She sucked on him, clasping the base of his cock and working it.

"Mistress...let me."

"Be still," she ordered. More evidence he was a true sub, not entirely comfortable with her servicing him like this, but her command sent him a message. Whatever she was doing to him, his reaction and surrender served her.

Wetting a finger, she traced it along his perineum to his rectum, and slid inside, earning a quiver and jump, a thickening of his cock in her mouth as she kept up her rhythmic sucking. His hands were on her thighs, clutching but not pulling. A reminder he was there whenever she was ready.

She smiled against his cock. Yeah, he'd never be totally good. She hadn't told him he could hold her thighs like that. But she knew he wouldn't force her down on him. She could feel the heat of his stare boring into her pussy as it shifted above his face; could feel his body shaking with the attempt to restrain himself. A powerful man held by her command alone.

As she'd said, there was no drug like it. It was sheer, fucking heaven.

Slowly, she brought her pussy down, down, down. "Now," she said.

He attacked like a ravenous tiger. As she went back down on his cock, she swallowed him with a gasp and a moan of pleasure. He wasn't as smooth in his ministrations now, but the erratic urgency of his passion aroused her even more.

Fuck, he had her so close in no time, and she could tell he was ready whenever she was. She straightened and took her pussy away, muscles tightening against his grip to tell him she was moving.

He resisted one heart-stopping moment, eyes wild, mouth set with determination to have his way. But because he was in that zone of service and need, not because he was wanting to prove he had control.

Still, that moment of defiance would be good for another five licks of the belt, but right now she had other priorities. When he released her, she flipped around to face the head of the bed. "Hands and palms up, shoulder width," she ordered, her voice heavy with her own urgent lust.

She already had her hands out, showing him what she wanted. She loved that his eyes lighted with fierce pleasure. She could have had him scoot up the bed so she could grab the headboard, but the only support she wanted was him.

She gripped both his upraised hands and used the strength of his lifted arms to straddle his face again and control her movements against his mouth. As his face pressed deeper into her pussy, she watched his mouth work over her cunt, his dark lashes fanning his cheeks. She'd left him hurting for his own climax, but she'd take care of that in a minute. Right now his job was to take care of her. That was what they both needed.

As the climax surged up and through her, her grip slipped and his went to her wrists, an arousing and intriguing dual message of who held control, who was caring for who.

She came with low, long cries, working herself against him, the morning beard adding an almost unbearable friction as she rubbed harder, intensifying the sensation. Fuck...her brain was going to explode, her whole body overcome.

When she came down, shuddering, the lingering effect was so strong, she didn't want to stop. She moved on his mouth in a slow, rhythmic cycle, humming her pleasure as he kept his tongue available to her, stroking with long, strong sweeps along her still spasming tissues.

"You are a treasure." They were the first words she could manage, sometime later, in a voice hoarse from screaming. She found the strength to move back, touched when his grip went to her waist and hips to keep her steady as she dismounted, putting both knees on one side of his body.

She wasn't done with it yet. Not by a long shot. She brought her mouth to his chest and worked her way down, a laborious inch at a time, tasting and exploring, kissing and biting, chuckling darkly as he jumped at the sharpness of her teeth and let out a low curse. When his hand grazed her waist, her hip, she shook her head against him.

"Grip the bedding above your head. Keep your hands to yourself."

He groaned again, a protest. She knew he wanted to touch her, and Goddess, did she want to be touched. But first, she took him in her mouth again, took him deep and sucked and nipped, hollowing her cheeks. She gripped his balls, stroked her thumb over his perineum. At the height of his arousal, when she knew how close he was, she eased three moistened fingers back into his rectum, just an inch or so past the erogenous ring of muscles, and fluttered and played.

"Go," she muttered, a vibration against his flesh.

He cried out, a deep, guttural groan as the climax took him, as he came in her mouth, his hands clutching the rumpled sheets, his body bucking up to her.

She let herself feel it, the bliss of commanding his response, of him letting it happen, of the two of them coming together the way it was supposed to work.

As all the gods and goddesses as her witness, she wanted him like she'd never wanted a sub.

It didn't have to make sense. Yes, he had a unique backstory. But his response to her wasn't unique, not if she was objective about it. God knows, she'd had others more accommodating, far less work, and just as gorgeous and hot, if not more so. But she hadn't wanted to plumb their hearts, minds and souls the way she did with him. Endlessly and forever.

This was the way it worked. She'd seen it happen between Mistresses and subs before. That click moment when a Mistress knew a sub not only was all hers, but she was meant to be his, too.

When she realized she loved him.

Damn it all, she was as sure of it as if he'd come to her with a bow tied around his energetic dick and her name stamped on his ass.

Hmm. There was an idea. New Orleans had a lot of tattoo parlors, after all...

CHAPTER FOURTEEN

*M*arius stood at the airport window, overlooking the area for private planes. He was in a VIP lounge where they offered sparkling water, gourmet coffees, wrapped chocolates and snacks way above economy flight peanut packet standards. A concierge stood at attention behind a desk, ready to call another someone to run and fetch whatever was needed for the small scattering of important people hanging out here, waiting for their planes to arrive or be ready for boarding.

Regina was on a work call as she sat by another window. She was canopied by a slender trio of indoor palms. Her laptop was open as she coordinated some changes to her presentation, per the client's needs. Leastwise, that was what he'd picked up from listening to this side of the call.

He should be checking out the view, watching the prep of the planes. Instead, as he leaned against the window frame, arms crossed over his chest and foot hooked over his ankle, he watched her.

Today she was in work wear, and damn, if it didn't conjure some heavy-duty fantasies. Black slacks outlined her trim figure and those long, long legs he could vividly imagine wrapped around his body in a vise grip as her cunt squeezed down on him.

She wore a silky ivory-colored blouse, open at the throat to show a necklace with a pendant of the red jasper she favored. A black blazer completed the ensemble with a small pin on the lapel. The silver and ceramic red rose was no wider or longer than her smallest finger. She wore small silver hoops in her double-pierced ears.

He recalled pressing his face into her throat below one of her adorned ear lobes earlier this morning. Her hair had brushed his face, her pulse pounding against his mouth. She was affected by him. She didn't bother to hide it.

Since the night in the hotel room, she hadn't hidden or walled off her responses to him. She was putting the attraction right out there without fear. Probably because she'd made it clear she would kick his ass sideways if he tried to mess with the gift of her vulnerability.

He couldn't help but wonder. If, by some miracle, one day she could trust him enough not to be on guard against his fucked-up-ness —if he could trust himself enough to let her—how far could they go together?

The thought was just another thrown on the pile of his WTF list. He couldn't think about anything long term with her. It was safer to keep thinking of the whole relationship as driven by The Zone membership thing. It had started that way.

He really didn't know what the hell it was now.

He thought of kissing his way up her spine, those delicate bones. She'd be lying face down, her fingers curling into the blue and green comforter on her bed.

Was it nuts that he found it incredibly hot, standing in a public place and watching her work? Her focus on her client, the capable way she spoke and tapped on the laptop, showed how comfortable she was with a job that sounded pretty impressive and demanding. Was it possible not to feel like a complete loser in comparison?

Was he his best self with her, in the words of the bullshit self-help books? Not even close.

He knew Lady Regina's rep. She took on hard cases and helped them become better subs. So he was her latest project. He'd been spiraling downward, and should be grateful for the interest. If she could help him figure out how not to go down that dark road with a Mistress, to twist one up because of fucked-up reasons of his own, then he'd get back into The Zone—on a couple levels—and be able to count her as something he'd rarely had in his life. A true friend.

A win-win. One that pissed him off. *Don't*, he advised himself. *Don't screw up today.* Even though so many of the things she'd opened in him were what twisted him up now, he knew those were his issues. Maybe for once, he wouldn't make them hers.

Her gaze slid to him, lingered. He knew what she was seeing. His body was easy on a woman's eyes. He had no false modesty about that. He was also good in bed. When he wasn't being an ass, he was more than capable of satisfying her sexually, exceeding her expectations. Was she thinking of his mouth between her legs, his cock inside of her? As her perusal of his shoulders slid down over his chest and abdomen, groin and thighs, and back again, he expected she was. It took his mind back to the last few days since they'd returned to Tampa, and particularly to how this morning had started...

After they came back to the city, he hadn't seen her for a couple days. She'd had to work on one of her consulting jobs. However, the day before the New Orleans trip, she'd told him to come stay at her house overnight. She'd warned him she'd be working part of the evening and, sure enough, when he arrived, she only had time to give him a quick tour of TV, kitchen and sleeping arrangements before she returned to her home office, telling him not to wait up for her.

He found out she'd cooked him an honest-to-God homemade pizza, and left it in the oven for him. It was better than any pizza he'd ever had, even if it did have broccoli on it. She'd left a sticky note on the oven. "No picking off the vegetables." Strict Mistress.

When he took some pizza and her preferred drink to her before he ate his own meal, he won a pleased if distracted smile. Returning to the living room, he wished she could take a break to join him. He indulged the unsettling vision, the two of them hanging out on the living room floor to eat pizza and watch movies. But their relationship wasn't about that, so he put it out of his head.

He ate the rest of the pizza, broccoli and all, while watching TV. Despite his best efforts to stay up for her, he fell asleep on the floor in front of it. He felt odd about stretching out on her furniture without her say-so.

When she woke him, it was nearly midnight. She clasped his hand, and led him down the hall, to her bedroom. Maybe because he was half-asleep, he was over the threshold before he could experience the volatile need to retreat he'd had last time she'd tried to take him there.

He'd been distracted from that by the sight of the pallet on the floor, next to her bed. It was made up with sheets, blankets and two pillows. He stared at it, bathed by the soft glow of the bedside lamp. He was being given a place to sleep. For the first time in a long time, it felt like it was in a place where he belonged. Where he was supposed to be.

That should have sent him in full fight-or-flight mode, but the sleepiness and excess of pizza were apparently dulling his survival skills. He was fully capable of undressing himself, but she brushed his hands aside and did it, taking all of it off.

"This is how my sub sleeps. No clothes but his Mistress's approval. And you don't put them on in the morning until I say so. If you get cold, you tell me."

She put firm pressure on his shoulder. "Down. Get in bed."

He complied, though being naked made him want her to get in with him. Tucking him in and brushing a kiss on his lips and forehead, she chuckled when he tried to tug her down.

"Sleep, bad boy," she murmured. He watched her move away. Cruel and blessed goddess that she was, she slipped out of her clothes where he could watch, but as if she was alone, unselfconscious, practical. Perversely, that made him harder. Her nightgown was an ivory thing with lace that showed the dark smudges of her nipples and cleft of her ass. She climbed into her bed, shut off the light...and went to sleep.

It should have been sexually frustrating, and it was, but another part of him was content. He listened to her breathe evenly, to the sounds of the house settling as he slid in and out of a doze. Eventually he dropped off, in that extraordinarily deep way he did around her. When he'd woken up in his car at the prison and seen her sitting next to him, he couldn't believe she'd been able to get in without rousing him. She didn't believe him when he told her what a light sleeper he was, and why should she? Around her, he slept like a baby in his mother's arms.

What he'd read it was like, that is. Remembering her humming the lullaby to him in the hotel, he was uncomfortably aware that what he'd experienced with her might be the closest thing to it he'd ever had. He'd seen the Mommy/little boy scenes at the club, and that definitely was not his thing, the thumb sucking and diapering and all that shit. But Regina had mentioned there were a lot of layers to that kind of play, something about the need of the male spirit to find and cleave to a Goddess Mother through a lover's arms...

She'd said that during some of their random pillow talk, laughing at his dubious and blank look. Her laugh was sultry and raspy, making him feel the way he did when her fingers caressed the base of his spine.

She woke him in the early morning light with those tempting fingers stroking the strands of hair away from his forehead, teasing his temple with the scrape of her nails. "Good morning," she said when his eyes opened. Her voice was calm and throaty, not too loud.

She straightened from her squat by his pallet. She was already dressed and sipping a cup of coffee. The brisk energy around her suggested she'd been doing some prep work for the trip today. He wondered if she'd gotten enough sleep last night, and if he could have done something other than watch TV to help her get ready for her trip. He should have asked.

"Take a shower in the guest bathroom," she said. "We leave in an hour."

He wished he'd woken earlier so maybe she would have let them shower together. It irritated him.

As he propped himself up on his elbows, she touched his jaw, her eyes darkening when he gripped her wrist. "You like doing that," she said softly. "Holding me like you've captured me, even though your nature is to accept a Mistress's dominion. You need something to help you keep things straight in your head." She nodded to the bed. "I've left out clothes for you. This trip, you're under my command and direction, unless I tell you otherwise. Think you can handle that?"

"And if I can't?" He rubbed his eyes. Sometimes, it was kneejerk to be a smartass. He really had to work on that too.

"You can," she said evenly. "So not an option. There are two items on the bed you'll be wearing, but they're not for you to put on yourself. You bring them to me after you shower and get dressed in the rest of the things I left you. You'll know which ones I mean."

Hooking the corner of the blanket with the toe of her elegant heel, she stripped it off the bed, leaving him lying naked on the mattress. Her gaze slid over his body, his morning erection.

"Beautiful," she purred. "Fold the blanket up and put it on the mattress with the pillows plumped up and the fitted sheet straightened. There better not be anything happening in the shower other than washing. Your hand stays off what's mine except for functional purposes."

She strolled out of the bedroom, leaving him wanting to fuck her brainless and yet do everything she asked. He'd lost his mind, and apparently handed over his man card to her on top of that. But he didn't feel emasculated from the way she looked at him, how she approved of his obedience. He felt more like a man when he pleased her than he ever had when he pounded bigger men than himself to their knees. Go figure.

He wasn't straight enough to marshal a plan to counter those feelings, and he didn't have much desire to come up with one. The grip on her wrist was the only evidence of his controlling behavior so far today. But it was early.

Suppressing a sigh and the thought, he got up to check out what she wanted him to wear. Nice stuff. A pin-striped blue button-down shirt to go under a gray silk vest. The shirt sleeves were designed to be rolled up to his elbows and secured with a button. Stressed jeans and a brown belt completed the look. All the sizes looked right, but he wouldn't have expected anything different. A package of black briefs took care of the underwear.

It'd been a long time since he'd bought new clothes for himself. These were new, but except for the underwear, they appeared to have been washed and pressed, because they didn't have the creases and new store smell. Instead, they captured the pleasant, clean scents of her home. Did she have a laundry or maid service who had done it? He'd be far more comfortable with that than the idea his Mistress had ironed and done laundry for him. Thinking about doing that for *her*, though, brought a whole different kind of feeling, not unpleasant.

Pretty much all his sub stuff, except for the occasional eye-candy wait staff job at an event like Tyler and Marguerite's annual Carnival, had been session- or demo-based. Not service stuff, caring for a Mistress. But sometimes he'd thought about what it would be like to care for one. Usually late at night, when he couldn't stop himself from having those kinds of thoughts.

When he lifted the clothes off the bed, he found the two items he wasn't supposed to put on himself, and they just amplified his crazy thoughts about caring for, and belonging to, a Mistress. A cock harness, and something in a small velvet bag. It felt like jewelry. He knew enough not to open it, but as he held it clutched in one hand, a surge of emotions shoved through him, that mix of good and bad. He was always unsure which was going to get the upper hand.

One thing was certain, though. He was going to have a hard time not jacking off in the shower.

Going to the bathroom, he laid all the items out carefully. He proceeded the same way with his shower, handling himself with studied functionality, refusing to let the thought of doing more with his cock than washing it even cross his mind. He wasn't going to defy her. He was going to show he could do this, be a "good" sub. The jagged-edged voices in his gut laughed at him. Yeah, it would probably last less than two minutes. Why did he care, anyway? What was so different about her?

Everything, asshole. Don't ruin this.

But that wasn't the problem, was it? She was amazing. He was the fuck-up. Wasn't it better to let her down sooner rather than later?

No. Shut the fuck up and get dressed.

He dried the shower and cleaned up after himself. As he brushed his teeth and hair and donned the clothes, he could hear her talking on the phone. Picking up the two items, he followed her voice to the kitchen. His nose directed his gaze to the bacon and eggs in a fry pan on the stove. His eyes went to her. She was sitting in a kitchen chair, legs crossed, body twisted around to type on her laptop as she spoke into a handsfree piece in her ear.

When she dipped her chin toward the oven, he opened it and saw a handful of flaky biscuits, still warm enough to give off the fresh baked scent. She'd cooked for him again.

Not like other Mistresses had done. With more than a twinge of guilt, he remembered Lady Di, who'd done things like this for him. But even if he was being an asshole, it had reminded him of the pathetic slavishness of a person trying too hard to win the affection of their favorite pet.

He didn't get that sense of dependence from the woman currently on the phone. Regina was taking care of him because...he wasn't sure why.

She'd said he was hers to command for the duration of this trip, which apparently included dressing him the way she wished. He'd never thought about being into that, but she'd bought him a good outfit, and telling him what to wear seemed to underscore the ownership arrangement.

That was also what her fixing breakfast said to him. She was in charge, which meant when she provided for his basic needs, or bought him clothes, she was reinforcing that he was hers. It also reminded him who he served in provocative ways, big and small. He served her, and she took care of him.

It was a new thought, and an unsettling one that aroused his body and mind, and made his soul even more hungry and messed up.

She gestured to him. When he approached, she extended her hand, slim fingers and glossy nails. As she continued to talk on the phone, he laid the velvet bag and cock harness in her hand. Her gaze shifted to the jeans, then back to his face, a command.

He unbuttoned and took down the zipper, pushing briefs and jeans to his thighs. She caressed his cock, scratching him with her nails. His cock jumped in her hand, growing thicker. He'd already been half-erect, just thinking about this. She put the harness on him, two crossed straps that went around the base of both his cock and testicles. He bit back a grunt as she took it one hole more than was comfortable in his current state.

"No, I think it's a good idea to hold the handouts until the first break. I want them to exercise their listening skills first, because that's key to the rest of the approach."

She gripped him, stroking. As if she was entirely unaffected by his state. It was maddening. Intolerable.

He yanked her up from her chair by the shoulders, planting his mouth on hers, discovering the heaven of her heated, damp tongue and lips, the scent of cinnamon toothpaste and sweet woman. She didn't struggle, didn't draw back, but gave as good as she was getting, her hand dropping to clamp down on his buttock. Which gave her better leverage to use the other hand to grip his cock and twist.

Fuck. He let her go, but since her weight was forward, he didn't want to unbalance her. He pushed through the discomfort, holding his position to ease her back to the chair. Her cheeks were flushed, her eyes heated and a little pissed. That made him harder. She pointed to the floor and now he embraced obedience, dropping to his knees. She shook her head, pointed to the floor again. She wanted his forehead on the floor, his ass in the air.

He frowned but did it. Inexplicable things uncoiled in him as she put one shoe on the back of his neck, the other against his side. The heels dug into both places. She continued her call for another fifteen minutes, using her bent knee as a prop to make notes on a pad, the heel on his side gouging in deeper between his ribs when she twisted around again to type. He held fast in that position, though, serving as her foot rest. His unfastened jeans stayed off his ass, his cock and balls trussed up in her straps.

At last she cut the connection and removed her feet. "Sit up and apologize."

"For what?" He hadn't meant to sound belligerent. He just couldn't seem to help himself.

"I've seen you brat, purposefully seeking punishment to yank a Mistress's chain. I know the difference between that and what you're doing now. Back down to the floor."

She didn't wait, clasping the back of his neck in a firm hand and shoving him toward the linoleum. He tried to push back and she just held him down with an admonishing noise. He could have gotten rougher, fought harder, but he didn't, and didn't examine why not. She rose, a click-click of heels across her kitchen, and he heard the clink of a utensil against the granite countertop.

"This will do the trick."

He bit back a snarl as she hit his bare ass with something metallic that felt like it cut skin. She did it to the other side and then held it to his flesh. The metal spatula she'd apparently been using for his breakfast was heated but didn't burn. However, pressing that heat on top of the sting intensified the temperature.

"One more."

He did his best to bristle, not flinch, but Christ, she knew how to deliver a blow. She landed this one smack in the opening between his thighs, so his balls got a glancing blow, a sting through the joining point of his sac to the rest of his more tender regions.

He could handle loads of pain, even more than this, but something was raw inside of him, making it hurt more than usual. Or maybe it was that it hurt in places that had nothing to do with his nerve endings.

There was a clatter as she tossed the spatula in the sink. Grabbing his hair, she jerked him up to his knees, holding him against her thighs as she wrenched his face up, using a grip on his throat and jaw. He was staring up into her face, which was cold and disapproving. A reaction that also hit him in the gut.

"I let you sleep in and made you breakfast. So what do you owe me?"

A million smartass answers fought for supremacy, and she saw it, because she got closer, her eyes boring into his.

"You let me see into your soul," she said in measured tones. "Doesn't matter what you do today, that won't ever change. Your cover is busted, Marius. I know who and what you are. How about you try out a different version of yourself today? One a lot closer to who you wish you could be, the person I believe you actually are. You can be mine today and for this trip, or you can hit the road. I won't put up with the attitude on a work day. So, last chance. Tell me what you owe me."

That grip on his jaw moved slightly. A brush of her fingertip on his chin. A caress, at odds with the freezing temps of her expression, the hardness of her hold on him. Two sides of the coin, and she would give him both or only one. He wanted both.

He put his hands over hers. Not to grip, but to express himself. "I'm sorry, Mistress," he said roughly, adjusting his gaze to her waist. "I owe you...respect. Good manners. I should have helped you more last night, too. Gotten up this morning and made you breakfast instead."

He didn't mean to say all that, but he did. He also had to suppress an urge to press his face into her midriff. She'd likely knee him in the balls. "I do like biscuits and gravy. Thank you for making them."

She sighed, and he thought he heard a half chuckle. "I thought you would, sweet boy. Pull up your pants. Go make yourself a plate for breakfast and stop tempting me to fuck your ass with an open bottle of Tabasco sauce."

He had no doubt she'd do it, and that was something he'd prefer to avoid. Releasing him to do as he'd been told, she returned to the table. He tilted his head to look at her out of his peripheral vision. She went back to her laptop, not a tremor in her hands, but he sensed...disturbance. He'd caused that.

Wrestling with an unfamiliar sense of guilt, he cleared his throat. "Can I make you a plate, Mistress?"

She nodded, her eyes on the laptop screen again. She didn't provide him additional guidance, but he'd gauged the portions she preferred from the last time they'd shared breakfast. He brought her the plate of food and a glass of juice before returning to the counter to make his own. Might be stupid, but it made him feel somewhat better to see her glance at the plate and then pick up her fork to dig in, his choices obviously meeting her approval.

She'd left him a place setting, but he took a seat cross-legged at her feet and began to eat that way. He was aware of her eyes on him. A long few minutes later, her hand fell on his shoulder and stroked him absently as she resumed her work. The straps bit into his cock and balls, which knotted things in his gut. He wanted to slide under the kitchen table, spread her thighs and give her pleasure again. But he hadn't been given permission to do that. He might have, if he hadn't messed it up. He'd denied them both with his bad behavior. And suddenly that mattered to him.

She'd pocketed the item in the velvet bag. No matter how crazy it was, how he told himself he'd never wanted something like what might be inside that pouch, he knew he did want it. But he'd screwed up. Maybe she'd put it on him later. If he could keep himself from screwing up again. Not much chance of that. He'd always known he was hopeless; had never cared if everyone else felt the same about him.

Until now.

Returning to the present at the airport, Marius found he'd started to get hard from his imaginings of her taking such absolute control of him. The response reminded him with sharp clarity of the strap cinched around the base of his cock and circling his balls. He didn't usually give a second thought to a hard-on, since most of his time was spent in places like The Zone or the fight ring. However, being in an airport lounge with people way above his class and station had him feeling more self-conscious. If he didn't keep a lid on it, they'd get an eyeful.

He looked up to see her studying him again. She closed the laptop, put away the phone and gestured to him. As he strode across the lounge toward her, he was aware of a couple women's speculative glances. Rich women, who appeared to be traveling on their own. Yeah, it wasn't the first time he'd run into that kind. Even The Zone had a few of those interested in owning a good-looking sub mainly as their show pony, and he didn't mean for pony play.

Regina had money. But she didn't give him the impression that was what she was seeking. She might like treating him like her boy-toy sometimes, but the way she might want to do that didn't bother him. Far from it.

He had to suppress a strange urge to drop to a knee at her feet, bow his head and wait for her to express her desire, the way he would at The Zone. There was more than one way it was hard for him to act civilized in the mundane world. So instead he sat beside her in a chair, stretching out his legs in his usual sprawled way and laying an arm on the back of her chair. Yeah, it was a less-than-casual possessive gesture, but there were also a few rich guys in the lounge who were too interested in getting a piece of the tall, dark and totally hot action that Regina represented.

She laid a hand on his thigh. "That should take care of work for a little while. Sorry I had to ignore you."

"Not the way it works, Mistress. I'm here for your pleasure."

Her eyes sparked, her mouth tipping up in a little smile. "You said that in such a nice way, I didn't mind hearing it."

She leaned back against his arm and he coiled his hand around her shoulder, playing with the ropes of her hair, winding them around his fingers. She didn't seem to mind that, either.

She stroked his thigh. "This outfit looks really good on you. You're a handsome man, Marius. I expect you know that."

He shrugged. "I clean up good."

Her fingertip slid along his lip, the twisted scar. "You're not pretty, though. Not like you were at one time. I saw pictures of you early on at The Zone."

"Well, fighting takes away some of the prettiness. It was an advantage when it was there, because they tended to underestimate me. Now, not so much."

"No, I imagine not," she said wryly. "You don't seem bothered by that."

"It's just skin. You take it off, what's under..."

A twitch went through his leg, his fingertips. It hit him unexpected, fast, hard, like a scary clown jumping out of his closet and landing full body on him in his small bed, a recurring nightmare he'd had as a child.

He was on his feet and didn't remember bolting from the chair. His throat closed, trapping air, his stomach coiled in a weird panic as a bunch of images he so-the-fuck-did-not-want invaded his head. Regina, on his father's work table, him using a curved knife to take away the skin in long, ribbonlike strips... Only it wasn't his father. It was him. Marius.

"Hey. No. Easy." She had maneuvered him into the corner behind the potted palms, not a great screen, but one that gave him the illusion of privacy. He slapped a sweaty palm on the cool window, using it to brace himself. His other hand was on her, clenching the lapel of her coat. He sought her eyes out like a drowning man.

She was speaking to him, one hand on his side and the other braced by his on the window, but not hemming him in or holding him. "Breathe, Marius. Come back to me. Right here. We're at the airport. We're going to New Orleans. You're a grown man, Marius. Not a child. He's dead. Look at me. Right now."

He was looking at her, but he knew what she meant. He surfaced from those memories with a gasp, pain spearing through his lungs. Her tone was sharp, but it contained something his subconscious clung to like a flotation device.

"Breathe with me. Nice and even. It's okay. We're right here. After everything you dealt with the other day, it's completely normal you might have a little post-traumatic stress, things dredged up from your childhood. Just breathe through it."

As things leveled, he managed to choke out a response. "I don't like this. I kept this stuff locked out."

"Locked down, not locked out. Big difference. Think how well that strategy worked out. All those healthy relationships you've had; I don't have enough fingers to count them all."

It pulled an unexpected chuckle out of him, grim though it was. When he pressed his temple against the cool glass, wishing he could strip down and put his whole body against it, and then against her, her expression softened, eyes showing pain and concern for him. It made his stomach and chest turn inside out, made it hard to breathe again, for a different reason.

Please don't love me. Please don't.

"People are probably staring at us," he managed.

"Fuck them." She gestured to his arm. "Give me your wrist."

"Any body part you want is yours without asking, Mistress."

"I didn't ask." She shot him a look of mild reproof. "Don't do the charm thing when you're feeling vulnerable. I can tell the difference."

Problem was, the vulnerability he was covering wasn't only the unsettling daymare he'd just experienced, but that he meant what he'd just said.

When he put his wrist in her grasp, she reached in her pocket with her free hand and withdrew the small velvet bag. She shook the contents into his palm.

Seeing what it was enhanced his defenseless feeling. An ID bracelet. The masculine-looking steel links hooked to the top slim rectangular piece, and were embellished with chips of silver to catch the light.

Picking it up from the cup of his hand, she fastened it on his wrist. It was a close fit.

"Look at the back," she ordered. She moved to grip his hand as he complied. The bracelet had enough slack to allow him to tip the rectangular ID part up but not turn it over fully. It wouldn't roll and reveal the back unless he did it manually, as he was doing now. The close fit also meant he'd feel the faint impression of the engraving more easily.

If lost, return to Lady Regina.

"Since we're going to a new place," she said with a trace of humor. "It seemed appropriate. Now read it aloud to me."

She coiled her fingers in the bracelet, tugging.

"If lost, return to Lady Regina," he said, low.

"I'm right here, sweet boy," she said, just as quietly. "So you're not lost. You're found."

Until he wasn't. He locked his gaze on her and whatever she saw there made her tighten her grip.

"You can choose to have a Mistress. You can desire her, have something for yourself. That's okay. You don't have to play her."

He didn't usually ask but he wanted to, to hear her answer. "Can I kiss you?"

"You may."

He gripped her shoulders, drew her to him. He had no plan for the type of kiss. He usually opted for the tongue-sucking, deep-penetrating, make-her-knees-weak kind of thing, but as he closed the distance between them, other desires took over. He pressed his mouth lightly, so very lightly, over hers, teasing her with a hint of tongue. His lips were trembling a little, or maybe that was hers. His cock swelled against the hold of the straps. It was crazy, how one teasing kiss could rouse him as much as a far more passionate one, as if that brief press of lips had whispered all sorts of things to him, things that made him wish they were in a far less public place.

Her hands came up to hold his elbows, caressing gently.

"There you are," she murmured as he drew back, only enough so that he could bring her liquid dark eyes into focus, the thick lashes and slim, silken brows. Her mouth was wet and lush, a plum color. "See? I knew you'd find me. When you came over here, you wanted to sit at my feet, didn't you? You feel steadier there."

He nodded. "But I get it. This is your job."

"We're not at my job yet. And it's not likely I'll meet anyone in this lounge that is. If that's the case, it wouldn't matter. I'd just say my male companion isn't comfortable in these cushiony chairs because they hurt his back." She flashed him a quick grin, but then the expression disappeared, replaced by all-Mistress. "Come."

When she returned to her chair, he followed. He sat at her feet, putting his back against the chair he wasn't using, his arms locked loosely around his bent knees, body against her knee where she sat on her hip on the chair, legs folded at an angle away from him. She played idly with his hair as she studied the view out the window. "I think I see Peter's plane coming in now. Have you ever met him or his friends at The Zone?"

She was relaxed, helping him to relax. As if him nearly freaking out was an okay thing, something they could move past without dwelling on it. He still had frogs going in his belly, and his lower back had dampened the shirt with nervous sweat, but he found he could follow her lead back to a normal keel.

"Yeah. They're a good group. Good Doms. Never had a problem with them when DM'ing or on security. Really protective of their hot sub wives."

She tugged his hair. "Figures that's what you'd remember."

He looked up at her with a trace of a smile, taking his time getting to her face. "Not appreciating a beautiful woman is a crime."

She sniffed. "Have you ever done an interrogation scene?"

"No. Witnessed a lot of them, though." He shrugged, feeling a trickle of uneasiness. "Wouldn't say no to you, but not sure if they're my thing. That sense of...being caught between a rock and a hard place, having to hold out as long as you can..."

"Puts you in a weird headspace."

"Yeah."

"Maybe you've had the wrong kind of interrogation." Regina considered, her fingertips drifting down over his ears and neck. "If it wouldn't have been too conspicuous today, I would have had you wear a collar. I like playing with it and tugging. Would you like that?"

The idea jolted him, so it took him a second to answer casually. It was also gratifying, having her ask his opinion. "Yeah. But I also like the bracelet."

"Who says you can't wear both?" She swept him with a your-ass-is-totally-mine look that cinched around his cock and balls even tighter than the harness. "A Mistress can put as many marks of ownership on her sub as she wishes, right?"

"Yes, ma'am."

"Good. Now, back to the interrogation thing. I thought I could pull in Mistress Lyda. I'd tell you a secret about me no one else knows. And you could reveal the secret to her, or follow her commands to top me."

His gaze snapped back up. "I thought you said...I didn't want to do that." He cleared his throat and said it for himself. "I don't want to top."

"Well, then, all you have to do is not reveal the secret." But her smile disappeared, and she put her hand on his shoulder.

"It was an idea I was playing with early on, when I wasn't sure if you understood that you truly had no desire to top. I'm not going to do that to you, Duncan. I think you've already been placed in enough untenable positions in your life. Some subs enjoy interrogation, the push-pull of their emotions. You wouldn't. I'm a hardass, but I'm not cruel."

Hiding his relief, he looked down at his hands. "But I've been cruel. So I'd probably deserve it."

"Karma deliverer isn't in my Mistress job description. What you and I do isn't about that. If you've been cruel, you make amends the right way." Her eyes twinkled, though her lips remained serious. "On your own time, not mine."

He laid his head back on the chair seat to look up at her. Her touch drifted to his throat, sliding down into the unbuttoned collar of the shirt to stroke him. He liked the way it felt, but her words couldn't help but open up a track in his mind that led back to those other Mistresses.

Could he make amends? How would he go about it? Maybe she'd help him understand the best way about it, if he raised enough courage—or enough trust—to ask. She'd said she'd be his friend, right? Was that what a friend could do?

He shifted uncomfortably. He was so wrapped up in her, and she was right; a lot of this was spillover from all that intense emotional crap. In a few days, it wouldn't be as intense. He might not be seeing things as clearly right now, making way more of this than it was. BDSM interactions could get way intense, but at the end of sessions, often people put on their clothes and went home to another, or by themselves.

"Will you tell me something about you I don't know yet?" he asked. His questions and thoughts sometimes came out of an abrupt place, not really connected to the conversation, and her surprised expression reminded him of that social awkwardness. "What I mean is, I know about your job, that you're pretty hot shit at what you do. Else you wouldn't be so flush and have people wanting you to travel all over the place to teach them what you know. I guess I just wondered who you are when you're not doing that or Domme stuff."

What the hell was he doing? "Forget it," he said before she could speak. "It was stupid of me to ask. I know this is...this is about The Zone, and club stuff, and you helping me out and challenging yourself as a Mistress. The personal stuff becomes part of that enough without even more of it getting tangled in and making this more than it's not."

Her expression was unreadable. He wished he could figure things out from it, but when she wanted to use it, she had a damn good poker face. "So you don't want to know more about me, personally?" she asked.

"No. No, I don't. It's okay." He rose to his feet and started to backpedal. "I'm going to go hit the restroom."

She ignored that. "My mother lives in Cedar Key, Florida," she said. "My dad wasn't part of the picture, so she was a single mom. I have a couple siblings. One's in New Hampshire working for a senator; the other's down in Texas on an oil rig. They're both married, with kids, and I love them all. I see my mom about once a month, and get together with my sister and brother whenever I can."

She took a breath. "I was married. Once. In my twenties."

He'd stopped as she started to speak, but that brought him a few steps closer again, his gaze fixed on her face.

"He left me because he said he wanted to be with a woman who knew how to be a woman. He was a vanilla guy who didn't get the Domme part of me. It was stupid for me to even try, but I apparently had to do it once to figure out that it was essential for me in a relationship. I loved him, but it just didn't work."

He couldn't imagine her hooked up with a guy who didn't crave the Mistress side of her. It would be a fucking waste. Moving back to her, he sank to his knees and reached up to cup her face in one hand, his thumb sliding along her jaw. "He didn't have to be a dick about it. Anyone who doesn't think you're a woman isn't paying fucking attention."

Her lips curved, the sadness in her eyes from the memory dissipating. "He was hurt, angry. We say the wrong things when we feel like that. Right?"

Yeah. He couldn't cast a lot of stones on that one, could he? But her tone wasn't reproving, a reminder of his faults. Just matter-of-fact.

"He didn't understand how much it hurt. He couldn't see inside me. That was when I realized I needed a submissive lover to unlock that part of me that allows a man to look inside. He was so macho and alpha, and he thought I was asking him to be less of a man. It was a weird, dysfunctional competition of sorts, where I had to stay shoulder to shoulder with him all the time, because if I gave way to him, he'd just take over and I'd be lost."

She curled her hand around his wrist, his palm still against her jaw. "For all the things I kick your ass about, Marius, that's not one of them. You get it, how being a man and a submissive aren't in conflict. That's part of why you're such a lovely sub...and such a dangerous man." She blinked, glanced toward the bathroom. "If you really do need to go, you might want to head off and take care of that. The plane's landed and they'll join us shortly."

Instead, he stood up fully on his knees to put his mouth on hers. Still on his knees, he held her with a strength and sureness her body registered with a gratifying tremble. When he pulled back, he held her gaze.

"I'd never want you to be less than you are, Mistress. You're a Domme, through and through, and I love that about you. I also love that you're strong enough to let me take care of you sometimes."

"I like that you're man enough to do it *and* kneel to me." Her eyes swept him. "You're doing both things at once, right now."

He smiled against her mouth and kissed her again, long and lingering. *I want to take care of you. I'd like the way that would feel, you trusting me to do that.* No way he could say that, because it was only a breath away from wishful thinking, but he put it in the kiss, hoping she heard him.

Her fingers slid around his waist and back and held him close. They were probably giving the rest of the lounge a show, but if she was cool with it, he didn't give a fuck about anything but her. At length and with reluctance, he eased back. "I won't be long," he said.

"Better not. I'll leave without you." She winked, plucking one of her trade magazines out of her computer bag. He felt her regard, though, as he moved toward the restrooms. When he reached the door, he paused and looked back. She made no attempt to conceal that she was ogling his ass. It surprised a smile out of him and she grinned back.

She'd kept him from being completely freaked out by that whatever-the-hell it was that had taken him by the throat. And then helped him realize they all had their demons, by sharing some of her own. She didn't have any problem showing her own vulnerabilities, because she saw them as adding to her strength, not detracting from it.

Something to think about.

When he returned, she wasn't alone. He regretted that, but put a good face on it, pushing down his uneasiness about his state of mind in mixed company. He wouldn't fail her. He wouldn't shame his Mistress.

He vaguely remembered Peter Winston and his wife, Dana, enough to recognize them as he joined them. Peter was a big son of a bitch with military-short dark blond hair and steely eyes. From club gossip, Marius knew he'd done two tours in the Middle East with the National Guard, before he'd returned permanently to fulltime work as a plant operations manager with Kensington & Associates in New Orleans. Yet the main reason he'd withdrawn from the military was Dana herself.

Dana had been in the Army, but had been disabled by an IED. She was blind, her hearing managed capably by a cochlear implant. When she and Peter played at The Zone, Marius's sharp eyes detected the faint scars revealed by her scant outfits. Scars that might have been far worse, but Marius suspected Peter's lucrative resources had paid for the plastic surgery that restored her striking features. Dana's sharp sensuality was deeper than the physical, though. As the petite black woman with close-cropped hair turned in his direction, he saw it in her body language. Like his Mistress, she had more than a skin-deep beauty.

She wore a purple flowing blouse and black slacks over trendy-looking ankle boots. A necklace with black beads and small silver charms led down to a pair of dog tags. The quick glint of light off the lettering showed they were Peter's. Since Marius knew Dana was a dedicated submissive, he suspected it was a day collar, a way she could wear a symbol of her Master's ownership without comment in the vanilla world. His fingertips slid along the ID bracelet on his arm. Much like what his Mistress had given him.

"I believe you've met Marius before," Regina said to Peter and Dana.

"Yeah. Marius." As Peter shook his hand, Marius detected reserve in the greeting, and speculative scrutiny. Not unfriendly but not a blank pass, either. Peter knew some of what had been happening with him, probably from The Zone scuttlebutt. Getting information about members of The Zone in the outside world would have been a challenge for the most secretive branches of government, because privacy was taken seriously at the club. But inside the club, gossip could be as rampant as in any other fishbowl. Marius tried not to let it bug him.

Dana extended her hand. "Glad you could join us today," she said. She wore dark glasses to cover her blind eyes, but looked toward him, following the sound of his movements. When he took her hand, instead of shaking his, she clasped and held it, pressing a warm grip upon him. Her quiet calm had an intensity to it that wasn't unpleasant, but it was unsettling, as if she was seeing things with her touch deeper than sight could provide.

"The pilot's ready to go, so let's catch up on the plane," Peter advised, gesturing them toward the exit door.

Marius had seen TV shows where the characters rode on private planes. The cabin area was smaller than Hollywood made it look, of course, but the space was still pretty impressive. The private plane had a conference room with all the modern technology to conduct whatever business could be conducted from an office. There was also a separate, comfortable sitting area with a well-stocked wet bar and a refrigerator full of snacks. Peter showed them into that area and let the pilot know they were ready to go.

Regina had gestured him into a window seat, taking the seat next to him. Since that seemed to be her preference, he didn't dispute it, and was glad he'd get a prime view of takeoff. As the plane rumbled onto the runway and then accelerated, he was nearly glued to the glass. Or whatever they used to make a plane window. He realized he had a grin all over his face, watching the world race by. Fucking awesome.

He couldn't pull his attention away until they'd leveled out. When he did, he found his Mistress had broken off her chatting with Dana. She was studying him with amusement. "First time in a plane, hmm?"

He nodded, trying to look a little cooler about it, but seeing her pleasure in his reaction, he decided not to put too much effort into it.

"This is the ultimate in flying," she said. "Flying economy to and from conferences is a lot less of a pleasurable experience, especially these days. But that's why I'm glad I have kind friends."

"We had selfish motives," Dana said, unfastening her seat belt and curling up on the cushion, her now bare feet tucked under her. Her shoulder pressed into Peter's side, because he had the arm rest pushed up from between them. "I wanted to catch up and see how you were doing. Last time we talked you had just started at the community college. How are you adjusting from corporate consulting to playing teacher in an academic setting?"

Regina chuckled. "Fortunately, the course I teach is geared toward people looking to upgrade their existing skill sets, so it's not much of a shift."

"What do you do to make ends meet, Marius?" Peter asked.

"A little bit of everything," he said, his standard answer. "Manual labor jobs, mostly. I work through a temp agency." It wasn't a lie. He just made better money at fights, and so did it more often than the other to pay the bills. He was aware of Regina's look but didn't make eye contact.

"Hey, do I smell chocolate?" Dana lifted her head, nostrils flaring. Marius was glad for the distraction.

Peter chuckled and opened the package of TimTams, shaking them onto a plate. "You're better than a bloodhound, sweetheart."

More general conversation revealed Dana was now a minister at a church in New Orleans, one smack in the middle of urban vice. She seemed suited for that, since the air she emanated said fear wasn't something she'd let get the upper hand on her. While Marius didn't expect she had any trouble standing on her own two feet, her Master's dedication and support seemed a key brick in that foundation. The guy was obviously devoted to her. He kept his hands on her pretty much all the time, one palm curled loosely over her folded feet, or on the curve of her hip when he sat back again and let her cuddle her barely five-feet-tall body against his bulk.

It was intimacy, comfortable knowledge of one another. The vibes were probably from being married, as well as committed Master and sub. It wasn't something Marius had ever let himself think about having, but he realized not thinking about it didn't mean not wanting. He was with a Mistress who had introduced him to the word *want* in a way he hadn't experienced before he met her.

His elbow brushed hers as she sat in the cushioned seat next to him, her legs crossed, opposite arm lying loose and relaxed. She looked exactly like what she was. She wasn't a planet needing to orbit around another. Just as she'd said that night not too long ago, she was a star, a sun, who gave or took away warmth according to her own schedule.

Almost as if she'd picked up on his thoughts, and was reminding him of the truth of them, she rested her other hand on his thigh, stroking as she spoke with her friends. He wanted to move to the floor at her feet again. However, though Peter and Dana were Dom and sub, he wasn't sure if a vanilla protocol was in place right now.

Regina answered that question. Her hand shifted to his shoulder. A quick flick of her lashes told him what she wanted, and he slid to the floor at her knee, bracing his bent legs by tucking his shoe tips under Dana's seat, since she had her limbs folded up underneath her. Regina's touch moved to that favored spot on the back of his neck, her fingers threading through his short hair.

After some additional casual conversation and catching up between her and Regina, mostly girl talk, Dana began to sit up. When Marius would have moved his legs out of the way, Peter shook his head at him, telling him it wasn't necessary. Finding him there, Dana propped one bare foot on each of Marius's knees and smiled.

"I like this kind of foot rest. You okay with that?"

"I am," Regina answered when his lips parted. Okay, they were in Dom/sub mode. He subsided, feeling an unexpected comfort settle over him, particularly as Regina continued the slow stroke of his hair. "Lay your head back on the seat, sweet boy."

Though she could be ruthless, there wasn't anything arbitrary or cruel about her. She was kind and loving, tough and fair.

She deserved way better than him. He didn't want the thought to intrude on this moment, but there it was, always waiting. He shrugged it off, twitching under her touch. The truth of that rankled, but it didn't matter, did it? This was all great, but when he got back into The Zone with her help—if he did—where did they go from there?

She was all class, style and money, with a fancy education. He was...him. She might keep him as a sub at The Zone, because she seemed to prefer to pursue her interests in that environment. He expected it was only his circumstances and her willingness to help him that had caused their interactions to happen outside of that.

He could live with being hers just at The Zone, right? Maybe that would keep him more manageable.

He ignored the instant *yeah right* total bullshit call that went through his brain. And pushed away the thought that the club itself, all the stimulation and choices, might have sometimes helped set him off. He was trying to protect himself, he knew it. He could see himself laying the bricks, each negative thought the slap of the mortar.

He needed to stop thinking, fast. Yet as he thought of life going forward without her in the near future—or as just one of her subs at The Zone—he had a sinking feeling it wouldn't take him long to revert to what he'd been. He'd be back to where he started within a few months.

He needed her to keep him on the straight and narrow. Which sucked, because he'd always refused to be dependent on anyone. And she didn't deserve a man who couldn't be a man on his own two feet.

Something had happened to him all those months ago, when he learned his father would be executed. A vital coping mechanism had snapped, and he couldn't seem to pull the cables back together again. It didn't seem possible to go forward the way he had been, even if he could go back to being just an advanced-level sub, rather than a destructive one. She'd said it herself. Locked down wasn't a healthy long term solution.

"So Marius is thinking about adopting a pet while we're in New Orleans," Regina said. "We're going to visit Dale's place."

"That's great," Peter said, as Dana made a noise of approval. "We adopted a pair of Jack Russell terrier mixes last year. They're terrors. Scared the bejesus out of me the first week I had them. I thought they'd be fine running around the property without much supervision while I was working on my boat engine. They cornered a fifteen-foot alligator. Tough little bastards. Stayed just out of range, running around him like a pair of ants bugging a bumble bee. Totally ignoring me when I was shouting at them and trying to figure out what to do to distract the alligator. Fortunately, he wasn't hungry enough to go on the attack. He just got annoyed and went back into the marsh."

"Peter was ready to jump in and wrestle the alligator, but he knew the dogs would try to help. He doesn't know how to handle someone who ignores his commands," Dana teased. "And who's impervious to his punishments."

"Unlike a sub who ignores my commands to *get* the punishments."

She dimpled, unrepentant, and directed another question to Marius. "What are you thinking you'd like to adopt?"

He kept his head back, his eyes half closed as Regina stroked him.

"I've thought about a chocolate lab. A buddy of mine has one, and it's real loyal and friendly. Sleeps with him."

Regina's nails scraped him as she added demand to her touch. He wondered if she'd just visualized what he had, him sleeping on the pallet on her floor.

"If you're in NOLA through Sunday, you could come to our morning service," Dana suggested to Regina. "We have an awesome Sunday morning crowd. Some of the local at-risk kids have been visiting, because our choir rocks the house. Traditional favorites mixed with Christian covers of popular Motown, that type of thing. Our lead singer is a twelve-year-old girl who can bring tears to your eyes. There's a potluck afterward, and you *will* eat enough to last you a week. Plus take home doggy bags." She smiled in Marius's direction. "Maybe for your real life new dog."

"Yeah, maybe." Regina's fingertips slid over his jaw again as he answered the blind woman. "I've just started looking. Probably won't get anyone right now."

"That's what everyone says when they go to an animal shelter," Peter warned. "You don't choose them. They choose you. And then you're in a relationship for life."

"Kind of like how you chose me," Dana teased him. She tried to pinch Peter, but he caught her wrist and gave it a squeeze.

"If I remember correctly, you threw yourself at me and I had no choice at all."

Regina huffed out a laugh. "That is such a lie, Peter Winston. The K&A Doms have a distinct reputation. When they see the woman one of them wants, they go after her like a pack of wolves. Good thing for them every one of those women have proven themselves to be she-wolves, able to hold their own with you overbearing bastards."

"Typical Mistress," Peter noted. "Demonstrating a complete lack of understanding of a Master's technique."

"What technique? Pull out your club, whack her on the head and drag her back to your cave, then wake her up to make you dinner?"

Dana chuckled. "That backfired on Matt. Savannah couldn't cook to save her life."

"That's all right. She's CEO of her own company," Regina pointed out. "She can pay for an army of cooks to keep him fat and happy."

"Marius, I need some male solidarity here," Peter said.

Marius grinned and brushed his lips over Regina's knee, curling his fingers around her calf. "I'm at her mercy. I take the fifth out of pure cowardly self-preservation."

Regina tugged his hair as they chuckled. "Smart boy."

Dana cocked her head. The sunglasses she wore disguised the motionless state of her filmy green eyes, but the movements of her head and body suggested she was looking toward both Regina and Marius. "The vibes coming off the two of you are wonderfully strong. You should think about keeping him, Regina. And Marius, you should think about being kept."

Her toes curled into Marius's knees playfully, her smile seemingly intended for him.

"She never behaves for long, does she?" Regina said to Peter, humor in her voice. She asked him something about his job, and the conversation continued.

Marius figured her intent was to move them off the subject. Maybe for his own comfort, but maybe she'd changed the subject for her own comfort as well.

Dana had made an impulsive observation, no harm intended. However, the light smile on Regina's face as she moved on bugged him. She'd neither accepted nor denied. It shouldn't bother him; maybe wouldn't have, if he hadn't been chewing on the same issue. That pallet on the floor was a temporary thing. Not a permanent home for him.

Dana leaned forward, speaking low to avoid disrupting Peter and Regina's conversation. "Hey, I didn't mean to put you on the spot. You both feel happy. I'm glad for you."

"Yeah. She's been good to me. Patient. I appreciate her helping me deal with some shit," he said.

He hadn't felt the anger today. Hadn't missed it, yet here it was, a familiar enemy, closest thing he had to a friend. What was he doing on this plane with Regina and her rich buddies? He didn't really know these people. They moved in the same circles as he did inside a BDSM club, but outside of it they were out of his league, as much as Tyler was. When Regina was done with him, he'd either be her success, able to behave within The Zone boundaries, or a lost cause, forgotten and shut out in the cold.

He moved away from Dana, pulling his knees up to his chest, readjusting so his arms were linked over them. It straightened him up so he was no longer leaning against Regina's leg, either, though her hand still rested on his nape.

"She's getting a good deal out of it, even if I completely fuck up," he said matter-of-factly. "Cock-on-demand until she kicks me to the curb. Or until I say fuck it and take my business to a club that's not populated by too many overly sensitive Mistresses who can't handle their shit. Regina's different. She can hold her own with an asshole like me and get some benefit out of it."

Stop talking. Stop. His mouth ignored his cringing mind. "But you said it. I'm a project. She can hand me back when she's done with me, lucky her. She's not looking at someone like me to get what you two have. What you have is the unicorn, though, isn't it? She deserves that, so I don't really know why she's wasting her fucking time with me, but maybe I'm better than doing nothing until the right guy comes along."

Dana's expression had moved from contrition to startled dismay. Somewhere along the way, big surprise, he'd caught the attention of both Doms, their conversation coming to a screeching halt. That was fine. He was on his feet and moving away.

There wasn't far to go, just through the partition that led to the conference room and the bathroom in the back. He was going in the right direction. He could shut himself in the bathroom until the plane landed, containing any more poison spewing out of his mouth. But he didn't make it that far. He stopped at one of the oval windows and stared at the clouds against a blue sky. Christ, he was up so high. Yet why did he feel like a leaden weight was holding him down?

He thought of the other night in the hotel room, the struggle between darkness and light, and how she'd brought him into the light. But the sun didn't really care about anyone specifically, did it? It shone because that was what it was designed to do. At the end of the day, it set and the darkness came. It always came.

He heard her come up behind him. He deserved to be Tasered, but in the absence of that, she might slap him, reprimand him for his abominable manners, all of which he'd deserve and which would feel worse than a far harsher physical punishment.

Instead, she put her hand on his shoulder and pressed. She wanted him back on his knees. He thought about resisting, but he didn't really want to fight with her. When he complied, sinking down, she kept him going until his palms and knees were on the floor. She sat down on the platform his back provided, using him as her chair, her hand clamped on his neck.

"As nice as those seats are, I think I prefer this one. If I was a petite thing like Dana, I could stay here for quite some time."

"Stay as long as you want, Mistress," he muttered. "I can handle it."

"I know you can. But I value your strong, beautiful back. It looks like we're going so slow, just drifting through the sky. When I was little and went on my first plane ride, I wondered why we never saw flocks of birds flying alongside us, and then my mother told me how fast we were going. She said the only thing that could keep up with us was a dragon, so I should keep my eye out for one of those, and draw what I thought it would look like. It was a way to keep me occupied and not nervous during the flight. But I was never nervous. Just like you. I liked the expression on your face when we took off."

She rose, stepping away as if she was going to sit in one of the conference room chairs. He curled his hand around the ankle of her boot, bringing her up short. She wore dressy, sharp-heeled boots under the slacks, much more delicate than what she wore for the club. He loved her Domme wear, but these looked damn good on her.

He held on, the side of his face against her knee. She'd tell him to let go and punish him for the infraction. Maybe that was what he was going for. Normally, it would be.

She pulled a chair closer and sat. Though he had to accommodate the motion, it left the leg in his grip. She'd picked up something off the table. A quiet snick and tap on his shoulder with it told him it was a thin metal pointer she'd telescoped out to its full length.

"You behaved badly toward our host's sub," she said mildly.

"Yeah. Yes, Mistress. My mouth isn't always that smart."

"Actually, I think your smart mouth is what gets you in trouble." There was wry humor in her voice. "But you will go apologize to her Master, and make amends as he requires. After I remind you how to properly behave when you are in my company, representing your Mistress with your conduct. The other night it was as much about enjoying the flex of your beautiful ass as it was about teaching you to ask before you put on your clothes. But this is different. This is like when you kissed me when I was on the phone. You've disappointed me. You know it, don't you?"

He nodded, his throat tight. "I didn't want to fuck today up. I really didn't."

A long pause, then she spoke, her voice neutral. "You haven't. You fucked up a few minutes ago, and I've told you how to make it right. First you'll take the punishment." Her tone stayed reproving, but her touch on his back was oddly gentle. "Open the belt and the jeans from your current position. Then put both elbows on the floor. Don't do anything else."

This wasn't a scene, a game. Her next words plucked that feeling right out of his head and gave it a shape.

"For many Doms and subs, any interaction, whether punishment or play, falls within the structure of a scene, an agreed power exchange, which keeps it at some level a game that can be called off with a safe word. I've never asked you for a safe word, have I? Because I know you've been playing a game for so long, that's the last thing you need. You need to belong to someone. If true ownership of another person was permitted, that's what you'd prefer. I know that, know it terrifies you and that's why you keep fighting.

"Belonging to someone you can trust would be a safety net for you, a cell from which you could handle the world in a way you've never been able to handle it. Very few people understand the complexity and simplicity of that need you possess so deeply inside. But I feel it, I do. Which makes you a lucky man, because I have absolutely no problem with owning your ass, head to toe, heart, body and soul."

Gripping the back of his loosened jeans, she tugged them and the dark briefs off his ass with one strong jerk that almost pulled him off his elbows. She pressed her knee between his shoulder blades as she took a firm grip on his hair. "If that's what you need to find yourself, then you'll consider yourself mine. You know how to bear pain, because the pain has always been part of the game. This isn't a game. This is punishment, because you failed to meet my expectations. It doesn't change how I feel about you, how much I care about you or want you. And yes, I do care about you. Three. Count them off."

Three wasn't so bad. What was bad was the roiling knot of emotions her words were creating in him. He'd let her down. She meant that. She—

Holy fucking Christ. Being struck by something like a broken off car antenna was painful as shit. He sucked in a breath, and barely remembered what she'd ordered.

"One." When he muttered an expletive, she hit him again, with just enough of a pause for the pain of the first strike to clear the field so he could fully feel the next one on the opposite ass cheek.

"Two." Fuck, that hurt.

The third landed on the juncture between thighs and buttocks.

"Three," he said hoarsely. He could handle pain, he could. So why did this hurt so much?

"Okay," she said briskly. "Pull your pants back up, then come and apologize."

She dropped a kiss on his sore butt, snicked the pointer closed and placed it on the table. Then she left the room with a no-nonsense stride.

He pushed himself back to his heels and got to his feet, using the chair to pull himself up. As he tugged the jeans back over his smarting ass and tucked himself back in, adjusting things and buckling the belt, he saw his fingers were shaking. What the hell... He raked his fingers through his hair, rubbed them over his face, and went into the bathroom to stare at himself in the mirror. A man with a cruel broken mouth and stark gray eyes looked back at him.

What would she do if he didn't comply? If he said screw it and just hung out back here until the plane landed? He'd never get back into The Zone. That was her leverage over him. Wasn't it?

Looking into a mirror made the truth even harder to avoid. He'd lashed out at the idea that he was just a project. But him complying just to get what he wanted from her, a favorable re-application to The Zone, pretty much made him a whore, right?

Unless he went in there and apologized because he'd been an ass, and because he'd disappointed her and he didn't like that feeling, fuck The Zone.

If he thought back through almost every exchange they'd had about it, he was the one who used The Zone issue as defense and conflict point most often. She didn't; had even suggested a couple times that things were obviously about more than that between them. So who was he really fucking up with that shit?

He washed his hands and ran damp palms over his face, because it

felt needed to wake him up, or wipe away...something. He hadn't cried
—God, he would have just thrown himself off the plane if he'd been
that much of a pussy, but he had that kind of drained feeling that
came to a kid in his bed after crying his eyes out.

He hadn't cried since he was nine years old. But he'd needed her to
put her arms around him afterward, hold him. Jesus. He didn't do
aftercare. Not like that. Plus, this had been punishment, not a session.

"Fuck it," he muttered, and left the bathroom. He strode across
the conference room, noting the pointer lying there, all neat and
aligned with a control box on the table, probably for the videoconfer-
encing capabilities a couple monitors suggested the room had.
Fucking cool, having all that up in the air like this.

He stopped abruptly, head whipping toward the window as something dark caught his eye, just a flash. All he saw were blue sky and
clouds, but he moved to the window anyway to look. Maybe they'd
passed one of those birds they were outdistancing. Or maybe Regina's
dragon had passed them.

The thought gave him an unexpected smile. Not on his mouth,
just a small one inside. He bet she'd been a strong-willed child,
because the woman was indomitable.

The sound of three voices chatting amiably struck the hollow pit
in his stomach. Was he nervous? Crap, he was. He was used to being
an asshole, and apologizing only in fake kind of ways. Being genuinely
contrite wasn't his comfort zone.

Regina hadn't left him a choice. With her combination of gentle
firmness, ruthless punishment and straightforward logic, she'd made
him truly sorry he'd been an ass. Afterward, maybe he could slink
back into the conference room, because they wouldn't really want to
be around such a jerk anyway. He wondered if he might be hitching
back from New Orleans.

Don't be a fucking coward. He stepped out of the conference room,
and the conversation ceased. Peter's gaze turned toward him. Cool
and steady, his jaw set. Full Dom mode. Male Doms usually raised
Marius's hackles, and he could feel his fists starting to curl, but he saw
Regina's glance go to them and he forced them to loosen. He cleared a
throat that was suddenly dry.

"I'm...uh, fuck." He closed his eyes. Boy, did he suck at this. He
forced himself to open them back up again and met Peter's gaze head

on. "I apologize. There was no excuse for that shit. I...uh...I didn't mean to disrespect you or your sub."

His gaze shifted to Regina. As hard as it had been to look at Peter, that had been a testosterone conflict. It was hard to look at her because he felt ashamed under her steady regard. He walked several feet into the room and dropped to a knee, bowing his head to her. "I particularly didn't mean to shame my Mistress. She didn't deserve that. No punishment would be sufficient, but however you want me to make amends, I'll do it."

"Did she punish you?" Peter asked, voice neutral.

"Yeah." If the guy asked him to take down his pants and show him like an errant schoolboy, he would belt him. He wouldn't be able to stop himself. Given Peter's size and military background, that probably wouldn't be a quick or easy fight. Fortunately, Peter didn't.

"With what?"

The question hadn't been directed to him. A little smile flirted around Regina's full lips, though her eyes remained serious and kept Marius within their span. "The pointer, on his ass. Makes a great switch."

"Ouch," Dana said, mouth twisting in a wince. "If you need someone to rub that to make it feel better..." She bit back what she was about to say as Peter's hand fell on her thigh and squeezed hard, her Master following up the gesture with his own warning.

"I'll apply double the same punishment to your sweet little butt if you don't behave," he said, his eyes glinting. Then his attention returned to Regina.

"Your sub's apology is accepted," he told her. "My compliments on your methods. And thank you for not asking me to watch."

Regina chuckled. "You and the rest of Matt's boys are about as straight as straight gets. Dana is the only one who would have appreciated the view I had." She gestured to Marius. "Come kneel by me again, sweet boy. Peter brought out some more snacks and there's beer. We're talking about some good places for you and me to eat while we're in the city."

And that was the end of it. When he came and settled at her feet, he was unsure of the atmosphere. But Regina pushed a platter at him that had a red-pepper and almond scented cheeseball surrounded by a variety of crackers. Dana offered him a soda when he declined anything harder, and the conversation resumed as if nothing had happened. Dana slid down to sit on the floor across from him and pressed her leg companionably against his as she slathered cheese on the crackers. When Regina and Peter returned to conversation, she touched his knee and spoke to him in a low voice.

"I'm sorry I hit some bad stuff," she said seriously, and now he heard the minister, not just the sub. "Here, have this cracker. You okay?"

She meant it sincerely, kindly. It made him feel like more of a shit, but also better, too, the two emotions not necessarily conflicting. "Yeah," he said. "I am sorry. Don't know why all that came flying out of my mouth."

She shrugged. "Sometimes, when we're working through things, we're like a soda under too much pressure. Shake us up and we'll spew. Regina is a great Mistress, and if you've got shit weighing you down, she'll shake it out. I've been there." Her smile was quick, with shadows around the corners. "Thank God for my Master, or I might have exploded with all my personal shrapnel. Are you eating these crackers? I'm making them and you're not keeping up."

"I'm eating, I'm eating. Pest." He flicked her knee and she kicked at him, grinning playfully. Then she sobered.

"I think however long it lasts, you'll be good for one another. So maybe you should focus on that, more than anything else."

Marius grunted through a mouthful of cracker. After a time, he was surprised to find himself starting to relax. When Dana drew him back into conversation with their two Doms, debating the pros and cons of seafood in Tampa versus New Orleans, it was four people keeping one another company, no longer Doms and subs.

Well, except when Regina's foot pressed against his side, her hand falling casually on his neck and shoulder. Or when she offered him a cracker, making him take it from her fingers and watching him with her beautiful brown eyes as he ate it.

At such moments he knew the truth. Even if he became just one of her subs at The Zone, she was his Mistress. One and only.

He would accept that, make that be enough. Because to want more would be to ruin what he had today.

CHAPTER FIFTEEN

*H*er presentation was scheduled soon after they landed, so Regina had them do a quick check in at the hotel to drop off their stuff, and then Marius accompanied her to the offices nearby where she was doing her workshop. After she disappeared into the building, he walked a couple blocks to Harrah's Casino.

He studied the opulent logo lit up in neon outside the Roman-looking building and wandered into the casino. The flashing colors and incessant noise reminded him of a fight crowd, one he couldn't tune out by immersing himself in preparation for combat. He liked the intricate sculptures hanging from the ceiling, though. One looked like a sea king's chariot, surrounded by mermaids.

He headed out of the cacophony and toward the riverfront, where he bought himself a sandwich and listened to some live music.

He didn't let himself think about too much. His ass hurt every time he moved, since the denim chafed against the raw flesh. Since he'd still managed to get a hard-on numerous times since this morning, he was certain the straps of the cock harness would leave a permanent impression when it was removed. He was ready for that. His gaze slid to his wrist. He wasn't ready for the bracelet to be removed. He hoped she required him to wear it for the whole trip.

Eventually, he returned to the big office building, sitting down on a bench in a landscaped area. He watched a mix of panhandlers, tourists, business and street people. The sunshine made him sleepy, so he dozed off and on until she emerged.

When she did, everything else around her disappeared. Well, in a way. It did something powerful to a man's insides, seeing a woman he felt was his—at least for the moment— out in public, dressed up for business, the whole world seeing only one side of her, when he knew so many more.

She'd removed her blazer, so the silky thin blouse molded to her curves with the fluttering breeze, the hint of her bra showing under the thin fabric. Her slacks outlined her hips, long thighs and incomparable firm ass.

But as good as all those things were, it was her face, the eyes hidden behind sunglasses, that held him. The auburn and black locs danced along her shoulders in shimmering ripples as she walked.

She'd seen him, her lips curving as if in genuine pleasure at seeing him waiting for her. When was the last time a woman had felt that way about him? And she'd made it impossible to tear himself down by saying she didn't know him well enough to know better. Because she did know him. Sometimes better than he knew himself.

When she sat down beside him, he presented her two gifts, a voodoo doll and a strand of sparkling beads. She held up the beads, her lips pursing. "Did they tell you women would flash their tits at you to get these?"

"Yes," he said solemnly. "I was told it works on any woman in New Orleans. So if I'm giving them to you, at some point, you'll have to show me your breasts."

"Look. They're right here. For all the world to see." She threw back her shoulders and posed side to side, making him chuckle.

"So unfair, Mistress."

"I know, I'm a bitch." She looked more closely at the voodoo doll and started laughing. "Who did this?"

"This guy up on Canal Street. You give him a few features, and he does the rest. He slaps the nametag on them, though, in case you don't recognize who it's supposed to be. I was pretty sure you wouldn't have that problem."

The doll's head was a ball of twine, the body of soft cloth. It appeared to have bulging biceps and was well stuffed under the denim trousers. It was also wearing a pair of handcuffs made out of a paper clip. She gestured to the distended groin area. "Someone may have exaggerated their attributes."

"Or underplayed them," he informed her.

She smoothed her hand over the paper tag that read *Marius*. Flipping it over, she noted the back said *Duncan*. Her gaze lifted to his.

"A voodoo doll is the ultimate gift for a Domme," he pointed out. "You can stick pins in it, tie it up, twist the dick into all sorts of knots, even when I'm not in front of you."

"It's far more fun to do it in person." She held the doll up next to him, comparing critically. "Still, the head made of yarn is a close match. And the biceps are pretty good." She tested his with her grip, caressing the muscles since he had his arm crooked on the back of the bench. Then she pinched the doll's. "They should have used something firmer, like concrete."

It pleased him, stupidly, he knew, so he pretended not to react to her approbation. "Well, he only had cotton."

"It's a very thoughtful gift. Thank you." She hung the beads around his neck, tugging on them. "Now you'll have to show me *your* bare chest when I demand it. I need to go to the room to change so we can head for Dale's." She nodded in the direction of their hotel. The Belle Maison was only a few blocks over from their current location. "Stay here."

"I could go with you."

"No." She gave him an appraising look, and the flash of heat in her eyes startled him. "If I get you in a room right now, we won't leave anytime soon."

He rose when she did. "I can take care of your needs pretty damn fast, Mistress. And not worry about mine."

Her gaze heated. "Now that *is* a gift," she purred. "How fast?"

He closed the distance between them. "I need to kiss you to say for sure."

Her lips were curving when he brought his to them, but the urgency he felt upon the contact made him tighten his hold on her waist. It got him going, the obvious evidence she'd been thinking about having him, while in her meeting. He wanted to move his touch all over, up and down, stroke and grip, but he stayed where he was, conveying his desire through his grasp and his, yes, sizeable response to her he had pressed against her hips.

He drew back his head, keeping his body against hers. "Five minutes from the time we get into the room," he promised. "I could get the job done faster, but I don't want it over too soon."

She stared at him. "You know, that was probably the worst presentation I've ever given. All I could think about was how much I wanted my sub. His cock, his clever mouth, his rough fingers."

Her parted lips and the desire in her dark eyes made him take the lead as much as the heady words. Sliding his arm around her waist, he propelled them into motion, pulling her laptop bag from her shoulder so she wasn't having to carry it.

"Next time, give me a burner phone and send a text," he advised. "I could handle your needs on your break, Mistress. Under the table, if it had a long enough table cloth. Or none. I don't give a fuck."

Her sultry laughter stroked his cock. As they reached the hotel and crossed the lobby, he was grateful they'd already checked in. Regina managed a cordial nod to the desk staff, while Marius didn't acknowledge them. Everything was about his Mistress and the need he'd promised to assuage for her.

When the elevator doors closed around them, Marius dropped the bag and seized her, lifting her against the wall and pressing his body between her legs, hiking her thigh over his hip. He went after her mouth with seduction, not attack. Stroking, nibbling, his tongue sliding in to play. His hand moved down her side, thin silk over heated flesh. She let out a pleased sigh, breasts pressing into his chest.

He palmed her backside as he pushed his erection against her core with relentless intent. "Nothing between us, Mistress."

The elevator dinged, and she started to move, but he kept holding and kissing her. "Not our floor," he muttered. "Two more."

"Oh—" It had surprised her that she'd been too lost in what he was doing to track it, but he reveled in it. Not because it meant he had power over her. It meant she was trusting him. He'd never received a gift so sweet, because for once, it had been earned. She'd helped him figure out how to earn it, rather than blowing it.

He didn't care who saw them as the door opened, or who might get on with them. If they were offended, they could get over it. He kissed her mouth, feeling like he could do just this. Much as he wanted to fuck her, this was good. So good. Her arm was around his shoulder, the other gripping his biceps.

He thought he heard a wry female voice say, "Only in New Orleans," and then the doors closed and they were headed up again. Regina choked on a laugh, breathless with arousal.

He put her down and flipped her around, pressing her face first against the elevator wall as he went after her neck next, pushing her hair out of his way and holding it in a fist as he bit, sucked, kissed, nuzzling the blouse out of his way to tease her collar bone with his mouth.

"Marius," she breathed.

He liked how his name sounded on her lips. It didn't sound wrong, fake. He ran his hands down her sides again, her hips, her thighs, and back up, keeping his body flush against her as he ravaged her neck. The door opened and they were at their floor.

He picked up the laptop bag and kept kissing her, turning her around in his arms so they did a waltzing kind of walk down the hallway. When they reached the room, he pushed her against the door so hard, it rattled.

"Open it," he growled. She found the key card, and he guided her wrist, steadying it so they put it in the slot together. The door opened, and they were inside.

He dropped the bag again. This time she backed away, her eyes bright and sharp as he sauntered toward her. He was good at this part. He'd always been good at it, once he figured out the sub angle in his nature. He loved seducing a woman, loved giving her pleasure. But she'd taught him it felt best when it was selfless, no motive, just the need to serve every desire she had.

Her lips were parted and he came at her again, gripping her face, stroking his hands through her hair in the way she and he both seemed to like. He slipped the buttons of the blouse and slid it off her shoulders, transferring the beads from around his neck to hers, letting them dangle as he unhooked the front fastening bra to reveal her breasts. A smile teased his lips as his gaze flickered up to meet hers.

"You got your way after all," she said with mock reproof.

"Only because you let me," he said, and scooped her up to lay her on the bed. He opened her slacks and removed them, then gazed down at her wearing nothing but a white filmy pair of lace panties, the crotch dampened with her arousal. She lifted her legs to place a foot on his chest. He resisted the pressure when she pushed against him playfully, turning his head to kiss her ankle, work down her calf and inside thigh. He nuzzled her pussy, sucking and licking it through the thin cloth, making her buck up against his mouth. Then he unbuckled his belt, opened the jeans and pushed them out of his way. But he took a folded piece of paper out of the pocket first and closed her hand over it, kissing her wrist and up to her shoulder, back to her mouth.

"What's this?" she breathed.

"What I said in the elevator. Proof that I can be inside you with nothing between us," he said, lips hovering over hers. "Your choice, Mistress. Hand, mouth, or cock?"

She crumpled the paper, and laid her arms above her head like a siren who knew her effect on men was irresistible, unconquerable. Because it was.

"We're near a casino," she said. "So dealer's choice. You have three more minutes."

"Not doing my job if you're watching the clock."

"Well, I wasn't going to say anything, but..."

He grinned and slid an arm around her waist, hiking her up so he could put a knee on the bed. Once poised over her again, he paused. Gleaming brown skin, long limbs, her dark eyes penetrating him in multiple ways, moist lips parted, her sex glistening with arousal. One leg still hooked over his hip, her foot rubbing the back of his thigh.

"You promised to bring your Mistress to orgasm within five minutes," she reminded him softly. "Do as you promised, Marius. And take off the cock harness."

He complied, wincing but enjoying her pleased look at his discomfort. The straps had left marks behind, and she seemed to like those as well. Bending, he captured her breasts in his hands and began to suckle the right nipple. At the same time he angled his hips and pressed against her opening, feeling the give of the moist tissues, readying themselves for his entry.

Fucking heaven. He slid into her, slow, savoring every inch of her slick channel, the squeeze of her muscles on him, the quiver of her body. He angled himself so the stroke of his cock inside would hit the right nerve groups, his pelvis rubbing her clit while he pumped inside of her. But if all it took was the right combination of physical factors, women wouldn't be such a mystery and pleasure.

The removal of the harness had only increased his girth and she moaned with pleasure at the fit. He captured her mouth again, finger tips curving around her neck and descending to stroke the outer swell of her breast, her side, ignoring the more obvious targets like her nipples or cunt.

"I love the way you smell. I love how you walk, the way you wear your clothes. The way you breathe and laugh. I don't have to look at you with my eyes. I close them and know that you're everything in my world...fucking everything."

He'd intended to stay with the practiced things that pleased a woman, things that told her that the man inside her wasn't just fucking her; he was her lover, aware of her at every level. And it wasn't a line; he meant all of it. But he hadn't meant to go so deep. The words were just there, leaving his lips, said and unable to be unsaid, because they were simple truth.

She put her hands on his face, framed it, bringing him down so every point of their bodies were flush against one another, including their mouths as she held hers against his.

"Go over with me," she whispered. "Sweet boy. Don't let me go alone."

She wrapped her arms around his back and he rolled them so she was sitting on him, his feet braced on the floor as he sat upright on the bed and brought her down on him with sure strokes. He could give her his strength. He might give her anything, because she left him no choice.

For the first time in his life, he truly belonged to a Mistress. In a few minutes, after the climax came, that would terrify him, and he would do something stupid to push her away. So he wanted to make this the best damn climax she'd ever had. Within five minutes, that is.

The time reminder gave him a desperate spurt of humor amid the arousal. He put his mouth on her breast, suckling, as she gripped his hair. He kneaded her ass, working her on him. Her pussy clutched his cock, those first ripples of orgasm about to take her. Obeying her command, he let go with her, pressing his parted lips hard against nipple and breast, his forehead against her chest, face held against her bosom by her clutching hands as he took her where he'd promised.

And she delivered him there right with her. God, he wasn't sure there were words for how it felt, his seed spurting inside her cunt, nothing between them. As if the gates of heaven had truly opened, like they said in the songs.

While they were both riding the aftermath, his arms tightened around her. A dozen things started to come to his lips, all of them wrong, all of them spurred by that demon in his soul that told him he couldn't have this, that he was just some toy she was playing with, that he was getting too deep and needed to push her away before he did her real harm...or got himself hurt beyond repair.

"No." She put her hand on his mouth as his lips parted to say the devil knew what. Despite the aftermath of the climax still gripping her, enough that her face looked soft, her lips still parted and eyes a little dazed, there was a sharpness behind that.

She eased off him, and he automatically helped her, steadying her as she made it to her feet, standing between his. "Don't speak and stay there."

She moved to her suitcase, blissfully naked. Their combined release marked her thighs in glistening tracks, making him lick his lips and need hit him hard anew. He was glad she didn't say he couldn't look at her. Not until she returned. "Close your eyes."

He did and she put a blindfold on him. "Put your hands behind your back."

When he complied, she attached a pair of thick cuffs to his wrists and locked them together. The hold pressed the ID bracelet into his flesh, a welcome imprint. "One more thing," she said.

The finger in the hinge of the jaw, anticipating his resistance, but this time he opened up to allow the ball gag to be seated. She buckled it so tightly around his head it cut into the sides of his mouth.

His cock, even spent, reacted to the restraints, to her taking full control. He could feel the spurt of pleasure deep in his gut, in the ripple through all his muscles.

"Good," she murmured. "For the next little bit, you'll simply be. You don't get to make stupid, snarky comments, or lash out at me. I've taken care of that. You can let it go. Come with me."

She put her hand on the cuffs, propelling him to his feet, and guided him to the bathroom. The shower started, her hand staying on him as she probably checked the temperature with the other.

"After I put on your blindfold, I was going to text Dale and ask if we could be an hour late," she said. "He'd already texted me that he needed to switch our appointment to late afternoon. So win-win. Step inside the shower."

She steadied him as the spray hit him, and then maneuvered him so the water jetted over his body, wetting down every side and angle. "Be still now."

She washed him, handling his genitals with practical efficiency and then scrubbing him head to toe as thoroughly as he could do himself. More so. The angry cycle of words, the things that tormented him, had no outlet, so all he could do was focus on her hands, and react to how it felt, being cared for and given no choice to speak or act except in response to her commands.

"Yeah, that's what I thought." Her voice had a sensual tag to it and she slapped his cock, starting to rise. "Get your mind on the right things, and you can't control that beast. That's your only job, Marius. Pleasing me, following my commands. That thing inside of you? It answers to me as much as you do, so you let it know that if it fucks with me, I will put it down hard."

She brushed wet lips over his, stretched by the gag. "If it fucks with my boy, I will destroy it utterly. I can see the dark side of the mirror. It won't ever be able to hide from me."

She put her hand on his chest and pushed him into the corner, angling a jet so it hit his shoulder and side, keeping him warm. "Down."

She guided him to sit on his ass, bent legs spread so she could tease his testicles with one questing foot. "You sit there and behave while your Mistress cleans herself. And no, you don't get the privilege of watching. You sit where I tell you and wait for me to want something from you. Other than sitting there."

He really wanted to watch her. If she'd cuffed him in front, he might have tried to lift his hands and sneak a peek from under the blindfold. But she'd anticipated even his smallest misbehavior. He listened to the splash of water, smelled soap and shampoo. She hummed, talked about things she wanted to see and do with him while here. Talked about previous experiences she'd had in the city. All as if having a cuffed, gagged guy sitting in the corner of her shower was the norm.

It felt that way to him. As he listened to her, imagining what she was doing, other things receded. He wished he could have done some kind of post-sex cuddling thing with her, but he would have messed that up, wouldn't he? She'd done this to him instead, which initially left him with resentment, then shame, then...quiet. She stroked his wet hair, used his bent knee as a prop when she shaved each of her legs. Then she teased him, straddling his body and pressing her cunt up to his gagged mouth, rubbing herself against it as she leaned against the tile wall.

"I could make myself come again just doing that," she said. "Looking at my sub sitting and waiting for me, pretty mouth all gagged and hands bound, his knees spread out so I can see the package and ass that's all mine... I might just chain you up in my house when we get home and never let you out."

He wondered if he wouldn't prefer that himself.

"All right." She shut off the shower and stepped out, the rustle of cloth telling him she was drying herself. She returned to lift him to his feet with one arm under his elbow, guiding him back out to towel him off. She made him put on his underwear and jeans blind. When he pulled up the jeans, she tucked his cock back into them with her caressing hands before zipping him up herself. Then she pushed him down into a sitting position on the end of the bed and removed his blindfold and gag.

She wore jeans and a lacy bra, a combination that he decided was his absolute favorite look for her so far. When she unlatched his cuffs, she tugged lightly on the ID bracelet. He reached for her, but she slipped away. "Finish getting dressed. If we're going to play with dogs, probably a T-shirt would be best. I need to handle about a half an hour of email before we head to Dale's. You can occupy yourself however you wish."

Her gaze flicked down. "But keep your hands off what's mine. That's not a permitted distraction." Her gaze glinted, anticipating his wicked thought. "Even if it's intended to distract your Mistress."

∼

"Eddie's Junkyard and Temporary Home for Good Dogs and Imperious Cats." Marius read the sign on the gate. The *"and Imperious Cats"* looked like it had been added, since it was in bright red while the rest of the lettering was yellow. It was also painted in more feminine, less blocky script.

The words were embellished with a whimsical cartoon of a car on one side and a dog and cat on the other. Beyond the sign, he saw several acres of junk cars. A two-story building near the gate looked like a combination office and residence. Another long, low building housed the dog kennels, evident by the row of about twenty chain link runs with dog-sized doors providing access to the building's interior. He saw some of the dogs lying in the runs on hammock-style bed frames.

A smaller building nearby had some tall, fully enclosed cages appended to it, but no animals in them right now. Just carpeted towers he recognized as the type of thing people bought for their cats. So that was the building where the cats were. His muscles knotted up, his breath clogging in his throat in a way that irritated him. He snapped his gaze away from that building. He didn't have to go in there. He was here for a dog. To look at dogs.

This was stupid. People with dogs had stable lives, regular schedules. Green yards with picket fences. They didn't have basement apartments with tiny, narrow windows so scuffed the sunlight that managed to get through was weak, diluted. What did he know about keeping a dog, anyway? He'd never had a pet. Though they probably taught you how to do it, right?

One day working with a road crew, he'd taken his lunch break sitting on the curb of a strip mall parking lot. He'd seen an animal rescue group outside of a pet store, having some kind of adoption day. A family was being introduced to their new dog, the volunteer handing them a plastic bag full of food samples and pamphlets.

Around the same time, another volunteer had been taking a dog for a quick walk and squat, and she'd come near Marius. When Marius met the medium-sized brown and black dog's eyes, something got caught up inside his stomach like a bird in a net, the sandwich halfway to his lips.

The dog hadn't made a sound, but he'd heard it anyway, an echo from his past. A dog whining, crying...a universal plea for help.

The dog cowered back from him, lips curling in a half snarl before he retreated behind the volunteer and tugged against the leash, trying to get away from Marius. The girl's startled glance had fallen upon

Marius's face. Whatever she saw there had a friendly reassurance dying on her lips. She'd managed a short nod without meeting Marius's eyes before she and the dog hurried away.

"We shouldn't be here," Marius said. "This was a bad idea."

"We're here now. Let's give it a go." Regina unbuckled the seat belt of the courtesy car the hosting company of the presentation had provided her. "Come with me. If nothing else, I want to say hi to Dale and give him a donation."

But he stayed in the car as she got out. When she paused in front of the grill, he lifted his gaze. Her jeans fit her well enough to destroy a saint's peace of mind. Her purple T-shirt had New Orleans printed across her high, generous breasts, surrounded by swirls of washed-out colors that gave it a vintage look.

It was the first time he'd seen her in sneakers instead of her boots or heels. She'd tied back the ropes of her hair in a loose tail, except for a couple she'd curled in corkscrews to frame her face.

He'd had her under him less than a couple hours ago, straining, gasping, moaning. Then she'd ridden him to a finish. After that, he'd been sure he'd screw things up, because the need to protect and distance himself had been overwhelming. She'd anticipated it, defused it, dealt with it. The gag and restraints had restored control of his thoughts and emotions again. But now she'd brought him here and shit was resurfacing. Could he trust her with what he was feeling?

He hadn't had that conscious thought before, and now he considered it, a new idea. She'd said he needed a friend as much or more than he needed a lover. Did she realize he was new to the idea of having a woman be either of those?

Putting her hands on her hips, she gave him a mock severe look. "Don't make me come pull your ass out of that car, young man."

His lips tugged and he put his hand on the door to get out. As he did, she came around and leaned on the front panel, tipping her head back and closing her eyes in response to the bright sunshine. "Feel that? What a gorgeous afternoon. There's even a bit of a breeze to cut the humidity. C'mon. It's a nice day for a walk."

When he closed the car door, she linked her hand through his elbow, as if he was escorting her. As if he was a man, and not someone who wanted to run as far away from this place as fast as he could.

He'd been quiet on the way over, and she hadn't seemed bothered by that. He was uncomfortably reminded of the quiet boy he'd once been. One who hadn't had a lot to say, but who watched everything and listened.

Then, it had been because of fear, the fear of being noticed. Now, it was because he liked listening to her. So he focused on that.

"Dale is a retired Navy SEAL. He's married to Athena, who is gracious Southern belle all the way. They're Dom and sub. He used to live out here before they were married, but he stays at her place now. Her estate." She dimpled at him. "She is mega loaded, so I like to tease him about being a kept man, which rubs his Dom fur the wrong way. He's pretty old school. Anyhow, I know male Doms poke at your testosterone reservoir, but don't fuck with him. He knows how to cut you up into pieces and make your body disappear. I like you assembled and present."

"I'm in favor of that myself," he said, and she grinned.

"I figured. Here he comes."

Retired or not, Dale looked like a SEAL. His capable, relaxed demeanor was a thin layer over a solid core of watchful preparedness. He had dark, close-cropped hair and eyes of a mixed blue-green color that reminded Marius of the sea. He was missing half a leg, his cargo pants pinned up securely on that side as he maneuvered smoothly toward them on a pair of crutches. The pants and his T-shirt highlighted a powerful body, despite the disability.

He had a ready smile for Regina that said he was fond of Marius's Mistress. The feeling was mutual, Regina taking his hand and brushing a kiss on his stubbled cheek.

"Did you get too bossy and Athena hid your leg so she could outrun you?"

Dale chuckled, an easy sound, though his gaze had already moved to Marius to do a quick, penetrating assessment, uncomfortably familiar. It was the way shrewder cops measured a guy, weighing his strengths and weaknesses and gauging both accurately, based on nothing more than experience and their reliance on their gut.

"I got an upgrade to the prosthesis this past week and the fit wasn't exactly right, so it gave the stump a couple blisters. It's healing up while they adjust the cuff."

"So is it a bionic leg?" Regina asked, eyes twinkling. "You'll be able to kick twenty guys' butts just by turning up the volume?"

"I can do that already, with only one leg." Dale winked at her snort. "How'd the presentation go?"

"Pretty good. Some promising talent in the group. Even if my teaching gig only lets me participate via videoconference, I hope I'll have the chance to rub elbows with them again when they apply what I've taught them to the new developments at their company. That's always the exciting part." Regina angled her body toward Marius.

"Dale, this is Marius, the man I told you about. He's thinking about adopting a dog." Regina shifted her attention to Marius. "Dale usually goes over a lot of background info with potential adopters before introducing them to the dogs, but I've asked him to approach things a little differently. He's going to let a couple of them out to interact with you first."

Dale nodded to Marius. "That sound good to you, son?"

Marius wondered what he and Regina had discussed about him beforehand. Dale didn't strike him as the type of guy who altered his protocol unless given a compelling reason to do so.

He should be offended or wary, but more dogs had emerged in the outdoor runs, watching the small knot of people. A couple barked. He could feel the familiar tension start in his gut, but he forced himself to sound casual.

"Yeah. Okay."

"Tempest and Shotgun are real friendly," Dale said. "The most socialized of my current group."

"Animals don't always take to me. I mean...they might see me as a threat. They usually do." This really was a mistake. He looked toward Regina, hoping the panic didn't show on his face and in his voice. "Maybe I should just go sit in the car while you guys visit. Do this another day. Or maybe not at all."

"Son." Dale shifted closer to him. Marius took a step back.

"I'm not your son," he snapped.

Dale stopped. Marius didn't look toward Regina. He was going to disappoint her, damn it. He shouldn't have suggested this, agreed to this.

"Fair enough," Dale said amiably. "But before you chalk it up as a bad deal, let's try something different. A little more manageable. All right?"

A firmness had entered his tone that was a shade different from a

Dom giving orders. Maybe it was the tone Dale used when explaining things to men under his command. Regardless, it took Marius's reaction down a couple notches.

"Why don't you go sit at the picnic table with your Mistress?" Dale gestured to it.

Regina hadn't introduced him as her sub, but he guessed Dale would know that was what he was. Regina reinforced it, touching Marius's arm. "Sit down with me."

Responding to her commands was familiar footing, so it helped as well. As Marius moved toward the table with her, Dale left them, headed toward the kennel. Marius didn't want to look toward Regina. He didn't know what to say, but she put her hand on his on the table, squeezing. He looked at her then and saw she wasn't angry with him. Nor pitying, which would have been worse. She looked as calm and easy as Dale had. They were handling him, but in a way his sub nature recognized and grabbed, not allowing the other side of him to implode.

"Breathe," she said. "You'll get through this. Just wait and see." She moved her foot so the toe of her sneaker was pressed against his beneath the table.

"So did he lose his leg as a SEAL?" he ventured, looking for a safe change of topic.

"Yes, I think so. He doesn't talk about it much. The first few times I met him, I didn't even know he had a prosthesis instead of a normal limb. It really is like a bionic leg. You don't even notice a limp."

The dogs had quieted, which was surprising. He would have expected they would have been barking more, excited to see Dale coming to them. He heard Dale issuing a few commands, the clank of a gate, followed by the patter of trotting feet, the measured tread of Dale moving on the crutches over the gravel driveway. Marius saw one of the dogs dancing around and circling Dale in a ponderous prance, the other walking in a proper heel next to him.

The black and gold Rottweilers had glossy coats, their eyes bright and inquisitive. The massive heads bobbed, taking in everything around them, as alert as Dale himself.

Dale sat back down on the bench across from Marius. "Down. Rest," he said. The dogs laid down on the ground at the short end of the table, one of them within inches of Marius's foot and knee. The creature's gaze moved to him and Marius saw that watchfulness, a watchfulness that would turn warier by the second. He'd seen it happen. He shouldn't be staring right at the dog, but he couldn't seem to look away...

"Breathe," Dale said. When Regina touched Marius's hand, he realized Dale wasn't speaking to the dogs. Regina squeezed Marius's fingers. The picnic table had plastic chairs at either end of it, to allow for more visitors, and Regina moved into one of them, so now she was sitting diagonally from Marius, her on one side of him, the dog on the other.

"Look at me," she said, and Marius did, resisting the urge to shut his eyes, close things out. "I want you to listen to Dale like you listen to me. Just for the next few minutes. He's very good at this. Relax and trust him the way you would trust me."

She'd made the assumption he did trust her. Well he did, more than he had any Mistress before, except maybe Marguerite that one time, but that wasn't saying much. Fuck it all, what was he doing?

"Keep looking at your Mistress," Dale said quietly. "Breathe. Just one-two-three in, one-two-three out. Regina says you fight profession-ally. What do you do to get yourself in the right headspace for that? Keep looking at her."

Marius's gaze had started to stray to the dog panting near his foot. The sound was like the chuff of a slowing train. He brought his gaze back to Regina. She had that faintly stern, set expression that could steady him because it said she had things firmly in hand.

"I go deep, ground myself, I guess. Hard to explain. Everything else disappears except pounding the other guy until he can't stand up anymore."

"Okay. Take the front end of that. Quiet is the key. I don't want you to look at Tempest. Just reach down and touch her back. Stroke her fur."

It was just petting a dog. What the hell? "Regina..."

Taking his hand, she lifted it to her chest, pried open the fist he didn't know he was making and laid his palm on the upper rise of her breast, over her heart. She put her own palm on his chest. "Breathe with me."

He did it, locking gazes with her, feeling soft flesh and her heart-beat. "You keep looking at me," she said. "And when it feels right, reach down and touch her. It will be fine. But right now, there's just me. Look at me and breathe. Remember when I had you gagged and bound in the shower this morning? Imagine you're back in that space. You can't speak, you can't free your hands. You simply have to do as you're told, but you're safe. Incredibly safe. You can do no harm here. I won't let you."

She was saying this stuff in front of another male, a Dom at that. He should be getting pissed and defensive. But her heartbeat was a steady thud under his palm, her eyes so intent and calm at once, telling him nothing else mattered but what she was telling him to do. It was keeping those images at bay, the cries of the past, trying so hard to form a hurricane in his head.

Marius focused on her mouth, the glitter of the beads in her hair. The cleavage her shirt revealed, the generous curves of her breast. "I feel like an idiot," he admitted. "I can't do what any kid can do. Pet a damn dog."

"Mice completely freak me out," she informed him. "Even Mickey. He gives me nightmares. Dana says I was an elephant in a previous life."

It made him smile, as he was sure she intended. He breathed and listened to her heart, as his own slowed. His thumb curved under the collar of her T-shirt to stroke in time with it. She didn't tell him that he couldn't.

He was aware of Dale sitting silently with them, the dogs panting, a rhythm that went along with the rest, slowed things down. Dale didn't have that irritating Dom vibe that seemed to take up too much space, pushing at Marius's defenses. The guy looked more than capable of it, but he could also be this. He guessed it was the same way Regina could be all different types of Mistress, depending on the moment.

He could do this. He could.

Keeping his eyes on Regina, he removed his hand from her to brace his palm on the table and leaned down, reaching blind with the other. "A little to your left," Dale said, wisely realizing touching him wouldn't be a good idea. Marius made the course correction and suddenly had his hand on the dog's head. Soft, sleek, alive and warm. He stroked down the thick neck, thinking of how he stroked Regina. Her skin was smooth and warm, much like the dog's fur. Tempest moved her head to accommodate his touch. Just the way Regina did when she liked what he was doing.

"When you're ready, look at her," Dale instructed. "Don't stare her down. Just make eye contact like you would the cashier at the grocery store, friendly and relaxed. Keep your mind empty if you can. If you feel yourself winding up, look at how you're petting her instead of at her face. If you're still getting uptight, look at your Mistress, and then try it again. We have plenty of time. If you get overloaded, we'll let them go play and bring them back when you're ready."

Marius turned his head and met the dog's gaze. Nope, too soon. It sucked him down immediately, that abyss, and he snatched his hand back as if burned, making both dogs jump. Dale settled them with a word and a touch as Marius jerked his eyes to Regina. His heart was thudding in his throat again, and sweat popped up between his shoulder blades, the creases of his palms.

"Hey." She grasped his wrist, stroking it before she put his hand back over her heart. "Again," she murmured. "As long as you want to try. No pressure, sweet boy. You're all right. You've got this."

He wanted to shake his head, say no way, but she was looking at him, believing he could do this, and he wanted to please her. It was petting a damn dog. That was all.

The second try lasted a few seconds longer, so he tried not to despair as he had to reel back his agitation again. He didn't want to inflict his sweaty palm on her clothes or skin, but Regina gave him no choice. She held her hand over his on her breast and wouldn't let him pull away.

"She told you about me, didn't she?" he said to Dale as his breathing leveled again. Marius didn't look toward him. He could only look at Regina.

"Yeah, but it was in confidence and goes no farther than here." Dale's voice was neutral, easy. "She knew I needed to understand where your head was at to walk you through this."

Regina didn't look as if she thought she'd betrayed his trust, and Marius guessed she hadn't. She'd shared the info to help him.

Once more. This time, when the dog's head turned to him, he met the gaze but imagined Regina's eyes, her curving mouth, the touch of her hand and her body. Supporting him, surrounding him, guiding him. He moved his attention to the massive head, the powerful body.

As he trailed his fingers over that terrain, Tempest seemed pleased, her panting mouth like a smile filled with laughter.

"She's liking it. My touch."

"You sound surprised." Regina's voice was gentle, teasing. "I like it very much. You have good hands, a good touch."

"You let a sub touch you?" Dale raised a brow. "Getting soft, Mistress."

Regina made a face at him and Shotgun sat up, eyes alight as if he'd been given an invitation to play. "Yeah, you've been good a whole five minutes," Dale informed him. "A miracle." He produced a ball and spoke two words. "Shotgun. Chase." When he fired it off toward the closest stack of junk cars, the male dog charged after it. Tempest remained where she was, placidly accepting Marius's stroking of her neck, his long glides down her smooth back.

"Shotgun's quite a bit younger than Tempest. Tempest is my matriarch. She's seven."

Marius sat back. He'd petted her, and she was acting friendly toward him, despite the churning in his gut. He hadn't been trapped in his memories, and he hadn't frightened her. He felt drained as if he'd run five miles at the height of a Florida summer. Sensing it, Dale took them in another direction.

"That's good progress. I'm going to let all the dogs out for their pre-dinner run around the yard. We'll take a break and talk some more. I have some fresh iced tea and sandwiches in my office. Athena keeps me well-fed. We can come back out later."

"How about it, Marius?" Regina asked. "You want to do that? Or do you want to take a little walk first on your own, check out the cars Dale has in the lot?"

She looked toward Dale to see if that met with his approval. The SEAL studied Marius. Marius wouldn't have been surprised if he'd said hell, no, but Dale nodded. "You don't have to interact with the dogs any more than you want. Some will try to get you to pet them, but if that bugs you, just say 'Free.' That's their command to go about their business."

"It's okay. They don't usually approach me on their own. Uh, yeah, I wouldn't mind wandering around." He needed some air and space. "That okay with you, Mistress?"

"Perfectly fine." Her eyes warmed in approval at his checking. "If you see any interesting car parts, Dale's still scavenging for the Frankenstein car float his SEAL buddies are putting together for the Mardi Gras parade."

"I find new stuff every day," Dale added. "I could be out here a hundred years and not uncover every treasure Eddie collected when he ran this place. I keep thinking I'm going to stumble on the Holy Grail. Or a body."

Despite the casual dialogue, Marius wasn't oblivious to the unspoken conversation going on between Regina and Dale, all handled with body language and eye contact. Dale rose, collecting his crutches, and headed for the kennels. Tempest followed at his heels and Shotgun emerged from the cars with a joyous woof and the ball, cavorting in circles around them.

Regina touched Marius's hand. "You're doing well," she said. "Don't push yourself too hard. Do as much as you can handle. You don't have to adopt anyone today."

"Like he'd let me. If I freak out at petting one, I'm not ready." He tried not to let despair close in at the thought. Two weeks ago, the decision to adopt a pet hadn't even been on his radar. Now it loomed in his mind as a pass-fail test of the kind of person he was. He needed to get some fucking perspective.

"Yeah, you might not be ready." She eased the gut shot impact of the short statement by tapping his jaw with a polished nail. "But that doesn't mean anything bad. You're here, you're trying to deal with something awful from your past that's been choking you. Maybe volunteering for a place like this at home, and then graduating from there to pet sitting for a friend, or volunteering your services as a dogwalker, is the way you need to go until you're ready for the next step."

"What if I hurt one?" The moment he blurted out the words, the tide rose and threatened to engulf him. He was up and off the bench, moving away from her, moving toward the car. "I can't. I need to leave.

"That's going to be tough," she said. "This place is out in the boondocks. Not a lot of hitchhiking options."

He turned and saw her jangle the car keys on her fingers. When he set his jaw, her gaze softened. "You need to breathe, tough guy. Just wander around the lot, or drink tea and have sandwiches with us.

Don't think about the past. Think about the now, and the future. You're not him."

When he shifted uncomfortably, neither confirming nor denying, her expression hardened. "You go down that road, I will tie you down and beat you within an inch of your life. You were already walking stiff when you got off the plane. Want to be hobbling?"

As his gaze narrowed, she dipped her head in a short, satisfied nod. "Keep it in mind. Your number one prerogative today and every day is not to piss off your Mistress." Her tone gentled. "And be true to yourself."

"I don't know who that is."

"Yes, you do." Rising, she closed the distance between them to grip his arms. "I see it every day I spend around you. If you can't have faith in yourself yet, have faith in what I see."

She released him, albeit with a reluctance that bolstered him. He wished she would stay with him, that they could leave and spend the rest of the day...doing nothing.

"Can we go to the waterfront later today and just...walk?"

She cocked her head. "Sure. If you buy me dinner at the French Market Restaurant. They have a great goat cheese and fried green tomato po' boy."

"Okay." He looked down at the ground, his gaze passing over the tempting terrain of her breasts along the way. He wanted to put his head there. Hold her, be held. But he was already feeling like a complete pussy. Couldn't barely pet a fucking friendly dog. "I'm going to go walk around. Look at the cars."

"All right."

Regina watched him go. She was sure he knew she wasn't fooled by the forced casualness of his tone, his pretense that yeah, hey, it was all good, but she knew when a sub needed some space. Hell, anyone who'd just done what he'd done would. He was unfortunately and obviously beating himself up about it, but everything she'd just seen was classic traumatic stress.

He *was* walking stiff, her sweet boy, but it wasn't because of those stripes she'd left on his ass. What he'd done in less than fifteen minutes had likely left him more drained and muscle sore than a three-hour session or even a fight in the ring. He still had a damp spot on the back of his shirt where he'd sweated through it in less than a blink. When she'd laid his palm on her chest to modify his breathing, his hand had been shaking, his eyes latched on hers like he couldn't look away without the world coming to an end. Then things had calmed and she'd seen the wonder in his face as Tempest had responded to him.

She'd had to blink back tears, fast, swallow over a thick throat. No good would have come from him seeing how hard it had been for her to watch his struggle. But Dale had apparently noticed. As he came back to the table and sat with her, he pulled a small flask out of one of the leg pockets of his cargo pants and proffered it. "You could use a little bracer."

Giving him a grateful look, she took a swallow of the strong whiskey. He took his own swallow, then tucked it back in his pocket. Following her gaze, he watched Marius ambling around the cars, his hands tucked in his jeans' back pockets, his head down. A couple of the dogs trailed him, but Marius had been right. None of the fifteen or so dogs Dale had released approached him, whereas several made a bee line to Regina, automatically gravitating toward the attention she willingly offered. It broke her heart a little, to be surrounded by the wagging tails and playful creatures, while the isolated man wandered in her peripheral vision.

"Do you know what you're doing?"

She lifted her head at Dale's question. His blue-green eyes were serious, concerned. "As much as any male Dom who takes on a troubled female sub does," she said mildly.

"Hmm. I've rarely had a sub who could overpower me. And that boy is dealing with some bad shit. He needs serious counseling."

"I'll ask him if his lucrative healthcare plan covers that."

Dale's gaze cooled and Regina shook her head. "You're not telling me something I don't know, Dale. But he's not open to that yet. Believe me, I don't have a messianic complex. I know he's got bigger problems than I can solve, but he has to figure that out himself before he'll accept help. I have two choices as a Domme...and as his friend. I can walk with him, and do what I can to help him get there. Or I can decide he's not worth the risk or trouble and walk away."

"Does he realize you're in love with him?"

At her expression, he blinked. "Let me revise that. Do *you* realize you're in love with him?"

She linked her fingers on the tabletop. *Yes. I just didn't expect anyone else to notice it so quickly.* "I know I want to keep him for the long term. I haven't been analyzing and dissecting the feelings that go along with it. Feelings take care of themselves."

"True." Dale's lips tugged in a faint smile. "No sense spending energy on what's going to go wherever the hell it's going to go anyway."

"Exactly." She took a breath. "This was a huge step today. But I don't know why what looks like a victory makes me uneasy."

"It's because you have good instincts. Breakthroughs can result in a lot of fallout as a person confronts what they've kept locked up, the stuff that shakes loose as things start breaking apart." He sighed. "You're a good friend, Regina. Just be damned careful with this one, okay?"

"I'm not afraid of the big bad sub blowing my house down. I'm a fortress, Dale. If he figures things out, I'll lower the gate and give him sanctuary. If he doesn't...I want to at least get him closer to help than maybe he's ever been before."

"You're a saint. You and Mother Theresa."

She snorted. "I'm not denying he's affected me. I'm more possessive with him than I've ever been with a sub. And yes, that gorgeous ass alone is worth the risk, but that's not it." She paused, suddenly not sure where she was going with it. It didn't matter, since Dale seemed to understand.

"Nope. You can list a million things about him you like, and none of that will be it. Because it's all of it, and then something more that can't be defined." He cocked his head. "You're in love, Lady Regina. It's so sweet."

"You're such an ass. I'm going to tell Athena some ways to cut you down to size. Because I know she's your blind spot."

"Blind spot and the best thing in my life," he agreed. "That's the way it works." He jabbed a finger at her. "Which is why I'm warning you to be careful. Don't be blindsided by him. Everything I've seen says he's got a lot of shit to work out before he's going to be able to handle a healthy relationship. Soon as you can get him to agree to it, get him into counseling. Someone who deals with PTSD, extreme trauma. Don't make the mistake so many military spouses make, being put off by the 'oh, I can handle it myself' routine. PTSD can be unpredictable in how it manifests. You've got zero personal distance from this guy. You read me?"

"Roger that," she said, borrowing some of his SEAL terminology. But she was taking him seriously. Marius's volatile reaction in the airport, triggered by nothing more than a casual comment, flashed through her mind.

Dale shook his head. "Come on, smart ass. Let's have sandwiches and tea while your boy clears his head."

~

Marius circled around it twice, three times. He'd told himself to stop. But here he was.

As he'd predicted, the dogs had stayed away from him, though it pleased him when Tempest fell into a walk near him. She kept pace as he wandered through the junkyard, absent-mindedly digesting the wide variety of cars. He found a junker of his vehicle, same make, model and year, and wondered if he could buy some parts off Dale to put away for a rainy day. But that wasn't the first thing in his head.

Eventually he was back at the cat building. He could hear the occupants, that tiny shrieking sound. It pounded behind his eyes, filled his ears.

When he dropped his hand, he was startled to find Tempest under his palm. His fingers coiled against her sleek fur. She stood silently as he stared at the screen door. Cats were behind it. And kittens. He was pretty sure those little shrieks were in the here and now, not back... then. For one thing they sounded different. Not...afraid, or hurting.

He backed up a step and almost trampled Tempest's paw. She adjusted, pressing against his leg. The sun-soaked dark coat penetrated the fabric of his jeans. He could feel her breathing, big rib cage expanding and releasing.

As he took several deep breaths, matching her, he felt like a bull, preparing to charge into a china shop. Only he'd be creeping into it, one weighted footstep at a time, not sure why he was doing it. He just had to.

He said "Free" to Tempest, but his voice was hoarse, indecisive. She gazed at him, then padded ten feet away and lay down, watching him with placid acceptance. Or maybe Dale had some freakish telepathic connection with her and she was here to rip out his throat if he did anything wrong.

Putting his hand on the screen door latch, he peered through the mesh. There were six or seven floor-to-ceiling partitions in the building, chicken wire and wood creating separate play and sleeping areas for the cats, and an open space in the middle. Taking a deeper breath, he stepped inside. He was sweating again, but he was determined to get through this, as Regina had said. Just get through.

Another screen wall and door separated this area from the middle corridor and the cat enclosures. It looked like he was standing where food preparation and supplies were kept. He guessed it also served the purpose of keeping the cats even more secure, so no one loose would have direct access to the door to the outside.

As he put his hand on that second screen door, however, he found that one of the enclosures had been opened to let the occupants play in the middle area, which was apparently communal play space. A dozen kittens, barely old enough to be weaned, turned from their various activities to run toward him, probably thinking he was Dale with food.

He thought of picking up one of the kittens and holding the small body in his hands.

Lifeless. Broken like the most fragile toy, the fur holding the pieces together. He'd closed his fingers over it, his boy's hand almost not large enough to cup the creature. But he was a man now. His hand could choke the life out of a grown man, let alone squeeze the life out of a kitten. He'd thought about choking the life out of Regina, his Mistress, only a handful of days ago. Had a terrifying moment when he'd *wanted* to do it.

He began to tremble. *Leave, leave, leave.*

But he was rooted to the spot.

CHAPTER SIXTEEN

hey'd brought the refreshments back to the picnic table. Dale sat down next to Regina on her side of the bench so they could both watch Marius's progress. They'd seen him wander through the junk yard, then approach the dog kennels, circle and pause at the cat building several times. Regina's brow creased as he at last moved toward the door as if he was being pulled there by rope. Then he disappeared inside.

Dale was already rising. Regina put out a hand. "Let me go see what's happening first."

Dale nodded, but continued to collect his crutches. "You'll get there faster, but I'll be right behind."

"He won't hurt them."

"You don't know that. Neither do I. I should have told him it was off-limits unless I was with him, but I didn't think he'd go in there, after his wariness of the dogs. Go."

She strode away at a fast pace, then broke into a jog. It didn't help that Tempest met her half-way and spun to lead her back, a worried look on her heavily jowled face. *Marius, please don't have done anything.* If he had, she'd seriously misjudged him, and would have to re-evaluate everything.

No, she hadn't misjudged him, she knew that. Yet Dale had warned her. They'd had a significant breakthrough, and there'd be fall-out. She knew as well as Dale did that PTSD could play tricks with a

man's mind, changing the reality around him as decisively as a hallu-
cinogen.

As she entered the cat building, she saw there was a second screen
door to access the cats. There was a kitten clinging to the mesh,
mewling at her, but Marius had made sure the screen door caught
securely, so there was no chance the creature could get out. She
turned the latch and slipped inside, detaching the tiny claws from the
screen and lowering the kitten back to the floor. "Marius?"

The adult cats were bathing, eating, or playing on carpeted towers
in their separate enclosures, about three or four cats per area. They
didn't seem agitated, which reassured her. She noted a giant brown
tabby tom cat with torn ears and a baleful yellow gaze eying her from
the top of one of the enclosures, rather than from inside. He had a
carpeted platform up there and was settled on his perch with his legs
folded beneath him. He reminded her of a Chinese emperor with his
arms threaded into his robes, staring down at his supplicants with
terrifying inscrutability.

She wrinkled her nose at him. "You don't scare me," she told him.
Never mind that he looked like he might pounce on her head and
gouge out her eyes. He lifted his back leg and started to bathe his
privates, which she assumed was the feline equivalent of arrogant
indifference.

Her gaze slid around the area. Had Marius gone out the back
door? Where... And then she found him.

Toward the rear of the building, there was a smaller enclosure,
probably intended for the corralling of the kittens when Dale was
cleaning or letting the adults out to exercise in the communal area.
The door stood open and a handful of loose kittens seemed to be
darting in and out of that space.

As she moved toward it, Marius came into view. He was sitting
cross-legged on the floor, against the back wall. She paused in the
doorway.

A black kitten with a couple sparse white markings on feet and
chest was sitting in his two cupped hands, bathing itself. Another one,
a yellow tabby, was on his knee, kneading his jeans. Two others played
with a yarn toy beside his hip.

His muscles were bunched, as if he were holding something much
heavier than a kitten, and he was quivering. His eyes were closed,

head bowed. As the kitten unconcernedly curled up, his fingers curved inward, making the nest more secure. She realized then his eyes weren't closed, just lowered, watching the animal. As she moved to stand before him and dropped to her heels, her breath caught in her throat.

The night he'd told her what his father had done, she'd heard the raw pain inside him, unable to be unleashed. It was too awful, too terrible. Tears were for things that could be healed, washed away. There was nothing to heal or wash away those memories, not in the re-telling.

But now, as she touched his chin, she saw silent tears running down his face. That was why his muscles were so tight. He was breaking apart from the inside, only his frame holding him together. He met her gaze, his gray eyes swimming.

"She came to me," he said brokenly. "Climbed on me like it was okay. She's so little, so easy to hurt, but she doesn't know it. She doesn't ever have to experience that fear. Not ever."

"No. She doesn't. She's in good hands." She touched his.

He swallowed. She moved her fingertips to his face, her thumb tracing the tear tracks. "Marius," she said softly.

His face got even tighter, more tears tumbling. "People who don't...who haven't been there...they don't know. They don't know how helpless... We're all like a kitten, no matter how tough and big we think we are."

His gaze snapped up to her. "They don't know what it's like to be pulled into something you can't stop, where you're paralyzed, you can't move."

"Duncan," she said gently, covering his hands with hers, drawing his attention down. "Ease up. You're trying to clench your fists."

He loosened his grip so abruptly he would have dropped the kitten if she wasn't holding both his hands in hers, a nest within a nest. He hadn't affected the kitten's repose, but she wanted to make sure he didn't do anything to disrupt what his mind was working through.

"If you really know," he said, gazing down at the kitten, "you don't talk about it, not to anyone, because there's a part of you afraid that you'll make it happen all over again. And plus, when you feel too much, you go back there in your head. Over and over. Less you feel, less helpless you feel."

"I know." She cupped the side of his neck, stroked him with a firm touch. "But if you're in good hands, just like that kitten is now, you can be truly helpless and find something good."

The words might or might not be penetrating. His gaze was haunted. "I never wanted a place to live, or to adopt a cat or dog. Not until you. Roots mean you stay still. I didn't want to stay still. Things catch up to you when you stay still. I don't deserve anyone's trust, especially not a Mistress's."

"That's for your Mistress to decide, not you." She stroked a finger along the furry back of the tiny creature he held. The kitten yawned and curled into a tighter ball, making her smile.

"She doesn't know I'm a monster," he said.

"You're not one," Regina said, sharply enough to draw his eyes toward her face. Her heart was breaking for him, but she wouldn't let him get away with that. She captured his chin, a gesture intended to pull him back toward the here and now. "You are *not* him, Marius."

"No. I'm not." His gaze filled with misery. "He wanted to be the center of everything, noticed. I don't want who I really am to be noticed...I want that part of me to disappear, but it won't. It keeps... when I'm with a Mistress, I can feel it trying to get free, but it doesn't deserve to be free. But I can't stop myself from reaching for it, so I trash everything."

"Stop this," she said softly. "You're talking nonsense."

She adjusted to sit next to him. As he quivered and a couple tears splashed down on his forearms, she turned to put her arms around him. He stiffened.

"I can't." He tried to push away from her, but he wouldn't disturb the kitten, and she wouldn't be denied.

"I'm here, and you can. Come down here. Let me hold you."

She brought him down like a slow falling tree, easing his head into her lap. Regina rubbed his back, his arm, and curved her body over him. "It's okay," she whispered. "You're okay." *I've got you.*

He'd kept his palms a joined cup for the kitten, and the creature wasn't giving up her spot, no matter his movements. When his knuckles hit the floor, his palms up, the animal merely adjusted to start bathing.

His eyes latched upon the motion, and then he pressed his face

345

into Regina's thigh. His powerful body vibrated like an electric current had passed through it, his eyes shutting tight.

Just like that, the flood came.

The shuddering through his shoulders became a jerking motion, and she tightened her grip on him. A sob ripped from his throat, more an animal sound than a man's. The storm of tears racked his body, and had her murmuring to him, rocking him. Tears tracked silently down her own face as she absorbed his pain and confusion, taking it within her. She would surround his heart, keep it together, so the broken edges wouldn't rip him to pieces from the inside.

She heard Dale come in and stop in front of their enclosure. She didn't look up, her energy dedicated to Marius, helping him get it out. The fierce, hard sobs were those that the child had carried all these years, until they were finally released by the man. Which was good, because she was pretty sure their force would have torn a child apart.

Seeing Dale, the kitten rose, stretched and only now left Marius, running across the enclosure to him with her several other littermates. Dale quietly closed the wire door, leaving the space to Regina and Marius. His hands now free, Marius curled them under her thigh and calf.

"Ssh," she whispered. "It's all right. You're safe. You can be helpless with me and not be afraid. It's all right."

At times, she thought he might make himself sick, choking on all his rage and tears, but finally things slowed down and he was quivering in her arms, face still pressed into her leg. Because she'd gone through that storm of emotion with him, she felt shaky, too. Glancing up, she saw the brown tomcat was on top of their enclosure now, studying her and Marius as if they were in a zoo.

"Look," she said softly. "He must think we're a strange new set of cats Dale's brought in."

Marius adjusted his head and glanced blearily up at the male. "I think he likes you," he said in a thick voice. "You're the one he's looking at."

"Well, I am irresistible to difficult and standoffish males," she said.

The black kitten was back at the door of the enclosure, pawing at it, and meowing plaintively. A glance showed Dale had left them to their privacy. Regina was surprised when Marius pushed himself up stiffly and leaned across the distance without getting up. He opened the enclosure, then stretched back out on his side in the same position with Regina, head in her lap. It touched her, though he looked so tired. She kept rubbing her palm in slow, soothing circles along his back. The kitten mountain-climbed Marius's knee, sidling up to his hip, settling there and looking pleased with herself.

"A female after my own heart," Regina observed. "She wants to be on top."

"Sure she's female?"

"Absolutely."

"I thought I was getting a dog," Marius said after a time.

"Looks to me like a cat chose you instead."

His throat worked as he swallowed. "She deserves better than me."

"That may be true, but since she's chosen you, sounds like you have one more good reason to get your shit together."

His gaze lifted to Regina's face and held there. "Yeah, maybe," he said.

"Yeah, definitely." She curled over him more tightly, putting his head and face in the cocoon of her body. "You're a far better man than you've let yourself be, Duncan Marius Walczek. I've every confidence you won't let me or her down."

Proving it a moment later, he adjusted his body toward her, lifting an arm and looping it over her bent shoulders, rounding out the cocoon their bodies and limbs formed. His fingers delved into her hair to hold and tug. He squeezed her hard, giving her his strength in return for her own.

He also surprised her when he at last shifted, making sure the kitten had a safe transition to the floor before he stood on his knees and wrapped both arms around Regina. Since she was still sitting, her head was on his chest, and he gave her that same sense of being surrounded by warmth she'd just given him.

"Thank you," he said thickly. "In case I'm an asshole later, which is a pretty sure bet, I wanted to say that."

"You won't be an asshole later, or I'll kick your ass. If that's what you need." She smoothed her hands over his back and pressed her face into his chest, liking his heated scent. "I promised you a walk along the waterfront. Why don't we go do that? We don't have to make any decisions here."

"No. Yeah." He sat back on his heels and considered the kitten, who was playing with one of her brethren, tumbling and posturing with an adorable fuzzing up of tiny tail and back. "I think if I don't set things in motion, once I leave here, I'll talk myself out of it. I want to do it."

"Okay." She put a hand over his. "Just don't push yourself to do too much, too fast. It might be a good idea to think it all over some before you make too many changes."

He shook his head, a stubborn set to his jaw. "I've been stuck in this fucking rut for so long, all this shit about my dad in my head, and I'm done with it. It's like you said. Time to start living up to the expectations of people I want in my life."

"Sounds like a great start," she said sincerely. And she didn't want to do anything to throw a wrench into it. But...

"What you went through, Marius. It's not something you decide one day it's over, pick up your life and go on. Just now, when you looked at the kitten, I could see the hesitation in your gaze, even though she was sitting on you just a few minutes ago. It's going to be there for a long time, what happened with your dad."

"So you don't think I should adopt her?"

He looked so crestfallen, it gave his face a youthfulness she didn't typically see in his tough, masculine features. "I didn't say that." Though she realized she did think it might be too soon.

"No. I think you should," she said firmly, hoping she wasn't mistaking soft-heartedness for good instincts. If she was, she had Dale as a safety net. "I just think you should also take it slow. Why don't we go take our walk, and let it all sink in? Though before we go, we can fill out all the paperwork and get things started."

He gave her a searching look, but nodded. "Okay."

Dale's standard process involved a lot of questions. Some of the more penetrating ones about Marius's living arrangements, finances and work schedule made her boy get more somber and quiet as the process continued. When it concluded and Dale met her gaze, Marius pushed back from the table abruptly.

"I know I'm a bad bet, so I get it. Whatever." He moved toward the office door, that belligerent set to his shoulders Regina well knew. Dale brought him to a halt with one question.

"Why do you want to adopt this kitten, Marius?"

Marius pivoted and faced him. "What does it matter? I'm not a good home for her. I can tell you think so."

"Maybe you're assuming things so you don't get punched in the face by a rejection. From what I understand from Regina, you're not afraid of getting punched in the face for real, so man up and answer my fucking question honestly. And don't presume to know what's in my head, son."

Marius bristled at what Regina was sure was Dale's deliberate use of the familiarity. His jaw clenched, but he didn't break the retired SEAL's gaze, which Regina knew was a good accomplishment when Dale was leveling that stare on someone.

"I would take care of her. I'd follow Regina's direction on the stuff I don't know about, and I'd learn how to be good at it."

"I'm glad to hear that. That's the kind of sincerity I want from someone who adopts an animal. But it's not an answer to my question. Why do you want to adopt her?"

Marius frowned. Sorting the thoughts and emotions to answer Dale clearly was an obvious physical effort. "I liked holding her," he said at last. "I liked how she trusted me. When she played, it made me smile. Those things felt normal. She made me feel like I could be a normal person, adopting a pet. I thought, for a minute, I could give her a good home. That we could be good together."

She saw a deep despair in his gaze. "But you're right. It's too soon and...just forget it. Thanks for your time. I'll be in the car."

He left the office, the screen door clapping against the frame as he released it and strode across the lot. A couple of the dogs approached him and then veered off.

"He's right. It's too soon," Dale said. "I'm sorry, Regina, but he's all over the map."

"What if I was the cat's primary guardian? If she lives with me?" As the idea formed in her mind, it made sense. Keeping the cat at her home for the time being would help Marius be less uptight about all the things that could go wrong. Give him breathing space to build the necessary bridges in his mind to see himself as a good risk as a pet parent. "I think he truly does want to learn how to care for a pet," she added. "But that would be less stressful, and good for him and the cat at the same time."

Regina was relieved to see Dale's expression ease into a tentative approval. "If you're wanting to adopt a cat, that could work. I'd need to be sure that if it never worked out for him, that you'd want to be this cat's long term home. I want her loved, not just tolerated."

"No problem there. I've thought about adopting one plenty of times, but until recently I traveled too much. The corporate outreach through the community college is looking like a two-year gig at least, and may lead to other consulting in the area. I'm over being on the road half the year."

Dale grunted. "I'd accept that solution, then. But it would be good if she had a friend to play with."

Regina shot him a calculating look. "Do I get a two-for-one discount?"

Dale shrugged blandly, but with a twinkle in his blue-green eyes. "It's a known fact that most dogs and cats are happier if they have another animal companion in the home, especially when most families have to work nine to five so they're alone a big chunk of the day."

"How about that striped brown tabby who looks pissed at the world?"

Dale chuckled. "That's Bad Attitude. I call him Badat for short. He's a feral who catches rats around the junkyard, though he's become socialized enough he'll occasionally let me pet his head and not try to take my hand off at the wrist. Some days, like today, he snarls at me until I let him into the cat building to hang out for awhile on his observation perch. He's pretty dug in here, and considers himself the lord of the cat habitat. Otherwise, I'd let you try your Mistress wiles on him. You seem to have a touch for the male hard cases."

He cocked his head, the light glinting off the silver strands in his short hair. "But the mom of that kitten needs a home. She's barely nine months old herself, so she still has plenty of kitten in her to be a good playmate. She's also a tough little lady. Reserves judgment and does some heavy screening of her own before she decides to be friendly with a human. I think the two of you would be a good match."

"All right." Regina rose. "I'll talk to Marius. I'll text you if we're coming back to pick them up before we leave. I can meet her then."

"No problem." Dale sat back. "He's a good kid who's been mind-fucked in the worst nightmare kind of way. He doesn't believe it, but I'm in his corner. I'd really like him to provide a home for this little mite. It's not a bad idea to have two imperious females in his life looking out for him."

Regina chuckled, and touched his hand fondly. "I know you're in his corner. And I appreciate you being straight about it. The truth is the best way to go with him, though his reaction to it can be challenging. He's a workout."

"Some of the best ones can be," Dale noted. "Good luck, Mistress."

She left the office, petted and spoke to the dogs lying in the shade of the rollout awning in front. As she walked along the gravel drive to the entrance, she saw Marius leaning against the back bumper of their car, gazing down the road. Sliding through the front gate, she moved to prop next to him, hip to hip. The New Orleans sun was starting to set, but the humidity was still high. She could see the dampness of the soft hairs on his nape.

"Hungry?" she asked. "Someone promised me dinner."

He lifted a shoulder and straightened. "Yeah."

"Hey." She stopped him, moving into his space. Cradling his jaw, she put a kiss on his tense mouth. It eased under the pressure of hers, and his lips parted. She swept in to tangle with his tongue and bring their mouths even closer together. It reflected the same closeness she was bringing to the contact between their two bodies, her breasts against his chest, hips and thighs brushing.

His hands went to her waist, holding her even closer. Making a soft noise of pleasure, she slid her arm over his shoulder, hand resting on his neck, stroking as she took the full measure of the kiss that spun out under a lazy, warm sun. She was vaguely aware of the sounds of frogs from a nearby pond, the rasping song of crickets.

When she lifted her head, breaking the kiss, his eyes held desire along with the confusion, but the confusion wasn't as jagged and painful. She stroked his jaw.

"Buy me dinner, sweet boy."

~

Food always seemed to level out even the most uncertain male temperament. Marius started out the meal cordial though quiet, but as it progressed, she made him talk about random subjects. She added in the reminder he had to be a good date or she'd leave him for one of New Orleans many street buskers. Under that kind of gentle teasing, he started to relax again. But it wasn't until they were done with their meal, and she was seeing the occasional smile out of him, that she decided to head back toward more serious topics.

"So I told you how I got into the Domme thing. How did you first figure out your submissive craving?"

They were walking along the outskirts of Jackson Square. They'd paused to hear the musical stylings of a man with Marley-style dreadlocks playing a trio of upside down buckets and improvising lyrics about the foot traffic around him. But as they moved on, she posed the question.

Marius shrugged. "Kind of fell into it. Regular relationships weren't working."

"Oh? How so?" She directed him up the ramp over the trolley tracks to the sidewalk that followed the river. It took them away from the Jackson Square congestion.

He didn't say anything right away. But she waited him out and eventually he collected his thoughts and gave her more. "Couldn't... you know. Perform. I'd get with a girl, start making out the way any other high school kid did, and all the stuff would pile up in my head, these images from the past, things she didn't know about me, and... nothing. I covered it by getting really good at getting her off."

A dry smile touched his lips. "Not a bad skill to have. One girl I was with for a little while, she enjoyed it a lot, and started being kind of bossy about it. Think I stumbled onto an aspiring Domme, neither one of us understanding then why we were so well-matched.

"She'd tell me what to do, how she wanted it, and the more she ordered me around...well, I realized I was getting turned on by it. First time I came while with a woman. All over her dress."

Regina winced and he chuckled painfully. "Nothing like being a teenager, right? After that, I figured out what my trigger was and could finally masturbate like a normal kid."

"You never had, until then?"

"Not successfully." A shadow crossed his expression and his gaze was elsewhere again. "I'd have the urge, but couldn't make it go anywhere. That mindfuck invasion from my past again." He cleared his throat. "When I turned twenty-one, I went looking for the pro-Dommes. I was more comfortable with that scenario than finding it through a relationship. But the pro-Domme thing only worked once or twice."

"Because they were a paid service."

He looked toward her, surprise flickering in his expression. "Yeah. They were there to take care of *my* needs. No matter how cloaked it was in me doing things for them, that was the deal. They were pros, so they could have been enjoying it, not enjoying it, and been tops or bottoms in their real lives, or neither."

He needed to serve a Mistress, really serve her, even if he was fighting through a quagmire of his own issues to get there. The thought gave her a firm surge of satisfaction, though she spoke casually. "So things flopped again, literally."

"Nice confidence booster there, Mistress," he said dryly. "But yeah. The first time, the pro decided what would work would be humiliation. Telling me I was garbage, didn't deserve to be born, that kind of thing."

He noticed her wince. "Lots of guys get off on that," he said mildly. "It wasn't a bad guess."

"Yeah. Guys to whom it doesn't hit so close to home to what they really think of themselves. Did it work for you?"

"No," he admitted. "Gave me a sick feeling in my stomach. She was smart, figured it out, sent me to another Domme who had me kneel at her feet, fucked me with a strap-on, let me eat her out while she sat on this throne like a queen. That got some response, but not much. Once again, she was a smart lady, so after talking to me about it, she figured out what I couldn't and suggested I hit the clubs, make myself available to Dommes looking for subs for a night of play. That's where I found the fit. My fit."

He gestured down the hill to a beer vendor. "If we're going to talk about my teenage struggle with impotence, I'm going to need a beer. Can I bring you one?"

"Sure. But from what I can tell, that issue is fully in the past." She gave him an appreciative look. "I've never had a problem noticing when you're inside me. You and your man meat totally get my attention."

He chuckled, but she could tell from the slight tinge of color in his cheeks she'd stroked his ego, in the right way. Boy needed the right kind of stroking, especially after admitting so baldly he'd had trouble getting it up most of his teen years. Most men wouldn't have done that.

She touched his arm. "You don't drink much because your mother did. To make it all go away. I'm guessing beer wasn't her preferred choice."

He met her gaze. "Yeah."

She did a quick stroke of his face with her knuckles. "Okay. Go get my beer."

She watched him stride down the hill, a handsome, fit man who caught female attention easily. He'd always been flirty inside the club, but she noticed here, out in the world, he didn't seem to employ those talents. Was that because he was with her, and he was being respect-ful? Or was it more of what he'd discussed, that he needed a Domme not just to trip his trigger, but to inspire him to even switch it on?

When he returned, she had another, lighter question for him. "So what happened to the high school girl? Were you together long?"

He sat down on the bench, handing her the brown-bagged beer after he twisted open the top for her. "The usual run for a high school relationship. A few months. I heard her joking with her friends one day. Saying, 'I just tell him, 'Boy, on your knees. Get down there and take care of that.' And he does. Girlfriends, he makes me see stars, no lie.'" He imitated the imperious female tone as he smiled around his beer. Regina rolled her eyes and elbowed him.

"Hey, I'm just reporting the truth. She said the others were going at it all wrong. That if they ordered their boyfriends around, rather than letting them fumble and stumble, they'd both be happier."

Regina chuckled. "Sounds like you helped give a young woman a stunning amount of self-confidence."

"I think she already had that. She reminded me of you."

Regina cocked a brow. "Was she a black girl, you bad thing?"

His lips quirked. "Yeah. But that wasn't what reminded me of you. It was...what you just said. You're always in charge, and so was she."

"Are you calling me a control freak?"

His eyes sparkled. "No, ma'am. Seriously, I'm not. You don't have a hang-up about relinquishing control, because it doesn't matter. Even when you let go, you're still on top. It's who you are."

"We make sense then. Because there are plenty of times that stubborn nature of yours tries to take control, but you never top. You don't have it in you, and that's not a judgment." She tapped her beer to his. "That's a part of your personality. I like many parts of your personality, including that one. You can take the attempts at control too far, into some dark areas, but there are other times it's fun, a challenge. I like a bad boy."

He seemed okay with that and they drank in silence for the next few moments.

"So what are you going to name your kitten?" she asked at last.

He shook his head. "We were just looking. I can't get one right now."

"Why?"

"She deserves...she deserves a really good home. And that means a place more like you have. Hell, that mean-eyed tomcat is more suited to my place, with the dark alleys and all that concrete."

"I've found street-wise tomcats like sunspots and safe places as much as kittens. Maybe appreciate them even more, once they relax enough to know they can trust the environment. And you don't have to have bunches of money and a nice house to give a pet a loving home. But why don't you let her stay with me until you feel more comfortable about it all?"

The brief flash of hope she saw in his eyes told her his heart had become set on this. He'd really wanted to adopt the kitten, and not simply as a prove-himself kind of thing. Tucking herself under his arm, she caressed his jaw. His gray eyes returned to the river as his shoulders lifted in a sigh, and he shook his head.

"I don't want to saddle you with something I may never be able to have. My landlady has a lot of health problems. She's talking about going into assisted living, and will probably do it soon as she finds a place that will let her bring her cats. When that happens, her son's going to kick me out and sell the house. I haven't really made a habit of living in the same place for long anyway."

From the fondness Mrs. Jones demonstrated for him, Regina suspected he would like to have the option of staying longer.

"I told Dale *I* want the kitten," she said firmly. "I've been thinking about adopting a pet for the past couple years, and this seems the right time to do it. If you never feel comfortable making her all your own, I'll keep her. I'm going to adopt her mother, too. As far as your living arrangements, Dale mentioned one of the men from his old unit recently moved to Tampa and is looking for a roommate to share expenses. I have his number. You could talk to him and see what you think. In the meantime, you can visit your kitten anytime you want."

He played with the neck of the beer, thinking. "I don't...I've never really let someone depend on me. Makes me antsy."

"Time to work on that, because I depend on you."

His surprised gaze swiveled toward her. "What do you mean?"

"I think you know, so I'm not explaining it." She put her feet on a cut log someone had left in front of the bench as a convenient footrest while watching the river's boat traffic. Marius had his ankle crossed on his knee, and she tipped her feet to the right to brush the sole of that shoe, a teasing admonishment. He grimaced affably.

"This is different from the things we've done lately," he observed.

"Yep. Doesn't have to be all about whips and chains."

He tracked a passing freighter, loaded with towers of containers headed off to ports unknown, but his attention was too fixed, alerting her of the import of his next deceptively casual question. "Is it part of your whole Domme therapy strategy? Doing so much non-Domme/sub stuff?"

She cocked her head. "Tell you what. If we drop the pretense of The Zone issue once and for all, what's the less scary answer to that question for you? Yes or no?"

"*No* is the scarier answer," he said. "But I don't like the *yes* answer much."

"Really?" She arched a brow, the expression deepening as he moved his arm from the back of the bench to drape it over her shoulders.

"No," he said firmly. "But what about you? Which one's the scarier answer for you?"

She made a *pfft* sound. "*No* falls well within the scared shitless territory."

She surprised a shy smile out of him, so at odds with his usual cocky confidence, it touched her.

"Is that because of what I've done to other Mistresses, messing with their heads, making them vulnerable and then taking advantage of that?" His eyes sharpened. "I won't do that to—"

She shook her head and touched his knee. "I've never feared that."

She turned her attention back to the river. He wasn't the only one who could use it as a buffer against stronger feelings and worries. However, she stayed leaning against his side, absorbing his heat and strength. "I'm falling in love with you."

At his jolt of shock, she laid her hand on his thigh, closing firm fingers on him. "I've no idea what the shape of that will look like. And I'm not asking you to do anything different. You also don't have to be scared about me making myself vulnerable that way. I'm not ever going to let you fuck with my head. You'll never treat me badly, or try to manipulate me, because I will shut you down and shut you out every time you do, until you purge it from your system and overcome those demons. But there's one thing I won't do."

She glanced at him, making sure she had his full attention. "Cut you loose. Not until it's my decision, or the right one for you."

"So if I don't think I'm in love with you, that's not a problem?" But she heard the trace of panic behind the edgy tone. She trailed her fingers over his mouth.

"No. Because I know you've fallen in love with me, too, even though you don't recognize any of the markers. You don't have any points of reference for them. But you don't have to worry about that, either. I can damn well take care of myself, and I see you, good and bad. I won't let the bad take over. I expect you to work on fixing the bad, but I'm your safety net, your warden, judge and punisher, until you figure it out." Her lips curved. "I have ways of punishing you that you haven't even seen yet, sweet boy."

"What if it's never the right decision to cut me loose?"

He had no idea how it pleased her, to hear the wistful note of hope he probably thought he had buried too deep for anyone to hear, even himself. She sighed and settled deeper into the curve of his arm. Turning on her hip, she put her head on his chest, her arm loosely around his waist. It was a very female pose to take, and she was further pleased when he set his beer aside and slid both arms around her. A quiver through them made her think he was a little overwhelmed at being allowed the rare chance to hold her in such a sheltering way. He was damn good at it.

"Well, if I never cut you loose, then I'm afraid you'll be mine forever. You'll have *Exclusive Property of Lady Regina* branded on your muscular ass."

"Okay." He pressed a kiss to her forehead, nudging so he could bend and kiss her mouth. She parted her lips, her arm sliding up to his neck to hold on. When she drew back after a satisfyingly long moment, she traced his cheek. "Dale *is* ready to let you adopt the kitten, if I'm the primary owner. Which I think is apropos, since I'm your primary owner. Unless you wish to dispute that."

"Well, I don't know, Mistress." He leaned back and sprawled out indolently again, looking like bad boy sex personified. But below the surface she could see all sorts of emotions churning, because she'd just rocked his world. It almost made her smile. "I'm not wearing your collar," he pointed out.

"Really?" Her gaze went to the ID bracelet on his arm. "I thought you were."

His eyes flickered. "I hoped that was what it meant," he said, low.

"Well, it does. But I'm a woman who likes backups. That bracelet says you're mine all the time, whether we're watching TV, I'm at work, or you're under me, being ridden until I wear you out." Unzipping the top of the small cross-body purse she wore, she produced a worn strap coiled in a neat circle. It was the collar she'd put on him for the pony play scene.

She'd surprised him again. When his gray eyes latched onto it with a raw hunger that took her breath, she had to fight to maintain her composure. "I don't need you to profess your love for me," she said. "But I want one honest answer. Let's put it to rest. Is this still about getting back into The Zone?"

She saw calculation happening amid the storm clouds. She refused to let it hurt, or create a sinking disappointment in her. She'd said it herself. He still had a long way to go, but they'd only get there step by step, moving forward.

"There's no wrong answer except a lie," she said. "You lie to me, now or ever, I will make you regret it. As many times as needed to teach you the lesson that you will never get away with that with me."

His gaze flashed at the challenge, and she had to suppress another smile when he slid his fingers along her shoulder in a sensual caress. An insolent one.

"What about you, Mistress?" he tossed back. "Am I still just some challenge to prove how badass you are to all the other Mistresses? The one that can bring the problem child back in line?"

"You've never been a child, Marius," she said seriously, tapping his sullen mouth. "That's the part they missed, no fault of their own, because you excelled at masking it and giving them what they wanted. Until suppressing all that other stuff started to surface and you turned mean."

She wrapped her fingers around his throat and shifted closer, pressing her breast against his chest, her mouth to his ear. As he stilled, she spoke with smooth conviction. "This is your real collar, my hand upon you, keeping you in line with a touch, a reminder of your submission to me. The collar, the bracelet, a cock harness...all of those are just symbols of this."

As she tightened her grip on his corded neck, his façade dropped. It revealed the man she'd seen break, the night of his father's execution. One she'd also watched hold a kitten in his hands. And pound on a man with breathtaking rage.

For good or bad, his most honest moments were his most brutal ones, the moments that had shown her who he was, as well as who he could be. Not because she could change or fix him, but because if he had someone to love him, truly love him, someone he would let himself love back, he could find his way on that path himself. She had faith in it, just as she'd told him.

"So much of what makes a healthy power exchange is the inner child, our deepest longings, fears and needs," she murmured. "Your inner child died a long time ago, Marius. Went dormant. But you're bringing it back to life. And I love watching it happen under my control."

He gripped her wrist, an unspoken message requesting her to ease back. As she did, he surprised her by moving off the bench, dropping to one knee before her. The significance of the gesture caught her breath, but he'd forgotten she'd set her beer on the walkway and his foot hit it. Though he managed to catch it as it wobbled, some of the beer slopped over his hand. He shot her a lopsided grin. "Pretty smooth and suave, right?"

"I'm all a-quiver." She brushed his face. "Why are you kneeling to me, sweet boy?"

He lowered his head, gazing at her feet.

"I'd like to wear your collar, Mistress. I care about getting back into The Zone. I miss it, miss the work, miss the connection, the way I felt there. Like I belonged. But that's not why I want to wear your collar."

"Good." She managed to sound calm, though her heart tripped. "Because that's not why I offered it. You were a challenge and a mystery to me at first. I expect that's the way a lot of good relationships start. But whether you get back into The Zone has nothing to do with me wanting you to belong to me." Letting the collar unravel, she slid the strap along his shoulder, a provocative tease. "Lift your chin."

He did. Even with the fastest image capture equipment currently on the market, no one could have caught all the emotions that went through his gray eyes in a blink. She didn't register them with her own vision; she felt them. He was light and dark and all shades in between, but those emotions could twist into the same arrow, pointing toward what he needed and wanted. The energy in his body gravitated toward her and that collar.

"Has a Mistress ever collared you like this? Not just as a prop for a scene?"

"No, ma'am." His voice had that roughness again, and when she shifted forward on the bench, spreading her thighs to flank him, he moved into the triangle of space. She threaded the strap around his throat. Most subs wouldn't touch their Mistress during such a moment, but she didn't correct him when he put his hands on her hips. He needed the contact, and she liked it too.

Did he notice that she allowed her cheeks to flush, her fingers tremble? Could he hear how her heart thudded extra beats? Since he dipped his head against her hand after she buckled the strap, she thought he did. She caressed his collar bone beneath the collar's hold, and the coarse hair curling near the base of his throat. She'd left only a finger's breadth of space and was pleased with the flare in his gaze at the constriction when she tugged on it. She also saw the momentary glazing that so many subs experienced when a collar was put upon them, as they turned inward to that deep-seated need to be owned and got lost in it.

She closed her fingers on the strap. It had been a long, long time since she'd claimed one for her own. And those relationships hadn't had half the impact on her senses that this man had had in such a short time. She told herself to get a grip and let go.

Let go of the collar, not the man. Maybe not ever.

"We'll work out what this means as we go, depending on what you need and I need," she said briskly. "And want. But for now it means that when you're wearing it, I don't expect to have to stay on you about the things I've made clear from the beginning. You're honest with me, and you don't bullshit or charm me." She tugged the D-link, pulling on the back of his neck, and clamped her knees on either side of his kneeling body. "When you want to take this off, you ask permission, unless it's a matter of your immediate safety. Your first job is always to take care of yourself, because you belong to me and I expect my property to keep itself safe and undamaged."

Her lips twitched ruefully at the flicker in his eyes. "Or relatively undamaged." She twisted her fingers in the strap beneath the D-link. "I know you fight for money. But fighting to deal with your emotions ends now. Anytime you want to take on a fight because of your feelings, not your bills, you call me first. I will handle whatever's happening in your head. If I can't, you can get to a fight afterward. But first option belongs to me. I'm your first drug of choice. Agreed?"

His gaze coursed up her body to her tight mouth and sharp eyes, and desire flared hot in his own, responding to the implication. "I can do something those fights can't, and you know it," she purred. "Wear you out, make you beg and take you down. And it won't hurt the next day. Well, not quite as much."

He smiled and moved closer. She spread her knees wider in accommodation. When he kissed her, he didn't ask, the need in his face overriding everything else. She was okay with that, because the right part of his soul had asked, and her own had given permission.

This was her boy.

~

She decided they'd walk back to the hotel, because she had somewhere else she wanted to stop. A tattoo parlor, one she'd researched on line for its five-star reputation. As she stopped in front of it and nodded to Marius to hold the door for her so she could precede him into the establishment, he raised a brow. "Decided you want to get that exclusive property tattoo already?" he asked.

"Tempting, but for the reality I want something a little subtler. Sit there." She pointed to a scarred metal chair, part of an ensemble of half a dozen of them. One was occupied by an older man in jeans and leather biker vest who looked like he was a regular visit to the parlor, if his spirited debate with one of the other tattoo artists about one of the popular reality shows was any indication. That artist, as well as two others, had customers in their chairs or on padded tables, depending on what body part was getting tattooed. Other people milled around, chatting and relaxed, friends of the artists or maybe waiting their turn—or both.

Rock music blared through the speakers. A flat screen was on mute, showing a basketball game somewhere. The walls were muraled with the artists' work. Those pictures were interspersed with snapshots of themselves at tattoo events, or with friends or family. The scent of ink pervaded the establishment.

When she approached the counter, which had a plethora of piercing jewelry on display beneath the glass, she found the inevitable thick books of tattoo ideas. Fortunately, they were categorized so she could find the theme she wanted quickly. In short order, she lifted her head and located an available artist, a wiry but sexy looking biker chick with lots of tatts, piercings and vivid violet eyes provided by contacts. She wore a black tank that exposed her flat belly and low-riding tight jeans. From the Internet site, Regina recalled she was a newer member of the business, but highly rated for her work.

Regina adjusted the book toward her so the woman could see what she was viewing. "I want to choose the one of these that will look best with his existing tattoo." Regina flicked her glance at Marius, bringing him to his feet and to the counter without speaking a word. It swirled something low in her belly. He really was so much more responsive than he realized. "Take off the shirt," she ordered.

While the artist or the others here might not be part of the BDSM scene, the tattoo world lived on the same edges the D/s world did. Regina didn't feel any reservations about exposing what her relationship to Marius was.

They'd cleared the air between them while sitting at the river, and she'd laid the groundwork for taking complete control of a situation like this. Now, as she waited to see how he would respond, her body vibrated in anticipation.

～

As Marius met her gaze, he had mixed feelings about getting a tattoo she'd chosen. Not opposed, just...fuck, he didn't know what he felt. But he wasn't saying no. Wasn't feeling no, either. Not when she issued a command like she just had, her eyes fixed upon him with that steady Mistress's regard.

As he stripped off his shirt with barely a blink of hesitation, her eyes sparked with the same kind of heat that surged through him in response. The tattoo artist's gaze roved appreciatively over his upper body, but her skill as an artist showed as she zeroed in on his existing tattoo and came closer, her fingers passing over it critically. "Damn fine work. I'm Jillian. I hope you want me to do what I think you want me to do. That's going to be kickass."

She discussed it with Regina as he stood silently listening. He saw Jillian's gaze pass over the collar on his throat, then go back to Regina. While it might just be a passing look, Marius took it as an acknowledgement of his Mistress's obvious lead role of the situation. That made his body tighten with a desire to do things for her that couldn't be done here.

Restraining himself for her only heightened the deep intensity of that feeling, keeping him quiet and in an almost meditative focus on her, a functional subspace he didn't mind experiencing.

But when he was sitting in the chair and the artist had finished the drawn outline, ready to begin the tattoo itself, Regina bent over him, touching her face. "All right with this, sweet boy?"

He glanced at Jillian. "Can you start while I'm kissing her? I want my mouth on hers when I feel the first touch of the needle."

As Regina's eyes flared hot with pleasure, the artist nodded. Though her expression was hard to read, he thought he detected a flicker of female approval. "Just tell me when you're going to stop. Unless you plan on kissing her the whole time," she added dryly.

It wasn't a bad idea. He saw the sensuous laughter in Regina's eyes as his thought obviously reflected her own thinking. Or maybe she just read his face.

Reaching up, he curved his large hand against Regina's delicate throat and brought her down to his mouth, taking a deep, demanding dive into that heated wetness, letting her feel it. He might be a sub, but there were times that need ironically drove him to take over, prove to her just how much testosterone was hers to call. She made a soft little moan, her fingertips curling over his hand, nails digging in. He felt the sharp burn as Jillian began the outline, and kept the kiss going a few seconds longer before he eased his mouth back enough to speak.

"Okay."

The tattoo artist let him readjust, and then resumed. Regina took a seat nearby, where he could look right at her. He didn't say another word; he simply kept his attention on his Mistress as the tattoo artist worked on him.

Regina engaged the other clients and artists in casual conversation without self-consciousness, but her gaze flicked back to him often and stayed, even when she was talking. He could feel it like a touch, meandering down his bare chest and muscled abs, lingering over his groin and thighs under denim. With the result he got fucking hard in front of everyone and wasn't the least bit repentant about it. Especially when he saw her lips curve with the knowledge of what she was doing to him. What she could do to him.

Anything. Anything she wanted. He couldn't wait to get back to the hotel.

The thought consumed him, and had only grown stronger by the time the tattoo was finished. Regina rose and came to inspect the work. Her gaze lifted to his, her brown eyes alight with fire. "Exactly what I wanted," she said in a husky voice.

Jillian positioned a mirror so he could see it better. It was a badass-looking black kitten, one paw raised in play. Yet the positioning made it look as if the small creature had been the one to shred through his skin and expose the armor beneath.

"Your first pet," Regina said, running a light finger around it. "If you take care of this one, maybe you'll eventually get to take the other one home."

The word hit him hard and low. To conceal his reaction, he looked down and slid his touch, not over the tattoo, but over her fingers. His Mistress was too sharp-eyed, though. She touched his jaw. "Look at me and say what you were thinking."

He shook his head. "I'll just ruin it."

"Say it anyway." Jillian had moved away to do clean up, giving them the illusion of privacy.

"She'll already be home if she's with you," he said. "That's what I want to think of as home. What I wish was my home."

He rose abruptly, reaching for his wallet. "No," Regina said. "I'm paying for this."

He shook his head, closing his hand over her wrist as she reached for her purse, his grip hard enough to catch her attention. "Not this time," he said.

He pulled out a couple crisp hundreds from a small wad of bills, and handed it to Jillian. "Keep the change."

When Marius tucked the wallet back into his pocket, he noted a pair of new arrivals on the scarred metal chairs. Tattoo parlors attracted some rough-looking types, but there was rough-looking cool, like the woman who'd just added to his tattoo, and rough-looking criminal. They could be wearing the same look of tattoos, piercings, jeans and T-shirts, but they pinged his radar with a warning of danger.

The smarter-looking one of the two seemed a little too interested in the wad of cash Marius was carrying, and had leaned over to mutter to his companion. Regina was offering her thanks to Jillian, engaging in the kind of conspiratorial female discussion that normally he'd enjoy observing. Any type of shared intimacy between two hot women had the potential to become wishful fantasy material. But he wasn't taking his eyes off these two lowlifes.

He expected Regina would have been savvy enough to mark the two as trouble if her gaze turned in that direction. Her nose for danger was pretty good, probably thanks to the prison guard stuff. Or correctional officer, as she preferred.

The thought gave him a grim smile, but didn't change his focus. Maybe the reason she hadn't noticed these two was because her subconscious knew she was with someone more than capable of protecting her from their type.

Because she damn well was.

As she touched his arm, letting him know it was time to go, he saw she was holding his shirt. When he reached for it, she hugged it to her, refusing to give it back, a little smile playing around her lips. He liked that, but when she would have drawn him toward the door, he squeezed her hand, a mute request to wait a moment as he handled what needed to be handled.

He caught her quizzical expression a flash before he turned and closed the distance between himself and the two men. One had started to rise from his chair, probably preparing to tail them as soon as they left the place.

Marius put him back down with a casual shove and got into the face of the seated male, the smarter-looking one. Though, on closer inspection, that wasn't saying a whole lot.

The deliberate act, as well as his expression and body language, created a sudden lull of conversation in the tattoo parlor.

"I earned that money from fucking up guys far bigger and meaner than you two assholes," he said. "So you want to go to the hospital, you follow me. And if either of you threatens my Mistress to get me to give it up"—his gaze hardened—"You won't need a hospital. The morning street crew can hose what's left of you down the fucking drains."

Straightening, he waited only long enough to confirm the message had been received. Then he rejoined Regina, cordially holding the door for her, his hand resting on the small of her back as she stepped out and he followed.

They'd moved into the awakening energy of a glittering New Orleans night, but his Mistress had other things on her mind. She walked less than two steps with him before pulling him into the lee of the building. Curling her hands in his shirt front, she kissed him hard and deep. He gripped her hips, wanting her to feel the urgency of his body, how much he wanted to serve her whenever, however. She'd said that was a drug to a Mistress. He wanted to be that drug for her.

"I'm not saying the testosterone surge always works on me," she declared as she pulled free. "But occasionally it does."

He grinned, and she sobered. "I like you thinking of me as your home, Duncan. Hearing you wish for that...makes me wish for it, too."

As always, such a gift from her had the ability to simultaneously arouse, thrill and terrify him. She touched his face, seeing all of it, if her words were any indication.

"I know you're still going to be a pain in my ass. I don't need you to be perfect to want you. I just need to know you're trying to be the best person you can be with me, and you're always, always trying to be honest."

He'd never wanted to be what a person wanted him to be. Probably because he'd never thought he could even come close. But as he felt the sunburn ache of the tattoo on his shoulder, and the weight of her fingers in his hand, the desire was there...and it wasn't a bad feeling at all.

He just didn't want to fail.

CHAPTER SEVENTEEN

*H*ell, why was he nervous? Why should he be nervous? He looked again at the message in his Zone account, which he'd accessed from the cell phone he carried now, more evidence of how his life had changed in the past month.

Temporary guest pass to The Zone has been approved. Your Mistress orders you to arrive at seven o'clock tonight. Wear what's in locker #23. DM will lock you in jail cage. Your Mistress will know when you're ready for her appearance.

He was surprised, but then he wondered if that was the plan. Regina volunteered to do one orientation a month for new Dommes at The Zone, which would have been tonight. However, last week she'd had to call another Mistress to switch dates. She'd claimed to have a class commitment that would run late. It wasn't even one of Marius's scheduled days to come see her.

He slept at her place three nights a week. She'd given him a protocol to follow. He could come over whenever he wanted on that day, watch TV, sleep, whatever, as long as he kept things neat. But when she texted him a thirty-minute heads up, he stopped whatever he was doing to run through the shower and shave. He would put on a ball gag and cuffs and get on the bed on all fours. He'd attach the cuffs to four chains he pulled out from the mattress at the corners, and hook his collar to the tether fastened to the center of the head board, a restraint screened by the colorful pillows she kept there.

He could do all that one-handed, because the cuffs were Velcro, not intended to keep him from getting out of them if an emergency required it in her absence. Their purpose was to switch gears in his head, become his Mistress's pure boy toy—or man toy, as she liked to call him—helping her defuse after a day at work. And fuck, serving such a functional, purely sexual purpose for her never failed to turn him on.

The schedule had led to the discovery of other, more surprising things that fulfilled him. Sometimes she left things undone, like making her bed or washing her dishes, so he could do those things for her. He liked serving her that way, too.

When he was on the bed and heard the lock turn, his cock would already be straining inside the condom he used to protect her bed linens. She'd put down her laptop case, glance through the mail he'd leave neatly arranged on the kitchen table. She'd hum a little tune when she came down the hall, and he knew she'd be untying her hair, letting it fall soft down her back and over her shoulders.

She'd shrug out of her jacket, slip off her slacks and pick up the lubed strap-on he'd leave sitting on the dresser. Sometimes he left other things for her. A couple chocolates, or a trio of roses he'd put in a vase he'd found in her cabinets. She didn't mind him being familiar with her home. Didn't mind him considering it his home. Or him leaving her little touches like that she didn't expect, so long as they didn't mess with her instructions.

Once she slipped on the strap-on with its clitoral stimulator, she'd put her knee on the bed, positioning herself behind him. He was required to stay quiet and still as she ran her hands over him, purring her pleasure.

Sometimes, if she was in a particularly sadistic mood, she'd have ordered him to wear the cock harness, buckling it tight enough it cut into him as he got harder and harder.

Other times he was required to don the stallion mask and insert the tail butt plug before she arrived, the thick hair sliding along the back of his thighs from his every move. When she got home on those days, she'd replace the plug with the strap-on.

If he'd been a pain in the ass, which still happened more often than he wished, the dildo was thicker on those days. As she fucked his ass like she was a beefy lumberjack, instead of a beautiful woman half that weight, she'd make him strangle out a muffled proper apology.

It all turned him on, but the most intense moments were those first few, when he shuddered with the anticipation of her being home, of her touching him. When she wouldn't speak to him directly, and wouldn't allow him to speak. He was there to relieve her sexual need after a hard day at the office, and he would serve her well. That was what was required of him. She'd slide the dildo into his ass with a hum of pleasure and start thrusting, undulating, a dance against his body as she let the stimulator get her worked up while she thrust and withdrew, thrust and withdrew.

His cock would ache, feel so hard it could split, especially as he listened to her start to breathe faster and heavier, little moans breaking from her luscious lips. He wished there was a mirror before him so he could look at her, but that wasn't permitted. Not until after.

When she came, sometimes it was like a dove's cry; sometimes a hawk's sharpness, a guttural shriek he felt all the way down into his gut and balls. He'd be so near that edge he almost couldn't hold back any longer. But he'd wait on his Mistress to relent.

"Come for me, sweet boy."

He would jet into the condom, his body humping and working the air, wishing he could be thrusting into her. That came later in the evening, if she welcomed him into her bed. If not, he at least didn't have to be far away from her. Unless he was *really* an asshole. Then she'd chain him up in the playroom for the night. He hated that, so he fought his demons extra hard to keep that from happening.

She'd moved the pallet on the floor of her bedroom next to her bed, so at night she could let her fingers trail over his shoulder, his side, as she lay on her stomach and they looked at each other in the dim lamplight, talking about whatever.

Christ, it was so many different things, belonging to her like this. He'd thought it wouldn't be much different from being in a club environment, but then he'd never been a Mistress's personal sub, in a relationship with her. Like so many things in his life, he'd had no way to anticipate what this would feel like. There was the sex part, which was mind-blowing. But it was the other stuff—room for tenderness, for practical moments, for laughter, for living a life with a woman he seemed to need like air—that blew away all his foundations, all the crap bullshit defenses he'd erected.

He'd named the kitten he'd adopted Dot. She lived at Regina's with Magenta, her mother. He'd expected Dot to gravitate toward Regina, but Dot made clear from Day One Marius was her person, in ways he thought only dogs did. She was in the window watching for him when he pulled up on his visiting days. She slept on the pallet with him. When he and Regina watched TV, she curled up in his lap or perched on the sofa back behind his head. Regina would recline against his side, her head on his shoulder. Life didn't get better than that.

One evening, when Regina was in the middle of her post-work fucking of his ass, Dot jumped on Marius's back, kneading and cutting a couple circles before she curled up in the small of it for a catnap, utterly oblivious to what they were doing, or the rhythmic movement of their bodies, though she did rub her face against Regina's fingers, gripping Marius's hip.

Her timing had been so perfect, Regina on the cusp of climax. His Mistress had muttered "screw it," laughter in her voice, and had her orgasm then and there, commanding Marius to come, which he'd managed, though they'd been laughing throughout it. Which had been silly and fun. Another surprise.

Dot also had a command post on the top of the home office chair, kneading his shoulder when he used Regina's computer with her permission and looked at job options. He was considering enrolling in a program to become a certified nursing assistant, with the thought he might be able to train to be a nurse if he did well as a CNA. Or become an EMT and train to be a paramedic, something like that. Regina had put him in touch with a job counselor at the community college where she was doing her corporate stuff, and that counselor had given him some material to study and work on until enrollment opened for the next semester.

Sometimes he thought he was crazy, but when he'd finally worked up the courage to tell Regina the options that interested him, she'd brightened.

"I think you'd be great in any of those fields," she said. "You like taking care of people, particularly women. Let me know how I can help."

She still kept after him about talking to a different kind of counselor, but he dodged it. The fights they had over it, how ugly he'd get, were what got him banished to the playroom most often. One time he walked out, and she texted him that he wasn't allowed to come home for a week. That had sucked so badly he'd vowed never to lose it like that again. But he still wasn't seeing a damn shrink.

He was doing fine. He was past it. Why could she see so much, and not see that? His father was dead and had no more hold on him. Everything was going in the right direction. He wasn't having any more urges to fuck with Regina's head, except for the occasional flare up that, like a headache, Regina could see coming and handled. And he was getting better at managing them himself, learning that self-discipline she'd talked about.

Yeah, he had some weird flashbacks sometimes, and more nightmares lately, which didn't make a lot of sense, because things were going right. But she helped him with those, too.

So he didn't need anyone else's help. All he'd needed was her, the chance to serve a Mistress who understood him.

He could pretty much pass as normal. So why the hell should he be nervous about a scene at The Zone, being conducted by the Mistress he'd learned to trust more than anyone he'd ever trusted in his life?

He wondered what she'd left for him in the locker. The question, as well as the rest of the text, had his cock hardening. Hell, lately it had been a matter of when was his cock *not* hard? She could get him erect as fast as a dog trained to beg. On command.

Maybe after tonight, she'd believe he was okay, too, and lay off the shrink stuff.

Then everything would be perfect. Or rather, far better than he'd ever expected his life to be—which was his definition of perfect.

Arriving at the club, Tina, the hostess, looked at his guest pass closely. Her brow creased over it, but she nodded cordially and let him in. Not overly friendly, but not hostile.

Yeah, that was going to be the awkward part of tonight. Everyone knew his situation and his shit. Thinking about how he'd acted, he really couldn't blame Tyler anymore for what he'd had to do. And Regina...Tyler had given Marius the chance with Regina, when he'd done nothing to deserve her.

But he'd changed since then. He'd prove it. Then those sons of bitches could say what they liked about him, shit on him as much as they wanted, to each other. But he'd be above and beyond reproach for his Mistress. She'd show them. He'd show them.

He didn't like the way the thought made him feel and didn't really want to examine the why all that closely. Even though it was early for too many people to be here, he felt like everyone was staring at him, particularly the Dommes, and he didn't want to get thrown off balance by that. He knew he'd done wrong things to them, but he was different now.

He remembered that night he'd wondered how to make amends. He hadn't gone back to that idea much since, but maybe he would at some point. For tonight, his focus was this. Doing what she'd told him to do.

Once he arrived in the relative privacy of the locker room, he could breathe a little easier. Until he opened the locker. He whistled, muttering an oath under his breath. His Mistress was pulling out all the stops tonight. Just a thong with a codpiece style front that would barely cover his dick.

This was all he'd be wearing? No, not all. His gaze flicked to his ID bracelet at the same moment he lifted his hand to the collar around his throat.

He only took them off to shower, with her permission. Or when he had his fights, which had been about once a week this month. So far he hadn't needed to call her to avoid going to a fight angry. The fights were still a channel for his aggression, yeah, some of his demons taking over as he hammered an opponent, but that had always been the case, making him a good fighter. It wasn't the same as going there all worked up. She didn't totally agree, but she didn't argue with him over it. Much.

As he put on the barely-nothing item and checked himself out in the mirror, he might have blushed, if he knew what modesty was anymore. He was bare-assed, and the cod piece revealed the creases between thigh and groin area, which would give anyone looking glimpses of his balls as he moved.

Closing the locker, he came back out to the floor and found Alex, who was the DM on shift. He didn't have to tell him what was needed. Alex gave him a polite but stiff nod and led him to the jail.

It was a tall rectangular cage, with enough height for a man to stand up in it, but not wide enough to sit down. Which meant a Mistress or Master could reach through the bars and do pretty much anything to a sub that was part of the scene. Electrical zapping, pinching. Sometimes a Mistress or Master might order a male sub to put his cock and balls out between the bars. Then they'd bind his waist and thighs flush against them with straps so he couldn't move, couldn't do anything to keep his hanging dick from being fondled, sucked or slapped by anyone passing by, if that was the Dominant's decision.

He wasn't sure if that was her intent. She hadn't seemed eager to let other Mistresses touch him ever since they'd gotten together, but maybe putting him in a public cage with that green light to the other Dommes was her way of proving he could pass the test.

"Did she leave any instructions on...access?" he asked Alex.

"No," the man said shortly. "But you can safe word out if it gets to be too much. Tell me what it is."

"Fight Club."

"Got it. Get in." Alex opened the jail cell door. Marius looked at it, suddenly feeling uneasy. There was a weird energy here tonight. Alex's distant behavior toward him was to be expected, so it wasn't that. Maybe he was feeling antsy because he'd been under Regina's dominion for weeks, and he wasn't used to trusting or following direction from someone else.

He thought about waiting until Regina showed herself. He'd assumed this whole thing was part of the reapplication process, some kind of test run Regina had arranged with Tyler. However, if he felt uncomfortable, she'd be all right with him waiting on her to show herself. She had to be watching because, even with Alex's supervision, she wouldn't delegate his care to anyone, though it might serve her purposes to stay out of sight.

She might punish him for not following her direction immediately, but if she knew he had an honest concern, she wouldn't chastise him any more than their mutual pleasure demanded.

Hell, he was being a chickenshit. If he got in and things bothered him, he'd only need to safe word out to Alex. He stepped into the cage.

"Wrists," Alex said shortly. Marius put them through the bars to be cuffed to them, his fingers curling as Alex decreased his mobility within the already small space. Looking at his impassive countenance, Marius felt a twinge of conscience.

"I'm sorry I caused you problems, Alex. I know I didn't deserve to be here anymore. I want to change that."

Alex's eyes shifted to his and held. Marius saw a coldness there, more than he would have expected. "I'm paid to deal with shit like you caused," the DM said. "You want to really change things and deserve to be here? Think about how to fix what you did to the Mistresses you fucked with."

So, okay, he'd been lying, somewhat, about not thinking over the amends issue much. He *had* thought about the things he'd done. Most often in the early morning hours when Regina slept and it was just him, stuck with the darkness of his soul. He thought of Siren, who'd been on board when his train derailed with his personal shit. Alex's words brought all that to the forefront, in vivid color.

He swallowed pride. "Okay. Thanks, man."

Alex's gaze flickered at the laconic but sincere response. Rather than answering, he checked that the cuffs were secure. They were threaded over a bar so Marius could slide them up and down, but not pull his hands and wrists back into the cage. "I'll be watching. Any problems, just signal me."

As he began to step away, Alex glanced over his shoulder at Marius, that cold look returning. "Are you playing Regina?"

"No." Marius's lips tugged in a grim smile. "I couldn't even if I tried, and I did try at first. She's a big part of why I'm here tonight, trying to be better."

Alex pursed his mouth. "She's one tough bitch, in all the right ways. You have a long way to go to deserve her."

When the man moved away, Marius thought about how he would have reacted to such blunt words weeks ago. With sneering hostility. Now, he knew it to be simple truth. And sometimes, uncomfortably, he knew he needed to be doing more to fix his shit. But he was, and would. Regina had helped get him this far. He could make this relationship work.

The protocol on the jail cell cage was anyone could reach in and touch if they wanted to do so. Only the sub's genitals were off limits to any but the Dom-in-command, so to speak, unless they were purposefully put on display in the way Marius had recalled. He was kind of glad she hadn't required that. He wasn't sure he really wanted some other Mistress's hands getting his cock worked up, particularly if his Mistress wasn't standing where he could see her, giving her stamp of approval to it. Maybe not even then.

On a normal night, a sub in the cage got plenty of attention, some good-natured teasing from passing Doms and even some subs. Yet though the room had become more populated, more people using the different stations, he was starting to feel invisible. Except to the Mistress who now stood in the doorway to this public play room.

He vaguely remembered her as a one-time scene. She'd gotten frustrated halfway through and simply cut him loose.

When she met his gaze, it was automatic to paste on the mocking, charming grin. He caught himself a blink later, realizing it for the defensive mechanism it was. Regina had taught him that bullshit was no longer acceptable. He was too late to fix it, though, because the Mistress had pivoted and disappeared, though he'd caught a hostile look in her gaze before she did.

Well, fuck it, what did it matter if he gave them his usual charm and fuck-you attitude? He wasn't here for them. He was here for Regina. She knew him, knew how to handle him, bring out the best in him.

Did he know how to bring out the best in himself? The question was unexpected and unsettling. She'd asked him that in a couple different ways these past few weeks. He hadn't been sure of her meaning, but the jagged feeling in his gut now was starting to give him a clue. This whole set up was making him face the painful truth that, while he might be at his personal best with her, she was the why factor. He was still who he was on his own. Someone who didn't have the respect of a guy like Alex. He'd been a shit to too many people here, disrespected what this was all about, as well as the job Tyler had given him.

Marius shifted. There was a spanking scene going on at a nearby station, a male Dom and female sub. Usually he'd enjoy watching the reddening of a pretty ass just as much as the next guy. But everything around him was turning gray.

Gray. Fuck. He tried to push down the panic the realization brought. How could it be so close, just waiting to resurface, unless he really hadn't changed that much, if all the shit was still there, waiting to grab him by the throat?

Had Regina arranged for this with Tyler? Maybe she'd anticipated him needing to do some reparation and suggested this as the best way to prove he could handle being here again. He wished she would show herself. He could handle most things if he could see her.

A glance to the left made him realize why no one had approached the cage. A red ribbon had been tied to the hook holding the keys. That meant a sub was on display only, no touching.

That should have made him feel better, but it didn't. Bad feelings continued to build, more uneasiness and a wrong sense of...helplessness. It underlined what he'd just realized. He was nothing without her. He was still that powerless kid, prey to the predator. Darkness started to rise, bringing fear.

"Exactly where you need to be."

He tuned in to see Siren standing in front of the cage, several other Mistresses arrayed in a semi-circle around him. He couldn't see Alex. Had he left the fucking room? He was there, Marius was sure of it. He wouldn't leave his post when sessions were ongoing, when he had been specifically charged to watch over a sub who couldn't get out of a cage without assistance.

Siren's eyes were fixed on him, her mouth tight. She had her hair pulled up in a severe knot, increasing the strain of her features. She was a beautiful woman, but an inner ugliness had taken hold. He was responsible for that. All he had to do was look to see the shattered confidence, the anger at what he'd done to her. She was carrying a dense veneer of righteous anger, but the hunger for revenge still bled through.

Withdrawing a folded paper from the bodice of her corset, she opened it, showing a printed news clip. She slapped it against the bars in front of his face, the writing on the page toward her so the other women could see it. Through the translucence of the paper, he got the gist of it, though.

"Murderer of Clerk Put to Death."

His stomach dropped.

"Look at the picture, taken when his daddy was put in prison. He looks like him, doesn't he?"

The women shifted, muttering and agitated. "You are him, aren't you?" Siren demanded. "Just a little psycho-in-training."

Pivoting, she looked up toward the darkened executive offices. Their vacancy didn't stop her from pointing an accusatory finger toward the space. "He never should have been here. And the owners of this club knew it. They had to have known it. He was their employee. They let this bastard be here, fuck with our heads."

"They didn't know," Marius said, fighting past a thickness in his throat. What the hell was happening? He felt like he was shrinking before their accusing eyes, shrinking back into that small boy, standing in a cold, desolate corner, watching, trying not to listen, not to hear... But he wasn't that boy. He was a man, and he wouldn't let Tyler get blamed for this. "None of them knew. I didn't tell anyone."

She turned and stared at him. "There's no way to make you suffer," she said dully. "Pain doesn't bother you. I could electrocute you, cut you, beat you, and you'd just take it all. You're not human. They should have strapped you in with your father so you two demons could go straight to Hell together."

"I'm not...him." He tried to summon the things Regina had said to him, how she'd touched him, what she'd made him feel. Siren was wrong about him and pain. He felt like he was being beaten the way his father had beaten him. His knees were weakening strangely, breath shortening, and the cell seemed three times smaller than it had a moment ago. "Alex. Fight Club." He wasn't sure how loudly he'd spoken, if the words had made it over the roaring in his ears.

He should have been able to handle this, would have, only a few weeks before. He would have leaned indolently against the bars, stared her down, told her to fuck off. Regina had taken away his shields and defenses, those bulwarks against anyone reaching him. He'd let go of them in favor of pleasing his Mistress, learning how to truly love her. But a boy cowering in a corner couldn't fight back or love anyone.

"Alex isn't here." Siren leaned in, her eyes glittering. "He had a problem he had to address in the other room. But if you scream like the little bitch you are, maybe he'll come. Eventually."

She wants the demon? Give it to her.

Those shields weren't as dormant as he'd feared. Siren had come too close. A short yelp was all she managed when he clamped his cuffed hands around her throat. The chain linking the cuffs to the bars made a harsh shriek as he yanked her against the steel. Fury and violence swamped him, despair clinging to the small sinking island of his consciousness that had hoped he could be something else.

Other parts of his black soul were far louder. Regina had put them to sleep, but Siren woke them with nothing more than a clap of her hands, showing they were as strong as they had ever been.

Just do it. Crush her throat. It doesn't matter. You'll always be connected to him, just as she said. Doesn't matter if you never did what he told you to do. He always knew you were the same. Regina wanted to believe differently, but she was as stupid as you were.

He shoved all that aside. He didn't want to think about anything, now or ever again, and this was the way to do that. He constricted his fingers on Siren's throat, making it clear he was too strong to be dislodged, and bared his teeth, savagely satisfied at the sudden fear in her eyes. But it wasn't her. It was his father, both afraid and laughing at him. He'd stop the laughing forever.

Some part of him was vaguely aware of someone trying to loosen his grip, but he wouldn't be budged. "This time we *will* go to hell together," he snarled.

Electricity shocked through him, propelling him back, loosening his fingers. His father was yanked away, and then disappeared, replaced by a dazed and pale Siren, held in the hands of the other Mistresses, all out of range. His howl of rage and despair sent them skittering back even more. Unfriendly eyes, angry faces. He saw a male sub—one of Siren's regulars before Marius—holding the hot stick. The man looked as if he thought he should hit Marius with it again, despite his imprisoned state. Marius snarled at him, daring him to do it.

He could hear sounds, that roaring, but words only distantly. Present kept disappearing into images of the past and returning, overlapping, making him feel dizzy and nauseous.

"Who's responsible for him? Who's looking after him?"

Alex was back, shouldering through a mob of shouting people, all of them too close. The inability to breathe, the sense of being buried alive, returned. He couldn't sit down, but he slumped against the cage side, grasping the bars.

"Move, goddamn it."

His Mistress. She sounded more pissed than he'd ever heard. But she also sounded frightened. He didn't like that. Why had she done this?

"He tried to choke her... Tried to kill Siren..."

"From what I picked up, she deserved it," Regina snapped. "I would have choked her myself, if I could have gotten here any faster."

She plucked the keys off the hook and unlocked the cell. When Alex came closer, she shot him a searing look. "You fucking stay back," she said. "You've done enough. Clear this damn room."

"Duncan," she said. "The door's open. Come here." She reached in, but it wasn't her again. It was his father, pulling him to the table, and it was Dot under his knife. He struck out, missed and hit the bars. The pain was welcome, bringing Regina and the present back into focus. He did it again, and wanted to keep doing it, just hammer his fists into blood and fragments of bone so the agony wouldn't let the past swallow him again.

But Regina's hands rested on his fists, curved over them. She held his gaze, wouldn't let him go away. She wasn't restraining him, but she didn't need to do so. He wouldn't beat on the bars if her fragile fingers were between his fists and the unrelenting steel. His gaze clung to her, the one thing of color in a gray world.

He still couldn't breathe. Regina eased him out of the cell and put him on his ass, using the outside of the cage to prop him up in a sitting position. She crouched next to him. She was still in her teaching clothes, her trim slacks and crisp blouse.

"Easy," she murmured. "It's a panic attack. Nothing's wrong with you. Just slow everything down. Easy."

He was gripping her too hard, though not as hard as he'd wanted to grip Siren's neck. "I tried to kill her," he rasped. "I tried..."

"She cornered you and broke every rule there is about how to treat a sub. It's okay."

"No, it's not. Why...why did you..."

"No. Not me." She touched his face, bringing his gaze up to her worried eyes, her tense features. "Someone pretended to be me, had the staff send you that text. I was expecting to see you at dinner tomorrow, our usual routine."

"So you didn't..."

"Mother of God, no. No, sweet boy. Sssh." She tried to put her arms around him, but it was too soon. He pushed away. She let him go, respecting that, but as he struggled to his feet and gripped the bars of the cage to stay on them, the darkness kept closing in on him.

"Not. I'm not that. I tried to kill her. Wanted to kill her."

"Duncan." Regina stood before him, giving him space but staying in his direct line of vision, keeping his focus on her. At least externally.

"You have triggers. You know that. She was so set on making you face what you did to her and taking her pound of flesh, she had no interest in why you did it or who you are. So she stomped on those triggers and set them off. You didn't want to kill her, Marius. You were protecting yourself."

Protecting himself? Regina hadn't been in his head, hearing those voices, feeling the drive to take life from someone who was mocking him. He would have done it and felt nothing.

He brought his gaze to Alex, who stood on their periphery. Though he was trying to maintain a professional DM façade, his unhappiness and unease suggested guilt. The sharp look Regina shot him said she'd also put it together.

"Taught me a lesson, did you?" Marius said softly.

He was aware of Regina moving closer, her tension increasing. She was worried he would launch himself at Alex, pound his self-righteous face into a wall. He could do it. Make him bleed. Make him beg.

Alex met Marius's gaze squarely, despite the shame and regret suffusing his features. "She's been so off her game since it happened, and this seemed a way to help her get peace about it. You said you were wanting to understand, you said you're sorry. She said Regina had asked for a temporary pass and knew about it. She didn't tell me it was going to be like this. Or about your father. And...I thought I'd be here. There was a problem in the other room—"

"A fucking distraction, you idiot," Regina snapped. "Which accomplished exactly what they intended. And the Mistress who knew I was working late tonight helps in The Zone administrative offices. She approved the fucking pass in my name. What got me here was Tina's text to confirm I knew about this, because she thought something was up. Apparently she has better instincts than the damn Dungeon Master watching the floor."

Alex nodded, accepting that, looking miserable. The rage

simmering in Marius had no target. He was weary. Too weary too care. "I'm going to go change," he said woodenly. Things felt very distant, as if Regina and Alex were tiny figures within a model version of The Zone, and he was floating somewhere around it, detached.

"Good. We'll go home," Regina said. He backed away, shaking his head.

"Not now." *Not ever.* The certainty of it was a rock in his chest where his heart should be. He stared at her, her beauty and strength, her glorious anger only exceeded by concern about him. It made everything inside him hurt. Abruptly, he dropped to one still quivering knee. "Thank you, Mistress. But we're done. I'm done. I don't belong here. Or with you."

He rose and strode away. As he passed through the club, through the quiet knots of people with accusing or curious eyes, he didn't pay attention to anything or anyone. He kept going, knowing if he stopped too long the lava inside him would explode, overflow, too many emotions to manage. But he knew where to find an outlet for those. He just needed to get in his street clothes and get the hell out of here.

As he went down the stairs to where the locker rooms were, he was brought up short by someone unexpected. Marguerite Winterman, dressed in white blouse and dark gold pencil-style skirt, her pale blue eyes focused on his face.

"You need your Mistress," she said quietly. "Don't run away from her."

He put his hands on her arms and bodily moved her out of his way. Albeit without malice or harm, it was still way outside of protocol for him to put his hands on her. But he was no longer bound by any of this. He'd proven once and for all it was something that couldn't keep him in check, no matter how much he had hoped for and craved the right to belong to a Mistress. He had no rights when it came to Mistresses. Not now, or ever again.

Marguerite reached out to hold his arm, but he pushed away, rougher this time, a warning. "You've always been just as fucked up as I am," he told her cuttingly. The pain of that truth swamped him. "You know I need to go."

"I know that's what everything inside you is telling you that you need to do," she said neutrally. "But it's wrong. You won't fix it until you stand in front of a mirror and stay there, as long as needed to fix the problem. You learned to look in that mirror with a Mistress by your side, but to deserve her, you have to do the scary part. Look in that mirror by yourself and see what's not fucked-up. What's worth saving. You."

She moved away, and he realized she'd bought Regina enough time to catch up with him. Stifling a curse, he marched into the locker room area, not at all surprised when his Mistress followed him.

Regina sat down on a bench as he yanked open his locker and pulled out his clothes. She didn't say anything as he stripped off the thong and put on underwear, jeans and a T-shirt. He stuffed his feet into socks and shoes. But when he closed the locker, she rose and put her arm in front of him, blocking his exit.

"What do you want from me?" he demanded. "I can't be it."

"Yes, you can. You are. But the real question is what do you want for yourself?" She caught his face in both hands, forcing him to look at her. He should shove away from her as he had Marguerite, but he couldn't seem to make himself do that. He had to curl his hands into fists not to clutch her wrists, bruise, manacle her to him forever.

"If you didn't want anything for yourself," she said, "if you weren't willing to fight through the demons to get it, then I would want nothing from you. But I know you're a formidable fighter. You've just always fought for and against the wrong things. And you're not going to go fight now. You're not in the right frame of mind. You could do yourself or others real harm."

"You think?" he snapped.

Her expression went hard and cold. She was going to get all badass Mistress on him, and he didn't want to feel the eagerness rise in him for that tough hand. It would fucking tear him apart, what he wanted eclipsed by what he didn't deserve.

It was as Marguerite had said. Maybe she'd meant it another way, but it boiled down to this. Was he only worth something if Regina was riding herd on him, taking care of him, being his warden? If so, she didn't deserve to have that shit dumped on her, and he couldn't handle the idea that that was the best he could do, all he could be for her. She deserved...everything.

"You're not going," she said firmly, stepping toe to toe with him.

Though he knew the concerns and genuine caring driving her, it merely emphasized his demoralizing thoughts.

"I. Don't. Need. A. Fucking. Keeper." He snarled it, punctuating each syllable by hitting the locker next to her with his closed fist. She flinched at the first blow, her body and face so close to the shadow of his rage, but then she locked it down and kept her expression frozen as he dented the metal with impressive force. It wasn't enough. It just made the violence rise even more. Fuck it. He had to deal with what was inside him, and there were two sure ways he knew how to do that. He wasn't going to risk her with the way she'd taught him to prefer.

Tal had gotten him on the roster for a fight downtown tonight. A shadier crowd than he usually dealt with, but good money. He could use that money to get out of town. Keep driving and driving and driving.

He pushed down a sudden absurd wrench in his chest when he thought of Dot waiting for him to come home. Regina would love and take care of the kitten. They'd take care of each other.

"You do need a keeper. Especially if the only solution you can come up with is running," she said shortly.

He curled his lip in a sneer and moved past her. She wrapped her arms around him so he'd have to physically dislodge her to leave. She felt so good, everything he needed to feel...right. But none of that came from inside him, did it?

He turned them, using his strength to overpower her, to shove her against the lockers, hold her there with her wrists pinned, his body pushed between her legs so she couldn't kick him. The brief flash of surprise in her face didn't come with panic, thank God. If he ever frightened her like he had Siren, he'd just kill himself. But he put his mouth to her throat, to the pulse there.

"I've always been stronger physically," he said against her skin. "You're stronger in every other way, all the ways that count. You're everything. I love you, Regina. I love you so fucking much. Enough to let you go. Don't follow me."

He pushed her away and left the locker room, aware of Marguerite still standing outside the door. Good. She'd be there for his Mistress. There was nothing he could give her, and the burning of his gut, carrying Regina's knowing yet stricken look with him, told him she'd given him everything.

~

Marguerite entered the locker room right after Marius stormed out of it. She found Regina on a bench, bent over double. She hurried to her side, concerned, but the woman straightened, drawing a deep breath. Although she had tears on her face, her eyes blazed with russet fire. "Where is that bitch?"

"Somewhere you shouldn't be right now," Marguerite said wisely. "Where's he going?"

"Probably to one of his damn fights to get his head beaten in. I dropped my phone in his car on the way in here. I'll give him enough time to get there and then call my locater service to find it for me and go after him. Where is she?" she repeated. "Tell me, or I will tear this fucking place apart to find her."

"If it wasn't right for her to go after Marius for revenge, it's no better for you to do the same."

Regina closed her eyes. "Sure, be fucking logical. Goddamn, Marguerite. How the hell did she know who his father was?"

But she already knew the answer to the question. Siren had likely been obsessing about Marius since their ill-fated night. Siren was a wealthy woman with deep pockets. If she'd wanted to dig up dirt she could use against him, it wouldn't have been outside her means. Maybe she'd even picked up a hint from the news reports of Larabee's execution, where they'd shown full color pictures of him when he was in his twenties. The resemblance to Marius was chillingly remarkable.

"Does she have any idea what can of worms she broke open tonight?" Regina demanded. "We were getting closer to him realizing he needs counseling. I could see him starting to figure it out, knowing he and I could only go so far." Renewed fury surged through her. "Sorry, I don't care how fucked up she is. I'm going to go fuck her up worse."

Marguerite sat down on the bench next to her, putting a restraining hand on her forearm. "Terry called Tyler and the other owners, and the club has been closed for the night. They're clearing it now, and Alex was told to wait for Tyler's arrival in his office. This is a very serious situation, and they'll get to the bottom of all who were involved in it. *They* will handle that. Your job is Marius. Take a breath.

You said he's made progress. Something like this, as horrible as it seems at first, can help."

"Yeah, maybe. Or it can go completely to shit."

Marguerite ran a light hand down her back. "You love him."

"Yeah." Regina snorted. "He loves me, too. Told me right before taking off. Stubborn ass. Men. Dumbass men."

"They have their uses."

"And after that fifteen minutes, there's the whole rest of the day to kill," Regina quipped grimly. Marguerite made an amused noise of agreement. They sat quietly shoulder to shoulder.

"I get it," Regina said at last. "He was a total shit to her and broke her, so this was evening the score. She did what she did tonight without any understanding or compassion for who and what he is, and he did the same thing the night he hurt her. But still..."

"Two acts of malicious harm rarely cancel one another out," Marguerite supplied the rest of what Regina was feeling. "Typically, they only make things worse on both sides."

"He was trying so hard. I can't even describe it."

"He would have faced this eventually. If not here, like this, in another way. The question is if he's progressed enough to find his way back without you guiding him." Marguerite nudged her knee with her own. "He's always focused on his physical strength. You helped him see he's stronger inside than he ever knew. It's what a Dom who loves you does. Have faith in that love."

Marius didn't want to think about faith, love, understanding or patience. He wanted to pound on flesh until he reached blood, bone and quivering muscle. He parked in the alley and beat on the back door, stepping back as it was opened by a tall, scarred Asian Indian man who went by the short name of Sisk. Sisk didn't speak, only nodded when Marius told him he was scheduled to fight and Tal was his manager. Marius stripped off his jacket as he moved through the dark, dank hallway that smelled of sweat and men. There were no show ponies here, no eye candy, no showmanship or good-natured characters like Top Hat.

This was down and dirty fighting where injuries and the occasional death was the norm. The bettors were the dark end of the spectrum high rollers. Crime lords and their underlings, drug dealers who liked fights of any kind, seedy, shifty-eyed guys like his father who did things in the shadows and came here to watch live violence for entertainment, the bloodier the better.

The first event was the appetizer and warm-up. In an open area loosely ringed by the shouting crowd of spectators, nearly a dozen guys were engaged in a violent brawl. Weaving, ducking, punching, kicking, biting—a brutal free-for-all. Anyone signed up to fight— meaning someone on whom the bookies had taken odds—could jump in the ring and just start punching. Perfect for his mood. He stripped off his shirt and shoved through the crowd, slamming his fist into the first jaw that presented itself. The hit landed so hard it took the guy off his feet, spinning him around with a spurt of blood. He face-planted on the stained concrete.

Someone recognized Marius and the cry was taken up, a hot wave of noise. "Rabid, Rabid!"

Shutting everything else down, he waded into battle. He would keep fighting until he stood on a mountain of bodies. Or they buried him under them.

Regina found his car as she was making a circle around the parking area littered with trash and no cars. Attendees must be parking elsewhere. It sent a ripple of unease through her, because though the other fight she'd attended had been illegal, there was illegal and there was criminal. This had the scent of the latter, which told all her smart brain cells she should get the hell out of here and regroup with Marius later.

But what happened if his state of mind kept him fighting until he was seriously injured...or worse? Not only was he spun up, but he was at a fight that might potentially have even less rules than usual.

The other venue had made it clear hot women were welcome at fights. She didn't know of many male-oriented events that didn't have the same policy. So ready or not, she was coming in. Parking next to his Civic and getting out of her car, she shrugged all her confidence and armor in place, marching up to the scarred gray alley door to knock on it.

"You lost, honey?"

She squashed a nervous start at the drawl. Turning, she saw a knot of men sitting in the shadows, sharing whatever their drug of choice was. The one who'd spoken to her was wiping the powder residue off his irritated nostrils.

"Not hardly," she said coolly. "I'm with one of the fighters. Rabid."

Another man grinned, showing oddly white teeth, a gold one winking in the middle. "Not here. No bitches allowed at this kind of fight. Rabid don't give a shit about you if he told you to come down here. Or he has a whore who likes being shared. Only pussy at this fight are fair game for all of us."

"Well, he didn't get the memo." She rapped sharply on the door again, without obvious hurry, and casually tried the latch, finding it locked. Praying someone would answer, she leaned on the wall next to the door, crossed her arms and eyeballed them with all the icy calm she was used to employing as a Mistress. However, the creeping fear sliding up her vitals told her that veneer wouldn't withstand the first man willing to break through it. She'd made a mistake. Now she had to figure out how to get out of it. Wits and calm were her best defense. Working in a prison had taught her that, too.

"I'll get my cell out of the car and call him," she said, putting bored annoyance in her voice.

As she straightened, they rose. Her panic climbed as others came out of the shadows.

"Yeah, you could make a break for that fancy car of yours," the ringleader said. He rubbed a hand over his crotch, a revolting gesture. He had a large, bald head, dark clothes and a sleeve tattoo that seemed to feature a lot of skulls. He could qualify as the poster child for lowlifes. "It's more fun to chase a girl."

"In your dreams," she said. Examining her nearest options, she saw a piece of rebar had been left next to the door, maybe to prop it open. There were a couple garbage cans, a small stack of bricks and a metal bucket with a mop in it. She picked up the rebar. "Stay the fuck away from me."

"Sure, honey." He nodded to the men on his right and put his hand on his belt. "I'm going to beat this bitch into submission and then fuck her ass. Take her down."

~

Blood. The repetitive thud of flesh on flesh. Screams as an arm broke somewhere. The roar of the crowd, like a TV gone to static late at night. When he was growing up, the old TV set in his room hadn't had cable, long past when everyone else had gotten their 100+ channels. One of the three channels it received played the national anthem in the small hours of the night before it went to that soft rush of white noise. He'd leave it on in the graveyard hours, so things couldn't get him in the dark. A futile wish.

"Look in that mirror by yourself and see what's not fucked-up. What's worth saving."

"What do you want for yourself?"

He'd dropped four before he tagged out of the ring and stood in the corner behind the crowd. As he caught his breath and knuckled blood off his chin, he watched the other fighters. He was scheduled for the fifth fight of the evening. But he already knew he wouldn't be hanging around for it. Tal would give him hell about it and they'd take some heat from the organizer. He'd figure out how to make it up to Tal. Fuck the rest of these assholes.

He'd tipped the top boiling rage out of his system, and other stuff was crowding in. Siren...all the Mistresses he'd harmed. He thought of Marguerite, who'd given him the first glimpse of what he really wanted. Regina had expanded that to a widescreen, panoramic view. She'd shown him it was okay for him to love and want. And maybe let himself be loved in return.

Your first job is always to take care of yourself, because you belong to me...

Hell. He put his hand to his throat, realizing he hadn't taken off the collar he wore for her. He was lucky someone hadn't grabbed onto it and used the hold to beat in his face. He'd remembered to put the bracelet in his pocket to protect it and he fished it out now, staring at the back.

If lost, return to Lady Regina.

He remembered the voodoo doll, the two names on either side of the tag, and her observation about his tattoo.

"You're the skin over the armor, being ripped away. Duncan is the armor and the man beneath."

He rubbed his hand over it, over the kitten she'd had added to it. He thought of Dot, curled up and purring in his lap. Of Regina, her head resting on his shoulder, body vibrating as she laughed at something on the TV. Their hands, casually linked and resting on his knee.

So what did he want?

He wanted her. He wanted to be hers. Needed to be hers. He needed her to kick his ass, not take his bullshit or be afraid of him. He needed her. Lover, mother, friend...Mistress.

He'd told her he loved her, told her she was everything. He'd meant it as a good-bye, but it didn't have to be. She'd known that. She wouldn't let him go. She'd probably followed him, figured out where he was by some diabolical...

"Fuck." His gut went cold, fear stabbing him. Her phone was in his car, tucked between the console and passenger seat. He'd noticed it when he got out. He thought she'd maybe left it there last night, when they'd gone to a movie and then stopped at a diner for pie. She liked apple cinnamon and had shared half with him when he thought he'd only wanted coffee. But the pie was too good. Sharing with her made it even better.

She could use the phone to track him, would use it. And this was not a place safe for a woman. Not safe for anyone other than people like him. She wouldn't know that. She'd only gone to the one fight, and didn't know that they weren't all like that.

If he'd led her into danger...fuck. Grabbing his shirt, he ducked the organizer's muscle and slid down the hallway, headed back the way he'd come. He shrugged into his shirt as he went. He was probably being an idiot. His Mistress was smart. If she was here, she was safely sitting in her Mercedes, waiting on him with that baleful, you're-in-deep-trouble look that stiffened his cock. He was already hard, the way he always was after a fight. He could give his Mistress a lot of pleasure tonight...if she accepted his apology. And helped him figure out this mess in his head maybe one more time.

Or maybe it was time for him to stop relying on her for that. She could do that in session as part of what they could do for each other, but maybe he should consider the unthinkable. Seeking someone trained to help his fucked-up head, and ease that burden on her. That was his job, wasn't it? To serve his Mistress, to take care of her. Not make her carry more of the weight than was her due share of a relationship.

He couldn't just bury his past and hope it would stay that way. You couldn't bury a demon without exorcizing it. Siren had proved that tonight.

Christ, Marius. Are you finally growing up? While the thought came with rueful humor, there was a poignant, painful component to it, a fierce and quiet victory. It was time to let the ghost of the child he'd been go and become the man he should be. Regina had shown him that, made that possible. To honor that gift, he needed to embrace it.

Sisk's lanky dark hair framed his scarred brown face and red-rimmed eyes. He was smoking a cigarette and gestured with it as Marius came up. "If you're going out for some air, the boys are having a little fun with some cunt who claimed to be here for the fights. Just stay out of their way."

Almost before he finished the sentence, Marius heard a scream. High and thin. Enraged, afraid, and in pain.

A million memories crowded in on him, with the same effect on his senses as an ignition switch to a rocket. He hit the door like a battering ram and charged out into the alley.

When he'd come here tonight, he'd had a lot of pent-up rage to vent. That vat of anger was nothing next to the volcano that erupted in him now. He had his hands on the first man standing between him and the struggling group on the ground before he even remembered leaping. He rammed a rupturing blow into his kidney, broke his knee with one sharp kick, and sent him headfirst into a group of metal trash cans, with a loud crash and howl from the injured male.

He took in the situation with one red-hazed glare. Even with the help of two men holding her arms, the bastard on top had his hands full, trying to force himself on Regina. They couldn't secure her kicking and thrashing legs, and some of her attackers were already bleeding. She was a fighter, his Mistress. Not a victim.

"Knock this bitch out," the man had just snarled, a sound that turned into a yelp as Marius landed on him. Tearing him off Regina, he tossed him across the asphalt, spinning to plant his shoe in the teeth of the one trying to pin one of his Mistress's long legs. It sent him arcing back and hitting the brick wall. Then Marius was on the others, kicking, punching, drawing them away from her, engaging them with a roar of pure rage and determination.

She'd been defending herself so vigorously, he had to believe she wasn't yet badly hurt. If he could give her the opening, she'd be smart enough to run for the car. Then there was a crack on bone as the man charging him from his right went down. He glimpsed her standing over him with both hands gripping rebar. But there were too many. She needed to run.

"Get to the damn car," he snapped at her, and then he had no time for anything as he was shoved back, two trying to pin him so two others could whale on him. Fuck, he'd spent so much energy in the ring, whereas these assholes were fresh and souped up on whatever they'd been snorting. Why the hell had he come here? He never questioned taking money from these scumbags, but he'd endangered his Mistress. If anything happened to her...

Adrenaline helped him tear himself out of their hands. Vicious satisfaction flooded him as a wrist bone snapped under his grip. The subsequent shriek of pain gave him even more strength.

He was in a blind haze of fighting, pummeling and snarling when another man was yanked off him and he realized unexpected reinforcements had arrived. Tyler dropped the guy with a blow to the chest that the bettors inside would have loved, particularly when the guy didn't get up. Marius instinctively went back to back with him and they faced down the remaining crew. More had come to join the fight, goddamn it all. Regina was at his side, the steel bar clenched in both hands, her eyes flaming like an Amazon warrior.

Fuck, he loved her. He didn't want her to be here, but she'd told him plenty of times, hadn't she? He didn't give the orders in this relationship. The only choice he had was to take out the rest of these assholes so not another one of them got near her. Fortunately, Tyler seemed to be on the same page.

Over the next few moments of intense hand-to-hand combat, Regina stayed in that ready position, her eyes darting, body tense, but no one got close enough. Marius made fucking sure of it. Tyler might have had something to do with it, too.

When the last body dropped, and all that remained were unconscious, groaning or fast-retreating men, Tyler gripped her arm and gestured to Marius. "Come on," he said, his tiger eyes sharp and cool as frost on an amber blade. "We need to be out of here."

No disagreement there. Marius hated that they had to drive separately. Regina seemed in good enough shape to get into her vehicle, though he worried she was running on adrenaline and might be worse off than she seemed. Tyler was right, though. Neither they nor their vehicles needed to be here.

Tyler led the way out, Regina's Mercedes in between their two cars. He took a few side streets before emerging smoothly onto a main artery. A half-mile down that road, they met two police units coming their way. In his rear view, Marius saw them turn onto the street that would lead them to the fight location.

About ten minutes later, Tyler pulled into the parking lot of an all-night diner, choosing a back corner where they weren't likely to attract much notice. As soon as they stopped, Marius was out of the car and at Regina's door, pulling it open. She was holding the wheel in both hands, and she was shaking. Shock. Christ, she shouldn't be driving at all. Feeling a mixture of anger, chagrin, and an overpowering need to gather her up and take care of her in whatever way she needed, now or forever, he knelt in the open doorway.

When he put his large hands gently on her face and upper arm, he wouldn't have been surprised if she'd recoiled from him like he was the plague. Instead her hands came up and gripped his. Her fingers were icy. She had blood on her, and he hoped to God it wasn't hers. She turned her head to look at him, her dark eyes a little glassy.

"O-okay?" she asked. Her teeth were chattering but she touched the cuts on his cheek and jaw, humbling him and giving him another helpless wave of fury.

"Very okay," he said, his throat thick. "How about you? Are you hurt? Any of that blood yours?"

She fingered the back of her head. Tyler had opened the other door. At Marius's gesture, he took a closer look at the area she'd been probing. "It's bleeding," he confirmed. "They slammed your head on the pavement when they put you down? Did you black out, even for a second?"

She nodded. "Y-yeah to the first. No, on the second. Assholes. Nothing else, though. They d-didn't get that far." Her gaze turned to Marius. "You came out. F-fast fight."

"I didn't want to fight anymore. I just wanted to be with you. I wanted to say I was sorry for being an idiot."

A ghost of a smile touched her lips, relief showing in her expression. "I should have trusted M-Marguerite. She said you'd figure it out if I j-just gave you some space."

"I figured it out, thanks to you. Hope she told you that, too." He bent his head to put his lips against her knuckles. She was still shaking and he hated it. He wanted to make her smile some more. "All I could think about was how I wanted to go home, let Dot curl up in my lap while you leaned against me, on the couch. Fall asleep in front of the TV together."

"That sounds really good to me." She looked at him a little hazily as he unbuckled her seat belt and he and Tyler maneuvered her over to the passenger side with gentle hands. "We're so d-domestic. W-worried about that."

"We usually start the night with you and the strap-on. I don't think the spark is gone just yet." The thickness in his throat had moved down to his chest as he passed gentle fingers over her bruises. "I wish I'd killed those fucking bastards."

"Me too. And that I'd helped. B-but you're okay. No more fights. None, you hear me?" She seemed to be rallying, her eyes glittering with the spirit he was used to seeing when she was pissed with him. It was as welcome now as the slick heat of her pussy around his cock. She gripped his forearms. "You w-will work at some crap minimum wage job until you get that nursing degree or p-paramedic certification. You will live with me if you can't make your rent. But n-no more fights. You promise me, here and now."

"No more fights. Only with you."

"Okay. I need to...damn it, I need to cry. And a shower. A shower that lasts an hour on a hundred and twenty fucking degrees."

Tyler wisely withdrew with a long look at Marius that said this was his area. Marius was more than glad of it. He'd take it as a lifelong responsibility if she'd let him.

He'd slid into the driver's seat, so he pulled her over the gear shift and held her, wanting nothing between them, but this would do for now. As the trembling increased, he ran his hands along her back and arms, then cupped her head tenderly with one hand. "I'm so sorry," he said again, wanting to say so much more, anything that would make it all right.

"It's okay. We're all fine. You were c-coming home. That's what matters. And you're not going to do that...anymore."

His heart did a slow roll. "Coming home. I like the sound of that. I never thought I would."

"That's because you had y-your head up your ass f-for so long. Until I took you in hand."

"Yes, ma'am. That's true." He pressed a kiss to her forehead, her brows, her nose and lips. Sitting back, he framed her face to kiss away each tear. "I'm so glad you're okay. So glad I came out when I did, though I wish it had been earlier. Wish you hadn't followed me. I was coming to you, Mistress."

He saw blood spots on his hand where he'd touched her head. That, and a glance at Tyler, standing quietly in the open passenger door, said they needed to get to an Urgent Care. One was fairly close by.

He'd dropped his touch to her wrists, but immediately let go when she winced. Lifting her forearm, he was ready to commit murder anew when he saw the chain of fingerprint-shaped bruises. But they'd had to hold her down so brutally because she'd fought them so hard. Tough mistress. Amazing woman.

He knew what he could give her, something even better than his violence. He touched her face to draw her gaze to his, so she could tell he meant it, that it wasn't just the intensity of the situation.

"I was coming to tell you something else. That maybe...I'm not saying I won't need some help staying on the right track, but you've taught me to trust you. It's time I start earning your trust, letting you know I can do the right things to be a better person for you...and for myself. You mentioned that lady that Marguerite recommended, the retired lady who does counseling. I think maybe...I should start talking to her. What do you think?"

It was the right call. It pulled her out of that alley and put her in the here and now. Her mouth softened, her heart in her eyes, which choked him up more than he wanted to admit. She'd helped him understand what serving a Mistress meant, what it could be. The more of himself he gave to her, the more she filled him up.

He could tell it mattered to her, that he'd asked her opinion, and felt like a hero just for having done so. She had that effect on him, too.

Regina stroked his jaw. "What do I think? I think that you're becoming the man I've always known you are. One I want at my side, and at my back." Her voice had steadied, another victory.

He dropped his head and pressed another kiss to her hand, to the abrasions on her wrists, and then lifted his face to her. "You mentioned a shower. After we get you checked out, will you do me the honor of letting me bathe you, Mistress?"

"We're going home. I'm fine."

He shook his head even before he saw Tyler's mouth open to issue the same no-go message. "Not going to order me around on that one. Unless your head is hard as mine, a head injury's nothing to fuck around with. You're going, even if I have to carry you through the doors."

"Oh, really? Think you can get away with that, do you?" She looked down her nose at him, a warning he'd pay for his high-handedness later. But her eyes were warm, her mouth still soft.

He reached over her, belted her into the seat as Tyler closed the passenger door, a sign he was assured the situation was well in hand. Which also bolstered Marius in ways he hadn't expected. But he kept his main focus on his Mistress. "If you go without a struggle, I'll give you a massage after the shower. I give a pretty good one."

"Really?" Her brow lifted. "That's a talent you've kept hidden."

He shrugged and slid his hand under the dark, slim ropes of her hair to fondle her neck, a move that soothed when she did it to him. "Most Mistresses only seemed to want my cock."

"Well, it's a very fine cock, but that's not why you kept the talent hidden. You wanted to keep it about sex, didn't you?"

She never let him bullshit her. Even now, she saw through any attempt to do so like she was a human X-ray machine. He bit back a smile. "Yeah. But I'd like to take it a lot farther than that with you, Regina." This time he purposefully used her name, putting them on equal footing. "Be like you said. The sub you can use and enjoy the way we both like...and the man you can depend on. I'll probably still fuck up a lot, but I want to at least say it, so you know I really want to try."

"Okay." There was a bated pause and she took a shaky breath, one that had him gripping her hand in concern. But she shook her head at him and sent him a watery smile. "Then we're going to start on that right now. I need you to get me through the whole Urgent Care thing and then get me home. Help me get rid of these clothes, and the stink of all of them, and wash me with your strong, warm hands... So when I go to sleep tonight, my head won't take me back there, to that..."

Tears were spilling down her face, scaring him, enraging him, and making him love her even more. He had his arms around her, his lips on her face, taking the tears away as he kissed the tracks, her lips, all so lightly.

"I will. I promise. You don't have to think or do anything but rely on me to get you home. To get us both home."

She might not realize it, but she'd just given him the greatest gift possible. Not just permission to help, to make it better—but the right to do so, to be that man for her.

"I'll take you home," he said. "And I'll take care of you. Promise."

CHAPTER EIGHTEEN
A Few Months Later

*M*arius leaned against the wall of The Zone's public play room, studying the scenes currently in progress. Some interesting needle play was happening at station three. All the Dominant players on the floor were veterans, though Mistress Zee had a relatively new male sub still figuring out his own head. She was showing the right amount of patience with him, taking it slow and staying alert to any cues that he might not be safe-wording when he needed to do so.

Marius shifted his attention to the smaller playroom behind him where a punishment was reaching critical mass on the versatile oak frame housed there. Red marks were multiplying on the bountiful pale ass of the woman bound to it. She was moaning with a mixture of obvious pleasure and reaction to the pain, so she was enjoying the scene, but he'd keep an eye on it because breaking skin was only permitted if approved in advance, and Sir Todd didn't have that clearance.

Marius didn't anticipate having any problems with him. Todd was a good guy and an intense Master. He just sometimes got caught up in Dom space and had to have a gentle reminder of the rules to bring him down to earth.

"I'd say about ten more strikes with that thing before one of us has to step in," Alex said, stepping next to him. He kept his voice low to avoid disruption of the sessions.

"Yeah. You here to relieve me?"

"Yep. Your shift's up, buddy. Your Mistress said to get your ass to her as soon as you were done. She has plans for it."

Despite the instant leap of blood, heart and cock, Marius sighed with dramatic effect. "Work, work, work. She's a slave driver."

"And you're her one and only favorite slave to drive." Alex paused, looking toward Todd's scene. The casual tease took Marius by surprise. Since Marius had come back to work at The Zone a few weeks ago, Alex had been reserved but cordial. Rumor was he was visiting Siren. Not in the dating sense, but as if the man kept checking in on her out of guilt for her state of mind. Marius carried the lion's share of that, and wished he could visit her, but Regina and Tyler had made it clear she wasn't ready for that. At least right now. He sincerely hoped Alex's visits were helping, though.

He'd pushed up from the wall, ready to take his leave, when the other man spoke.

"Thanks for saving my job, man. Tyler gave you a second chance for the right reasons. I didn't see that, but since they reinstated you, I've seen the difference." He cleared his throat. "Siren let me read the apology you wrote her. I also heard about the tea party you threw for the Dommes. And the afterparty."

Marius remembered that afterparty vividly himself, so he was glad Alex didn't expand on it. Though he wished he could ask how Siren had reacted to the apology, his Mistress had forbidden him follow-up of any kind. But Alex did throw him a bone.

"All good steps, man," the DM said. "My thanks is way overdue, but I mean it. It's good to be working with you again."

It felt damn good to hear it said straight out, but Alex wasn't done. "I'm sorry I let my feelings for her interfere with my judgment. I should have verified with Regina when she told me Regina knew about the plan. I should have called someone to take over monitoring you when I saw the situation in the other room was going to take longer to resolve. I fucked up on every level. Even with your input, I'm surprised Tyler didn't fire my ass. Not so sure I wouldn't have fired me if I was in his shoes."

Marius shook his head. "You were trying to help out a Mistress you cared about, who needed to get her confidence back. You didn't realize how far she was going to take it that night. So you deserved the second chance far more than I ever did. If we're talking degrees of asshole."

Alex digested the comment. "Just so you always remember who's the bigger asshole of the two of us," he advised.

That was that. The switch flipped, male conflict resolution accomplished in that simple way that always mystified women. He and Alex were good again. Nothing else necessary but male razzing.

"I know a Mistress or two who'd be willing to don an elephant dick strap-on and stretch yours out some."

Alex chuckled. "Yeah, that's never happening. You sub boys have bigger balls than I do."

"Don't you forget it. Pussy." Grinning, Marius gave him a nod and headed toward the exit to the public play area. He paused at the door, though, doing Alex the professional courtesy of keeping an eye on the other sessions as he moved to talk to Master Todd. When the Dom nodded agreeably and put down the whip to pick up a soft flogger instead, Alex came back to the post where he had a full view of all scenes and gave Marius a thumbs-up. He was clear.

Management had hired Marius back, but he wasn't a full member again. And he wouldn't be, by his own choice. He was part of Regina's family membership, a membership dependent on her being his Mistress and him always being in her company when at The Zone on his leisure time. He had no interest in playing with anyone but her, unless it was under her direction and driven by her desire.

That had been part of what the counselor had helped him understand. He needed the structure of that one-on-one relationship, the safety of it. Learning how to handle one very important relationship and all its many variables was plenty to manage. Except for that after-party Alex had mentioned, Regina rarely invited another Mistress into their play. When she did, she remained in control. As long as that constant never changed, he was good with that. He'd learned it was okay to put his hard limits out there. His Mistress encouraged him in that, made him feel proud of himself for doing so, for not risking his soul to prove he could be more badass than was good for their relationship, or himself.

Marius had advocated for Siren as he had for Alex. While Tyler had heard him out and thanked him, she'd still been expelled. It had bugged Marius deeply enough that Regina had made a point of helping him understand why Tyler and the other owners had made the decision. And that had led to the things Alex had just mentioned. The apology, tea party...the after party.

As he moved through the club now, Marius remembered that conversation. They'd been out on Regina's sunporch on a Sunday morning, shortly after the ruling about Siren had been made. Regina had made him breakfast and then ordered him to strip out of everything but his collar and bracelet. Following her commands, he'd lain on the cushions of the chaise lounge on his stomach, soaking up the sun on his backside. She'd said him being naked enhanced her view of the canal, as she propped her feet on his bare ass and read a book. But at length, she'd realized he was stewing about The Zone decision, and had set the book aside...

$\sim$

"I'm not going to ask why it bothers you so much," she said quietly, fixing her gaze upon his brooding face. "Because I do understand that. But maybe you're too focused on your own need to make reparations, and missing that the decision was a necessary one."

He had his arm over the side of the lounge to play with Dot, moving his finger in circles around the tile floor while she batted at it. "But Alex didn't lose his job."

"No, he didn't. He should have, and probably would have, if not for you, and a couple other factors Tyler took into consideration." His Mistress's lips pursed, her eyes flashing.

He rocked his hips, moving his ass under the soles of her feet to tease her. "He's a good guy. You really should forgive him, Mistress."

She would in time, he knew. She was a hardass, yeah, but she also had a good heart. She was as protective as a mother bear, which gave him some mixed feelings, knowing it was on his behalf she still held a grudge.

She sniffed. "I told him if he'd let Mistress Helen do electric play on his testicles, he would earn my forgiveness. He's still deciding if my forgiveness is worth that. That's neither here nor there. Alex made a stupid, terrible judgment call, but he was misled as to Siren's intent. She told him she wanted you in the cell to make you listen, and that they were simply going to talk about the way you'd treated them. Like an intervention. Still inexcusable, since he didn't clear it with me and I was supposedly the arbiter of the whole thing, but intent was the key difference."

She took a breath. "Siren lied to Alex and forced you into something against your will. That made her infractions worse than Alex's, but it wasn't that which prompted her expulsion. Tyler said he banned her for essentially the same reason he banned you. She needs help to work through what happened and get her head straight about it. Yes, you broke something inside her, but something in her let it escalate to where she took it. It's up to her to address that in the right way, with counseling, like you're doing."

He frowned. Even if he'd found a weak spot in her behavior as a Mistress, he'd exploited it, stuck a knife into it and twisted, making the wound bigger.

"If I apologized to her, really apologized, do you think that would help her get back to a better place?" Maybe he could find out where she lived and go mow her lawn for about five years. Take out her trash, do things to make her life easier. A spurt of frustration told him that wouldn't work. Rumor had it she was extremely wealthy, so she'd have landscapers and other people to do those things for her.

Regina tilted her head. "Turn on your back and start stroking your cock," she said with gentle firmness. "What's the rule?"

As she adjusted her feet to the edge of the lounge's long seat cushion, he complied, his hand gripping his shaft. His cock was already starting to come to life. All it took was his Mistress's command. "I don't come until you say. If you take me all the way to the edge, but pull me back, over and over, I still don't come. Because it's your cock, your ass, your body, to do with whatever you want."

Her lips curved. "Yes. Good. And every time I order you to say that, you get harder, even if you're not touching yourself."

"Yes, Mistress." He looked at her as he stroked, because she hadn't said he couldn't. He stifled a groan as she slid the loose neck of her bathrobe to the side, exposing one full breast. She began to play with the nipple and the full curve.

He was trying not to be a selfish bastard, but when she answered his question, he had to remind his lust-fogged brain what the question had been.

"Yes. If done right, a sincere apology would help." She leaned forward and met his gaze. "Stop. I want you to hear this."

His hand stilled. He wanted to fire off more ideas, ways to convince Siren of his intentions, yet with the one word and her direct look, his Mistress stopped the words from leaving his lips. "Sometimes penance is as much about having to carry guilt and regret, as it is about fixing what created the guilt," she said. "Those feelings can serve more than one purpose. They help drive the type of person you truly want to be."

She sat back, tapping her long fingers on the table. "Later down the road, once she's at a different place in her head, you might have the opportunity to do more for her. For now, you'll prepare an apology and I'll deliver it to Tyler to pass on to her. That will be the end of it, for the time being. Do you understand?"

She didn't usually pull the Mistress card on something like that, but her tone of voice said she meant it. And forced him to face the truth.

She was right. His desire to fix it was as much because the gnawing ache in his gut about it woke him in the middle of the night, or hit him when he thought he was doing better, knocking him down again with self-incrimination. Learning to live with that, manage it, was part of getting better. While that seemed counterintuitive to his male need to fix, he was also learning to trust her when he couldn't make sense of things on his own.

Trust was the key. His heart and soul struggled with it, but when he met her gaze once more, and connected to all the emotions he saw there—her care for him, her understanding of what was inside him in ways even better than he sometimes comprehended them himself—he capitulated.

"Yes, Mistress."

She nodded. "So the question is what can you do in the interim? What other things can you do to make things better, right now? Start stroking your cock again."

"I hurt her the worst, but I think..." His breath caught in his throat as she opened the robe fully. Sliding her touch down to her cunt, she played with her clit, her lips parting in aroused reaction. Her gaze was on the movement of his hand, the flex of his body as he pushed up into his grip. Fuck, she knew he didn't multitask well. It was why she did it, though. Dommes were sadists, after all...

"I want to say I'm sorry to all of them in some way. And I'd like... your help. You're a Mistress, so you'll know the best thing. Will you help me figure out how to do that?"

She rose from the chair, leaving the robe behind for Magenta, who immediately transferred from the cushion on the adjacent chair to curl up on body-warmed terry cloth. Regina moved to straddle him, one leg folded up against his side, the other braced on the floor. With no more than a look, she had him move his hands out of her way. "Hold onto the top of the lounge," she instructed.

When he did, she pushed herself down on his cock, a nice slow, Sunday morning slick glide. "Fuck, you feel good," he growled.

"Same goes, sweet boy." She began to ride, up, down, squeeze, rotate, as his hands flexed on metal and his body thrust up into the heated wet grip of hers. His gaze stayed glued to the quiver of her breasts, the sinuous motion of thighs and stomach, the glint of the silver spiral charm at her navel.

"Yes," she said breathlessly, right as the orgasm took her. "Yes, I'll help you. Always."

~

Making amends. It was a lot harder than it sounded, because it wasn't some stupid-ass politician standing up and saying, "I'm sorry if I offended someone," arrogant words that didn't express regret at all.

But Regina helped him figure it out, just as she'd said she would. He did the written apology to Siren. After about a hundred painful drafts, he passed it on through Tyler. It felt inadequate, but it was something.

As far as the other Dommes, with some suggestions from Regina, he worked out an idea, then consulted with her and Marguerite to set up the whole thing. The first step was renting Marguerite's place for a tea party with all the trimmings.

Since the organizers of that last fight had made plenty of money on him in the initial free-for-all, they hadn't thrown too much of a shitfit about him ducking the scheduled fight. He and Tal had settled with them with some left over, and Marius used those leftovers to pay for the event.

Tal didn't act too mad that he'd decided to retire. He seemed pretty pleased for Marius and told him that he and his wife would have them over for barbecue sometime soon.

Regina had at last made him tell her what he did with the money he won from his fights. For years he'd dropped big chunks of it anonymously at one of the local animal rescues. Some of the rest went via money order to the shadow's sister to help with...his mother's care. It had taken time for him to finally call her that, but the counselor had helped.

After that pivotal night where he'd learned his father's pro-bono lawyers anticipated losing their fight to keep him from lethal injection, Marius had started giving almost all of it away to both those causes. He hadn't really cared about where he lived, what he ate. That gray pall had stayed on everything.

Until Regina had helped him start seeing, feeling and tasting in vibrant color again. Calling the shadow what she was—his mother—and telling Regina about the gray curtain and what he did with his money? Those types of breakthroughs made him feel better than he expected.

He also discovered a pleasurable kind of nervousness with her, a desire to please, to not fail her. Even as he also enjoyed yanking her chain sometimes. She knew how to get rough with him. She liked setting a bad dog back on his heels...and he liked it, too.

A different kind of nervousness started manifesting when Marguerite issued the invitations to the tea party, and almost all the Dommes RSVP'ed that they'd be there.

The day of the event, his Mistress chose his clothes. A white dress shirt, black slacks and jacket, shiny shoes. Dark brief shorts and a cock harness under the slacks. Though he wasn't sure the latter was needed, since he felt like his privates wanted to turtle right up into his body, Regina proved otherwise when they arrived at Marguerite's and his Mistress took him into the back room to give him another once-over.

Once there, Regina removed the light wrap that had denied him a full view of what she'd chosen to wear. All he knew before they left her place was it was red satin and short, and she was wearing elbow-length black gloves. His saliva had dried up, looking at how the fabric molded her long, feminine fingers and forearms like a second skin.

The dress she revealed was a short wrap-around style that hugged her curves. The black bra she wore beneath pushed her breasts up on tempting display, the lace edges providing a trim to the deep vee neckline of the dress. Her necklace was a delicate gold chain, the pendant a tiny gold and black kitten playing with a ceramic red rose. She wore strappy red heels with black soles.

That cock harness was going to get one hell of a workout.

He was still nervous as hell, but the surge of lust and alpha *mine* vibes surged up over that like a wave, making him restless enough to want to push through limits and take her against the wall, here and now.

She saw it, moistening her crimson-painted lips, her brown eyes measuring him as she tested his self-control and came closer. "Turn around," she commanded.

He pivoted, slow, not wanting to take his eyes off her any sooner than necessary.

As she stepped behind him, he smelled her perfume, a haunting scent he wanted to taste on her skin. She ran her hands over his shoulders, down his back and under the jacket tail to mold her hands over his ass, his hips, and press her body against his. He drew in a breath, and it sounded like a growl. She chuckled, a low, husky note.

"So you like the dress, sweet boy?"

"Fuck, yeah," he muttered.

She tsked and gave his buttock a light slap. "Clean up your language. This is a formal tea party. Best behavior. You're going to have to work very, very hard to earn the right to take me in this dress. Are you ready to work very hard?"

"I'll do anything you want, Mistress."

She pressed her mouth to the back of his neck. "I remember the night I gave you the flogging for putting your feet on the wall. You said things like that. But you didn't mean them. When you say that now, I get all wet and slippery for you." She rubbed her mound against his ass, her teeth nipping him. Fuck, she was going to kill him.

He'd gotten a haircut and the skin was so clean and smooth on his neck it made the touch of her lips all the more potent. His hands closed into half fists.

"We've talked about your hands, haven't we?"

He loosened them with an effort. Though he'd been struggling for control of his lust, the fist clenching sent mixed signals to his mind. In a nerve-wracking scenario like he was facing in the next few minutes, that trigger could open the gateway to the side of himself he was learning to manage...and she was helping him to heal.

"Good." Regina slid her arms all the way around him, and began plucking open the buttons to the white shirt. "I'm taking this off. I want you in the slacks and shoes only, and so do our guests. No. Leave your hands as they are. I want to do it."

She did it thoroughly, caressing his chest, nipples and abdomen, stroking his arms as she slid shirt and jacket off of them. When she commanded him to turn and face her, he knew his eyes reflected the desire to have her. As she palmed his cock, he bit back a groan. Her eyes sparked.

"You arranged this, Marius. You want to make amends, to say you're sorry. But what do you need to remember above everything else? The most important thing?"

Would she ever understand how grateful he was to say it and mean it? It still felt like a miracle to him, that he had reached the point he could do it.

"You're my Mistress. I serve your will."

She leaned in, brushing her sinful lips against his temple, his cheek. "Actually, what I intended you to say was 'I'm yours.' Possessive man."

He grinned, things loosening in his lower belly. "Sometimes a sub has to remind a Mistress she's his, too."

She pinched his side with sharp nails. "Bad boy. You'll pay for that in a lot of different ways today." She sobered, laying her hand on his jaw. "That's why I want you to remember you belong to me. You're making amends, doing what a man should do. This is the right thing to do, and because it's the right thing to do, you don't stand alone. Understand?"

He wasn't sure he did, but her words settled things in him. Her penetrating look said she knew he was uncertain about it, and she didn't push him to answer. "I'm going to go sit down. In five minutes, you come out and get things started."

He nodded, but when she started to step away, he was holding onto her waist. She raised a brow.

"May I kiss you, Mistress?"

"You may."

He focused on her beautiful lips, her warm skin, the vibrant quality that infused her dark eyes like sunlight. While he wanted his mouth on every part of her, he knew what part of her he needed to kiss right now. Dropping to one knee, he bent and kissed the top of her foot, pressing his lips there hard, his forehead brushing her shin. He heard the little catch of her breath and knew he'd pleased her, which was the best feeling there was.

It would carry him through anything less than that in the next couple hours.

∿

Even before he emerged from the back room, the wave of female chatter told him they'd arrived. Seventeen women, including his Mistress. Though he was supposed to do the bulk of the serving, Chloe and Melissa, Marguerite's staff, would be helping.

He glanced down at himself. Upper body bare and dark, close fitting slacks belted at the waist. Shiny shoes. His cock was still semi-hard in the harness, thanks to his Mistress's parting words.

"While you're serving those other Mistresses, I'll be thinking about how every inch of you is mine. When your penance is done today, you'll know it, too. And next time I ask you what the most important thing is to remember, you'll say it the way you should."

He stepped out onto the main floor, and that chatter slowly died down as seventeen pairs of eyes turned and came to rest upon him. Neutral, assessing, the way Mistresses did. These were damn good Dommes, and he was hit anew by how he'd disrespected them, and the gift they could give a sub open to receiving it. He thought of how he'd feel about anyone who disrespected his Mistress and the surge of near-violence unsteadied him.

Multiple five-seat round tables were decorated prettily with flowers, napkins and delicate dishes. He'd helped handle the set up last night, polishing everything and following Marguerite and Chloe's direction for the arrangement of both furniture and place settings, but until he stood at the front of the room and took it all in, he hadn't recognized the final, impressive results. Things looked nice, classy. Feminine.

Marguerite was sitting at the table with his Mistress. Lyda was on Regina's right, and their expressions, even Regina's, were quiet and waiting. Expectant, intimidating and measuring, as Mistresses could be. In the right ways.

Regina had walked him through what he wanted to say. She'd helped him get it clear in his own mind so it would come out sincere and from the heart, even if he stumbled a couple times.

He cleared his throat. "Thanks...thank you for coming today. I... uh, wanted to do this because I know I didn't do right by you when you gave me the honor of your attention in session. I disrespected you."

A scoffing sound, laden with contempt, caught his attention. Mistress Tia was one of Siren's closest friends, and her expression wasn't neutral. That was okay. Despite the drop in his stomach her brief reaction caused, he pressed onward.

"I was pretty messed up. That's not an excuse; just the reason. I don't think there's any right way to say I'm sorry for how I acted. Maybe it just has to be that way, you always disliking me because I was an asshole. I accept that, and I'm still sorry. I was wrong. What I did was wrong, no matter the reason. But from here forward, you can expect the courtesy and respect from me you all really deserve. I know only time will help you believe that, but this is the starting line for proving that to each of you. If there's anything I can do to earn your forgiveness, I'll do it."

Regina cleared her throat and he glanced her way. "I mean, if my Mistress agrees."

Chuckles rippled through the women. Not for him, but for Regina, showing their Domme appreciation and understanding of what limits a Mistress might impose on how generous her submissive could be in his reparations.

"Yeah, you bitches don't get a blank check," Regina confirmed with good humor. "But this is a two-part apology. After the tea party, we'll be adjourning to The Zone for a private event before the club opens for the night. I believe what you're offered there will meet your approval."

That was also part of the reparation plan they'd discussed. He'd wanted to do something like this, the tea party, but he also wanted to offer something...more physical, to make amends. He hadn't known how to make that work, because he was in a situation now where he only wanted to serve one Mistress. And he definitely didn't want Regina thinking he felt differently about that. Fortunately, when she'd walked him through the quagmire of what he was trying to say, she'd understood. He wanted to offer something like what he should have given them before. Surrender to their demands; provide reparations in a way that matched the crime. She told him she would handle the second part.

"Will you accept what I decide?" she'd asked. "Without knowing what it will be until it's happening? No foreknowledge to prepare or shield yourself. Anticipation and dread should be part of the process."

"Yes, Mistress." Though now, at the glint in her eye, he had the good sense to feel a ripple of trepidation. No matter the purity of his intentions, his need to offer these Mistresses a sexual reparation meant his Mistress would take a pound of flesh in exchange for her permission to allow him to do so. A balance he'd need, so he was glad for it. Even as he dreaded the unknown.

The Dommes murmured their appreciation, and he was surprised to see some assessing looks of his person as they anticipated what might be offered. Most of them had had nothing but contempt for him for months. But many of these women were also Regina's friends or confidantes, so maybe she'd been letting them know how things were going.

As Chloe rolled out the first trolley of tea and hors d'oeuvres, he began to serve. He'd been a waiter before, not just at Tyler and Marguerite's Carnival, but at a couple different area restaurants, before he got into the fighting. He wasn't bad at it; had particularly liked waiting on the female customers. Big shock there. They'd appreciated him as well, though not for the same reasons that Regina or any of the ladies here would have. At least not consciously.

Today, no one offered him up any warm fuzzies, nor had he expected them to do so. Reparations didn't mean instant forgiveness. But they were cordial and spoke among themselves as he'd expect,

Mistresses accepting a sub's service to them and reinforcing the role by seemingly ignoring him as long as he performed as he should. All while they tracked his every movement, that stirring duality. No one watched him more closely than his own Mistress, which stirred him up the most of all.

Mistress Tia asked for iced instead of hot tea. He lifted the pitcher and poured some into her glass, with a rattle of ice and smooth fountain sound. "Lemon?" he asked.

She picked up the tea, sipped it. Then her gaze lifted to his. He was a fighter. He could read the tells of an attack, a punch about to be thrown. Therefore he steeled himself as, in the next breath, she dashed the contents of the glass directly into his face with a shock of cold water and ice.

Gasps, a scraping back of chairs. Her table fortunately had three occupants, rather than five, and he'd stood before the two empty chairs, so the other Dommes had been mostly out of range of the fallout. The only one affected was him, her, the floor, and the section of the table nearest them. He understood and accepted why she'd done it —no matter the sick frog jump in his gut—but he thought it had been a rude thing to do in Marguerite's place.

That wasn't his call. As the tea dripped down his face, he pulled the towel off the cart and dropped to one knee before her, keeping his eyes down. "I apologize the tea wasn't to your liking, Mistress. You got some of it on your arm. May I dry that for you before it gets on your clothes?"

The stillness in the room had weight.

His unexpected reaction didn't seem to defuse her emotions, however. When his gaze flicked briefly to her face, he saw the cold anger.

"You aren't touching me. You're a useless mongrel who should have been put down."

Chloe approached with more towels, but at Tia's words, she came to a halt, her expression tightlipped. He saw her shoot a glance over her shoulder, and he expected she was looking to Marguerite for direction. Later, he would realize the expression on Chloe's face was akin to *"Tell me I can put this bitch in her place,"* a championing he hadn't expected.

Now, though, he offered his hand towel to Chloe and took the ones for the floor from her. "So Mistress Tia doesn't have to suffer the offense of my touch," he said quietly.

Chloe passed the towel to the Mistress, but when she started to kneel to help with clean up, he made a sharp, quelling sound, and shook his head, reaching up from his half kneeling position to clasp her arm briefly, a way to keep her on her feet. "If you and Melissa would start pouring the tea so the ladies aren't waiting for me, I'll clean the floor."

He felt like every eye was upon him as he started mopping up the liquid. He wondered what his Mistress was thinking. His gut was cold, a lot of things buzzing in his head trying to drag him down into darkness. *A mongrel who should be put down.* Had Tia deliberately chosen an animal reference, or was it just fate that took him back to that part of his life? No, he wasn't going there right now. He couldn't. Yet he couldn't erase the overlapping of voices in his head, telling him he was nothing and she'd treated him just as he'd deserved.

Maybe he should take his self-flagellation as an improvement. Before, the darkness would have surged forward, compelling him to use anger and cruelty to hide his feelings. He was embarrassed she'd done this in front of his Mistress. He could tell himself that Regina saw all of him, dark and light, but in a moment like this, it didn't feel that way. He felt ugly before her, and since she was the only one in the room whose approval counted, it weighed him down, hurt his heart. He didn't want to put on a mask, but he wasn't sure how he was going to get up off the floor and do this without putting on a face not his own.

"That's more than enough." He saw her feet clad in the sexy strappy heels stop at his side, and inhaled her scent with a flood of relief. He was ashamed at how welcome her presence was, her touch, when her gloved fingertips grazed his back and bare shoulders.

He wanted to tell her not to interfere with this, that he'd prove he could handle anything they threw at him. He'd show her how much he'd changed, that he could do this. The slight tightening of her fingers on the back of his neck told him to be still. He didn't always obey her, but this time the pressure convinced him to stay silent, kneeling. When she'd touched him, he'd automatically assumed a submissive posture, hands flat on the tile, head bowed.

"He wants to show me he's changing, becoming a better person,"

Regina said. "I told him once that the most important thing to me was that he was trying to be the best person he could be with me. That's what this is about, even more than making amends to all of you."

He swallowed. It sounded kind of bad, put that way, but hearing it said straight out, he knew she was right.

"Because I think most of you understand the significance of that," she continued, "you know I don't bring it up as an ego stroke to me or a cut against any of you fine ladies. It's progress in the evolution of a human being, which I believe deserves a certain level of respect."

"I had—" Tia started to object.

"Shut up." Regina spoke in such a chilling voice that Marius himself froze under her hand. "You want to keep your nose in its current shape, I'll have my say, and then you will leave."

Tia wasn't all that physically imposing, and next to Regina, that difference would be enhanced. Especially with his Mistress emanating a low-level fury that did odd things to Marius's gut.

"I was not in time to stop Siren from what she did to him," she said, her tone sharp as a razor blade. "As Dominants, we are not immune to being fucked over and fucked up. But we appoint ourselves to a position of control, where we trust our instincts and our nature to dive deep into the mind of a submissive, figure out his twists and turns. There are risks to that, on both sides. But we're all big girls, aren't we? We wouldn't be Dommes if we didn't accept the consequences of taking that control.

"One of the gifts that comes with that risk is a sub like this." She stroked his hair, and he couldn't resist the desire to lean into her touch, shoulder pressed to her thigh as his head remained bowed. "We all know there are times a sub might need a light to guide him to the true expression of his submission, to bring him peace and pleasure as we bring it to ourselves. Sometimes he's too fucked up, and he needs a therapist to break some things up first. But if he's a true sub, once he finds that help, a Domme can help him get the rest of the way there."

She took a breath. "What he did to Siren and the women in this room was wrong, but he knows that. Which is why he's trying to make amends. You had the right not to come today. To refuse those amends. But you did not have the right to come here and attack him. So I want you to leave, Mistress Tia. Go contemplate what true repentance is. And look up the meaning of grace while you're at it."

Tia's chair scraped back and she rose. A tense silence reigned as Marius saw the legs and feet of both women in a squared-off position. Then Tia's closed-toe black stilettos changed direction as she claimed her purse off the back of the chair.

"I'll see you at the club, Mistress Tia," Regina said formally. "Thank you for coming."

A bitten-off reply, and the woman was leaving, her heels clicking across the floor. Regina waited a beat, then trailed her fingers over the juncture between Marius's bare shoulder and neck. "The ladies are waiting for you to serve them tea," she said in a neutral tone.

"Yes, Mistress." He bit his lip, but couldn't not say it. "You didn't need to interfere with that. It was okay."

She squatted, cupping his jaw to bring his face up to meet her gaze. He was right. She was angry enough to spit nails, but there was a tenderness in her eyes that made him swallow and want to look away for reasons that had nothing to do with protocol.

"Who decides upon your proper care and discipline, Duncan?" Her gaze held his in a lock, and what he saw in it made his stomach do a flop.

"You, Mistress."

"That is correct. Tia disrespected me in a manner that was unacceptable to me, and to the other Dommes here. Not that I owe you an explanation. Do I?"

"No, Mistress."

She nodded. "I'll punish you later to help you remember that. For now, resume your duties."

The other women had remained silent until Tia's departure, which left him uncertain of whether they had supported Tia's action or disapproved of Regina's. Until Marguerite spoke.

"Ladies, you'll find we've provided four types of tea for your enjoyment. I encourage you to sample them all, but your server will explain to you what they are so you'll know what might best suit your preferences. He'll also explain how particular hors d'oeuvres will bring out their flavor. Marius?"

She had coached him closely on the differences between the teas, how their origins and preparation impacted the taste; which ones could be enhanced by milk and sweeteners, or the foods, as she'd just said. His Mistress rose to her feet, tugging his hair, and he took a steadying breath. Right. Time to get back to it.

But Lyda had something to say first. "Lady Regina," she said. "It appears your sub's trousers are soiled from his thorough clean-up of the floor. Might he discard them? And I particularly like being served by a barefoot slave."

Marius lifted his head and saw his Mistress's eyes light with warmth at her friend's way of switching things to a better footing. A wave of sensual laughter ran through the room and expectant eyes turned to Regina.

"An excellent point, Mistress Lyda. Marius, remove shoes, socks and trousers and put them here beside me."

"Not everything?" Lisette queried, amused disappointment in her voice. The Domme in her well-tended sixties had her dyed blond hair drawn back in a smooth chignon that worked well with the snug skirt and blouse she'd worn. She'd given Marius particularly thorough workouts in the past.

"Erect appendages knocking over tea cups or dipping into sugar bowls don't meet health code requirements," Marguerite said demurely. The comment set off peals of laughter, which broke into resumed conversations and restored the earlier mood.

He rose, removed the trousers, socks and shoes, and brought them to his Mistress, crossing the ground in his dark, snug brief shorts only. The cock harness beneath it didn't do a great job minimizing his reaction to his Mistress's command, which only added fuel to the mirth over Marguerite's comment. A wolf whistle came from one of the tables. He was a bit mortified to find himself blushing, something he never did, but it seemed to give all of them pleasure.

His Mistress closed one hand over his on the clothes, and reached up to hook her fingers in his collar, which she'd of course required him to wear today. She increased her grip on his throat, a move that shot straight to his cock.

"Sweet boy," she murmured, and he had all he needed to proceed. Her approval.

~

Over the next two hours, he worked hard to meet their needs. They were demanding, keeping him busy. But unlike Tia, there was no pettiness or hostility. It humbled him, the respect they were showing his Mistress, and the kindness they were offering him.

Forgiveness. It was a balm over the raw place Tia had opened, and they were all administering it, with every even-handed command and some sparse but sincere praise when he performed to their expectations. It made him work all the harder for them. When they at last adjourned to take the party to the club, he was worried, but even more determined to do whatever Regina would require of him, to show her and these Mistresses who he truly was, what kind of sub he could be for Regina.

He'd worked quickly to handle clean up, which went faster than he expected because he found out Marguerite had excused him from dish duty. With a wink and quick grin, Chloe had shooed him off, explaining that the Mistress of Tea Leaves hadn't gone easy on him by letting him out of the task.

"Washing her delicate tea sets requires special training. It's a huge badge of honor, to be trusted with it. She still does certain ones herself."

So he took himself off to The Zone. The Mistresses, including his own, had gone on ahead, carpooling to keep a festive atmosphere. Once there, though, he was more relieved than expected to find Regina waiting for him in the foyer. Maybe she'd known he would feel somewhat uptight about crossing the threshold for the first time since Siren had trapped him in the cage. He could do it; it was just nice to see her there.

She pressed herself to him for a warm kiss, reassuring him and re-stoking his confidence with one gesture. "Follow me," she said, and turned to lead the way.

She brought him to the main playroom. "Strip," she commanded, and pointed to a bench with adjustable side pieces. "Then lie down on that, face up."

The bench had adjustable side pieces. She strapped his calves to those pieces and raised them, tying him down so he looked like he was sitting in a chair, only he was on his back and his knees were bent and thighs spread so his cock, balls and ass were vulnerable and exposed.

She even strapped down his head to keep it motionless at the end of the bench. The bench had separate pieces, so she could tip his head and neck down. A much better angle to provide oral pleasuring, which gave him an idea of what she had in mind.

During that process, some of the panic he'd felt when he realized Siren had him trapped returned, but his Mistress picked up on it, stroking him and making eye contact often, reminding him this was not that. In case he wasn't completely aware of it, when she was done binding him, she bent to speak softly in his ear.

"There's nothing you can do to disappoint me, Marius. Safe word if you need it. You will only fail me if you don't care for yourself the way I require you to do."

Yeah, everything began and ended with her. And maybe, at a deeper level, with himself. The counselor had implied the same a few times and he'd shied away from it. He shied away from it now, but that didn't mean her insistence that he keep himself safe didn't help steady him.

"Ladies?" Regina drew their attention without much effort, since they'd been milling around, sipping their wine and watching her restrain her naked sub with frank gazes of appreciation. "I see some of you have asked your subs to join you here, as we indicated would be welcome. While you well may be occupying yourself with them during our lovely couple hours of private time here at The Zone, may I please extend the use of my sub's extremely capable mouth to you as an added perk?"

With a series of sultry movements, she loosened the hold of the elbow-length black glove on her right hand and skimmed it off her elegant limb. Sliding her now bare palm along Marius's side, she reached his face, traced his lips. As he parted them, she dipped her fingers inside and he automatically sucked on those slim digits, teasing them with his tongue. It scrambled his brains and made him care less that some of the subs gathered around were smug-looking males.

"You're welcome to straddle his face and let him give you pleasure. While he does that, you may also play with his body as you wish, with the exception of penetration. And no male/male play." She tossed the audience a feline smile. "As hot as I'm sure we'd all find it to watch, it's one of my sub's hard limits."

She bent and kissed his mouth. It took him by surprise, but he caught up fast, tasting and tangling with her wet heat as much as she'd let him before she drew back a few inches and studied him. The black bra and hold of the red satin dress gave him a sweet view of her generous breasts, but her dark, rich eyes were what mesmerized him. "Make me proud, sweet boy," she said quietly. "Every time a Mistress puts her cunt to your mouth tonight, I will fuck you afterward with a nice, oversized strap-on. When I get tired, as I'm sure I will, because all these Mistresses look like they plan on using your mouth, I have a fucking machine standing by to take up the slack for me. But I'll never be farther than a yard from you all night long. Understand?"

"Yes. Fuck." He stared up at her. How had she known that was the part that had worried him the most? He wanted something else, too, and was concerned it made him seem weak to ask, but he did it anyway. "Could...when the other Mistresses are using me, could you be touching me some way? So I can feel you?"

For all that asking made him feel like a total coward, her reaction flipped that over and made him feel like a hero. Framing his face with both hands, she put her lips on his, this time a slow, lingering kiss that spun out and snared him in a web of her making. One he embraced. His cock and heart jumped as she gripped his collar, holding it tight.

"Yes."

Slapping his stiff and cruelly harnessed cock, pinching him, using impact play toys on him... Whatever kink pleased each Mistress was explored, though all under Regina's watchful eye.

The night Siren had set him up, he'd come to the club so full of himself, so certain about handling his own shit without actually handling it. Now that he was, he realized the two feelings were all the difference between what was on the surface of the earth and what lay beneath it. It was a tough road, but he had a couple good reasons to walk it.

The first reason was the one that jumped to his mind first, last and always—his Mistress. She knew how to torture him on every level, break him open so it was a true punishment, his suffering evident to all of them. A few weeks ago, she'd compelled him to tell her what position made him feel the most vulnerable and foolish. This was it, making him feel like a damn baby in a crib, getting his diaper changed.

So of course that was the position she chose to fuck him and allow others to watch or enjoy his discomfort...or his tongue and lips.

Having her orchestrate so much of his torment was an inescapable reminder this was more than making amends. He was serving her will, always. Despite the humiliation, he'd gotten aroused again and again. Not when a woman shoved her cunt in his mouth, but when his Mistress fucked him, or watched him give oral, or touched him with trailing fingertips, reminding him everything he did was at her command.

When the night was over, he was sore and raw everywhere. He also had the worst case of blue balls he thought he'd ever experienced, since of course he wasn't permitted to climax. With the invaluable assistance of the cock harness, his Mistress had stopped short of every near miss that happened when fucking him or letting the machine do so.

But that didn't matter. He'd pleased her, he could tell. She unstrapped him, bade him get dressed. After he did that, he knelt at her feet, head bowed, as she made her farewells. He registered some good words about him from the Mistresses, but no one addressed him directly. That was fine, because he wanted to stay in full submission mode with her, his cock, heart and soul all of one mind in their focus on her.

He had to follow her home, and the separation was as painful as the dig of the harness. When they cleared the doorway, he dropped back to his knees, his head bowed and knuckles of one hand pressed to the floor. "Mistress."

"You're deep in a functional kind of subspace, aren't you?" she mused in a purr. "What do you want to do for me, sweet boy?"

"Everything. I want my mouth between your legs. I didn't want my mouth on anyone but you tonight. Please, Mistress." He was begging for the privilege of giving her a climax before tending to any of his own needs. Begging in a hoarse voice, throat and chest aching with all the emotions she'd summoned from him today. And given him.

She made an approving hum, but when she moved her foot so the toe of her shoe prodded and stroked up his engorged cock, he choked back a groan. "Mother of God," she breathed at his size. "Follow me."

He followed her to her room. Another time, perhaps she would have drawn it out, for both of them, but the whole night had been an erotic feast, and she'd only let herself come once or twice herself. It was clear she wanted him all to herself, to let the full strength of a satisfying climax take her. He could help with that. He was the only damn male he ever wanted to have that honor again. If any guy thought differently, he could remove a few limbs to prove a point.

Mine, mine, mine.

Hers. Totally fucking hers.

She'd taken off both gloves at the club, and now she unwrapped the satin dress, let it whisper off her skin to the floor. He devoured her with his eyes as she unhooked the black bra and shimmied out of the panties. When she put one knee on the bed, she was briefly on the mattress on all fours, a position that made his brain lock up entirely and his body howl with savage needs. She tossed her hair over one shoulder, and sent him the kind of look a lioness would have.

"You'd like to take me like this, wouldn't you?"

He nodded, his fists starting to clench. He made them stop, but from the light in her eyes, he could tell she registered his animal hunger.

She turned, slid under the covers and then lifted them, inviting him under with a pointed look down her body. "Come impress me," she said, with a feline smile and heated eyes. "And then you can have whatever you want."

He obeyed. For the next blissful, endless time, he was buried under the soft covers of her bed, his arms curled over her spread thighs as he lay on his stomach and dedicated himself to her pleasure. Licking, nipping, stabbing into her folds. Stroking her legs and stomach with his hands that she miraculously seemed to love, despite their roughness.

But in the end, she didn't want him to bring her to climax with his mouth. And though he believed she would let him take her from behind, that wasn't what she wanted right now, either. Face to face, heart to heart; that was her desire.

She gripped his shoulders, his hair, telling him to come lie fully upon her. Clamping her hands firmly on his ass, she wrapped her legs high on his back and pulled him inside her. A groan tore from her that matched his.

"Fuck me, sweet boy. Hard and deep. Keep it going."

He did, thrusting inside her cunt until they released together, with harsh cries. When she demanded the answer this time to what was the most important thing for him to remember, now and always, he didn't think at all. He just said the simple truth.

"I'm yours. All yours, Mistress."

He could die without complaint. Or, for the first time in his life, the unbearable pain of regret.

CHAPTER NINETEEN

*M*arius's mind returned to the present as he paused in the archway to the social room. He found her without any difficulty, and not just because she usually favored the horseshoe booth which could accommodate her, Lyda, Marguerite, Lisette and Violet most comfortably for their regular get-togethers in The Zone lounge.

She was a total cock tease tonight, even more than usual. Wet black latex from ankle to waist, and a velvet vest over it that had a deep plunge neckline and mesh sides that hinted at the swells of her breasts. Her boots were needle stilettos with tiny little ankle chains strung with several glittering red gemstones. She had matching tiny red beads dangling from her earlobes.

He'd put those on her tonight. He'd also helped her dress as she'd required, only allowed to touch her as was necessary to prepare her. After he'd zipped the boot over her latex clad leg, she'd angled the sharp heel and pressed it into his testicles, accessible to her because he was naked, kneeling and knees spread so she could play with him as she desired. Sometimes he wore clothes at home, sometimes he didn't. It was up to her, and earlier tonight had been a no-clothes night. That usually meant she was in the mood to be extra demanding and domineering.

Since he'd committed to a three-hour shift at The Zone, it had only increased his anticipation, thinking about what she might require from him when his work was done. He came to her now, kneeling at her side without interrupting her conversation. Her hand dropped onto the back of his neck, sliding under the strap of his collar to hold it and let him feel the pressure of her ownership. Whenever he was away from her for any length of time, he always felt a release of tension at the vital reconnection.

"Shep, Tyler's partner, is finalizing the gladiator night protocol," Marguerite was saying. "Men or women fighters permitted, certain rules to prevent serious injury, but it would be primal play. Winner fucks the loser in whatever manner that winner's Dom wants. Oral, ass, genitals, etc. Obviously, the participants would be subs without hard limits involving those conditions."

"That would be a hell of a sight," Violet said, a purr in her voice. "If it stays manageable. Things can already get pretty intense in primal play."

"Well, Tyler's thinking is that Marius has a lot of experience in fighting, so if he wanted the extra pay, he could be the referee and call it if things are getting too out of hand. And they'd have the usual DMs watching to help break things up if needed." Regina ran her fingers along the hair at his nape. "What do you think, sweet boy? You have my permission to talk."

He'd stiffened at the initial mention of it. He didn't want her to order him to fight. He'd realized that the fighting was his way of purging his demons, battling them back, but the violence that swamped him during it had often kept him firmly in their grasp. But as he realized that wasn't what was being expected of him, he relaxed, and chided himself for thinking she would feel otherwise.

"I could do that, Mistress," he said. He turned his face to nuzzle her, kiss the soft underside of her forearm. When he tested her, using some tongue, she tugged his hair a little harder. "Don't push. Else I'll slap a cock harness on you."

Which she also knew only made his dick jump to higher attention. He wanted to serve her. He wanted the other Mistresses to go about their business so he could do what he'd wanted to do all night. To bring her to screaming, clawing orgasm with his mouth, his cock, his hands, his submission...whatever got her off, he wanted to be the source and the drive for it. If that made him a selfish bastard, a pushy bottom, he was okay with that, because if it was wrong, she'd make him pay for it. And he was okay with that, too. So he muttered his response. An infraction, but soft enough that it wasn't intended to challenge her. Just goad her and give her an excuse to be even tougher with him.

"Promises, promises."

She sighed, but he caught the quirk at the corners of her lips. "Have to take this pain in the ass in hand. See you later, ladies."

"Need any help?" Mistress Lisette examined her nails. "That post tea-party event was very memorable. Wouldn't mind a repeat."

"Not tonight," she said. "Tonight I want him all to myself."

"Selfish bitch," Violet said, laughter in her voice.

"Yeah, like you share. Mac has been off the market to anyone since you claimed his fine ass. Don't want to hear any BS about *my* selfishness."

"It's what happens when you ladies get all monogamous," Lisette said, chuckling. "Since she has two subs, I'd ask Lyda to support me on this, but she's almost as possessive with them as you two are with your one-man shows."

Regina rose, the banter continuing, and bade Marius rise to his feet. He followed her, any teasing disappearing from his mind as he watched the sway of her hips in the leave-nothing-to-the-imagination latex, the brush of her hair on her shoulder blades, and inhaled her scent. His heart leaped as she took him down the hall to the private rooms. That was what he wanted, too. Just her.

When she stopped in front of Room 11, he opened the door for her. Her eyes warmed in approval. She preceded him in and he followed, closing the door behind them.

There was no equipment in the room, though there was a cabinet he was sure had some toys in it. She might have stashed some of her own there. On the floor was a cushioned mat. Multiple embedded rings with attached cuffs were at the corners and sides of it.

"Take off all your clothes and lie on your back on the mat. Cuff your ankles and one wrist, and lay your other in the last cuff."

He stripped The Zone T-shirt and his jeans, shoes and socks. She hadn't let him wear underwear tonight. He felt the telltale quiver in his fingers as he obeyed her. It didn't matter that they'd been together for months now. She had this effect on him every time she exercised a Mistress's rights. As the counseling did its work on his head and heart, it was only getting stronger. Sometimes he thought he was going to explode with all the things he wanted to do for her and with her.

And the "with her" part was becoming just as important to him. They'd taken Dot to get spayed last week. The two of them, concerned pet parents, had watched over her the night she came home glazed and groggy. He'd held her in his lap, Regina cuddling Magenta as they watched TV and didn't do much else, wanting to keep an eye on her. It was what a family did.

But his identity as her sub, her property, was an equally big part of who he was for her. They both liked it that way, and the second she actively exercised it, his mind shifted into that mode, like now.

As he locked the wrist cuff onto his arm, he was stretched out on the mat, naked and under her view. Straddling him with her mile-long legs, she looked down at him from a standing position. He felt like he was looking at one of the vintage soft porn pictures that offered a straight-from-the-ground shot of a woman, an erotic view of her crotch, overshadowed by her tilted-up, exaggerated breasts. Only nothing was exaggerated on his Mistress. She was every inch the fantasy material she appeared to be. Her moist lips pressed together as her brown eyes slid over his body with leisurely, possessive pleasure. Bending, she buckled the other cuff to completely lock him down. She avoided the curl of his fingers, trying to caress her hands, with a short sound of reproof. Rising, she pressed the toe of her shoe into his scrotum, earning a wince.

"Did I give you permission to touch me?"

"No, Mistress."

"Hmm." She brought a long, rectangular stool with short legs over, designed to be placed over his chest, the front legs pressed against his arm pits. She sat down on it, which positioned her so he was staring up at her above him. An adjustment of his gaze could have him looking right at her latex-clad cunt, inches away from his face.

"I know you're not staring at my pussy."

"No, ma'am," he said immediately, snapping his gaze to her face.

"Lying. That earns you another punishment."

"Can't help it, Mistress. I want to play with it. Eat it, fuck it. It's all I think about."

"I can tell. You did a crappy job washing the dishes this morning. I found a speck of egg on one plate." She leaned forward, eyes gleaming, and he had a tempting view of her breasts, the shape all but revealed from the deep neckline. "Now you're ogling my tits." She sighed. "Am I going to have to blindfold you?"

"No, Mistress. Please don't. I love looking at you. I can make up for it."

"You're trying to be good, trying to be Duncan. But I know when Marius wants to come out and play." Reaching back, she took a firm grip on his cock and twisted, pulling a groan from him. "So stop blowing smoke up my ass, Marius. Tell me what you're really imagining in that disobedient brain of yours."

He leveled his gaze on hers, feeling that aggression surge up. "Let me go and I'll show you, Mistress. Or are you chicken?"

Her lips curved, the gleam in his eyes matching it. At one time, he would have turned and twisted a Mistress's feelings with that aggressive feeling, taking the scene in a wrong direction. She accepted his aggression and they explored it together, in some fucking memorable ways. She was more than a match for him. Far more, most times. Even when she wasn't, he could never hurt her. He'd throw himself off a bridge first.

Rising, she moved to the cabinet and came back, holding a hood. Though he fought to pull his head away, she had it down over his head in a blink, tying the drawstring so he was plunged into darkness.

She moved the bench over his knees. When she touched him now, he bit back another groan. She'd donned a pair of vampire gloves, the silver barbs embedded in the fabric probably catching the light as she clamped both hands on his sides, hard enough the barbs dug in.

"Fuck." He cursed and shuddered as she dragged them downward. Regina was cleared for blood play, because Marius could take it, absorbed it. Ate it up.

He breathed through the thin fabric of the hood that increased the sense of heat and enclosed space around him. His pulse crashed against his throat. "Chicken, hmm?" she mused. "Good thing I have a big, strong man to protect me. One I can tie up and make helpless whenever I wish. Can't I?"

"Yes, Mistress. Fuck, yes."

"No editorializing. Just yes or no."

"Yes, Mistress, argh..." He strangled on it as her hands moved down to his hips, and then one was circling his cock. Oh, crap...

His hips jacked up as she closed her hand on him, letting those tiny barbs dig in all over his rigid member.

"No words. Be silent," she said sharply. "Take it. Take it as long as I want to do it. You serve me, don't you?"

He nodded, obeying her mandate.

"My sub. My slave? My property?"

He nodded again, emphatically. God, so much violent need surging up in him, hard and throbbing as his dick. This was a simple scene, straightforward, but that was all he wanted and needed. It was more about how it was between her and him than elaborate plans. He was good with anything as long it was with her. He was going to break free and fuck her. He strained against the bonds, all his muscles called into action.

"Did you want to fight as my champion in the gladiator fights? Take down some big strong male and fuck him at my command, showing your dominance over him, your submission to me?"

He quivered at the idea of it, the two sides of him warring over it. Yes and no. He knew it wouldn't be good for the shit that lurked inside him. But though he'd gotten somewhat better at the hard limit thing, anything she asked of him, he wanted to do. His mouth confirmed it.

"I'd do anything you command, Mistress."

"I believe it," she said, but with a mild rebuke in her tone that told him, as usual, he couldn't get anything past her. "I won't command you to do that. Because I know that's not good for my sub. But I do like the fantasy. It gets me stirred up. I know you could take down almost any male sub in this place, subjugate him to your will. Except maybe Mac. That would be an interesting fight."

Yeah, because Mac would have to be unconscious, his head beaten into pulp, before he'd let a live dick anywhere near his straight ass. But what made Marius hot was hearing how the fantasy turned her on. She'd be so wet, watching him shove some guy to his hands and knees, hold his neck in one hard hand as he shoved his cock into him with the other. It ached in the hold of the vampire glove. Fuck, it hurt. And yet he was so fricking hard...

She released him, scratching his upper thighs with the gloves, causing another little shudder. Standing, she moved the bench off him. When he heard a rustling, he didn't dare hope, not until she'd straddled him again and confirmed she'd removed her clothes. She was still wearing the gloves, though, making him bite back more curses as she curled the barbed fingers around him again, goading him as she guided him into her pussy and sunk down on him.

Putting both hands on his chest, she dragged them down over his pectorals, snagging his nipples. He snarled, writhed and bucked at the stimulation and discomfort while she rode him, clutching his cock with her slick muscles.

She was killing him.

She rode him hard and long, and kept tormenting him with the gloves throughout, pushing out his climax farther and farther. He was growling, lifting his hips to push into her, being just as aggressive as she was. He wanted his hands free and fought his bindings, which she didn't release.

"Let me go. I want to fuck you. Bite your nipples. Make you scream."

"Bite my nipples hard?" she whispered, bending down to bite his ear. She drew back when his teeth snapped close, trying to return the favor.

"Yeah."

"Well you don't get to do that, right now. You're mine, and you'll serve my pussy as I say, not you. Right?" She snagged his nipple again and he swallowed another creative curse.

"Yes, Mistress."

She rode him as she wished, taking him up and back, up and back, until he was crazed with animal need. "Go," she said.

Insane as he was, he knew it was a trap. She'd done it before, a playful mindfuck. He shook his head. "Not before my Mistress. She's taught me better than that."

"Yes, she has. But it may take her awhile. She's enjoying her ride too much to cut it short. So let's use this..."

She snapped the cock ring around him, having to push and pull on him some to make it work, since he was already so erect. He grunted his discomfort, and then she was back to rising and falling upon him, speaking to him in a breathy voice that morphed into long, low cries as she came, her orgasm gushing over his cock.

God, yes... He was dying, his balls and cock throbbing like a damn toothache. "Fuck...please..."

"Please what? You want to come?" She was breathless, bouncing on him, pushing down hard, slapping her clit against his pelvis. "Spill all that messy seed of yours inside your Mistress?"

"Please...I'll clean it with my mouth."

"You bet your ass you will." She unsnapped the ring, and intense pleasure flooded her tone. "Come for me, sweet boy."

Sometimes he thought he might explode from the force of the climaxes she could pull from him. He punched up into her, again, again, her sharp gloves digging into him as his climax jetted forth. He shuddered and convulsed from the intense pleasure of it, the pain of the barbs, the indescribable bliss of her cunt holding him.

It went on endlessly, and yet was always over too soon. When his mind stopped spinning, he realized she'd removed the gloves, and was running soft fingertips and palms over his abraded chest and legs. "There we are," she murmured. She straddled his face. "Clean me through the hood. I don't think you've earned using your tongue directly on my flesh. I'll have to take you home and teach you some more manners before you get that reward."

If he could have forced his tongue through cloth he would have. For now, he was just thankful the hood was thin enough he could smell her arousal, feel the wet heat of it soaking through as he licked and sucked on her cunt through the fabric. She quivered and jerked, still sensitive after her climax, so he gentled his touch. When she at last removed the hood, he found she'd turned off the light, so it was the two of them in darkness. He wanted to see her beautiful body. She laid down upon him, though, her hips between his spread thighs, the energy around them becoming even more weighted as a result of that darkness. She freed one of his cuffs so he could curl an arm around her, hold her tight against him.

"I love you, Mistress," he said quietly against her hair. "I hope I pleased you."

"You do, and you will continue to do so. Else I'll take it out of your hide." There was a smile in her voice, and tenderness...and love. "I meant it, Duncan. I would never make you fight in those fights. You never have to fight again."

He was silent as her fingers stroked him, her lips moving against his flesh. He closed his eyes, savoring it, feeling the twist in his heart and his gut. She was smart, his Mistress. She knew what happened in his head, what his silences meant.

"You don't agree. Speak to me. Tell me what my sub is thinking."

It took him a few moments, but he answered her, though the words came slow because they weren't easy. Nothing important was. "I do have to fight again, Mistress. Every day, against myself, and whatever else comes along. To serve you, to keep earning your love."

She slid her arms fully around him, held him even tighter for a long pause before she answered. "You know, all that time, the wonderful, charming things you said? They don't hold a candle to how you make a woman feel when you're speaking straight from your heart. So mind you only say such things to me, unless you want to be in big trouble."

It was a teasing though serious warning, one that made him smile, content. "Don't want to say it to anyone else." He paused, the humor disappearing. "All those years I was teaching myself to fight, thinking it was to go up against my father if ever he tried to make me helpless again... Sounds stupid and obvious, but it's only lately I realized that wasn't what I was fighting."

She nodded against his chest. "What was it, sweet boy?" Her voice was a whisper in the darkness. He closed his eyes.

"It was my memories, my anger at my father. So much futile shit, stuff I was fighting *against*. But the night they tried to hurt you..."

His arm constricted around her, an automatic reassurance to them both that that horrible moment was a memory, well in the past. He still had to take a steadying breath before he could continue. "That night was the first time I'd ever fought *for* something. The difference was the difference between choking and breathing. That's the one kind of fighting I'll do now and forever, Mistress. Always *for* you." He took another breath. "And for myself. The right way."

When she released the other cuff, he sat up in the darkness, and gathered her to him. She didn't mind being treated like a girl, his Mistress, and when he had her cradled in his lap, his arms surrounding her, she rewarded him, both for his care and the words.

"I'll hold you to that," she said quietly, stroking his chest, his jaw and throat. "Because I think I'm keeping you forever. I may even marry you."

"Do I have any say in it?" he asked.

Her voice had a smile in it. "Not a damn bit."

He sighed. "Thank God."

* * *

WANT MORE NATURE OF DESIRE SERIES? Ending up in a wheelchair wasn't part of Rory's plan. And as if the Fates really want to screw with him, his sexual tastes apparently run on the Dominant side.

Daralyn, a family friend with a horrific past, needs a Master who can help her thrive in a world that terrifies her. Her desperate need to trust, her eyes full of hunger for what love should be, are keeping him up at night.

He's going to be the man to give her that. She's going to find everything she needs in his arms.

CLICK HERE TO READ NOW
IN HIS ARMS

Reading this in print format?
Look for it at your favorite book vendor!

AUTHOR'S NOTE

As I mentioned in the Acknowledgements, a lot of random research goes into a book. This time, there was one piece I could not fact-check. The discussion between Regina and Marius in the Florida State Prison parking lot was a key scene, so I left it as it was written, with him concluding the conversation and walking from the car to the main building to be escorted to the witness gallery.

However, the actual procedure by which family members of death row inmates arrive at, and are escorted to, the witness gallery for the execution is confidential, for security purposes and to protect the family members. After the kind and patient folks at the Florida Department of Corrections advised me of that precaution, I chose to respect that, and didn't dig for further information.

So, if the information is incorrect, there are very good reasons. However, if there are readers who have inside knowledge of that process, my apologies if any inaccuracies pulled you out of the story.

ABOUT THE AUTHOR

Having penned over fifty acclaimed BDSM contemporary and paranormal titles, which includes six award-winning series, *Joey W. Hill* has been awarded the RT Book Reviews Career Achievement Award for Erotic Romance. A submissive herself, Hill brings authenticity to her intensely emotional love stories.

She is grateful for the support of a wonderful and enthusiastic readership, which allows her to live on her beloved Carolina coast with her even more beloved husband and menagerie of animals.

- On the Web: https://storywitch.com
- Twitter: https://twitter.com/JoeyWHill
- Facebook: https://facebook.com/JoeyWHillAuthor
- Facebook Fan Forum: https://facebook.com/groups/JWHMembersOnly
- MeWe: https://mewe.com/i/joeywhill
- GoodReads: https://www.goodreads.com/author/show/103359.Joey_W_Hill
- BookBub: https://bookbub.com/authors/joey-w-hill
- Amazon: https://amazon.com/Joey-W-Hill/e/B001JSCIW0

ALSO BY JOEY W. HILL

Mirror of My Soul

Mistress of Redemption

Rough Canvas

Branded Sanctuary

Divine Solace

Worth The Wait

Truly Helpless

In His Arms

Ignition Sequence

Naughty Bits Series

Naughty Bits

Naughty Wishes

Vampire Queen Series

Vampire Queen's Servant

Mark of the Vampire Queen

Vampire's Claim

Beloved Vampire

Vampire Mistress *(VQS: Club Atlantis)*

Vampire Trinity *(VQS: Club Atlantis)*

Vampire Instinct

Bound by the Vampire Queen

Taken by a Vampire

The Scientific Method

Nightfall

Elusive Hero

Night's Templar

Vampire's Soul

Vampire's Embrace

Vampire Master *(VQS: Club Atlantis)*

Vampire Guardian *(VQS: Club Atlantis)*

Vampire's Choice